Praise for *Liar City*

"This promising series opener is packed with action, interesting metaphysical abilities, and a fully realized world with political divisions that feel relevant to the current political climate. The developing romance is likely too subtle for romance readers, but urban fantasy fans will be thrilled with the possibilities for future entries."

—*Library Journal*

"Evan and Reece's chemistry crackles throughout *Liar City*'s nonstop action."

—*BookPage*, starred review

"Therin conjures up an almost *Twin Peaks* literary vibe for the launch of her new Sugar & Vice series, which is set in an alternate version of contemporary Seattle. Pair this with the author's flair for crafting captivating characters, as well as her ability to deliver fun, flirtatious bantering between Reece and Evan, and you have a paranormal-infused crime novel that will not only intrigue mystery readers but also offer some crossover appeal to fantasy and romance fans."

—*Booklist*

"Reece is an appealing viewpoint character, and chapters from Jamey's perspective are equally engaging. Evan and Reece's chemistry crackles throughout *Liar City's* nonstop action, but be warned that they do not exchange even one intimate touch. However, as this fantastic paranormal is the first installment in Therin's Sugar & Vice series, hopes abound for the future."

—*Publishers Weekly*, starred review

Also available from Allie Therin and Carina Press

Magic in Manhattan

Spellbound
Starcrossed
Wonderstruck

Roaring Twenties Magic

Proper Scoundrels
Once a Rogue

Sugar & Vice

Liar City
Twisted Shadows

And don't miss the third books in both the Roaring Twenties Magic and Sugar & Vice series, coming soon!

TWISTED SHADOWS

ALLIE THERIN

Recycling programs for this product may not exist in your area.

ISBN-13: 978-1-335-62196-2

Twisted Shadows

For questions and comments about the quality of this book, please contact us at CustomerService@Harlequin.com.

® is a trademark of Harlequin Enterprises ULC.

Carina Press
22 Adelaide St. West, 41st Floor
Toronto, Ontario M5H 4E3, Canada
www.Harlequin.com

Printed in U.S.A.

For a dream and a promise on 7th Street.

CHAPTER ONE

Three weeks after the brutal murder of Senator Hannah Hathaway, best known for authoring a bill introducing the country's strictest anti-empathy laws, the mood in Seattle remains tense.

"People are scared," said a source from within Hathaway's office, who asked to remain anonymous. "They're saying some of the executives at Stone Solutions were linked to the murder, but how could they be? Stone Solutions makes the empaths' gloves. They keep us safe from empaths."

"American Minds Intact has always stood for the right to privacy from empathy, and we will always stand with Stone Solutions," AMI president, Beau Macy, said. "We continue to call for an ongoing investigation into Seattle's empaths, who will always be this city's greatest threat."

No new information has been shared on the condition of Stone Solutions CEO Cedrick Stone, who was reportedly hospitalized the day after Senator Hathaway's murder. Hathaway's bill, S.B. 1437, recently passed in the Senate and will be up for a vote in the House.

—**THE EMERALD CITY TRIBUNE**,
"Seattle still reeling from November's murders and empath controversies"

IF EVAN GRAYSON had been someone other than the Dead Man, he might've felt something about spending yet another day of inaction in an eighteen-degree Washington, DC. Where he was yet again crammed into the smallest—and most isolated—conference room, with an overflowing table of bickering directors representing all the various empathy-related organizations.

Someone else especially might've had feelings about a room of wealthy, high-powered people shooting him dirty looks when they thought he wouldn't notice. But Grayson didn't make decisions to make others happy for the same reason he had no feelings about the size of the conference room, or the endless sniping, or those glares. Holt Traynor, director of the Empath Initiative, had requested he attend this latest meeting; all the Dead Man was concerned with was learning why.

He leaned back against the conference room wall, listening.

"I agree with you, as I usually do," Director Traynor was saying to Director Victor Nichols of the Polaris Empathic Research Facility. "But a United States senator behind a controversial anti-empathy bill is dead, and the head of the country's biggest anti-empathy defense facility has been implicated in the murder. EI is under a microscope; the public needs to believe we're acting."

Traynor was a former army general; a big man with a crisp suit, close-cropped brown hair, and a perpetual poker face, maybe from years of hiding his feelings from empaths. Unlike Traynor, Nichols had an openly bitter expression, his brown hair uncombed, his skin pale under the fluorescent light as his glasses slid down his sweaty nose. His gaze darted to Grayson, then back to Director Traynor. "The public is EI's problem, not mine," Nichols said. "I was not expecting more *guests* at Polaris and I'm expected to believe I have Cedrick to blame."

His tone was deeply sarcastic. *Guests* was a euphemism, as was *Empathic Research Facility.* Polaris was the facility for corrupted empaths, ones who'd been twisted from harmless pacifists into sadistic paranormal killers. Polaris was part of the Stone Solutions web but created and run like its own kingdom by Nichols for more than twenty years.

Or it had been, before Grayson had come along. He wasn't much older than Polaris itself but had a lot of opinions about how empaths were treated, even the corrupted ones. The Dead Man also had the dubious privilege of being completely unique among the country's anti-empathy weapons, and so Traynor had forced Nichols to listen to Grayson's conditions. Nichols wasn't very fond of Grayson, but being liked was just one more thing Grayson had no feelings about.

Next to Nichols, the president of Stone Solutions Canada, Vivian Marist—American, not Canadian, despite her role—raised a perfectly arched blond eyebrow at FBI Assistant Director Jacobs, who nodded solemnly, like he'd understood whatever invisible message she'd passed him.

"All of us in this room know that a corrupted empath was behind the murders that took place that day, but Cedrick Stone is taking the blame because he masterminded it," Director Traynor said. "Yes, the empath used emotional control to thrall a senator, and turned several other thralls loose in a bloody rampage, but we have undeniable evidence that Stone was part of the group that chose to corrupt that empath."

Traynor looked like it pained him to admit it, and maybe it did. Traynor had had a long military career before he'd been appointed to run EI and had known the Stones since their defense contracting days. When you got to the heart of things, empathy organizations were run by money and nepotism, same as most big corporations and government agencies Grayson knew of.

"This room is aware of that little distinction," Nichols said. "But your precious *public* isn't. They only know Stone Solutions lost three of its executives three weeks ago, and the country is outraged and terrified. Everyone wants to know: Who's going to keep them safe from empathy now?"

Grayson's watch silently vibrated on his wrist. He glanced down to see a text.

Reece.

Marist cut her eyes to Grayson, then lifted her chin. "Stone Solutions will rise to the occasion, as we always do," she said loftily, and no one would've missed her implication that the Dead Man sure wasn't rising to the occasion. "But as long as Cedrick is still alive, we are not replacing him with a new CEO. The accusations and implications can continue, but Stone Solutions will continue to deny his involvement; anything else would be tantamount to admitting the empaths have won."

Grayson's watch buzzed again.

Reece: You around? I don't know what time zone you're in.

The Dead Man had a job to do, and no time or desire to spare a thought for anything else. And thus Grayson never shared his personal phone number outside of a select, trusted network of folks in the same business he was.

At least, that had been the case up until three weeks ago.

"EI should release a statement of support for Stone Solutions as a company. There's something you can do to set people's minds at ease." Jacobs gestured at Marist. "You couldn't ask for a better figurehead to manage this crisis than Vivian here. American Minds Intact loves her, and it would send the right message to the public, to see EI supporting AMI's top choice."

And the choke collar on the empaths would stay tight, like EI preferred it.

Marist gave Jacobs a bright smile as Grayson pulled his phone out of his pocket, keeping an ear on the conversation as he tapped out a response to Reece.

Grayson: How do you have time to text? Thought you were moving today.

Some of the directors exchanged nods and glances. "Finally, a voice of reason," Director Nichols muttered, as he pushed his glasses up again, his nose still shining with sweat, pale blue eyes bloodshot behind the lenses.

Reece: I'm packing.

Grayson: As in still packing or just started?

Reece: There's barely anything. You could probably carry everything I own in one trip.

"I support Stone Solutions denying Cedrick's involvement, as obviously we can't have the truth getting out," Traynor said. "But we do need to keep up the messaging that empaths are pacifists."

"Some might say the paranormal ability to read others' emotions without consent is *de facto* aggressive, regardless of what the empaths claim to be," Marist said delicately. "But you should of course endorse the messaging you feel best, Director."

Grayson flicked his gaze up to Marist. After a moment, he looked back at his phone.

Grayson: Only probably?

Reece: Yes, only PROBABLY– I own a car.

Grayson: Debatable if that tiny thing you drive counts.

Reece: Bigger is only better if we're talking MPG averages.

Always with the sass. Reece's willingness to fire back on things he cared about, no matter how scary the target—it tickled something at the back of Grayson's brain, reminders of other empaths he'd met. He ignored the memories, and they disappeared, unexamined, as his watch vibrated.

Reece: My new place is downtown.

Reece: Downtown where there are lots and lots of people.

The sublet he was taking over was in a high-rise only blocks from the Seattle Police Department's headquarters.

Grayson: Good. You're an empath, you need people around for all that empathizing.

Grayson wasn't someone an empath could empathize with, but he was supposed to have been one of those people around today. He'd had a flight to Seattle booked for that afternoon before Traynor had asked him to come back to DC instead, though Grayson had yet to see what about this meeting required the Dead Man's presence.

"Maybe we could use this opportunity to lessen the public's fear of empaths," Jacobs said, but he sounded dubious.

Nichols frowned. "I don't think we want to do that. We still don't know exactly what happened to Cedrick Stone, but multiple eyewitnesses place a Seattle empath, Reece Davies, at the scene on the roof of Stone Solutions—"

"Mr. Davies wasn't responsible."

All of the heads at the table snapped in Grayson's direction. Several eyes narrowed.

And this was the crux of why the room was unhappy with Grayson. They didn't want Cedrick Stone to be responsible for Senator Hathaway's murder; they wanted a comfortable scapegoat, someone who wasn't a billionaire, a CEO, and their golfing buddy.

Too bad. They didn't get an empath.

Nichols cleared his throat. "Eyewitnesses do say that Stone had blood on his face—"

"He did," Grayson said. "He also had a head wound." Grayson ought to know; he'd put it there after Stone had taken a shot at him.

"So you still don't think the empath should at least be investigated?" Marist said, mild and sweet, like that hadn't been yet another unsubtle reminder that Grayson was the only one in the room with that opinion.

"No." Reece already had enough anxiety to power a grid. He didn't need extra stress.

Nichols turned to Traynor. "Reece Davies was at the scene—"

"Director Traynor, perhaps you could remind the room what I do and where I was," Grayson said dryly. "I realize our Polaris director is accustomed to the *other* kind of empath and may have trouble remembering what the pacifists are like, but last I checked, Director Nichols wasn't the empath specialist who was also at the scene with Mr. Stone and Mr. Davies."

Nichols folded his arms, but he didn't speak.

"The empath surrendered," said Grayson. "There were a dozen police officers there, easy targets for thralling. But even though nothing that had happened was his fault, even though he believed I'd *killed his sister*, he surrendered. Not sure why I have to keep telling y'all that Mr. Davies is harmless, but he needs to be left alone."

Nichols and Marist both looked to Traynor.

"Evan's right," Traynor said, and he didn't sound happy but he did sound firm. "Yes, we monitor empaths, but EI policy is not to interfere unless there's a reason we should."

"All of them are eventually going to give us a reason," Nichols muttered. "It's just a matter of time."

There was a murmur through the room.

"Funny, the way I see it, the empaths themselves will never give us a reason to worry," Grayson said. "I keep my eyes on the folks who can't stop messing with them."

The room went silent.

Grayson leaned back against the wall again, arms folded. Everything he'd said was the truth. Reece himself hadn't given anyone a reason to worry. He was another victim in the whole mess, targeted by unethical people who had wanted to see if they could use a stranger's pain to corrupt him. Completely innocent.

Well. Except for two tiny snags that none of these directors knew about.

For a couple minutes on the roof, Reece had taken full control of Stone's emotions.

And Reece could hear lies.

"Look," Traynor said, addressing the table. "If there was any chance the empath could be dangerous, Agent Grayson would have taken him down. He is the best defense we've ever had against empathy, and there's no one we can trust to make a rational, unemotional decision more than the Dead Man. If Agent Grayson says we need to leave Reece Davies alone, then we will."

The Dead Man wasn't supposed to hide things from the empath agencies, especially not secrets about empaths. But empaths had never before been known to develop an ability like hearing lies without also becoming corrupted. Reece had somehow managed it; was caught in some kind of liminal state where he had some of the enhanced abilities that made corrupted empaths so dangerous, but with all the pacifism of an uncorrupted empath.

It was supposed to be impossible. Reece's existence disproved countless papers out there. Every scientist at EI and Stone Solutions would want to know how it had happened.

Might want to know if it could happen again. Might be willing to chance making more corrupted empaths—or finishing the job with Reece—to make it happen.

Grayson had seen firsthand in November that not everyone in the empathy defense circles could be trusted, and so he wasn't going to trust anyone else with the truth about Reece.

Was Reece at risk of becoming actually corrupted? Absolutely. Was Grayson going to keep an eye on him and make sure that wasn't happening? Obviously.

Was the Dead Man going to step in and stop Reece if corruption did set in?

Without question.

Grayson's watch buzzed.

> Reece: Jamey and Liam went to find more boxes, it's too quiet. What were we listening to in your truck a couple weeks ago, while you were flagrantly violating all of my city's traffic laws? The one in Spanish, I want to play that.

But unless Reece became an actual threat, Grayson would see to it that he was left alone to bitch behind the wheel in peace.

He texted Reece the name of the Puerto Rican artist as the meeting broke up around him. But as Grayson pushed off the wall, Director Traynor called his name. "Evan! A moment?"

This was going to be the real reason Traynor had wanted him at the meeting. Marist was also lingering as Grayson strode over.

Traynor gestured at one of the vacated chairs. "Have a seat."

Grayson had flown too much and driven too many rentals in the three weeks since he'd left Seattle. Hours crammed into plane cabins made his body restless, and his six-foot-five-inch frame was too tall to drive most cars without his knees constantly banging the steering wheel. He'd had the driver's seat adjusted in his truck, but he'd left that back at the Seattle airport. "I'll stand."

"Suit yourself." Traynor reached down to grab a laptop bag from the floor and extracted an accordion file. "Here."

Grayson took it. "What's this?"

"Everything EI and Stone Solutions have been able to learn about the empath found murdered in Burlington this morning."

Grayson's gaze snapped to the folder. He reached in and pulled out the first picture. White woman dressed for winter, maybe late twenties or early thirties, her face bruised and cut. She was lying on ice-frosted grass, brown eyes staring into space and bloodstains soaking the snow under her head. Her gloved hands were crossed on her chest.

He set the picture down on the table between Traynor and Marist. "I don't recognize her."

"She's not one of the American empaths—they're all accounted for," said Traynor.

"We think she's French Canadian," said Marist. "It's an easy trip to Vermont from Montreal; she could have been down for a visit, or to see American family."

"Could have," Grayson repeated. "You don't know?"

"Perhaps the Dead Man believes he can cross borders with impunity, but Canada is, in fact, its own country with its own laws, and Stone Solutions must operate within them," Marist said, as she folded her arms. "Canada is taking cues from Europe, getting stricter about empath privacy, and Quebec has its own empathy agency that is notoriously difficult to deal with."

"Pretty sure that Canada also regulates empaths at the federal level, not the provincial level," Grayson said.

"Yes, and Stone Solutions has contacted Affaires D'Empath Quebec to demand records access. We *are* trying." Marist tapped the picture, right on the gloves. "In the meantime, however, we have these. The serial number is faded, but the first few numbers align to Stone Solutions' make, from a shipment sent to Toronto two years ago."

With the way the empath's gloved hands were crossed over her chest, the body had to have been deliberately posed. Had the killer wanted it known she was an empath? Grayson pulled the next picture out of the folder, the woman's body on a stainless steel table. The blood had been wiped away. "How did she die?"

"Blunt force trauma to the back of the head. Facial injuries are suspected to have happened when she hit the ground." Traynor leaned forward. "We don't have the weapon or leads. There are American empaths in Albany and Concord, but they weren't aware of any other empaths visiting Burlington."

Grayson glanced up. "Were these pictures shown to empaths?"

"With her injuries?" Traynor shook his head. "Obviously not."

Grayson wouldn't say *obviously*; his faith in both EI and Stone Solutions to do their jobs right was on shaky ground these days. "Were the empaths told she was murdered?"

"Of course not," Marist said, with a touch of impatience. "You wield a lot of influence within the Empath Initiative, Agent Grayson. Everyone is aware of how delicately you think empaths should be treated." Her tone made it clear that wasn't a compliment.

"But Evan," said Traynor warningly, "if we don't figure out who she is and why she was killed, we *are* going to have to start interrogating the other empaths."

The murdered empath stared blankly at Grayson from her photo. Traynor didn't know there was an empath in a never-before-seen liminal state in Seattle—that if Grayson was in Vermont, it'd be even longer until he could check on Reece.

But an empath murder needed to be investigated by the Dead Man—especially one where the killer had made the gloves this obvious.

Grayson's gaze lingered on the picture. "You book my flight to Burlington already?"

"Leaves in two hours," said Traynor.

Grayson nodded. He walked across the room to pick up his bag as the others stood. After Marist stepped out of the room, however, Traynor joined him at the wall.

"You know, when I created the role of the Dead Man, it was to put non-empaths first," he said pointedly, as the door closed. "Some of our directors feel like that's not your priority anymore."

Grayson could just make out Marist speaking to someone in low tones outside in the hall, not loud enough to be picked up by Traynor's normal hearing but the words clear to Grayson's sensitive ears. *Has someone arranged your flights back to BC?*

First thing tomorrow. That was Dr. Nichols. He must have been waiting for Marist in the hall.

"I'm not in the business of feelings, or making the agencies happy," Grayson said, even more pointedly. "My job is making sure folks aren't in danger from corrupted empaths. That also means making sure people don't get to thinking about corrupting empaths—even if some of our directors would rather I stopped after part one."

Protection, Reece had called the Dead Man, *for the world and for empaths.* It was a very pacifist way to describe Grayson, and no one in the room today would have agreed. Reece himself didn't have any business thinking of Grayson in such warm terms, not when the Dead Man was the closest thing the country had to an empath hunter, but that was an empath for you, not a lick of self-preservation or defense.

"Yes, Evan," Traynor said impatiently, "but if you keep defending the empaths—"

"Respectfully, Director," Grayson said, "you of all people know exactly how far I'm willing to go to defend people from empaths."

Traynor closed his mouth. His lips were pinched, but he didn't argue any further. He hadn't made a move to leave, though, so Grayson tilted his head. "Something more I can do for you, sir?"

Please tell me you're not flying commercial, Marist said to Nichols, out in the hall.

Traynor seemed to be weighing his thoughts. "There's some new research you should read," he finally said. "We don't have time to get into it before your flight, but I'll forward it over."

"Never a shortage of folks who think the empaths are a riddle to solve," Grayson pointed out.

"I know," he said. "But this new theory might make you think twice about your *job*."

The last research paper Traynor had sent Grayson had been written by Nichols, speculating on the possibility of a parasitic relationship between empaths and their siblings. Grayson's name hadn't been stated outright in the research, but only a handful of siblings had developed enhanced strength and senses while growing up alongside an empath, and it wasn't hard to guess the sources behind Nichols' conclusions.

Only one of those empath siblings had become the Dead Man, after all.

But that was in the past. Grayson's brother was gone, and if Traynor thought sharing new theories could change how Grayson saw his job, he was wasting both their time. The Dead Man didn't care about hypotheticals and what-ifs; all he needed to know was if anyone was sharing those conspiracies outside of their circles.

Out in the hall, Marist was still talking to Nichols. *There's no need for you to wait until morning. I have the company jet and*

I'm heading to Seattle tonight; we can arrange your other flights from there. Director Traynor mentioned he was heading out to Seattle as well; I bet we can convince him that it makes sense to share the plane. The chef is planning surf and turf—a favorite of his. Why shouldn't he join us?

Why not, indeed. Just the pesky little question of impartiality from government employees dining on steak and lobster in private planes owned by corporations that wanted to ensure their taxpayer funding never dried up.

Grayson grabbed his duffel bag off the floor and tucked the accordion folder into it before he hoisted it onto his shoulder. As he left the building, navigating the snowy walk toward his rental, his watch buzzed with another text.

Reece: You know, it's not good for me to be living around other people when I might be dangerous.

Grayson had emails to read. He needed to get to the airport. He needed to call Dr. Aisha Easterby, doctor turned medical examiner and one of his few trusted contacts, to tell her about the murder and see what she thought. She might very well want to hop her own flight east.

Except as he climbed into his rental car, he found himself texting Reece back.

Grayson: But that's why you've got my number, right? There is nothing you can do that I can't stop. You can never be more dangerous than me.

He turned the engine over.

Reece: I thought I had your number because you know you're a menace behind the wheel and someone needs to remind you of those pesky public safety laws you ignore.

Unbelievable.

Grayson: I just told you I'm more dangerous than you and your response is to backseat drive from across the continent?

Reece: I think we need to have a conversation about your driving.

Grayson: No, we need to have a conversation about your complete lack of survival instinct.

Reece: Sorry I care about the SURVIVAL of the people who have to share the road with you.

If Reece thought that was gonna get a rise out of Grayson, he had the wrong man. Grayson didn't feel annoyance, or aggravation, or frustration, or anything else. He couldn't.

The Dead Man was able to do his job because he'd been changed by his now-gone empath brother, and he was no longer capable of feeling anything at all.

And that was never gonna change.

CHAPTER TWO

Case Number: 2282023

Reporting Officer: J. Stensby

Incident: Assault on the rooftop of [REDACTED]

Details of the Event: …[REDACTED] was on the roof as well, kneeling next to [REDACTED]. His hands were on his head in a position of surrender. There was blood all over [REDACTED] face.

I wanted to bring in [REDACTED] but was told not to interfere, arrest, or even question him. We were never told why [REDACTED] was on the roof, or why he got away with it.

—SEATTLE POLICE DEPARTMENT REPORT

REECE AWKWARDLY BRACED his knee against the door, using it to balance his box of craft supplies as he fumbled in his pocket for the key to Liam's studio—about to be *Reece's* studio, at least for the next six months.

When Jamey had broached the topic of Liam moving in with her when his lease expired, she'd been adamant that Reece didn't have to move out.

Liam knows you live here, she'd said. *He knows what he said yes to. You don't have to go.*

She'd been nervous but excited, happy in a way Reece hadn't seen her in years. *If Liam had someone he trusted to sublet his place*, he'd asked, *would you two still be waiting another six months to live together?*

Oh no, she'd said. *He'd move in tomorrow.*

Which was how, one week later, Reece was letting himself into his new apartment. On the fourth floor of a high-rise.

Downtown.

The keys jingled in his unsteady hand as he unlocked the door. *My new place is downtown*, Reece had texted Grayson. *Downtown where there are lots and lots of people.*

Good, Grayson had texted back. *You're an empath, you need people around for all that empathizing.*

Except *no*, it *wasn't* good. Reece had seen what corrupted empaths were capable of, and it was lurking inside him too. He was too dangerous for downtown.

But Jamey and Liam were nearly giddy. Reece had heard Liam lie loud and clear about the rent, giving a figure that was probably half of what the lease actually cost, because he wanted to move in with Jamey so much he was trying to secretly subsidize the rest so Reece could afford it. How could Reece change his mind and keep them apart?

He stepped fully into the studio, letting the door swing shut behind him, and surveyed his new place. A kitchen area was built in along the wall to the right, with shiny new appliances and two stools at a bar-height counter. There was a wide couch and good-sized TV, and a tall folding screen in the corner to block off a double bed. Big windows directly in front of him, a sliver of ocean visible between buildings but the view mostly of another high-rise, probably also filled with countless innocent people.

No, Reece could not actually afford to live here, in any sense of the word.

His arms were now unsteady too. He set his box down on the coffee table, hearing the crochet hooks clink together. *Pick a hobby to be your anchor activity*, his new therapist had said. *It will help you manage your anxiety.*

Reece hadn't mentioned that the level of anxiety he was currently managing was *might turn into an evil doppelgänger of yourself at any moment*, but he'd dutifully picked up six different arts and crafts, just in case.

He walked over to the window, glancing down through rain-streaked glass. Despite the December cold, several people were walking on the sidewalk four stories down. A couple was laughing as they darted down the street, trying uselessly to dodge the rain before they climbed into an Escalade together. Three people in fancy coats stood in a tight knot, holding cups from the coffee shop in the bottom of the high-rise across the street and taking selfies, while a fourth man in a camouflage coat and black balaclava was leaning against the wall next to the coffee shop's decorated windows, talking on the phone, outwardly relaxed but his inner mood betrayed by the tense set of his shoulders.

Reece touched his pocket, like a reflex, feeling the outline of his own phone. He'd been so close to calling off the whole move earlier that he'd found himself texting the Dead Man for reassurance.

But that's why you've got my number, right? Grayson had said. There is nothing you can do that I can't stop. You can never be more dangerous than me.

Reece leaned his shoulder against the window, eyes still on the street. The Escalade had pulled away from the curb, and the man in camouflage was looking up the side of the building, phone just visible against his ear as he gestured with a gloved hand at Reece's building.

Grayson's text had helped, the reminder that there was an empath hunter out there who could—and would—stop Reece if he turned. But as dangerous as Grayson professed to be, Reece was the one who could be walking among those people below like a wolf among sheep. Who could take complete control of someone else's emotions with nothing more than his touch. Who could fill them with unwavering devotion to only Reece, fuel their strength with rage, then use his thralled army to tear the city apart—

The studio door opened behind him, his thoughts fading as Jamey's and Liam's voices filled the space.

"…can turn the dining room into your office." Jamey had Reece's duffel bag on her shoulder, a laptop bag on the other shoulder, and was carrying a stack of boxes higher than her head. Her ringlet curls were still perfectly in place and she wasn't the slightest bit out of breath. "For when you work from home."

"Our home." Liam was the same height as Jamey but carrying half as many boxes, looking at her with poorly hidden awe.

Reece folded his arms. "Should you be carrying that much where other people can see you?"

"I'll just say it's clothes or something." Jamey set the stack on the ground with a heavy thud that made it clear nothing as light as clothes was in the boxes.

"When you're also carrying a duffel?" Reece pointed out.

"No one was around," Jamey said. "Look, it's nice to not have to hide for once."

Reece could grudgingly accept that. She'd never told anyone about her unnatural strength and senses until Liam.

Liam set his boxes next to hers. "I think it's hot."

Not a lie. Reece made a gagging sound.

"Mature," Jamey told him, as she picked up two of the boxes Liam had carried and headed over to the kitchen, her movements confident and familiar, because she'd been here far more than Reece. There was a clink as she set the boxes on the counter. "Have you been in the kitchen yet this morning, Reece?"

"It's a studio," Reece said. "So technically I've been in all of it just by walking through the door."

Jamey raised her hands over the bar-height counter to show them a bright green plant in a cheerful pot. "But you haven't seen your housewarming gifts?"

"Housewarming gifts?"

He headed to the kitchen area, Liam with him. And sure enough, tucked behind the counter's edge, next to the sink, was a giant basket with a bow.

"Who is this from?" Reece said incredulously.

"Isn't it obvious?" Jamey said. "Who knows you're moving today, knows you would want a basket made of ethically sourced sustainable bamboo from a locally owned business, and has the kind of Southern manners that require giving housewarming gifts?"

"This is why she's the detective." Liam glanced at Jamey, pushing his glasses back up his nose. "*Was* a detective," he corrected, "and now is going to do some other super-badass thing," he added, which drew a little smile from Jamey.

Reece reached for the basket and pulled it over to himself. "You think Agent Grayson sent this?"

"A peace lily and vegan candy." Liam took the plant from Jamey. "I could see myself buying these for another man."

Reece side-eyed him. "You could?"

"Sure. If he was my *boyfriend*," said Liam, which made Jamey snort.

Reece huffed. "You can get each other plants and candy even if you're just friends." Or frenemies, or mortal nemeses, or whatever he and Grayson were. He ran gloved fingers over the basket's bow. "I mean, obviously you don't actually believe there's a chance Agent Grayson is even, like, bi or whatever. Um. Do you?"

"Where on earth would I have gotten the idea that the two of you have a relationship that's not completely straight?" Liam said dryly. "Could it be the giant hoodie he gave you? Or is it that he calls you *Care Bear*?"

"He *loaned* me that hoodie," said Reece. "I'm going to give it back." *Lie.* Well, shit. "And Agent Grayson probably calls all empaths Care Bear," he hurried to add.

"Gay, straight, bi, none of the above, it doesn't matter," Jamey said. "Grayson is literally the most emotionally unavailable man on the planet. He is the last person an empath would get involved with; he doesn't have feelings."

Possibly ironically, the reminder gave *Reece* feelings.

"He could be into Reece for non-feeling reasons," Liam said.

Reece furrowed his brow. "Like what?"

Jamey and Liam gave him identical stares.

"Oh. You mean—*oh*," said Reece. "Look, that's not the first place my empath brain goes, okay? But yeah, lust and all that can be separate from emotions. Not that that's the case here," he hurriedly added.

"He's still the Dead Man," said Jamey.

"Still an empath hunter—and you're an empath," Liam said. "Would the two of you be against the rules, like a *no fraternization with the enemy* type of thing?"

"Whoa whoa whoa, how did we get from peace lilies to taboo hookups?" Reece said. "He needles me about the empath sweet tooth and it's an easy-care plant. That's all this is."

"What's Grayson up to right now, anyway?" Jamey said.

Reece shrugged lightly, like he wasn't usually wondering the same thing at any given moment these days. "Classified Dead Man business he thinks I shouldn't know about, probably. Why?"

"Aisha Easterby asked if I could give her a ride to the airport at an illegally early hour tomorrow," Jamey said. "I got the sense it's for something related to their whole—" she waved a hand, faux-casually "—investigating empathy-related crimes, protecting the world, whatever she and Grayson do on that whole super-secret Vanguard team."

Jamey was trying to play it off like she didn't care, but Reece caught the note of longing underneath, how much she missed detective work. A pang of guilt hit him; if it hadn't been for him breaking and entering into Stone Solutions in November, trying to learn how another empath had been twisted into a killer, Jamey would still be a detective. "It doesn't really seem super-secret when we're talking about it over caramel corn made with plant milk," he said, trying to match her casual tone. "But I still don't know who to thank for the new gloves or the therapist, so maybe they are pretty secret."

"You have a spot on that team if you ever want to join," Liam said.

"So Grayson said." Jamey's gaze had gone to the gift basket. "But I'd have to trust him to work with him, and that's never going to happen."

"Not like you trust Lieutenant Parson anymore either," said Liam. "The force wants you back, though. Stensby keeps asking me about both of you."

"Aren't they all just glad I'm finally gone?" said Reece. "The only thing Lieutenant Parson ever said to me was *you need to learn to keep your damn mouth shut.*"

Liam coughed.

"Don't say it." Reece pulled the gift basket closer. "Ooh, gelatin-free gummy bears."

"And this is the problem, right here," said Jamey. "No, I don't trust Parson anymore, but I trust Grayson even less. He's sending housewarming gifts when I know he'd slap handcuffs on Reece again without hesitation."

"Maybe we should be glad about that," Reece said pointedly, meeting her eyes as he pulled the gummy bears out of the basket.

It had been just Jamey and Reece for years, until Jamey had started dating Liam. He'd gotten a crash course in *putting up with your girlfriend's high-strung empath half brother*, but unlike any of her prior boyfriends, he'd accepted their weird, messy world—and become part of it. He was Jamey's confidant now; knew all about her enhanced strength and senses, her innate resistance to empathy.

But Liam didn't have any of those defenses. Reece wanted to believe that even if he became fully corrupted, he would still never hurt Liam, but how could he know for sure? He needed Grayson between him and the world, willing to do whatever it took to protect Liam and others from Reece.

He frowned harder than he probably needed to at the gummy bears, still sealed away in their packaging, which slipped uselessly against his gloves.

Liam gestured at his hands. "You know I don't care about the gloves, right? You don't have to wear them just because I'm here."

"What if I trip and accidentally touch you without them?" Reece said. "I would know every single thing you're feeling."

Liam shrugged. "I think it would bother you more than me."

Not a lie. Reece frowned. "How?"

"I'm really into your sister."

Jamey laughed and leaned in to kiss Liam as Reece groaned. "You two are so gross."

There was no response, because they were *still kissing*.

"Oh my God, get *out*," said Reece. "Thank you for carrying my stuff, now go slobber on each other somewhere else."

The studio felt very empty after they'd left. Reece pulled off his gloves, tossing them on the kitchen counter before grabbing the basket and carrying it over to the couch. Outside the rain-streaked windows, the nearby buildings were shiny black against the wet, gray afternoon. He needed to start unpacking, but instead he pulled out his phone.

If you need me, call me, Grayson had texted, when he'd left Seattle three weeks ago.

Any reason? Reece had asked.

Any reason.

Reece was taking him at his word and texting him daily. Maybe it was weird, and a little bit pathetic, but the Dead Man wasn't the bogeyman anymore; these days, he was the only thing that seemed to make Reece feel better.

But as he unlocked his phone, he found he had an email: a single line from a gibberish address.

We're watching you.

Reece frowned. Threats and hate mail didn't usually make it to him. People tried to send them, he knew that much, but Jamey routinely added all kinds of filters to his accounts to screen it out. But someone had gotten through to his email address to send this; maybe a reader of the *Eyes on Empaths* blog—their whole schtick was, after all, that they had their *eyes on empaths*—or maybe it was still fallout from having his face plastered all over the news the day Hathaway died.

It was a shame that people got so worked up about empaths; Reece was way too familiar these days with how bad stress was for your body. If the sender of the email had used a real email address, he had lots of good websites for meditation and mindfulness he could have shared.

As he went to hit Delete on the email, Grayson's voice echoed in his mind, words he'd once said from the passenger seat in Reece's car as they'd driven to a coffeehouse.

If anyone's ever bothering you, you should tell me about it.

Reece paused. Then he shook his head. Even Grayson probably couldn't find this person so that Reece could recommend a therapist.

He opened his texts, but just sent a quick message instead.

Reece: Gift basket?

He kept his ears open for any sounds of people around, maybe footsteps overhead or a voice in the hall, as he settled into the couch. But beyond the occasional honk or shout from outside, it was quiet, like the high-rise's residents were at work—like he was in a building with normal people who could keep a job, who weren't just anxious, unemployable pains-in-the-ass.

Reece set his phone on the coffee table and picked up the remote, opening his favorite streaming service on Liam's television, the one that had recommendations tailored for empaths. Actors faking recorded emotions paled in comparison to the real thing, but at least it would be noise. He flipped through shows, letting the previews play.

He paused on some kind of Western in black-and-white. He watched for a moment as a cowboy on a horse tipped his hat at a woman in a bustled dress.

He wouldn't mind hearing Grayson's deep Texas drawl right about then.

On-screen, the scene changed. The cowboy was now stepping into the center of town, reaching for his holster. Shit, shit, *shit.* Fiery pain tore Reece's chest in the path of a phantom bullet, like burnt flesh and torn skin and shattered bone.

The same pain he would have caused Grayson on the roof of Stone Solutions if Reece had made Cedrick Stone pull that trigger.

Reece's chest burned, his head too light and black dots creeping into the corners of his vision as he scrambled for the power button, his arm not wanting to work—

A flag popped out of the end of the gun, inscribed with the word *bang.*

"A joke," Reece said out loud, like his racing heart cared. "Fake gun. *Fake.*"

He smashed the power button anyway, shutting off the television. He tossed the remote somewhere at the end of the couch as he flopped back against the cushions, the studio gone silent again, making his rapid breaths seem even louder.

Jesus. He couldn't even handle a fake gun these days.

He flung out a hand toward the coffee table. Most people Reece met were sick of him within minutes; he couldn't blame them, he was made of sarcasm and anxiety, it was an acquired taste. But Grayson had said he didn't think Reece was annoying, had told him to text for any reason. And maybe Grayson had also said the Dead Man didn't have friends, but Reece didn't have friends either, except for Grayson now. He could send more bullshit texts, or reread old ones, or—something. Anything that reminded him that Grayson was alive and unhurt and would help.

As Reece's hand closed around his phone, it buzzed with an incoming text. He raised it to his eyes.

Grayson: Housewarming gifts are customary.

His heart rate seemed to slow, just seeing Grayson's words on-screen. He could almost pretend he could hear that drawl, even if Grayson couldn't possibly believe Reece was actually that gullible.

Reece: Please. You just wanted to send me BEARS.

Grayson: Admittedly a bonus.

Reece cracked a smile. He let his head fall back against the couch, taking a few deep, slow breaths as he reread Grayson's words. They made Reece feel less alone, even if he had no idea where Grayson actually was.

Reece: So where's the Dead Man tonight?

Grayson: You know I'm not gonna tell you. Where I go is classified.

Reece: Can I guess? Are you at the graveyard? Hanging out with your zombie pals?

Grayson: You're about as far off as you could be.

Reece furrowed his brow. What would Grayson think was the furthest thing from graves—oh. Of course.

Reece: Maybe sky-zombies are a thing. Zombies on a plane.

Grayson's next message took a moment to come in, like he hadn't expected Reece to get it right.

Grayson: You're good at guessing games.

Reece was excellent at guessing games, thank you very much, not that he should be advertising that to the Dead Man.

Reece: Just got lucky.

Reece: So where are you flying to?

Grayson: You already got more than enough information for one night.

Reece: Night? It's late afternoon by my watch. You're on East Coast time, then?

Grayson: Care Bear. Be a good empath and stop guessing national secrets.

Reece snorted. His gaze lingered on the nickname for a moment. *Did* Grayson call all empaths Care Bear? He had to, didn't he? Why would Reece have anything that was special, that was just for him?

He set the phone down, taking a slow, deep breath. He rolled onto his side on the couch, eyeing his duffel full of clothes on the floor where Jamey had left it. After a moment, he bent down and unzipped the duffel. He didn't have a ton of clothes, so it was easy to find what he wanted: an oversized University of Texas zip-up sweatshirt, still soft with newness. He pulled off his own raggedy hoodie and tossed it to the side and then slipped Grayson's on over his T-shirt instead.

Jamey was right; an empath pining for the world's most emotionally unavailable man would be the icing on Reece's endless cake of bad decisions.

So it was a good thing Reece was smart enough to keep everything platonic. Grayson was a *friend*. Reece could platonically text Grayson while eating candy from Grayson's platonic gift basket in the hoodie that he had borrowed from Grayson. Platonically.

No feelings involved. Totally fine.

CHAPTER THREE

Readers are always hungry for any kind of news about the Dead Man, and here at Eyes on Empaths, *we deliver like no one else!*

WHAT WE KNOW: Agent Evan Miguel Grayson is from Texas. He's TALL. And he's HOT.

WHAT WE DON'T: How did he become the Dead Man anyway?

Rest assured Eyes on Empaths *is always hunting for the story behind the Dead Man. WHO or WHAT could have transformed a tall, hot Southern gentleman into a shadow agent and defender of the world?*

For in-depth coverage of my three-minute LIVE encounter with Agent Grayson, read November's four-thousand-word feature story with its EXCLUSIVE photo. (Please give the page time to load; there are a lot of comments.)

—GRETEL MACY, BLOGGING FOR *EYES ON EMPATHS*

GRETEL SAT IN the back row of the cavernous conference room on the ground floor of Stone Solutions, attention mostly on her phone as her dad addressed the full crowd of American Minds Intact members.

"We have been dealt the deepest of wounds," Beau Macy was saying. Every chair was full, with spillover guests lounging against the walls. "Losing so many of our champions in barely more than a day."

A notification lit Gretel's phone screen; a new comment on the blog.

You write the best Dead Man stories!

A tiny smile curled on Gretel's lips, disappearing as her gaze went back to her draft for the day's blog post. Her dad's monologuing made for pretty dry copy.

"An unthinkable tragedy," said Beau. "A critical blow."

She tilted her head back, gaze skimming the crowd. The new cop was here again, one Officer Stensby from the Seattle Police Department. He'd been coming to most of their meetings the past three weeks, since Senator Hathaway's murder. He was usually with one of the regulars, a big, blond ex-military type who still wore camo everywhere, but tonight Stensby was alone.

"A grievous setback." Beau leaned forward on the podium. "An almost insurmountable barrier."

Nothing new to add to the post, and nothing but increasingly dramatic ways to say *we need to regroup*. Not much here to interest *Eyes on Empaths* readers; they liked speculation and theories, going especially wild for anything about the Dead Man.

The most popular post of all time was, of course, the picture she'd taken of the Dead Man pinning a handcuffed empath, Reece Davies, over the hood of a Smart car outside of Senator Hathaway's building. It was hard to see the Dead Man's face, bent as he was over Reece. But it was still a hell of a shot.

And yes, a small but enthusiastic group of her readers thought the picture was hot. Which was not the point of the picture; the point was to show the Dead Man in action, righteously defending the world against the empath threat. But try telling that to the person who had written fanfiction and shared it in the comments.

"An effort to bury us—" Beau enunciated each word into the microphone "—the likes of which we've never seen before."

To be fair, Gretel wasn't sure what to make of Reece anymore. It was true that he'd thrown on a disguise, taken off his gloves, and snuck into Stone Solutions. She'd seen it with her own eyes.

But she'd also seen that he hadn't fought back against the guards who'd caught him, even when they'd gotten rough. So yes, maybe he had dangerous powers, but the pacifism was real too.

"But even though we face unimaginable adversity..." Beau paused for effect. "AMI will not be defeated."

A cheer rose up in the room, the audience breaking into applause around her.

Gretel sighed.

She sat through another thirty minutes of her dad's speeches before the meeting finally adjourned. Gretel polished off her last sentence and posted the article to *Eyes on Empaths*—she'd definitely written better, but this meeting didn't deserve better anyway—then stood, smoothing her pencil skirt and picking up her bag.

She made her way toward the door, where Beau was standing in a knot of people, shaking hands and exchanging serious nods. Paying absolutely no attention to her. Perfect.

But as she passed, he turned his head in her direction. "Gretel!" he called. "Come say hi!"

Gretel paused, plastering a smile to her lips. "Hi," she said to the group of various men and women, giving a polite wave.

Beau had his company smile on, as fake as hers. "We were just talking about the privacy conference—"

"At Rainier University on Monday and Tuesday, the one AMI is sponsoring," Gretel finished for him. "Vivian Marist, president of Stone Solutions Canada, is presenting the keynote in place of Cedrick Stone. The Empath Initiative just released a statement half an hour ago backing her oversight of the US side of Stone Solutions while Stone's condition remains uncertain. She's been your friend since her staffer days for Senator Hathaway, right, Dad?"

Beau looked pained at her interruption, as he always did when Gretel accidentally overshared about her special interests and endangered her ability to pass as normal in public. "Gretel is a very thorough researcher," he said quickly to the group. "She runs a little side project for AMI all by herself, you know."

The smile abruptly left Gretel's face.

"In fact..." Beau shifted closer. "Did you get an article about tonight up already?"

Ah. He hadn't stopped her to introduce her to his colleagues; this was all he wanted. "Of course," she said coolly.

"Great. Make sure that gets sent out to all of our AMI listserv subscribers." Beau turned right back to his circle, giving her no chance to explain that *Eyes on Empaths* wasn't part of AMI.

She gritted her teeth and stepped out through the doors, pulling her phone back out as she did so. She stopped by the wall for a moment and opened her email app, navigating to her dad's email.

Sure, she'd send out the article and make him look good. She'd also take a quick glance through Beau's mail for anything that would make a more interesting blog post than that speech.

Her eyes scanned the subject lines in his inbox, then paused.

Empath found murdered in Vermont

It had come from someone with an *empathinitiative.gov* email address. Gretel's eyebrows flew up.

"Gretel Macy? From *Eyes on Empaths*?"

She turned in surprise to see a good-looking guy coming her way. He was probably a few years younger than she was, early twenties maybe, with blond-brown hair, hazel eyes behind glasses, and an apologetic smile.

"I'm so sorry to bother you, you must get swarmed everywhere you go," he said, stopping a couple feet away. He had a trace of an accent, like he'd grown up in the South, and he still wore his winter coat, hat, scarf, and a pair of black gloves, like he'd just walked into the building from the cold evening. "Everyone probably wants to ask how you run something as big and important as *Eyes on Empaths* by yourself."

"No, no, it's fine," Gretel hurried to say, as she quickly stuffed her phone back into her purse. She straightened, which in her heels made her taller than he was. She was going to read that email, but most of AMI thought she was nothing but a useless and entitled daddy's girl. This guy had her complete attention. "That's very kind, thank you."

"No, thank *you*," he said. "I can't believe I get to meet you."

There was something familiar about him. It took her a moment to place it, but then it came to her. "I think I've seen you before," she said. "You were here a couple weeks ago, weren't you? The night that empath broke in?"

"Oh, you remember me?" He looked surprised and pleased. "I wanted to say hi that night, but things got a bit out of control, didn't they? I was covering the conference for my blog. It's a small one," he added. "Nothing like *Eyes on Empaths*. You're number one in the Pacific Northwest for a good reason; the gold standard for empath blogs."

"You run an empath blog too?" No way she was leaving without this guy's number. Gretel had a real smile for him as she shifted her bag to her shoulder so she could hold out her hand. "I'm sorry, I don't think I caught your name."

He took her hand with his own gloved one. "I'm Alex."

Burlington was even colder than DC, the snowflakes smaller and icier. The wind had an almost glacial bite, like a front had come to Vermont by way of the Arctic, stinging Grayson's face the instant the airport's automatic doors opened and he stepped outside. He ignored it and crossed the street, the keys to his rental in his pants pocket.

The parking lot was brightly lit against the dark night sky, and as he came up on his SUV, he caught his reflection in the window. His new hat wasn't particularly flattering; like most things designed to fit average-height people, it was too small, stretched too tightly over his head. But it was all they'd had available in the shop in Dulles.

An image rose in his mind and he let it fully form: Reece, caught on the Stone Solutions security footage, wearing Grayson's old hat with its stains from the spilled caramel almond milk steamer. Reece's eyes had been wide and frightened behind the borrowed glasses as three angry guards got off the elevator.

Obviously an empath wasn't supposed to be breaking and entering into the nation's number one empath defense facility. It had shocked almost everyone, because most folks thought empaths were unwaveringly law-abiding. But that was bullshit; empaths followed laws, sure, but they were truly driven by their own moral compasses. If the law and their morals were ever in conflict, they immediately and unapologetically shifted into pint-size pacifist vigilantes.

Reece had been in Stone Solutions because he wanted to help, wanted to find answers to explain how his friend became a sadistic murderer overnight. But the guards who caught him had been needlessly rough, and Grayson had found Reece bruised and bleeding. Empaths made easy targets, after all—unwilling to chance hurting others and completely unable to defend themselves.

But that's when the Dead Man stepped in. Grayson could hit back.

He stuffed his duffel in the backseat and then slipped into the driver's seat. As he let the engine idle and warm, he sent a pair of texts.

> Grayson: I don't put my keys in my coat pockets anymore.

> Grayson: Guess whose fault that is.

He pulled the SUV out of the rental lot and onto the road. A few miles passed as he cranked up the heat and found the rental's high beams, and then the reply came in.

Reece: I don't know. Someone who's a better driver than you?

Grayson should have known that was coming. Most people had too much survival instinct to taunt the Dead Man, but Reece was basically a sarcastic lemming.

Grayson: You're the one who commits grand theft auto—of MY truck—but I'm the one getting sassed again?

Reece: Are you texting from behind the wheel right now?

Grayson's gaze jerked from the phone screen to the road.

Maybe he wouldn't reply to that one.

Thirty minutes later, Grayson was pulling into a small parking lot at the far end of the park along Lake Champlain, where the body had been found. Unlikely to be much left at the crime scene, especially after a day of snow, but there certainly wouldn't be clues at the hotel.

He stepped out of the SUV and down to the parking lot. The snow was slowing but the wind was even colder here, coming off Lake Champlain with bits of ice in it. He zipped his coat all the way up to his chin and walked into the park. The trails were buried by snow and the moon was only a sliver, the night dark enough that Grayson flicked on the tiny flashlight he kept on his key chain.

His watch buzzed.

Reece: Since you dodged my question, I know I was right about you texting while driving. Did your plane land already? Are you out on a hot date or something?

Grayson glanced up. The park was dark and silent, empty besides him. The flashlight's bluish glow illuminated a sea of spindly trees, their bare branches casting twisted shadows on the untouched snow blanketing the grass. A messy rectangle of yellow police tape was woven through the trunks up ahead, marking off where the body had been found. There was nothing to hear but his footsteps crunching ice or the occasional car in the distance. Even the edges of the lake were frozen, no waves lapping at the shore.

Grayson: Not exactly. Are you?

Seattle was full of waterlogged numbskulls if no one was taking Reece out on a Friday night. It'd be good for Reece, of course—he was an empath who'd feel better around other people, would probably be downright delighted if he got to read someone.

But happy as Reece would be, anyone crawling into an empath's bed was going to leave a thousand times happier. Empaths read emotions, not physical bodies, but they could figure out what a body liked by following the feelings, and you'd end up with an empath drunk on their partner's pleasure and a blissed-out partner who'd just had the best night of their life.

At least, for most people. Obviously not Grayson. But it wasn't like that mattered; no empaths were looking to get in bed with the Dead Man and he couldn't have touched any of them anyway.

The response came in.

Reece: Yeah right.

Clearly Reece lived in Soggy Idiot Town.

Grayson: You ought to have plans tonight besides complaining about my driving.

Reece: We don't all have a line of people hoping to get in our pants.

Grayson: You think I do?

Reece: I bet the traffic to your dating profile could crash a server.

Grayson stopped at the edge of the yellow tape to tap out a response.

Grayson: What dating site do you imagine the Dead Man would use?

Reece: Corpse Match? Single Brain-Eaters? Plenty of Zombies in the Graveyard?

Grayson: I should not have given you that opening. Rookie mistake.

Grayson shined his flashlight's beam on the ground. The body had been found that morning, but according to the day's weather report, it had been snowing intermittently ever since. There was nothing to see now, not even an impression of the corpse left behind. Hopefully local PD had taken pictures and samples before it all got covered up.

He straightened, shining his flashlight around the trees. Bare branches stretched in every direction, their shadows distorted, falling in unexpected patterns. Someone had murdered an empath and left her body in this park. It wasn't a huge park, and it wasn't immediately within the city, but people had to come and go. As hiding places went, this one sucked.

Not hiding the body, then. The killer wanted it to be found? Wanted people to know they'd killed an empath—might be looking to kill another one?

He spent a few more minutes walking around the scene, but there was nothing to see, hear, or smell beyond fresh snow. Nothing he could do here tonight; might as well hit the hotel after all, maybe get a few hours' sleep.

He headed back to his car. As he reached the door, he got another text.

Reece: I mean, you do date or whatever, right?

Grayson raised an eyebrow as he opened the door. He climbed into the car, turning the engine on and the heat up.

Grayson: Think that depends on what you mean by "whatever."

Reece: Empath here. I can tell you that biological drives and emotions aren't the same thing. Some people want feelings before sex, some people want sex without feelings, some people don't want sex OR feelings, and so on. I don't know where you fit in, but if sex IS on the table, why wouldn't you have a dating profile?

Grayson leaned back against the driver's seat as he responded.

Grayson: I'm still stuck on who exactly you think the Dead Man is gonna date.

Reece: Well, if zombies aren't your type, who is?

Memories teased at the back of Grayson's mind: a girl in a cheerleading uniform, grinning as she hit a pike on the sidelines of a college football field; a boy in sunglasses and a damp T-shirt, basking under the Hill Country sun on a reddish-brown rock at the edge of a giant lake.

Grayson blinked and the memories vanished.

Except now he was remembering Reece, overgrown dark hair and giant brown eyes, lectures and grudging smiles from behind the wheel of the Smart car.

Grayson ran his thumb along the edge of the phone and then typed out his text.

Grayson: Backseat drivers.

He pulled out of the parking lot as the response came in.

Reece: You think you're funny, don't you?

Grayson: The bossier the better.

Reece: Yeah, well, I hope you don't fuck as bad as you drive.

Grayson: Keep talking dirty to me, sugar.

CHAPTER FOUR

From: Holt Traynor <director@empathinitiative.gov>
To: Beau Macy <beau.macy@americanmindsintact.com>
CC: Vivian Marist <v.marist@stonesolutionscorp.ca>
Subject: Empath found murdered in Vermont

It hasn't hit the news yet, but it's just a matter of time. There's no way to keep something like this quiet. If AMI wants to make a statement, I'll have my secretary reach out.

VIVIAN MARIST FELT the pressure change in her ears as the Stone Solutions corporate jet started its descent into the Seattle area. She set her wineglass on the table as she smiled at Empath Initiative Director Traynor, who had just put his phone away. "Stone Solutions does appreciate EI giving AMI a little warning about this empath murder," she said.

They'd chosen to sit in the grouping of four seats that flanked the built-in conference table at the rear of the plane. In the leather recliner to Marist's left, Victor Nichols was on his own phone, ignoring the window and the lights of Seattle's outskirts as they came into view.

Traynor shrugged. "You made a persuasive argument," he said. "And you're right; we can't keep it quiet forever. AMI is going to find out anyway, and it hurts nothing if we're the ones who tell Beau Macy."

Marist nodded. A murdered empath risked stirring up public sympathy, and AMI and Stone Solutions both would need to be ready to counter that. "It hurts nothing, *and* it keeps AMI friendly toward EI," Marist said. "AMI has got quite a lot of sway in Seattle, you know."

"Believe me, I know," Traynor said dryly. "And it's only gotten stronger since what happened to Cedrick and Senator Hathaway."

On her left, Nichols tapped away at his phone. "I still don't understand what happened in this city last month."

Traynor snorted. "And you don't like anything you don't understand."

"If that was the case, Victor wouldn't like empaths," Marist pointed out.

"You said it, not me," Nichols muttered.

She laughed. "Beau was just telling me they've had more police officers enroll in AMI since November. I sent Victor here the list." The air pressure was building; Marist reached for her purse. "Quite good news, isn't it? How nice it would be to have more allies of the, shall we say, *alpha* persuasion? Law enforcement, military, special agents, that kind of thing."

On her left, Nichols looked up. "Too many scientists at our meetings for your tastes?" His tone had a sarcastic edge; the man was a scientist himself, after all.

"Jacobs has been with us this week, he's FBI," Traynor pointed out.

"Perhaps we include him more often," Marist said, trying to bury the eagerness in her voice. She withdrew a small pack of gum from her bag. "I'm simply saying we could use more *real* muscle, to protect people from empathy. You were a general, Holt; I'm sure you agree."

She wouldn't have said that around a public roundtable and Traynor wouldn't have publicly agreed. In the privacy of the jet, however, over the last of his whiskey and crème brûlée, he smiled wryly. "I don't disagree by any means," he admitted, drawing a side-eye from Nichols. "Though you're not going to get much more *alpha* than the Dead Man."

"Untenably so," Nichols said. "Fascinating, how much he's been altered by empaths, and yet unlike others, he continues to survive."

Marist schooled her distaste off her face, but it was one thing to talk about the empaths like science experiments gone wrong. Agent Grayson, however, had been a normal child, changed against his will by his own sibling.

Marist held out the gum to Nichols, who straightened and took a piece. When she offered it to Traynor, he shook his head. "Landings don't bother me."

He'd also picked one of the rear-facing seats at their table, seemingly unbothered by motion sickness. Perhaps in his army days, he'd spent time in planes of all sorts.

"Speaking of Seattle and empaths and Evan…" Marist hesitated. This was going to be a delicate question. "Do we really agree the wisest course of action is to ignore a potential threat posed by Reece Davies?"

"It would be the height of foolishness to ignore any potential threat," Traynor said flatly. "Evan is entitled to his opinions and of course EI gives those opinions a lot of weight, but he and I have diverged on this issue."

"And does he know that?" Nichols said.

"He'll figure it out," Traynor said.

He'd finished three glasses of top-shelf whiskey with his dinner and seemed to be in an honest mood. Maybe it was a good time for another, even more delicate conversation. "Evan makes a lot of people nervous," Marist said casually. "Never you, though."

"He's unsettling, I can admit that," Traynor said. "But it's hard to be afraid of someone you knew back when he was just a college student who felt EI needed to *mind their own business* when it came to his little brother. Victor, you remember Evan before he became the Dead Man, don't you?"

Nichols grunted. He'd drunk nothing but sparkling water and a cup of black coffee, which was still half-full and sitting on the table in front of him. "I remember a lot of people the way they used to be." He folded his arms. "My entire job is, after all, running a facility for empaths who aren't quite themselves anymore."

"Evan was different then," Traynor mused, almost to himself, as if he hadn't heard Nichols. "A good kid, even if he had no respect for the authority of the Empath Initiative."

"Prototypical empath sibling, from the metamorphosis to the attitude," Nichols said. "That *little brother* he was so protective of was a parasite."

"That's still technically just one theory," Traynor said.

"Is it, though?" Nichols said. "When you consider Agent Grayson's prior behavior, the way he insisted on defending his brother?"

"Evan might have done so. The Dead Man certainly didn't," Traynor said, with an edge.

"Whatever the cause, some people do feel Evan's inclination to protect the empaths hasn't changed," Marist said carefully. "Look at this mess in Seattle, the way he's making conditions around Reece Davies—"

"No." Traynor abruptly and firmly shook his head. "When push comes to shove, Evan will do *whatever* it takes to save people from corrupted empaths. We all know what he's willing to sacrifice and how far he'll go."

Marist pursed her lips. In the seat next to her, Nichols shifted.

Traynor shook his head again. "The Dead Man is the best weapon we have ever had against the empaths. And Evan's devotion to the job is not up for debate."

Marist let her gaze drift to Nichols and found him looking at her. She gave the tiniest shrug. If Traynor was thinking about Grayson's past, he wasn't going to listen to any concerns about the priorities of the present, whether they were brought by Stone Solutions or Polaris.

And at the end of the day, Agent Grayson was still the Dead Man. Still absolutely unique and absolutely necessary.

She smiled at Traynor. "Of course, Holt," she said. "There's no cause whatsoever for debate." She turned to Nichols. "I'll have my assistant arrange your flight to Prince Rupert for the morning."

"No need." Nichols' gaze was on Traynor now. "For the moment, I'll be staying in Seattle."

Liam's old bed was a lot more comfortable than Jamey's couch—some kind of fancy pillow-top-foam-gel-who-the-hell-knows thing that would have put most people right to sleep. Unlike Jamey's too-quiet house, the bar on the ground floor of Reece's new building served up constant noise, Friday night revelers whooping as they left, cars honking as they picked up passengers.

A few months ago, Reece might have welcomed all of it, but tonight his stomach and chest hurt from anxiety, and thoughts crowded his mind so loudly he couldn't find peace.

They don't know they're in danger.

That you can hear their lies.

They don't know what you did to Cedrick Stone.

He forcefully rolled over onto his side. He'd pushed the folding screen out of the way so he could see the lights he'd left on under the kitchen cabinets, which gave the studio a soft glow. At least Jamey's house had had Jamey in it. Now, he was alone, no potential for the phone to ring with a new gig for the SPD, and no one to celebrate Friday night with. Not that it mattered what day of the week it was; he had no friends or job expecting him anywhere, not tonight or tomorrow or Monday. It was just him, the only empath in Seattle now, with more empty days ahead.

And that was how it needed to be. He knew the truth about himself now; that no matter how hard he tried to cling to his pacifism, there was another side to him. And no one else should be put at risk.

His gaze went from the kitchen to the couch, then up to the television mounted on the wall.

Can't even handle a toy gun anymore.

Because you almost shot Evan.

He abruptly sat up, so hard the bed frame creaked. Insomnia won this round; he wasn't going to fall asleep anytime soon if his thoughts had gone *there.*

He got out of bed. There was a lamp only a couple feet away, on the living area's side table, and Reece flipped it on, then reached for the hoodie that was draped over the couch's arm. He slipped it over his shoulders and zipped it up to his chin, like the soft fleece inside could somehow surround his thoughts too, a constant reminder against his skin that he hadn't pulled that trigger, that Grayson was alive.

Rain had started up at some point, soft taps against the window edged with a louder staccato from the flecks of sleet, which left translucent specks of white on the black glass. He grabbed his phone from where he'd left it on the coffee table and flopped onto the couch, pulling his legs up under him as he opened his most recent text chain with Grayson.

Reece: Well, if zombies aren't your type, who is?

Grayson: Backseat drivers.

Reece's lips grudgingly twitched. "Dick," he said out loud, but it sounded a little bit like an endearment. It helped, pretending he heard Grayson in his head when he read his texts, the memory of that low drawl loosening some of the tightness gripping his chest.

He leaned back into the cushions, the sleeves of the Texas hoodie sliding down his hands as he scrolled through their messages. Reece really didn't have any business asking about the Dead Man's type, but it sounded like Grayson wasn't dating at all. Maybe he couldn't, because he was the Dead Man and supposed to be all spooky and classified. But how would that be fair? Grayson *wasn't* dead. He deserved to be able to try to meet someone if he wanted to, same as anyone else.

Whoever it was Grayson would want to meet. Normally Reece could guess someone else's tastes in partners, but the Dead Man was still an enigma in too many ways. Maybe he went for people who were tall and hot like him. Stoic and rational. Poised. Polite. Able to watch an R-rated movie. After all, it wasn't like anyone had *short neurotic pacifist* on their dance card.

Reece scrolled further back through their texts.

Reece: I mean, you do date or whatever, right?

Grayson: Think that depends on what you mean by "whatever."

Well, Reece hadn't meant *line dance*. But it didn't matter if Grayson was celibate or railing half the East Coast; the Dead Man's sex life was also none of his business. Even if Grayson did have sex, and even if his type miraculously included anxiety-addled empaths, they couldn't touch each other. Grayson wouldn't *want* to touch Reece anyway.

Reece would just be glad they were friends; he wasn't sure how he'd be surviving these days without Grayson in his pocket.

He raised his hand to send a message, then lowered it. If

Grayson was on the East Coast—and Reece was ninety-nine percent sure he'd gotten that guess right—then it was going on four a.m. He had the same sensitive hearing as Jamey and a text might wake him up. Reece could wait.

He glanced at the coffee table, where his box of anti-anxiety arts and crafts still sat where he'd left it. He owed Grayson a hat. He had some rainbow yarn and crochet hooks—maybe he should practice some half-double stitches. Put on the song Grayson had sent him, let the Spanish take his brain south, somewhere the nights and people were warm.

But as he was reaching for the box, an email notification lit the screen, from another gibberish sender. Reece pursed his lips, then opened the email.

We are always watching you.

Reece frowned. Was this the same jerk from earlier? It was easy to send hate to targets you imagined were weak, to those you didn't expect to fight back. Nothing brave about punching down.

It was a creepy email, but no one could be *really* watching him. If they were, they wouldn't be trying to scare him with stupid emails. This coward would be way too chicken to mess with Reece if they had any idea what they were really up against—if they knew what he could do.

He reached out toward the message, but the sleeve of Grayson's hoodie slipped down over his hand again, blocking his fingers.

Reece stared at the hem for a moment, the fleece inside the sleeve soft against his bare fingers, light as a ghost but taking him back to the moment he'd gotten the hoodie, in the warm cab of the big black truck after Grayson had taken Reece's side against the world.

He blinked hard, then shook his head.

It was good the email's author didn't know how dangerous Reece was now. They'd be terrified of him, and he didn't want to make anyone feel scared. Obviously he didn't want that.

Still, he'd gotten a similar message twice now, and maybe he *should* tell Jamey, or even Grayson. Once it was a reasonable hour and he wasn't going to wake them up.

He swiped the notification off his screen and reached for his crafts.

CHAPTER FIVE

...welcome back to Fiction with Feelings, *the only podcast that focuses on empath-approved reads. Our panelists are here today with an exclusive early look at* A Study in Sentiment, *the historical thriller that reimagines the mysteries of Sherlock Holmes if empaths had emerged in the 1880s...*

—EXCERPT FROM THE EPISODE 79 TRANSCRIPT

GRAYSON OPENED HIS eyes at six thirty a.m. to a world made of white: white hotel walls, white hotel sheets, white snow outside a window with white curtains.

His dreams, on the other hand, had been gray. It was all he ever dreamed of anymore.

The hotel bathroom was closet-sized, the showerhead not much more than chin-height. He had to duck to rinse shampoo from his hair, but the pressure was good, and the hot water relaxed his shoulder, which was still a bit stiff in mornings from the bullet wound he'd taken from that FBI agent at the Seattle marina. It was healing well and quickly, though; soon all he'd have was the scar where his chest and shoulder met.

A scar Reece could obviously never see. The less he thought

about that night and the mess that had followed on the Stone Solutions rooftop in the morning, the better. Empaths had no business being exposed to that much violence; Grayson knew that all too well. That was how they ended up corrupted, like Cora Falcon. Like his brother.

Reece wasn't corrupted, but he was in a liminal state that made him dangerous to everyone in Seattle. And Seattle was dangerous for Reece right back: AMI was always there, but now Director Traynor and Vivian Marist were too. If those two ever discovered the truth, it wouldn't matter that Reece was still a pacifist, or that Cedrick Stone was responsible for his liminal state; they'd send Reece straight to Victor Nichols at Polaris, the corrupted empath prison.

Grayson needed to be here in Vermont, to solve this empath's murder, but it left Reece vulnerable to all the wolves circling empaths. The Dead Man could hit back where an empath wouldn't, but Grayson couldn't fight by text.

After the shower, Grayson shaved in front of the mirror, one of Reece's texts rising up from his memories.

I mean, you do date or whatever, right?

That one had been a funny text. No, the Dead Man didn't *date.*

But that hadn't been the whole question, had it?

Grayson tilted his head to glide the razor over his jaw. Bodies were also funny. You could be sitting on a chair, minding your own business, and then if someone came along and tapped your knee just right, your whole leg would jerk, all on its own, no thoughts or feelings needed.

Once upon a time, he might have looked at a person and thought *I want to be with them because they make me happy.* He didn't think things like that anymore, but if someone hit him just right, his body still jerked. Still sat up and took notice and *wanted.*

And Reece? Hit *exactly* right.

Grayson had, at first, done a good job of ignoring it. Sure, Reece was cute—really fucking cute, all overgrown dark hair, giant brown eyes, and fiery personality. He'd been cute glaring at Grayson from the other side of a table in the Seattle Police Department and still cute running his motor mouth in the Smart car.

Didn't matter. Lots of people were attractive, and the Dead Man was there to do a job. Reece was a potential suspect.

Then Reece had seen a book about torture in an office at Stone Solutions and been thrown into a panic attack. No one knew the exact parameters of corrupting an empath—maybe it could happen from a graphic enough book, or maybe not—but Reece had been hyperventilating and Grayson had intervened, gotten down in front of him and tried to bring him back.

Miraculously, it had worked, and Reece had stayed with him, had calmed down and even been able to laugh. And for a moment in that office they'd been so close they could have touched, empath body heat radiating off of Reece like a micro furnace, their eyes locked together, his smaller frame fitting perfectly into the space made by Grayson's body.

Grayson rarely got that close to anyone anymore, unless handcuffs and an arrest were involved. And it had gotten a lot harder for Grayson to ignore his attraction after that.

But it still didn't matter. Just because your body wanted something didn't mean you could or should have it. Grayson didn't chase his body's desires, because the Dead Man didn't have time for anything but work. That work was protecting the world from corrupted empaths, and nowhere in his job description was there room for anything else—*especially* where an empath was concerned. Grayson had to be ready to stop empaths if the corruption set in.

Not to mention there was never going to be a chance Reece would be interested. Grayson was as repulsive as a rotting corpse to empaths: a face they couldn't bear to see; a voice that made them sick; a touch so rejected it knocked them out.

An empath would never be interested in the Dead Man, and

good thing too, because he didn't have any business climbing in bed with one.

He looked himself in the eyes in the mirror.

No business. None whatsoever.

The hotel lobby had a breakfast buffet, about half the tables full. A woman with a messy topknot and pink pajama pants side-eyed Grayson as he grabbed three plastic-wrapped hard-boiled eggs and a yogurt before filling a paper coffee cup, skipping the half-and-half and instead adding milk from the cereal station. As he headed out to the rental car, his phone rang with a call from Dr. Easterby.

"You're already awake?" he asked, as he answered. Wasn't even five a.m. yet on the West Coast. "You got an early flight?"

She made a sound of affirmation. "Jamey's on her way. Got your coffee?"

Grayson sipped the weak, lukewarm drink. "Supposedly."

"Hotel coffee is never up to Cuban or Lebanese standards. Our mothers would have been disappointed," she said. "And I need you to ask for more blood tests for the murdered empath."

"Whichever ones you want. Any particular reason?"

"I looked at the pictures you sent over. Her eyes are as bloodshot as a case of conjunctivitis," said Easterby. "Empaths don't do drugs on their own. I want to know if someone slipped her something before they bashed her over the head."

"I'll make sure they work up a panel, if they haven't." Grayson had to use a little extra force to get the icy car door to open. "But then that begs the question—why drug an empath before you kill them? They're not gonna fight back or even defend themselves."

"Because you're afraid of empaths," Easterby said bitterly. "The kind of creep who not only murders an empath but takes the time to position her corpse to make her gloves obvious." Her voice dropped a little lower. "You're going to get the bastard who hurt this empath, right?"

A memory flickered like a movie projected on a distant screen: an underground bunker, people screaming, fire everywhere.

Grayson, in the center of the room, a Magnum .44 in hand and nothing in his heart.

He blinked and the memory was gone. "It's what the Dead Man does." He hesitated, then said, "I realize I'm the last person on this planet to advise anyone on feelings. But don't push yourself too hard here."

Easterby's voice was quiet. "You know I can't promise that, Evan."

After they hung up, Grayson sat in the SUV as the windshield defrosted, flicking through his phone. Gretel Macy had put up something new on the *Eyes on Empaths* blog the night before, a few dry paragraphs on AMI president Beau Macy's remarks at Stone Solutions' headquarters. AMI membership was skyrocketing on the West Coast; an empath had been murdered on the East Coast. Tensions around the empaths were higher than ever, the empath agencies tightening the leashes while people like Cedrick Stone ran secret experiments and tried to justify it as necessary to protect non-empaths.

And in the middle of it all were the pacifist empaths, who kept getting hurt.

One thing was certain: the Dead Man's complicated job wasn't getting easier anytime soon.

It was still the predawn dark of a winter morning as Jamey turned down an unassuming Capitol Hill street, her GPS landing her in front of a redbrick building with stairs leading up to the front door. Small businesses lined the other side of the street: a teahouse, a combination books-and-gifts shop, a fashion boutique.

She pulled Liam's Corolla to the curb. She'd given her previous Charger back to the Seattle Police Department but hadn't replaced it yet. At least she wasn't borrowing Reece's little Smart car, where her head came close enough to the roof that speed bumps became a hazard to her skull and the keys would only be handed over with an unsubtle list of safe driving rules.

She put the car in Park, idling in front of the redbrick building. Leaving the force had been the right decision, but what did she do now? For as long as she could remember, she'd wanted her job to involve protecting other people. She'd become a detective like her dad so she could stop murderers; transitioning to private investigator sounded like she'd spend too much time snooping on people having affairs.

There was, however, a different job out there. And if she was being honest with herself, she couldn't seem to stop thinking about joining whatever Grayson's *Vanguards* were.

But she was never, ever going to trust Evan Grayson.

She glanced out the windshield just as the door at the top of the stairs opened and a pretty woman stepped out, dressed in blue jeans and a pink puffy coat with a bright purple scarf and matching weekender bag on her shoulder. Her deep brown hair was swept up in a ponytail and her coffee-colored eyes were framed by thick black glasses like Liam's, and she was waving at Jamey with a big smile.

Aisha Easterby, on the other hand, Jamey *did* trust. Maybe it was working a case together, maybe it was having Aisha's help when Jamey was teetering on the brink of madness, but somewhere along the line on that wild November night, they'd become friends.

"I think this is the first time I've seen you out of a lab coat." A light but cold rain fell on Jamey's hair and neck as she got out of the car, opening the backseat door and holding out a hand for Aisha's bag. "Did you coordinate this outfit with the bisexual flag on purpose?"

Aisha passed the bag to Jamey to put on the seat. "That depends."

"On?"

"Who's asking and if she's cute."

Jamey grinned. They got in the front and she started heading back to the interstate. "What's the emergency that's got you hopping a flight to Ottawa, anyway?" she asked, as she waited at a stop sign for a couple to push their stroller through the crosswalk.

"Stone Solutions has a couple Canadian offices. I'm going to dig into some things," Aisha said. "It's really good to see you, by the way. You were way too close to the end of the road last time we talked. But you look so great now." She winced. "In a friend way, not a hitting-on-you way—not that I'm saying you don't look good enough to hit on," she hurriedly added. "I just—yeah." She winced again. "Have I mentioned most of my coworkers are corpses and I'm not very good with the living?"

Jamey snorted. "My brother can't keep his mouth shut for anything; I'm immune to social awkwardness at this point." She glanced at Aisha out of the corner of her eye. "You didn't say what you're digging into."

Aisha's mood instantly sobered. "Someone bashed a French Canadian empath over the head and left her body posed in a Vermont park."

Jamey's eyes widened.

"Grayson goes any time a crime involves empaths, doesn't trust anyone else to handle it," Aisha added. "They always assume empaths are the villains, you know? But Grayson knows it's more complicated than that."

The rain was still dotting the windshield; if the temperature dropped another degree or two, they'd get snow. Jamey turned the wipers on. "Cora Falcon was responsible for a lot of deaths."

"*Corrupted* Cora Falcon was responsible," Aisha said. "You and I both know that if Cedrick Stone and his cronies had just left her and her fiancé alone, they'd be wedding planning and caring for veterans, not locked away in British Columbia and six feet under, respectively."

If Stone would have just left empaths alone, Reece wouldn't

have been put into his liminal state between pacifist and corrupted empath either. "Any update on Stone?" Jamey said neutrally, like she didn't have a personal vendetta against the man.

Aisha shook her head. "He's still comatose. The president of Stone Solutions Canada is running things for now. I don't think Grayson is putting much trust in her either, though, and I'm guessing the feeling is mutual." Aisha had unwound the scarf from her neck as the car warmed, revealing the edge of a thin scar that twisted close to her jugular vein, the one that looked like it came from a knife. Jamey had never asked how she got it, or gotten the story of how a sweet, bubbly doctor had ended up working with the Dead Man. But Aisha was so firmly on the empaths' side that Jamey couldn't help but wonder if there'd been an empath in her life, once upon a time.

And then if something had happened to them that brought the Dead Man calling.

She didn't voice the thoughts out loud, instead saying, "I'll be honest, I don't know how *you* work with Grayson or trust him."

"I don't trust him at all," Aisha said, surprising her. "He's dangerous, and he's absolutely ruthless. He'll tell you himself never to trust him. On his advice, I'm prepared that one day he might be my enemy."

Jamey thought that over as they passed downtown, the high-rises on the right jutting up above the highway.

"Grayson isn't my boss. I have never needed to trust or take orders from him." Aisha had pulled off her gloves and had her phone out. "He and I both want to protect people from corrupted empaths, and to protect empaths from the people who want to corrupt them. Everyone else who knows the truth stops after part one."

"So it's just you and Grayson?" Jamey said skeptically. "Because I had assumed someone else sent Reece those new gloves in November. Unless glove-making is your hobby?"

Aisha shook her head. "It's not just us; there are others. But their names aren't mine to share." She glanced over at Jamey. "For what it's worth, they know Grayson is different, and would understand that you're different in the same way. You wouldn't ever have to cover up all the amazing things you can do the way you had to hide with the SPD."

Point to the Vanguards; Jamey could barely imagine not having to constantly check herself. Did Grayson's trusted circle know *why* he was the way he was? Did they know that Jamey's empath brother had changed her the same way Grayson's brother had changed him?

Jamey hadn't told Reece that truth yet. She needed to stop putting that off. He wasn't going to take it well, but he deserved to know; it would be a terrible secret to keep from him.

The exit sign for Sea-Tac was just up ahead. "Grayson still arrested Reece twice," Jamey said. "I haven't made up my mind about working with him. But if *you* want some backup on this murder in Burlington, I'm in."

Aisha's smile grew. "I'll take it," she said, and Jamey found herself grudgingly smiling back.

Grayson arrived at the Burlington police station just after eight a.m. The Empath Initiative had prepared them for Grayson's arrival and he was taken to wait in a small side room.

He left the door open, keeping an ear on the activity around the station as he scrolled through his phone. There was an email from Marist—she'd apparently finally gotten records from the French Canadians and sent over everything about the murdered empath. One Marie Pelletier, age thirty-two, a librarian at a local branch in Montreal. Single with no children; her friends and roommate had been contacted to learn her last known location.

There were pictures of her, probably taken from her social media accounts. Empaths were just as diverse as all of humanity, but Ms. Pelletier had dark brown hair and big brown eyes, just like Cora Falcon. Just like Reece.

Footsteps echoed in the hallway, approaching, accompanied by the sound of wheels on linoleum. Grayson lowered his phone as two officers came in, a short woman with an accordion folder and a man pushing a small cart with two shelves. They introduced themselves as Officers Maguire and Fortin.

"Everything we recovered from the body and the scene is on the cart," Officer Maguire said. She held out the folder. "These are the pictures of the scene. We're still waiting on lab results for soil and blood."

"Thank you, ma'am." Grayson took the folder. "We're gonna need samples sent to the Empath Initiative as well."

"We're on it," Officer Fortin promised. "You need anything, you just ask."

They left Grayson alone in the room, and he began to methodically work his way through Marie Pelletier's possessions. There was a winter coat, a scarf and hat set—no matching gloves, obviously, since she'd been wearing the empath ones. The hat was torn in the back, and everything was splattered with blood. There was also a small canvas satchel, which hadn't held a wallet or phone but did have lip balm, a few nice pens, and a paperback novel with a crisp, new spine. He examined the book, but there was no receipt within it, and the novel itself looked to be some kind of sweet, cozy romance, exactly the kind you'd expect an empath to have.

There were no rings or bracelets, but they weren't very convenient for empaths, with the gloves. No earrings either, but piercings and tattoos tended to be a mixed bag—empaths could tolerate their own pain, but not the sight of it happening to others, so you'd never find one in a tattoo or piercing parlor. The only jewelry was a gold necklace with a small heart pendant. Grayson turned the pendant over and ran his thumb over the engraved *3:16* on the back.

He moved on to the empath gloves, laying them out palms up. No bloodstains, but if she'd died quickly enough, she wouldn't have had time to touch the wound on the back of her head. No dirt stains either. There'd been snow on the ground, maybe enough that the gloves hadn't touched grass or mud.

He turned the cuffs down to show the serial numbers. As Marist had said, they were faded to the point they were impossible to read in places. American empaths would never have gloves long enough to fade like this; they got new pairs every year. But then, too many Americans were also paranoid, and the public needed reassurance that the empaths were wearing the very latest anti-empathy technology, even if there were no upgrades some years. The wastefulness had been a heated point of contention with the empaths until Stone Solutions had promised to upcycle the old ones.

Marist had said these gloves were linked to a shipment to Toronto two years ago. Except the rest of the gloves were in perfect condition—not only clean, but no noticeable wear and tear like you'd expect from an item worn daily for two years. Maybe Marist had the shipment number wrong. It wasn't like you could see the whole serial number.

He took pictures and sent them to a heavily protected contact in Portland who specialized in empath-related research and development. Grayson added a note with it: *How old do these look to you?*

He picked up the right glove to better see the fading on the serial number. Most folks didn't realize that empath gloves had a faint metallic scent from the heavy metal threads woven in—it wasn't a strong enough scent to be picked up by normal people, but Grayson's sensitive nose always caught it. As he breathed in the faint, penny-like scent, however, he picked up a hint of something else from the inside of the glove—sharp and medicinal, reminiscent of hospitals and rubbing alcohol.

The footsteps came down the hall again, and Officer Maguire knocked on the door before opening it. "The witnesses are here," she said. "Whenever you're ready."

"Thank you, ma'am." Grayson gestured at the gloves. "Were these cleaned?"

"Absolutely not." She looked bewildered by the question. "The evidence has been left as intact as possible."

Interesting. He snapped a couple more pictures, then followed Officer Maguire deeper into the station.

The witnesses were a pair of women who'd arrived together, marathoners who'd been at the park to get a run in before the snowstorm hit. They'd just returned to their car in the parking lot when a man had staggered out from the tree line.

Grayson questioned them separately, but they told a similar story: the man hadn't talked or made any noise, but he was bleeding profusely. They both had assumed he had a head wound, but when Grayson carefully pressed, both admitted they hadn't seen a cut, just blood all over the man's face.

The women had called to him, but the blood-covered man had ignored them, scrambling into a car and driving off. The women had immediately called the police, who arrived fifteen minutes later and found the body.

After the interviews, Grayson sat in the quiet room for a moment, thinking.

An unresponsive man with a bloody face could have been an empath's thrall, bleeding from the eyes. Could Marie Pelletier have been corrupted and somehow her thrall had turned on her and murdered her? Grayson had never seen or heard of that happening. And yes, Reece had taught him that the Dead Man didn't know everything about empaths, but a thrall's devotion was absolute; hard to believe anything could ever make one turn on their empath maker.

There were many others in the field who might hypothesize that the corrupted empath was a second empath, who'd sent a thrall after Ms. Pelletier.

But Grayson had been building a private theory over the last several months, and he didn't think he believed there was a second empath either.

He finally left the station with more questions than answers, but maybe the morgue would hold another clue.

It didn't matter how many times Gretel explained to her dad that *Eyes on Empaths* was an independent blog; Beau still expected her to show up and help when American Minds Intact hosted an event. Which meant she was on her parents' couch way too early on a Saturday morning, supposedly reviewing the privacy conference's registration list but actually secretly working on her latest blog post on her phone, when she heard Beau on his own phone in the dining room.

"I always have a minute for you," Beau was saying.

He had a tendency to orate like he was at a podium, even on the phone. Gretel kept an eye on her phone and the article from yesterday's local Burlington paper, about a woman's body discovered in a park just outside the city—edited an hour after it had gone up, maybe to remove any reference to the victim being an empath?—as she reached into her bag for her headphones.

"Naturally I continue to be devastated by what happened to Hannah," Beau said dramatically. "And of course, I would never call it a boon, but yes, we've certainly been making friends since her death."

Gretel paused.

"Obviously more senators signing onto her bill," Beau went on, "and AMI has enrolled record numbers the past three weeks with no sign of slowing."

He seemed to listen for a moment, then chuckled. "Yes, well, as Cedrick Stone was fond of saying, *the best defense is a good offense.* AMI has always agreed. As you know, several of our local members are active or retired from duty, and we're up to four officers in the Seattle chapter now."

Gretel straightened, leaving her headphones untouched.

"Mind you, even with police members on our books, I haven't been able to get a decent account of whatever happened to Cedrick on that roof," said Beau. "We've filed five public records requests but every document we get back is redacted to the point of useless. I don't suppose there's anything you can do about that?"

Gretel strained her ears.

"Ah well. It was a long shot, but I always have to ask," Beau said ruefully. "Of course I can get you an AMI member list."

He was moving into his office now, his voice quieting. Beau had always spouted off the lines about AMI needing a good offense, needing to take the fight to the empaths, and that had seemed logical enough. Except now, Gretel had seen for herself what happened when people took a fight to an empath: Reece Davies had paranormal abilities and he'd still let three guards at Stone Solutions rough him up instead of fighting back.

Her gaze went back to her phone and the article. This empath found murdered in the park would also have been a pacifist, like Reece. These were people who wouldn't even defend themselves because they were afraid to hurt you—what kind of offense did you really need?

A multibillion-dollar one, apparently, judging from the size of and funding behind Stone Solutions.

Her phone vibrated in her hand.

Alex: Hey, genius.

Alex: What are the chances I could buy you brunch tomorrow so we could chat about blogs and empaths and AMI?

She broke into a smile. It was from the cute blogger she'd met at the AMI meeting the night before, Alex. He'd only given her his first name, and she'd forgotten to ask for a last, too distracted by the Southern accent and hazel eyes and the rare pleasure of meeting someone who seemed genuinely interested in her work.

Gretel: Ten a.m.?

CHAPTER SIX

American Minds Intact is proud to sponsor Privacy in the Digital Age, a cutting-edge conference that asks the hard questions about how we protect our minds and thoughts when intrusions are everywhere. Don't miss our special keynote on Monday, now from Vivian Marist, president of Stone Solutions Canada!

Notice: Conference registration is required. We collect a broad range of personal data, which may be shared or sold at any time to third-party organizations, affiliates, advertisers, apps, internet service providers, and others. All registrants will be automatically added to our mailing lists and considered to consent to all terms and conditions.

—DIGITAL DIRECT MAIL MARKETING CAMPAIGN

JAMEY HAD JUST gotten home from dropping off Aisha when her phone chirped with an incoming text.

Stensby: Can I talk to you?
It's about empaths.

It was from one of the SPD officers she'd worked with over the years, Jared Stensby. As she closed the front door behind her, she could hear the shower running at the back of the house. Surprising Liam sounded like a much better time than talking to any of the SPD's officers, but she reluctantly dialed Stensby.

"Jamey." Stensby sounded relieved. "Thanks for calling. I know you're not on the force anymore, but I don't have anyone else I can try for this."

Jamey frowned. "What's going on with empaths?" she asked, as she stepped into the kitchen, following her nose to the coffee maker. She and Liam liked the same local roastery and he must have started a pot before getting in the shower. She already loved living with him.

"We got an APB from Port Angeles," Stensby said. "An empath is missing."

"Who?" Jamey said. "I've never met an empath from Port Angeles."

"Canadian tourist. Port A PD doesn't have anyone who knows anything about empaths," Stensby said, "but with you gone, we don't either."

Jamey pulled a mug out of the cabinet. That was true. The only person she would have trusted besides herself on anything empath-related was Josh Taylor, and he'd been another victim of November's mess. But Aisha was on her way to investigate a Canadian empath's murder; what were the odds another Canadian empath just happened to be missing in the States?

"For the record, it's been nuts around here since the Great Empath Shitshow that was the Hathaway murder," Stensby said. "We get questions every day wanting details about what happened on the roof of Stone Solutions."

The SPD didn't know an empath was responsible for Hathaway's death, but they were aware it hadn't been a normal case. Jamey's memories from the roof were blurred, thanks to having Cora Falcon's empathy in her system at the time, but she knew the SPD had arrived to find Reece kneeling in surrender at Grayson's feet next to Cedrick Stone's unconscious, bloody body. It couldn't have looked good. "And what are you telling them?" she said coolly.

"We have a script we have to stick to."

"And you're all sticking to it?" Jamey pressed. "Because no disrespect, but you've never really seemed like the type who cared about empaths. I know you never liked Reece."

"Because your brother is annoying as fuck," Stensby said bluntly. "But come on, Jamey, I still care about my *job*. I care about missing people, even if they're empaths."

Jamey glanced through the window at her pine trees, a rich deep green against the gray day. "So you want me to go to Port Angeles and look for this empath?"

"You don't even have to tell local PD you're there. I can send you everything we have, the name, the last known locations. You can do whatever you want with that information and I can sleep a little easier knowing you're on the case."

Jamey lingered at the dining table after hanging up with Stensby, drinking her coffee and tapping out a text. Aisha hadn't mentioned a second missing empath on the way to the airport. Was the case that fresh? There was no way the SPD could know about a missing empath before Grayson, could they?

She sent the message to Aisha, then glanced out the window again at the cold and wintery landscape. Jamey had been born in Atlanta and made all her earliest memories there, before her dad had died when she was five and her mom had gotten a too-good-to-pass-up job offer and moved them to Seattle.

In her most conspiracy-driven moments, Jamey sometimes wondered at the coincidence: her dad's sudden passing, her grieving mom lured to Seattle with a dream job, then hooking up with a stranger and just happening to get pregnant with an empath. But back then, Jamey hadn't been thinking about that. She'd been changing faster and more intensely than other kids, her strength increasing exponentially fast, her nose and ears becoming so sensitive that she spent most evenings in tears at the sheer overwhelm of the world.

They hadn't known what was happening to her, but Reece's empathy had also manifested by then, and their mom had accepted her kids were different and done her best to do right by them. Housing had been cheaper then, and their mom had scraped together enough for a fixer-upper bungalow on three peaceful acres of forested land outside of the city. Even all these years later, it was still Jamey's refuge; a place she never could have afforded on a detective's salary, the tranquility worth every minute of the commute.

She drummed her fingers on the table. Now she knew why her ears and nose were so sensitive, why she'd had the strength to help renovate the house, even as a preteen.

And Reece still didn't know he was the reason.

She picked up her phone. If Liam didn't want to come to Port Angeles, she'd need to borrow the Smart car, and it was better to tell Reece everything this way, actually, where he couldn't hear it if she lied. Not that she was *planning* to lie; she just had no intention of telling him both possible explanations. As far as she was concerned, the second one was a fucked-up load of paranoia not worth mentioning.

The phone rang several times before Reece picked up. "Jamey, what the hell," he said blearily. "Some of us sleep."

"Not you."

"There's nothing wrong with going to bed at one. Two. Four. Whatever. Why did you call?"

"I might need to make a day trip tomorrow," she said. "Which means I might need to borrow your car."

"Where are you going?" Reece said. "I'll highlight all the road hazards for you."

She pinched the bridge of her nose. Please let Liam want to join her. "I can't tell you where I'm going."

"Oh, come on—"

"It's not the driving lecture." Mostly not the driving lecture. "It might be case-related."

"What case?" Reece said. "You're not on the force anymore. Did you decide to work with Evan? I can make a map for him too; he also needs to practice his cornering."

"I'm not—wait, what do you mean, *also*? No, actually, never mind," she said. "There's something else I need to tell you before I go. Something more important than safe driving."

"What's more important than safe driving?"

"*This* is."

"Fine." She heard rustling in the background, sheets moving, maybe. Or maybe he was wearing Grayson's hoodie again, the one he thought she and Liam hadn't noticed was essentially Reece's security blanket. "I should tell you something too. But you first."

She took a breath through her nose. "You know I'm—not normal. And neither is Agent Grayson. And you know we're *not normal* in the same way."

"I told Evan once that he kind of reminded me of you," Reece said.

"Yeah, well. I know the reason now." She bit her lip, then said, "Because of our brothers."

The other end of the phone went eerily silent.

"It's not a bad thing," Jamey said quickly.

"Why do I feel like that's bullshit?" he said, with an edge. "Are you telling me this over the phone because I would have heard you lie just now?"

She winced. He was so damn intuitive when he wanted to know something. "It's not bullshit and it's not a bad thing," she insisted. "Apparently baby empaths have a lot of love but not much control. The empathy spills over onto their sibling and can impact their limbic and endocrine systems."

"Like with Cora's *thralls*?" Reece sounded horrified.

"No," she said. "Totally different. Cora changed them on purpose."

"But Jamey." Reece's voice had gone quieter, hoarser. "Changing people isn't something empaths do until they become corrupted. How do you know it wasn't the corruption inside me that changed you? Cora made her thralls to protect herself. What if the corrupted part of me wanted to make you strong because it knows I'm weak?"

Well, shit. Jamey hadn't been planning to tell him that theory, that most scientists thought the corruption caused the change so the sibling would protect the pacifist empath. *Parasitic relationship*, Grayson had said the scientists hypothesized, but she was never going to say that word to Reece. "You're not *weak*," she said. "And the idea that the corruption was behind the change is fucked up. It is fucked up to think a tiny kid could be capable of that, even unconsciously."

Reece's voice wasn't much more than a whisper. "I don't know what I'm capable of anymore, Jamey."

"Hey," she said. "Knock it off. You're not going to become corrupted. Grayson's whole job is to stop that from happening, and even if he somehow failed, you've got me. I got an hour-long lecture from you because I once went out of turn at a four-way stop sign. If I let you burn down Seattle, you'd never let me hear the end of it."

"Not funny," said Reece.

"Kind of funny."

"...maybe," he grudgingly admitted. There was a pause, then he said, "But you do need to know that when two cars arrive at a stop sign at the same time, the person on the right—"

"Oh my God, *stop*. I got my lecture already and we're not doing it again," she said. "What was it you wanted to tell me?"

"It's my email. I keep getting—" Reece seemed to stumble on his words. There was a pause, and then he said, "I, um. I keep getting locked out; you know how bad I am with tech. But it's fine. I'll figure it out."

"You sure?"

"Yeah, yeah," he said quickly. "I think I just need to reset my password or something."

"Okay," she said. "Let me know if I can help."

"Of course I would let you know if I needed your help with something," Reece said, still quick. "Have a good trip, and don't let Liam text and drive. And don't you text and drive either. And if you have to have music on, keep it at a reasonable volume and—"

"Bye, Reece," she said pointedly, and hung up.

At the university hospital, Grayson lingered in the parking lot for a moment, checking his messages. EI said the blood tests he had asked for were delayed, but they had the lab's every assurance that they would be done as soon as possible.

He'd never had any issues with delays before.

Eventually Grayson went into the hospital and followed a petite resident in blue scrubs down to the basement morgue, leaning against the back wall of the elevator so he didn't loom over her.

"Does the staff who looked at the empath have any thoughts?" Grayson said, as he held the elevator door for her.

The resident glanced up at him. "You read the report, right?"

"I did," he acknowledged. "But it helps to hear theories." And it helped him gauge how much the staff might know and how much cover-up was gonna be needed.

He got the door to the morgue for her, and they entered. "Her fingernails are a mess," she finally said.

Grayson raised his eyebrows.

"I mean, I know empaths *say* they wear their gloves all the time," she said, more quickly. "But her nails look all chewed up, like she's a nail biter, and how could she be biting them if she was wearing her gloves? Are we sure they *really* wear them all the time?"

An image of Reece rose in Grayson's mind, curled up on the

passenger seat of the truck, bundled in the sweatshirt Grayson had tossed in the backseat long months and miles before. Reece had been chewing on his thumb, because sometimes even empaths who dutifully wore their gloves sought outlets for their anxiety.

Granted, Reece *hadn't* been in gloves at that moment, and that particular bout of anxiety was probably because he'd caused a world of trouble that night. He'd been cute in that hoodie, though.

A few minutes later, Grayson had on a pair of latex gloves at least two sizes too small. The resident had wheeled out Marie Pelletier's body on its stainless steel table, covered to the neck with a sheet. Ms. Pelletier had the brown curls she'd had in her social media pictures, but her features were less recognizable, scraped and bruised, nose maybe broken from a face-first fall.

The resident disappeared into the room's tiny office as Grayson stepped over to the body and picked up the empath's left hand. Contrary to AMI's ramblings, there was nothing you could immediately see with your naked eyes to know an empath's hand from anyone else's. They had extra friction ridges, which made ink fingerprints appear smudged and inconclusive. Marist had promised that Stone Solutions Canada had received digital versions of Ms. Pelletier's for analysis.

The resident had been right, though. Ms. Pelletier's nails were bitten to the quick.

Grayson lifted her right hand, then hesitated. It was hard to pick out in a hospital morgue that used chemicals to stave off decay, but the scent from the glove was here too.

He bent closer. It was stronger than it had been in the glove and seemed to be coming from the back of her hand.

He glanced up, but the resident had closed the office door, her profile partially visible through the office's glass window.

He reached for his coat and withdrew his pocket flashlight. Turning so his back blocked his actions, he picked up Ms. Pelletier's right hand again and flicked on the blue light. It lit up like Christmas: UV marker on the back of her hand. A loop like a messy, lowercase "L" that looked like it had been hastily hand-drawn.

Keeping his back to the room to block the resident's view, Grayson snapped a couple pictures. It was the kind of thing clubs or events might do, to mark people who were old enough to drink, or who'd already paid and could reenter. He might be able to find the club that marked hands like this.

But Ms. Pelletier would have had to take off her gloves to get this mark, and an empath going without gloves was illegal—illegal in Canada too. An empath wouldn't do it.

Another memory of Reece came to mind, this time the security footage of him walking bare-handed into Stone Solutions.

Well. Most empaths wouldn't do it.

Reece skipped his new building's elevator, bypassing the little lobby on the fourth floor and heading toward the end of the hall instead. He didn't want to be in a closed-in metal box with other people, didn't want to meet the eyes of the lobby's doormen. The fire stairs were a better exit; they didn't use electricity, they led to the ground floor of the parking garage, and best of all, they were empty.

He made his way to his car and a few minutes later, he was driving south on I-5 without a real destination, one thought overriding everything else.

He'd changed Jamey. *He* was the reason she was the way she was.

Eventually he took an exit, heading west as he wound his way through some of the towns that scrunched together to fill the corridor between Seattle and Tacoma. The direction was reflex as much as anything else; maybe it was because he'd been raised near the ocean, but when the world stopped making sense, his instincts led him to the water, to watch the endless waves and let them carry the weight of his thoughts.

He ended up at a small park along the sound, where the shore stretched beyond sight in both directions. The tide was out, leaving behind glistening gray rocks under a lighter gray sky. He followed it, leaving the car behind to walk down to the beach, hands stuck deep in the pockets of Grayson's hoodie. He was mostly alone; just a bird-watcher with binoculars and two sets of parents investigating the tide pools with their toddlers.

He sat down on a mostly dry rock, watching the families for a moment. Jamey had a picture of them on the beach that their mom had taken twenty years ago, when they were six and twelve. Back then, he used to talk to everyone he saw, learning the complexities of emotions the way other kids learned colors; purple was made from red and blue, like hurt might be made of betrayal and loneliness.

Reece would wander too far, and inevitably either tire himself out or piss someone off, and Jamey would show up and rescue him. The picture was of one of the countless piggyback rides she used to give him, because she'd already been as strong as an adult at that point. And that was his fault—he'd been changing her, morphing her into the perfect protector. Had she even wanted to rescue him? Or had he given her no choice, fucked up her instincts along with her strength and senses?

He wanted to believe he would never. But corruption had turned Cora into a killer, and he already knew it was inside him too.

He'd been about to tell Jamey about the emails, but how could he? For fuck's sake, she'd become a detective so she could protect other people as her job. Had he made her want that? How could he ask her to rescue him yet again when the only reason she might want to was because he'd changed her?

How could he ever ask Grayson for help when Grayson's brother had done the same thing to him?

He glanced down at the hoodie he was wearing. The one he wore because it made him feel better. That maybe Grayson had only shared with him because his empath brother had made him want to protect empaths.

Reece tightened his jaw and looked out at the ocean. Maybe AMI and Stone Solutions were right. Maybe empaths were too dangerous. Abominations that shouldn't even exist.

Maybe it was pointless to fight the corruption. Why resist so hard if he'd been evil since he was a kid? He could let go, just let it take over—

His phone pinged.

Reece blinked, his thoughts slipping away like the tide rolling out, and picked up the phone.

Grayson: You ever go to clubs?

Reece blinked at the text.

Reece: Why? You planning an outing for us that doesn't involve handcuffs?

Grayson: When I get sass instead of answers?

Grayson: No.

Reece cracked a smile.

Reece: I've gone. Very occasionally.

Grayson: If the club wants to stamp your hand, what do you do?

Reece: I just have them stamp high up on my arm instead. Obviously empaths don't take the gloves off in public.

Grayson: Obviously. Except for that one time when you did. And it made the news.

Reece gave the phone a dirty look.

Reece: Did you text just to remind me what a failure of an empath I am?

Grayson: Failure? Care Bear, a pair of gloves isn't what makes you an empath. Your compassion never got left in the glove box of your Micro Machine and towed to Tacoma.

The knot in Reece's chest loosened. His gaze lingered on Grayson's text. *Care Bear.* Such a ridiculous thing to call an empath when the Dead Man knew better than anyone else exactly how *un*-caring empaths could become.

And yet. He still used it for Reece, even though he knew Reece's secrets now.

He looked at the text another moment, then shook himself irritably. Grayson probably used that nickname with all empaths. Nothing more than habit.

A light drizzle was starting. Reece pocketed the phone and stood up from his rock, pulling the hood of Grayson's sweatshirt up over his hair as he started back to the car.

Aisha sighed and took off her glasses, setting them on the mattress next to her so she could rub at her eyes.

Grayson had forwarded the empath's name, and Aisha had gone to Stone Solutions Canada's Ottawa office straight from the airport for a copy of Marie Pelletier's records. Now she was working on two lap desks on the hotel's king-size bed, her Stone Solutions laptop on one and her personal laptop on the other, curled up under the covers with her printed pictures and handwritten notes spread out around her on the glaringly white comforter. Night had fallen and the curtains were still open, the window a square of black glass dotted with Ottawa's city lights.

She let her head fall back against the pillows stacked behind her and stared at the blurry TV, which she'd left soundlessly playing a station that ran old sci-fi movies.

Some creep had smashed an empath over the head and left her dead in a park. Why? Marie had been absolutely harmless, as far as Aisha could tell. The national file kept in Ottawa was slim, but it seemed she'd gone to every appointment Stone Solutions Canada had asked her to and worn gloves without complaint. She'd had one sibling, a sister, and several cousins, but no other empaths in the family.

Grayson had also forwarded Aisha the records from Quebec. Aisha read over Marie's job history, but again nothing stood out. She'd moved to Montreal from a smaller city for graduate studies at McGill and had been a librarian at the same facility for four years. She fostered cats for an animal shelter and seemed to have spent most of her free time volunteering at food banks and senior citizens' organizations.

The world was almost certainly worse off for her loss. Why couldn't people just leave empaths alone?

Aisha put her glasses back on and picked up her phone. Grayson had texted to say he might have a lead on Marie's location the night before and was checking all the clubs in Burlington. Jamey's text had asked if she knew anything about another Canadian empath gone missing from Port Angeles.

Aisha had sent the query on to Grayson, but he would have already said something to her if he'd heard anything. Stone

Solutions Canada should have already been on top of it, like they were supposed to be with Marie.

She looked at Jamey's message again and then hit Call. "Hey," she said, when Jamey picked up. "You hear anything further about the empath in Port Angeles?"

"No." Jamey didn't sound happy. "Still waiting on Stensby to send over the details. I'm planning a day trip tomorrow, leaving in the morning with Liam. Any luck in Ottawa?"

"No." Aisha wasn't happy either. "But we did finally confirm the murdered empath was from Montreal. I'll probably head over there tomorrow."

She glanced at her personal laptop, where Marie's social media was splashed across the screen. She looked like she'd been a sweetheart, with big brown curls and glasses, smiling at the camera with a cat in her arms.

"Speaking of Canada's empaths." Jamey sounded a little more hesitant. "Cedrick Stone had said Cora Falcon was being sent somewhere in British Columbia. Are there any updates on her? I haven't heard anything since the night we—well, you remember."

Aisha wasn't going to forget it. Jamey and Cora had faced each other in November, but they'd been too evenly matched: a corrupted empath versus the natural immunity of an empath's sibling. Cora had tried to thrall Jamey and ended up knocking herself out; Jamey had teetered between sanity and madness until she'd finally fought off Cora's empathy.

A lot of people would blame Cora for everything that had happened the night of Senator Hathaway's death. But Cora had begun that night as a kindhearted therapist before a pair of rich creeps had tortured and murdered her fiancé to create a corrupted empath; Aisha put the lion's share of the blame on Cedrick Stone's machinations.

"Obviously it wasn't a fun night for me, but what happened

to Cora and her fiancé was—well." Jamey sighed. "Just tell me she's not, like, suffering."

"She better not be," Aisha said. "Corrupted empaths are kept at the Polaris Empathic Research Facility in British Columbia. When the Empath Initiative created the role of the Dead Man, Grayson had conditions, and several of them have to do with the living conditions at Polaris. All the rules were being followed last time I checked."

"You've been there?" Jamey said, sounding surprised.

"The visitors' list is minuscule but Grayson got me on it," Aisha admitted. "There are only three empaths there—well. Four now, with Cora."

"And they're all as dangerous as Cora?"

"Yeah," Aisha said, more quietly. "But they've all been hurt too. I'm not making excuses for their crimes, but none of them corrupted themselves."

Jamey sighed. "I want to make a crack about what kind of living conditions an empath hunter would insist on for the empaths he hunts. But I'm guessing Grayson actually improved things for the empaths?"

"He definitely did," Aisha said. "And he's making Polaris search for a way to reverse the corruption."

"I thought Grayson believes it's permanent."

"Oh, he does. He believes down to his soul that once an empath is corrupted, there's no going back." Aisha cleared her throat. "He made that condition for me. Because *I* want to believe we can get the pacifists back."

"So do I," Jamey said firmly.

That made Aisha smile. "You should see how much Victor Nichols, the Polaris director, hates Grayson for coming in and disrupting his kingdom up at Polaris. But Nichols doesn't have a choice; there's never been anyone with Grayson's complete immunity to empaths before. EI and Stone Solutions know he's unique and they *need* him."

"Reece said it was Grayson's corrupted empath brother who took away his emotions and let him become the Dead Man." Jamey's voice had gone—not soft, exactly, but softer, with something like sympathy. "Had EI already created the Dead Man role before that happened?"

"No," Aisha said, with the same pang she always got when she thought about it. "I don't know much about what happened to the Grayson brothers beyond it being some bad, twisted shit. But when everything came to light and EI Director Traynor discovered what Grayson had become, he swooped in to capitalize on the opportunity."

"Like vultures," Jamey muttered. "But then, as you said: there's no one else like Grayson. Guess they couldn't pass that up."

After they hung up, Aisha tabbed over to another social media account, this time Cora Falcon's, which hadn't been updated since that November night. Aisha scrolled through the first few pictures, all of Cora and her fiancé, John. John had been a doctor at a veterans' hospital, Cora a therapist. They looked so happy together, gazing at each other like they couldn't believe they'd gotten so lucky.

Aisha ran a hand over the scar on her neck. It *was* unbelievable luck, to be loved by an empath.

Her gaze lingered on Cora, the obvious adoration for her fiancé in her eyes, the sweet expressions on her pretty face, the way she'd rested her head against John's as they took another beaming selfie.

Marie Pelletier had been horribly lost and now Cora was a murderer.

"Some of us know you're a victim too," Aisha said out loud, to Cora's picture. "They better be treating you okay out on the North Coast. We're going to solve this murder, and then afterwards, I'm coming to make sure they are."

CHAPTER SEVEN

Again and again, society expects monsters to do them the courtesy of looking like monsters. People want evil to be ugly; to judge on sight; to be spared the effort of thinking for themselves. They want to pick a team, and then fervently believe the bad guys are, of course, only on the other team.

They're so woefully unprepared for REAL monsters.

—EXCERPT FROM UNTITLED BLOG

DIRECTOR TRAYNOR HELPED himself to another bite of the Wagyu beef tartare, gaze occasionally stealing to the sprawl of Seattle's night lights far below. The restaurant's lighting was dimmed to allow the view to take center stage, the white tablecloths softly glowing around the room as candlelight reflected off the cocktail glasses on most tables. Marist certainly never skimped when she invited him to join her.

Nichols was with them again as well, ignoring both his companions and the rotating view of Seattle at night as he tapped on his phone.

How many times had the three of them dined together now?

Traynor had lost track. He'd made the requisite protests early on that it was unseemly for the head of the Empath Initiative to accept expensive trips and dinner from Stone Solutions, but Marist knew exactly the right responses, joking that Stone Solutions ought to be buying him plenty of drinks to make up for all the headaches they gave him. Traynor *deserved* these dinners, she would say, delivering the line with a laugh.

She was very good at the game. Forceful means would have been obvious, but couch it all in friendly smiles and bright tones of voice, and it was easy to give in to her gifts and entertain her every suggestion. Marist could have been a politician; her constituents buying into whatever lies she sold because she delivered the message so kindly.

Marist glanced at Nichols, then, who was still on his phone. "Victor, we have the director of the Empath Initiative *right here*," she said playfully. "We're plying him with foie gras and cognac; this is the moment to ask EI for whatever you want."

She winked at Traynor, making it a joke despite every word being stone-cold truth.

"Polaris needs more funding," Nichols said, not looking up from the phone. "A lot more funding. Our new guest, Cora Falcon, was responsible for a senator's murder, after all."

"Yes, look how busy Victor is," Marist said. "Poor man is working through dinner."

Nichols glanced up. "Conducting stress tests," he said. "Somehow I always end up being the one stuck doing the, shall we say, delicate work?"

All of them knew Traynor would never ask for details. Plausible deniability was a very important part of the balance. The actual mechanics of any tests were the domain of the scientists; the Empath Initiative director simply approved or denied whether they took place.

Traynor picked up his drink. "Tell me more about how much funding you need."

★★★

Reece was overly familiar with places vegan insomniacs could haunt in Seattle, and went from the beach to a coffeehouse by Rainier University that was open late and did fair trade hot chocolates with house-made almond milk. He spent the evening hunched over a table at the back, scrolling through job postings on his phone with increasing hopelessness. He'd dropped out of college junior year—thanks, anxiety—and was inept at tech. What was he even qualified to do besides consult on nonviolent crime and nag about traffic laws? And Jamey had texted to say Liam was going with her to Port Angeles in the morning and she didn't need Reece's car; who was he supposed to nag now?

He of course had kept on his gloves inside the coffeehouse, trying to ignore the attention they drew. But there were only so many nervous, distrusting, sometimes flat-out hostile looks Reece could stand in one evening, and he left sooner than he'd planned, making it home a little after eleven.

He parked in his spot on the second floor of the high-rise's garage, his beat-up Smart car flanked by a Mercedes on one side and a Lexus on the other. His side of the garage overlooked the same street as the studio, and as he climbed out of the car, he paused.

A white man in a camouflage coat and balaclava was across the street, leaning on the dark windows of the closed coffee shop. Despite his outwardly relaxed position, his shoulders were tensed.

He looked *exactly* like the man Reece had seen yesterday, the one who had been lingering and smoking outside the same coffee shop, watching Reece's building in *exactly* the same manner.

Reece walked straight up to the edge of the garage. "Sir!" he shouted down, and the man startled. "Sir, are you all right? Are you here again because you have nowhere else to go?"

The man's eyes widened and he hastily shoved off the building.

"Is your face all covered up because of the weather?" Reece asked loudly, as the man scrambled to pull his hat down to his brows. "Do you need to get off the street? Need somewhere to stay or a ride to a shelter?"

The man was already hustling down the street. "It's very cold outside tonight," Reece called after him. "I can help you find a place to get warm!"

The man increased his pace, disappearing around the corner without ever saying a word. Maybe he did have a place to go after all.

Reece shut the car door. He paused for a moment, staring at his rear taillight suspiciously. He took the covers off to replace the bulbs on a regular schedule, but now it was missing one of the screws. Had someone else taken it off—to put something inside, perhaps? His toolbox was still at Jamey's; he'd have to make time to drive out to her place to check his car.

Up in the studio, he tossed his gloves on the kitchen counter and got a bowl of cereal with several extra teaspoons of sugar before curling up on the couch with his phone. He hadn't texted Grayson since the beach and his last text was still on-screen.

Grayson: Failure? Care Bear,
a pair of gloves isn't what makes
you an empath. Your compassion
never got left in the glove box of
your Micro Machine and towed
to Tacoma.

Reece's gaze lingered on the message. These days, the empath hunter had more faith in the empath than he did in himself.

He shook himself before he could have any feelings about that and sent a much grumpier text instead.

Reece: Do you and the Empath Initiative really think I won't find a tracker in my rear taillight?

He had just finished his cereal and was contemplating his anti-anxiety arts and crafts stash when he got a response.

Grayson: If EI put a tracker on you, then I wasn't made aware. I told them to leave you alone.

Reece blinked. He hadn't been *made aware* that Grayson had told EI to leave him alone. But no, there would be no thinking about that, just like he wasn't thinking about Grayson having faith in him. He settled a little deeper into the couch cushions, pushing the too-long sleeves of Grayson's hoodie up his arms to keep his hands free so he could text back.

Reece: So did you visit the clubs you were asking about?

Oh, that had been a bad question to ask. What Grayson did with his nights wasn't any of his business. Even if apparently some of those nights he was telling EI to fuck off and standing between Reece and his demons, promising Reece that he wasn't a complete failure of an empath. None of his business. Absolutely none.

Reece's phone beeped.

Grayson: In a sense.

So Grayson *was* out tonight. Maybe he was having drinks. Dancing. Deep in a throng of people who could all touch him without blacking out.

Reece: Bet your hair was excited to show off how pretty and perfect it always is.

Grayson: Oh look, you don't guess everything right. It's a mess right now.

Reece frowned.

Reece: Who messed up your hair?

Whoops. He hadn't thought that text through. Did that sound territorial? Just because Reece couldn't touch him didn't mean other people had the same problem, and just because Grayson didn't have emotions didn't mean he was celibate. He could totally be having sex with those other people. The ones he could touch. Who weren't Reece.

Grayson: Hotel gym.

Grayson at the gym.

Shit.

Muscles weren't something Reece thought much about, but a post-workout high—he could drown in those endorphins until the world disappeared. He tried to push aside the fresh rush of interest that had suddenly unbalanced him. Even after a workout, Grayson probably didn't get any kind of emotion Reece could pick up—and Reece couldn't touch him in the first place. He needed to remember those things, just like he needed to respond like a normal person who had normal reactions to the thought of their platonic not-quite-friend at the gym.

Reece: Oh yeah? Why the gym?

Reece: Wait, are you still on East Coast time? It's like two a.m. for you.

Grayson: I struck out everywhere I went tonight. Needed to think.

Another frown creased Reece's face. So Grayson had been at a club trying to pick someone up? Who?

Reece took a breath through his nose. None of his damn business, that's who. He wrote out an appropriately platonic text, the kind a normal frenemy might send. If there was such a thing.

Reece: How the hell did YOU strike out? I've seen the way people pant in your direction.

Grayson: Not people. LEADS. I don't know why you keep thinking the Dead Man dates.

Oh. Well, then. Reece tried to wipe the smile off his face as he texted back.

Reece: So you're on a case? An empath case?

Grayson: What else would I be on?

You could be on me—no no no, delete delete DELETE.

Texting Grayson late at night was a bad decision. Reece was an empath; he knew better, knew this was when his own inhibitions went down. He needed to plant himself firmly on Team A, the normies who were smart enough to be afraid of

Grayson, and stay the hell off Team B, the fruit loops who'd add *Grayson* plus *sex* and come up with *yes, please.*

Reece: So you went to the gym to think? Why, do you think better when you're lifting those things that weigh more than me?

Grayson: They'd have to weigh a lot more than you.

Reece paused, looking at the texts that echoed the conversation they'd had in November. At the time, he'd thought Grayson was exaggerating. But Grayson was like Jamey—which meant he might actually be *downplaying* his strength.

Might literally be able to toss Reece around without breaking a sweat.

Reece: If you're really that strong it would make that second-date hate-sex interesting.

Reece stared at the text he'd just sent Grayson. Shit, he hadn't thought that through either. Well…fine. This was fine. No big deal. Platonic frenemies joked about hate-fucking each other.

Probably.

Grayson: First of all, why do you keep saying IF? Second, the moment I touch you, it's gonna knock you out again, and isn't that the part that would make hate-sex interesting?

Grayson: And finally, we aren't at a second date. When was the first? The dinner you ran off halfway through to commit a felony?

Reece let out his breath in a huffed half laugh. There. See? Grayson wasn't making it weird. Just your casual everyday hypothetical hate-fuck between not-friends.

Reece: Maybe I was playing hard to get.

Grayson: Guess a lot of empaths play hard to get with me then.

Reece snorted.

Reece: I got used to your voice and it doesn't bother me anymore. You never did tell me if the same thing would happen if we touched enough times.

Reece: Hypothetically.

Reece: Obviously.

Grayson: Nice try, sugar. But that is one of the Dead Man's anti-empathy defenses and you don't get the answer to that question.

Reece's lips turned up, a tiny bit sly.

Reece: So there IS an answer, and you know what that answer is?

Grayson: I told you to be good and stop using those empath skills to guess national secrets.

Grayson: You're not being very good.

Reece: Sure I am. Being bad would be completely ignoring all that stupid confidentiality crap around your location and asking for a picture of you lifting the weights that weigh a lot more than me.

Reece: Which you could send. Just saying.

Son of a bitch. Had Reece really just asked the Dead Man for a picture? Was he thinking any of these texts through or had his brain short-circuited somewhere back at the idea of getting tossed around in a friendly hypothetical hate-fuck?

Grayson: Pictures of me are classified.

Reece sat up, frowning.

Reece: What, seriously?

Grayson: The less people know about me, the better. I'm a weapon, remember?

Reece: No, you're a person. You can't take or share pictures? Not even with family?

Grayson: Haven't you worked out that there isn't any family anymore?

Reece pressed his lips together.

Grayson: I know you're an empath, but don't get upset. It's not a big deal. I don't have family or friends. I don't date. There's no one to want pictures of me. I might as well be dead—and that's the point of the Dead Man. It's not like it bothers me.

It bothered Reece.

Reece: Send me a picture.

Grayson: I just told you I can't.

Reece typed back so quickly his fingers stumbled on the letters.

Reece: I don't care about some stupid policy or national security or whatever the bullshit reason is.

Reece: I want a picture of you, Evan.

He sent the text and then stuck his thumb between his teeth, chewing on the tip. The thought of Grayson being so isolated he couldn't even share pictures of himself—

Grayson could say *don't get upset* until his Texas cows came home. Didn't matter; Reece was pissed.

He waited, but a couple minutes ticked by and there was no response. Maybe he'd pushed too hard—

His phone screen lit up, and there was the selfie of Grayson he'd asked for, of his reflection in the mirror in a small hotel gym. A water bottle and folded sweatshirt were set off to the side, and he was standing next to some cardio machine, maybe between reps or sets or the hell if Reece knew the lingo when the biggest weight he lifted was the spoon in the sugar bowl. Grayson had a towel draped over one of his shoulders, his sleeveless shirt damp and molded so closely to his torso that Reece could almost feel the contours of his body under his fingertips.

But his gaze was drawn to Grayson's face. A picture couldn't be read like a person anyway, so in a still image like this the lack of emotions could be mistaken for a blank expression. And without the distraction of the void of Grayson's missing emotions, Reece could pick out little things he might not be able to notice in person—that Grayson's hair still looked photo-ready, even mussed and damp with sweat. That his face was flushed, not red like Reece got but a tawny pink, and that he had a five-o'clock shadow a few shades deeper than his hair. That there were dark circles under his eyes, like most anyone would have when they hadn't slept enough.

Reece's gaze lingered on the dark circles, the reddish tint to the whites of hazel eyes. As far as he could tell, Grayson had been traveling since he left Seattle. Maybe he hadn't had much time to rest. Did he ever go home? Where was his home these days? Still Texas?

Reece tightened his grip on his phone.

And then he hit Call.

It only rang once before Grayson picked up. "Hey, Care Bear."

Jesus. Reece *really* liked that deep drawl.

He shook himself. Not the time to let his mind go down that road when his thoughts were already veering from Platonic Avenue. "Thought I should call and tell you that you've fallen right into my trap. I'm going to sell this picture to *Eyes on Empaths* and make enough money to retire young."

"Please. If you suddenly came into a lot of money, you'd donate it all to charity."

Reece huffed another half laugh. No one got him like Grayson. "I like the picture."

"I'm a sweaty mess."

"Shut up," said Reece. "I know your looks are wasted on me since I barely notice that kind of thing, but even I can tell that *Eyes on Empaths* readers would lose their shit over you." He shifted to lie flat on his back on the couch, the hood of Grayson's sweatshirt bunched under his head. "So. Where did you send this hot classified selfie from?"

"You think that's not classified too? Or are you about to call *national security* a bullshit reason again because that empath compassion got needlessly riled up on behalf of a man without feelings?"

Reece ignored that. "I know it's a gym in a hotel."

"That's already more information than you should have."

"And yesterday you texted about being across the continent and you didn't deny still being on Eastern time. Can we play twenty questions? Do the people in your current state sound like you?"

"I don't sound anything like someone from the Carolinas or Tennessee or Georgia."

"That's cute, that you think I would be able to tell the difference." Reece closed his eyes. "You've got a water bottle but you're not sentimental enough to keep a favorite one with you. You were getting on a plane last night, so I bet you bought it in an airport gift shop. I don't know what that 'W' on it means, but from what I know about you, I bet it's for sports, maybe football, and the only thing with a 'W' I can think of on the East Coast is Washington, DC."

Reece opened his eyes, staring up at the ceiling. "Except you're standing next to cardio equipment, not weights, which you said would have to weigh more than me to help you think. So maybe the weights are too basic for you, which makes me think basic hotel, which makes me think you flew somewhere from DC and now you're in a smaller city. You brought a sweatshirt with you even though presumably you didn't need to leave the hotel to get to the gym, so you probably flew north where the buildings aren't warm enough for your Southern tastes. You keep harping on about national security, as if it's top of your mind, as if whatever you're up to is a little more *inter*national than usual, so maybe you're up by the Canadian border. I'm bad at geography, so I'd have to look at a map, but maybe somewhere in Vermont or Maine?"

The other side of the phone was silent.

"Am I close?" Reece prodded.

He heard Grayson exhale. "You're being careful, right?"

Reece frowned, stung. "What do you mean? I'm not using any extra abilities. I wouldn't—"

"Nothing would work on me, but I know you're not and I didn't mean it like that," Grayson said, which made Reece feel better. "I meant you're not doing stupid things like running off by yourself or trusting strangers, are you? You gotta know there's a lot of people who'd like to get their hands on an empath as intuitive as you. Tell me you can stay out of trouble until I can get back to Seattle."

Reece broke into a smile. "You're coming back to Seattle?"

"Did you hear any of the other words I just said?"

"When?"

"Are you being careful?"

"Soon?"

"Reece."

"What?"

"Try to find even a thimble's worth of the survival instinct everything else on this planet's got," said Grayson, "and promise me you're gonna be careful."

Reece rolled his eyes. "Fine, yes, I'll be careful."

Lie. Oops.

"Uh-huh." Grayson sounded completely unconvinced. "Did you just lie to me?"

"No." *Lie.* Reece winced.

"You're still lying, aren't you."

"You know you have to come see me when you're here," Reece said, instead of admitting anything. "I'll give you back your hoodie." *Lie.* Oh, come on. He wasn't actually keeping the hoodie. Was he?

"I kinda thought it fit you better."

That made Reece smile again even while he scoffed. "You remember how big I am, right? Or not-big, in this case?"

"Fit isn't just about size," said Grayson.

"Pretty sure there's a sex joke in there. A hate-sex joke, even."

"What, like how no part of me would ever fit in any part of you?"

That startled a laugh out of Reece.

And sent a shiver up his spine.

"Don't flatter yourself," he said.

"I'm not," Grayson said dryly. "You remember how big *I* am, don't you?"

"Are you kidding?" said Reece. "That's a feature, not a bug."

"This, right here, is that empath lack of self-preservation we just talked about."

"No, this is you threatening me with a good time again, like we talked about."

This time Grayson scoffed. "I got close to a foot and a hundred pounds on you, and you know my strength is all jacked up."

"Yeah, you really don't know the difference between a threat and a good time," said Reece, "because every word you say just makes it better."

"I know how empaths work, Reece." Grayson's drawl was deep and gravelly in his ear. "Wouldn't matter how good a time I wanted to give you—*you* get in bed with someone to lose yourself to their emotions. You make them feel the best they've ever felt because you get all those good feelings back tenfold. But I'm not like other people. You wouldn't feel a thing from me."

"Nice try, sugar," Reece said, mimicking Grayson's accent. "But you don't guess everything right either, because that's not how empaths work and I'm frankly surprised you didn't already know."

"Then how—"

"Yes, the ricochet is amazing but it's *making someone else feel good* that really gets us going, and you're goddamn right I could make you feel the best you've ever felt. And for the record, right now I'm *not* lying, and I'm still not lying when I say you don't need emotions for me to have the time of my life wrecking you until we broke the fucking bed."

There was a pause.

"Hypothetically," Reece said quickly.

"Hypothetically," Grayson said, almost at the same time. "We can't touch."

"We can't touch," Reece agreed, "and you're an empath hunter."

"I'm an empath *specialist* and you're an empath."

"I'm an empath and I'm supposed to run away from the Dead Man."

"You're supposed to run away from the Dead Man who's supposed to be doing his job," said Grayson.

"So obviously it's a completely hypothetical hate-fuck."

"Obviously."

There was another pause.

"It's getting late," Reece said, right as Grayson said, "I should hit the shower."

"Bye."

"Bye."

Reece quickly hung up. He set the phone on his chest, face down, and looked up at the ceiling.

Wouldn't matter how good a time I wanted to give you.

Hypothetically. Grayson had been speaking hypothetically, just like Reece had been speaking hypothetically when he talked about making Grayson feel so amazing they broke the bed.

Because he had been. Speaking hypothetically. Obviously.

He snatched up his phone and lit the screen, which filled with the gym selfie Grayson had sent. No hint of the emotionless Dead Man in a picture, just Grayson, easy for Reece to take in every detail of his body, his eyes, his lips.

Reece took a breath through his nose. Grayson was attractive. Reece could admit that. And so obviously yes, the picture was hot; hot enough someone else might shamelessly save it as his background so he could enjoy the sight every time he picked up his phone.

Someone else might do that. But not Reece. Reece was an emotionally sophisticated empath who knew better than to pine after an empath hunter. He was *Team A*.

He stared at his picture of Grayson, flushed and sweaty, his hair mussed, probably exactly like he'd look if Reece spent a night wrecking him.

"Son of a bitch," he muttered out loud.

CHAPTER EIGHT

...but subject so far remains unconscious. Until he wakes, we cannot be sure exactly what changes have—

Hello? What's that sound?

...is someone there?

—PARTIAL RECORDING, MADE AT [REDACTED], TEXAS

GRETEL PULLED INTO a metered spot near her favorite brunch place, idling for a moment as she checked her makeup in the rearview mirror and whether it was at least somewhat camouflaging how little she'd slept last night. She'd posted the article about the empath's murder in Vermont, but her dad's comments about a *good offense against the empaths* had stuck in her head and next thing she knew, she'd spent six hours down a research rabbit hole, from Cedrick Stone's roots in defense contracting to the Empath Initiative appointing a former general as director to Vivian Marist's master's degree in strategy and foreign policy.

She'd made notes for a new post. It wasn't the kind of thing she would normally write for her blog; not the wild theories and Dead Man stories that got her the most traffic. But it just seemed odd, to keep turning up military ties and funding connected to the organizations that monitored pacifists.

As she stepped inside the restaurant, her gaze went past the hostess to a table along the window, and she broke into a smile. "Alex," she called.

But he'd already stood up, waving at her. When she joined him, he got her chair for her. "I want to protest this archaic ritual of the patriarchy," she said, as she sat. "But it kind of feels like you just did this automatically."

"Guilty as charged," he said, his words shaped by that subtle accent she'd noticed at the AMI meeting. "My dad was really strict about manners. It's kind of a thing, where I grew up."

"Where was that?"

"Texas." He flashed her an apologetic smile. "Would it make it better if I told you I do it for boys too?"

She had to smile. "Maybe," she admitted.

They ordered brunch—California omelet for her, avocado toast for him. As the waiter left, Alex held up his phone. "I just finished your latest post. Who's killing Canadian empaths in Vermont?"

"You saw that already?" she said. "I just got that up. You're so fast."

"*You're* so fast," he countered. "The news doesn't even know about that yet. How did you find out so early?"

Gretel shrugged. "Local gossip blogs, that type of thing."

Alex propped his chin in his hand. "You don't have to lie to me, you know," he said wryly. "I care about the information; I'm not gonna ever scoop your stories or judge how you got it."

How had he known that wasn't the truth? She probably should have been annoyed, or angry, but Alex's wry tone and smile made her feel like they were coconspirators, and she'd never really had one of those. She pursed her lips, but then admitted, "I find out from AMI. Well, usually my dad. He makes me send out notes to AMI as if they're from him, so I have his email password and I read all his emails."

"Oh, that's clever of you," Alex said, and it sounded admiring. "And not very nice of him, to take credit for your work. No wonder you started your own project."

"I need to start telling him *no* and completely break away," she said, sighing. "My dad's a giant fucking hypocrite and I hate it. So was Senator Hathaway. She claimed to hate empaths because of privacy violations, but then voted for all these bills that let the police monitor citizens and corporations buy up our data. She was voting away all our protections, it's right there in public records, but my dad never cared as long as she kept up her anti-empathy rhetoric. Cedrick Stone was the same way. The three of them would have dinner, parties, vacations—expense it all to Stone Solutions, of course, which means it got funded by the Empath Initiative, which means it was all actually taxpayer money. They used to laugh about it."

"Charming," Alex said, in a voice that suggested the opposite.

The waitress dropped off Alex's juice and Gretel's cappuccino. "I'll give Senator Hathaway this, though," Gretel said, as the waitress left. "Unlike the rest of them, at least she was anti-war. You ever go diving into the military connections behind most of the people at Stone Solutions or the Empath Initiative?"

Alex shrugged. "I'm probably more familiar with those connections than most people," he said lightly.

"It's wild, right?" she said, reaching for the cappuccino like it was a caffeinated lifeline. "Like why would you ever need all those military ties when the empaths are such pacifists? I feel like there's a story there, like there's something someone isn't telling us." She shook her head. "Sorry," she said sheepishly. "I got lost in research last night and now I'm off on a tangent."

"And I'm hanging on every word," Alex said. "I invited you here because I wanted to listen to whatever you had to say."

That made her smile. "Tell me about your blog," she said. "What's it called?"

"I haven't been bold enough to name it," he admitted. "It's just a place for my thoughts right now, really."

"But you've got to be working on a story," she pressed.

"Well," he said, "I was actually thinking about writing a piece on Stone Solutions' security. Supposedly it's this state-of-the-art empath defense company but we were both there the night an empath broke in during the AMI strategy meeting."

"Oh, I'd definitely read that," Gretel said. "Because it does make you wonder, doesn't it? Their security can't be very good if Reece Davies managed to get past it."

Alex tilted his head. "You don't think Reece is very smart?"

She snorted. "I don't want to be mean, because I don't *hate* him. But have you heard the kind of shit he says? Seen the comments he leaves on my blog? It's like his brain doesn't even work." She paused, replaying her words in her head, then winced. "Ugh, you know what? I take that back. Reece is just being an empath, wearing his heart on his sleeve, and I *am* being mean." She made a face. "I sound like my dad when I trash him like that, but Reece has never done anything to deserve it. To be honest, he's the only one in the city who's ever noticed that *Eyes on Empaths* is its own thing that I run myself. Well." She smiled again. "Until you."

"I bet Reece has a lot of hidden depths that no one's ever seen. Most empaths do." Alex reached for his orange juice. "You mentioned AMI and Cedrick Stone. I hope it's okay if I ask—do you think your dad knows anything about Stone Solutions' security?"

"I bet he does; he's there all the time," she said, picking up her coffee. "You want to ask him tonight? He's having a dinner for some colleagues at the steak house in the Leviathan Hotel. I could drop by and you could be my plus-one."

"Could I really?" Alex said. "Are you sure I don't need to, I don't know, joust with ten other bloggers to win the privilege first?"

She laughed. "All you have to do is let me read the story." And if it was any good, she could invite Alex to guest post it on *Eyes on Empaths*. Maybe ease her readers into the idea that she might be posting more critical and analytical content. Hell, if Alex's article was accompanied by a picture that showed how hot he was, her readers would probably eat it up; they loved eye candy, couldn't get enough of her picture of the Dead Man.

He raised his glass. "It's a deal," he said, and they clinked their cups together.

Jamey and Liam had been five minutes outside of Port Angeles when Stensby finally sent the details about the missing empath. And it turned out to be a flood—the empath's name and at least a dozen different addresses for various houses and businesses he had visited over the past few days.

Jamey had shown the list to Liam, frowning. "This is going to take all day. At least. We're going to need a hotel."

"I told Lieutenant Parson I'm here as long as you're here," Liam had said. "Stensby's the one who asked you to come on this goose chase and everyone on the SPD knows you just gave back your car. Parson can deal."

They'd gotten a room for the night and Liam had stayed there to catch up on work. Now Jamey was sitting in Liam's car, looking over her list again. The missing empath was from Victoria, according to Stensby's notes. Mr. Rodriguez had spent three days visiting national parks before disappearing.

It wasn't Jamey's preferred hiking weather, but maybe this particular empath loved the snow. Maybe he'd gotten lost or stranded. Olympic National Park was about as far as you could get from Vermont in the continental United States, so maybe this Canadian empath's disappearance from Port Angeles had nothing to do with the Canadian empath found murdered in Burlington.

Maybe.

Jamey forwarded the information to Aisha. Hopefully Grayson's team could dig up better information while Jamey followed the trail.

Victor Nichols sat in the backseat of Cedrick Stone's Maybach, letting the driver deal with the I-5 traffic as they crept north. Marist was at her hotel, working on her keynote speech for AMI's privacy conference, while Director Traynor was in Bellevue, visiting Stone Solutions. Obviously Cedrick himself wasn't using his car these days; shame to let it go to waste.

Shame to let any of Cedrick's other things go to waste as well—namely, his research projects. Research projects like Cora Falcon.

And if Ms. Falcon was known to be one of Cedrick's projects, then the same could possibly be true of Reece Davies.

Nichols reopened the police report on his phone, from Officer Stensby. Stensby had arrived onto the Stone Solutions rooftop and seen Davies next to Cedrick Stone's bloody and unconscious body, in a position of surrender at Agent Grayson's feet. None of that sounded like the actions of an innocent.

And yet Grayson continued to claim Davies was harmless.

Nichols' lip curled. Cedrick had been cagey and paranoid, unwilling to ever show all of his cards, but he'd at least understood the need to leash the Dead Man.

Nichols switched to his texts and the messages he'd sent that morning.

Nichols: Agent Grayson continues to insist on his own agenda that prioritizes the safety of empaths, even in a situation such as the Davies case. The Dead Man has become more dangerous. Cedrick never trusted him and perhaps he had the right of it.

He eyed the response.

I will always agree that Agent Grayson is complicated. But he's on our side.

Nichols stretched out his legs in the Maybach's spacious backseat.

He wasn't so sure about that.

Grayson sat at the desk in the hotel room, laptop open in front of him. The desk hadn't been designed for someone of his height, and he kept banging his knees on the underside while he hunched over to see the screen. But Director Traynor had sent over another research paper on the emergence of empaths that morning—the authors had so far declined to be credited; that was interesting—and Grayson was reading it through a second time.

I'll give you the short version of this new theory, Traynor's email had said. Humanity's scourge on the planet has finally led nature to evolve a predator for our species, ones that are perfectly hidden until their transformation into corrupted empaths.

Predator theory. The level of bonkers was almost impressive; people had started cults on less.

But if Traynor thought this theory would make the Dead Man *think twice about his job,* as the parting remarks in Washington, DC, had implied, then Traynor was gonna be disappointed. Far as Grayson was concerned, this changed nothing. This theory obviously wasn't true, and even if it had been, all anyone would've had to do would be leave empaths the hell alone so they didn't turn.

Protecting non-empaths was always gonna mean protecting empaths from the people who wanted to hurt or corrupt them. That was the entire reason he was here in Burlington, visiting clubs and trying to track down a killer.

Not that he was having any luck. Four of the establishments

he'd visited the night before used UV stamps for their patrons, but none marked hands with the looping lowercase "L" he'd seen on the empath's hand. An easy solution here in Burlington might've helped solve the case. Now he'd have to expand the search to everywhere within a few hours' driving distance.

Maybe farther. UV stamps could last a couple days; Marie Pelletier could have gotten it in Montreal before coming down, or six hours south in New York City. The internet hadn't been any help at all when he'd tried looking for places that marked hands with an "L." His search could take ages.

Just like it was taking ages to get the bloodwork he'd asked for.

He switched over to that email, which had come in twenty minutes ago. The empath's blood tests were delayed. The fingerprint records were delayed. French Canadian privacy laws, all the emails had complained.

That excuse was sounding real damn convenient. Especially considering someone had gone and tagged Reece's car again when Grayson had explicitly said Reece should be left alone.

He pulled up the empath-tracking website. The map of North America filled his laptop screen, small blinking dots scattered across it, all glittery blue except for a tiny concentration of four red dots on an island along BC's North Coast. Grayson zoomed in on Seattle and there was Reece's, right on his high-rise downtown.

Reece, who by rights should have been in purple, teetering too close to corruption and who didn't need the stress of discovering he was being watched.

Grayson picked up his phone and called Dr. Easterby.

"You have bad news, don't you?" she said glumly, as she answered.

"How'd you guess?"

"Because I haven't found shit." Computer keys were clicking in the background. "I went back into the Ottawa office, but there's nothing about Marie Pelletier heading to Vermont and no records at all about the other Canadian empath that's gone missing from Port Angeles. I'm sending you what I have, but there is nothing helpful here on either empath who apparently crossed the border into the US from our northern neighbor."

Grayson glanced out the window at the snowy parking lot a story below. "We don't actually have anything about Ms. Pelletier except her name and the body. No blood tests, no fingerprints, no proof she crossed the border. And what's the latest in Port Angeles?"

"Someone Jamey knows from the force asked her to go down and poke around, on account of no one in the Seattle or Port Angeles police departments knowing much about empaths. Officer Stensby sent her a bunch of info this morning; Jamey said it's going to take forever to check everywhere and got a hotel in Port A with her boyfriend for tonight. But I don't know where the SPD is getting its intel when I can't find anything."

A family was coming out of the lobby, a girl of maybe seven dancing around while one of her moms pushed a toddler in a stroller. "There's something else that's not adding up." Grayson stood up from the desk. "The witnesses at the police station described a man stumbling out of the park, didn't respond to their calls, blood on his face."

"Could be an empath thrall?" Easterby said. "Was Marie Pelletier already corrupted, and her own thrall turned on her? That seems highly unlikely to me, though; thralls are completely devoted to the empaths who made them. So—a different corrupted empath, then?"

"Maybe," said Grayson. "But in all the time we've been doing this, have you ever seen an empath's thrall attack another empath?"

Easterby hesitated. "I don't think I have."

It was time to share his private theory with her. "You ever even heard of a corrupted empath causing the death of another empath?"

"Cora Falcon lured Reece Davies to her to—" Easterby cut it off. "Not to kill him. To *change* him. To make another corrupted empath—shit, Evan, you think they want to make more of themselves?"

"I started to wonder after San Francisco." He sat down on the edge of the bed. "Seattle makes it seem even more likely."

"Everyone's been assuming they operate as isolated killers, but we always stop them early. If their intent is actually to seek each other out..." She let out another quiet curse. "Have you told anyone else?"

"How well would that go over?" he said dryly.

"I don't even want to think about it," she said. "I saw the email you forwarded from Director Traynor, with that batshit predator theory. If some of the scientists at Stone Solutions or EI get both these theories, they'll claim empaths are out there hunting people like wolf packs—claim we have to go on the offensive against them, and it's the pacifists who'll get hurt—"

"I know," Grayson said. "I don't plan on telling the agencies. But it means I don't believe that any empath's thrall killed Ms. Pelletier here in Burlington, and I'm real curious why someone made sure witnesses saw a man who would appear like a thrall to those in the know."

"I was thinking the killer is someone who has it out for empaths," said Easterby. "But barely anyone knows empaths are capable of making thralls. So what kind of killer are we even looking for?" She sighed, short and frustrated. "I'm heading out to Montreal," she said. "Picking up my rental car in thirty minutes. Drive shouldn't be too bad except it's snowing again. I'll call you later."

After they hung up, he set his phone on the bed and stared at the artwork on the hotel wall, a print of Lake Champlain in the vivid colors of a Vermont fall. The empath-tracking map was still open on his laptop on the desk, blue dots sprinkled over the satellite landscape like the bluebonnets of a Texas spring.

They now had two empath cases, both complicated by international factors that kept Grayson in the dark. He was out here chasing leads in Vermont, Easterby between cities in Canada, St. James and Mr. Lee kept busy in Port Angeles.

Grayson's gaze drifted to the map's West Coast and the solitary dot in Seattle. Reece, an empath in a liminal state between pacifist and killer, all by himself now.

Really, truly, all by himself, actually, with both his sister and Grayson out of his reach.

Grayson paused.

That sure was a coincidence.

He reached for his phone again. It was early afternoon on the East Coast; over in Seattle, even an insomniac like Reece ought to be up by now.

As he unlocked the screen, the picture of Marie Pelletier's hand lit up, the last thing he'd been looking at.

Grayson paused again. The mark was hand-drawn and messy, but now, with the phone at a diagonal, it no longer looked like a lowercase "L."

He turned the phone fully horizontal. Ms. Pelletier had been wearing a pendant with *John 3:16* engraved on the back, and with her hand at the new angle, now Grayson was looking at a symbol to match.

He tossed the phone on the bed and crossed to his laptop. He closed the tracker, then pulled up a search engine. This time, he found what he needed within minutes. He scrolled through the social media feed of Disciple Road, a Christian rock band that had performed at St. Sebastian's University outside of Burlington the night before, scanning pictures of the set. They'd performed in the chapel: there were crosses on the band members' shirts, painted on the drums, emblazoned on the banner hanging behind the band. A giant carved wooden cross, including the body of Christ, hung from the ceiling over the stage.

He slammed his laptop shut, grabbed his duffel and rental keys, and was out the door three minutes later.

CHAPTER NINE

All predators can be defeated. It's simply a matter of finding something more dangerous to take them down.

And if you can't find a bigger monster to fight them?

You create one.

—COMMENT BY [REDACTED] ON [REDACTED] MANUAL

THE MIDDAY SKY was a lightish gray as Reece drove north on I-5 toward the doughnut shop Officer Stensby had named, replaying their conversation in his head.

Can you meet me in person? Stensby had said, when he'd called earlier that morning.

I guess, Reece had said, even though he was hellishly confused. He and Stensby had worked several cases together and knocked heads on every one. As far as Reece could tell, Stensby didn't much like or trust empaths, but he'd been the first one to try to pressure Reece to cross boundaries when it came to witnesses.

Look, I can't talk about it over the phone, Stensby had said that morning. *But it has to do with your sister.*

There better not be anyone messing with Jamey. All empaths had their trigger points, after all, and Reece was all too aware another move against his sister might send him spiraling to a place he couldn't return from.

Even on a Sunday there was enough traffic that it took Reece an hour to reach the shop in the northern suburb. And sure enough, there was an SPD police cruiser idling in a parking spot. Reece parked in an open spot and got out of the car, striding up to the police cruiser to bang on the driver's door.

Stensby turned his head in surprise. His green eyes were bloodshot, the same red as his hair.

"You could have turned off your car and gone inside," Reece snapped at him through the window. "You're wasting gasoline idling like this."

Stensby's eyes narrowed and then quickly relaxed, like he was trying very hard to keep from revealing his irritation to Reece. Good luck with that. Reece had years of experience with that particular emotion; at any given moment, most people in his vicinity were some degree of annoyed with him.

Reece stepped back and folded his arms, watching Stensby awkwardly extract his long limbs from the cruiser. He wasn't quite as tall as Grayson, but he lacked all of Grayson's grace, his movements sluggish and dragging. Combine that with the bloodshot eyes, and Reece would venture to guess Stensby was yet another person who hadn't been sleeping much.

"What's going on with Jamey?" Reece said, as Stensby stepped onto the sidewalk and shut his door.

But Stensby just waved down the street. "Is that your Smart car?"

He was already walking toward it. Reece huffed and followed. "Yes. Why?"

"You don't see a lot of these on the road anymore."

"And?"

"And is being a gearhead a crime?" Stensby said testily, over his shoulder. "I'm into cars."

Lie. Jesus, what was the point of lying about that? Was this some kind of masculinity pissing contest? Reece couldn't care less if a man preferred turbos or tutus.

Stensby was eyeing the Smart car. "These are funny, right? Battery in the passenger footwell, engine in the back?"

"Yes," Reece grudgingly admitted.

"So if you run out of coolant you have to add it in the trunk?"

"No, the fluids are up front."

Stensby tilted his head, surveying the front of the Smart car with furrowed eyebrows. "Where?"

Reece sighed. He stepped forward and tapped one of the panels between the headlight and front license plate. "Wiper and brake fluid are behind this one. Engine coolant is behind that one," he said, pointing to the other panel. "My car also averages forty-one miles to the gallon on the highway, forty-three if I draft. Unlike your cruiser, which gets—"

"How about we go in?" Stensby said.

Inside the doughnut shop, Stensby got a coffee while Reece got a cinnamon raisin bagel, and then they stood across from each other at a bar height table. Stensby picked up the sugar canister. "Has Jamey said if she's coming back to the force?"

Reece gave him a withering look as he pulled off a piece of the bagel. "Why would she? It's Lieutenant Parson's fault she left." He popped the bite in his mouth. "I'm the one who fucked up and Parson took it out on her."

"Guess he did." Stensby poured sugar into his coffee. "Funny, I still don't know how you got out of a felony without so much as a slap on the wrist."

His tone was light, but his shoulders tensed. Maybe he wanted Reece to think it was a joke between friends, but his body language told his true feelings loud and clear. Stensby didn't think he should have gotten away with it.

Reece pulled off another piece of bagel. "The whole thing was just a misunderstanding." *Lie.* He tried not to wince. Grayson hadn't misunderstood a damn thing.

And he'd still taken Reece's side.

"So you didn't actually commit a crime?" Stensby said skeptically.

"Of course not." *Lie.* Reece gritted his teeth.

Stensby was watching him closely. "I never saw you do anything special," he said suddenly. "I watched you work our cases, and all you could do was figure out how people were feeling."

"Yes," Reece said bitingly. "Because that's what empaths do."

"Some people think empaths can do a lot more than that," Stensby said.

Reece huffed. "You mean AMI thinks that."

"AMI has a lot of theories," Stensby said. "They say empaths are probably hiding the truth about all their powers from the rest of us. You know that saying, *the best defense is a good offense*? They say we need more offense against *you*."

Reece's jaw tightened. Stensby was spouting AMI paranoia, but he wasn't wrong; Reece was probably more dangerous than Stensby's wildest theories.

He forced a casual tone. "What did you want to say about Jamey?"

Stensby glanced around, which was unnecessary—there was no one within ten feet of them. He still leaned forward and said, more quietly, "Rumor is the department is opening an investigation into her entire career."

Lie. Now it was Reece's turn to narrow his eyes. "Are they," he said flatly.

"That's what I'm hearing." *Lie.* Stensby gave him a sympathetic smile that wasn't remotely real. "A lot of people are suspicious of her because of you."

That part was true. It was also something Reece already knew and despised himself for. "And?"

"You don't seem very upset," Stensby said suspiciously.

"Because I don't believe you," Reece snapped. "Jesus, you're not even subtle. I wouldn't have to be an empath to know you're lying. Why are you making up some department witch hunt over Jamey? What do you really want?"

Stensby's mouth flattened into a thin line. "I want to know how you weaseled out of a crime that everyone saw you commit," he said. "You were on the *news* breaking and entering into Stone Solutions. And then I saw you up on that rooftop, with Cedrick Stone and that big secretive guy. I know he's the one they call the Dead Man, and I thought he'd arrest you and deal with you, but next thing I know, the whole SPD is ordered to forget any of it ever happened."

"Well, you're doing a shit job of that, aren't you?" Reece said, before he could stop himself.

"I'm not going to forget what I saw, Reece." Stensby's eyes had narrowed. "I thought the Dead Man was supposed to protect innocent people from empaths, not the other way around. People say maybe the Dead Man can't be trusted to do his job anymore."

Anger flooded Reece's stomach. "Who the hell is talking like that about him? *AMI?*" he said, before he knew he was going to speak. "AMI should shut their mouths about Agent Grayson. They have no idea what they're talking about. No idea what empaths are really capable of. And they better—"

And they better hope I never decide to show them.

Reece slapped a hand over his own mouth before the words escaped. He could feel his blood pressure rising; sweat prickling despite the cold. He mumbled some kind of excuse and stumbled away from the table, not looking back.

Reece found a short hall and the bathroom, a single room

that was claustrophobically small and heavily scented with disinfectant. He bolted the door and leaned on the pedestal sink.

His reflection stared back at him from the streaked mirror. His skin was too pale, with a greenish pallor in the fluorescent light and purplish dark circles prominent under his eyes. His pupils were blown, too big for such a bright room, and his hair was sticking to his clammy forehead.

Empaths didn't make threats. Not even in their heads.

Reece stared into his own eyes. How bad was it really, though? AMI thought worse about him. Wasn't it exhausting to constantly watch his thoughts, to care so much about the safety of others and never his own? To care so much he concealed his own abilities, just to make others more comfortable?

He reached out to the mirror, touching his gloved finger to his reflected one.

Grayson's drawl echoed in his mind, louder than his thoughts.

Care Bear, a pair of gloves isn't what makes you an empath. Your compassion never got left in the glove box of your Micro Machine and towed to Tacoma.

Reece blinked. He stared at his reflection in confusion.

What had he just been thinking about? Gloves? The circles under his eyes? He tried to concentrate, but his thoughts slipped out of reach, the way impressions of a dream might fade the harder you try to give them form.

With a sigh, he gave up. He splashed cold water on his face and then stepped out of the bathroom to find Stensby had vanished.

Grayson strode down the packed corridor, duffel over one shoulder, laptop bag over the other, making his way past gate after gate. As he walked, he called Kenji Ohayashi in Portland.

"Hey." Kenji picked up right away, sounding surprised. "What's going on? How's Burlington?"

Grayson sidestepped a couple with a giant double stroller,

quickly twisting so he didn't bump into their third kid, who was pulling a tiny pink suitcase. "Nine hundred miles behind me."

"Wait, what? Why is it so loud? Where are you?"

"O'Hare."

"O'Hare?"

"Fastest connection back to Seattle." Grayson picked up the pace, passing a group of high schoolers in matching dance troupe shirts, chattering by the gift shop. "I think it was a setup. In Burlington."

"The murder wasn't real?"

"The murder was real, and someone's gonna answer for it," said Grayson. "But I don't think the victim was an empath."

"But the gloves were real," Kenji said. "So you think—what? That someone put empath gloves on a decoy murder?"

Grayson slipped behind two elderly ladies in flowered pantsuits and hats pointing up at a Departures sign. "The victim had an ichthys drawn in UV ink on her hand."

"You mean a Jesus fish?"

"That's right," Grayson said. "I found the band that was using the symbol to keep track of entrants for a sold-out show. Christian rock. They performed in a chapel last night with crucifixes everywhere."

"Oh." Kenji was married to an empath; he understood right away. "Maya can't even bear the ones without a body; she looks away every time we drive past a church. An empath's not going to a show in a chapel without a nervous breakdown."

"I think whoever put the empath gloves on the victim couldn't see the UV mark and didn't know it was there," said Grayson. "I could just barely smell it."

"But why?" Kenji said. "Why would you ever want someone to think a murder victim was an empath?"

"I don't know." Grayson came to a stop at his gate. "But I know I was going to be in Seattle and I ended up in Burlington instead, because the Dead Man always goes when the crime involves an empath. And whoever set this murder up knows enough about empaths to fake a thrall."

"Not a good sign," Kenji muttered. "What's going to happen with the Marie Pelletier case?"

They were already boarding the last group. "I'm gonna send it to the FBI," Grayson said, keeping an eye on the end of the line. "But if someone out there wanted the Dead Man in Burlington, I'm gonna keep my itinerary quiet until I understand what's going on."

"Copy that. But if the body was someone else, then we've still got the problem of a Montreal-based empath who hasn't been seen in days. Were those Ms. Pelletier's gloves?"

"Stone Solutions Canada called the results inconclusive," Grayson said, "which is just another way to say someone probably scrubbed most of that serial number off on purpose, so we couldn't confirm who they were stolen from."

"So we're talking about someone who knows enough about empaths to fake a thrall and knew they needed to sabotage the serial numbers," Kenji mused. "Someone who wanted you in Burlington?"

"Or maybe just not in Seattle," Grayson said. "And not just me—Detective St. James is somewhere in Port Angeles. My calls are going straight to her voicemail and I think she might've been set up too."

"But why would anyone want you both out of—oh." Kenji groaned. "Seattle has the empath in the liminal state—Reece Davies. If someone wanted to target him, they'd definitely want the two of you out of the way first."

"Mr. Davies has got no sense of self-protection whatsoever," said Grayson. "If he's alone, he's a volatile target but also an easy one. All anyone would have to do is ask him to get in a car so he didn't make his kidnappers sad. He'd do it."

"And then next thing you know, Seattle's got another serial

killer loose." Car keys jingled in Kenji's background. "Did you get in touch with him?"

"I got his auto-response." Grayson was going to have words with Reece about that. "EI stuck another tracker on his car, though. He's up in Everett. Couldn't tell you why, and probably won't know until he stops driving and checks his messages."

"I'll see if I can get ahold of his sister," Kenji said. "But I'm three hours away and Aisha is out in Montreal. If you think Davies could be a target and you've got anyone else who can run interference tonight, you better call them."

As they hung up, Grayson stepped to the back of the boarding line, phone still in hand, considering his options.

Back in November, he'd had background checks run on all the employees at the fake empath club, McFeely's. He hadn't expected to discover the bouncer was vastly overqualified for the job. Grayson was still putting together how an ex-marine with Diesel's record had ended up bouncing at a club modeled on empaths, but he might be able to manage the one empath Grayson would try to send his way.

Jamey stood in the light snow that coated the grass at the shoulder of a narrow road and eyed the third destination on her list: a hiking trail in Olympic National Park. In the summer, it was popular with Washington residents and visitors alike.

In the winter, it was deserted.

Why would an empath tourist have been here two days ago? Or at any of the other destinations she'd checked, like the empty park cabin that hadn't had a renter since October? Or the tackle shop she hadn't bothered to go in—very few people were fishing in Washington in this weather, and an empath in particular wasn't fishing at all or even setting foot near the unfortunate worms used as bait.

Who exactly had given Stensby these addresses?

Jamey irritably reached for her phone, planning to call Stensby and get more answers.

Her lips pressed together as she saw she had no signal. Again. Like she'd had no signal at any of the other places she'd gone.

She'd been off-the-grid all day.

This didn't feel right. Forget the rest of the list; Jamey was going back to Port Angeles. She climbed into Liam's car and pulled back onto the empty highway. As soon as she had a signal, she was calling Aisha, and Reece didn't need to know about her calls behind the wheel.

About thirty minutes into the drive, her phone went off like a college band after a touchdown, a flurry of notifications hitting all at once.

Well, shit.

She grabbed her phone to find missed texts from Liam, Aisha, and someone named Kenji.

And one very ominous message from Grayson.

I think we were set up.

CHAPTER TEN

Ten Signs Your Date Might Secretly Be an Empath

1. They wear gloves indoors (although bear in mind that it IS a chilly December).

2. They pass on the hard drinks but can't get enough sugar.

3. They listen when you talk about your feelings. (Okay, yes, all your dates should be doing this but you know they don't.)

—EXCERPT FROM AN ONLINE LISTICLE

THE STEAK HOUSE in the Leviathan Hotel's lobby, the Ranch, was all dark woods and glass, more reminiscent of a wine cellar underground than anywhere outside. A tasteful sign had been set up in a glass stand at the front: *Welcome to our AMI guests! Join us in the Live Oak Room.*

As Gretel and Alex waited for the hostess to return, he pointed up above the sign. "We're on camera."

A small black circle with a red dot was set into the ceiling. Gretel grinned. "Should we pose?"

"Great idea," Alex said, like he thought that was funny.

They put their heads together and looked up at the security camera, waving.

A woman cleared her throat. Gretel turned back to see the hostess watching with a very blank expression. Gretel should have been embarrassed, but being around Alex made her want to drop her masks and just be who she was for once: an obsessive oddball who'd quit regular journalism to run one of the country's biggest empath blogs. Why did she try so hard to seem like a normal person?

"We're here for the AMI party," Gretel said.

"Follow me," the hostess said.

They were led to a side room with a private bar, where about twenty of Beau's AMI cohorts were already standing in tight knots around the small space. The waiter came by with a tray of champagne. Gretel grabbed one of the flutes and used the distraction to lead Alex over to the wall. "My dad is a huge talker and bragger," she said in a low voice. "We just need to get him going."

Alex nodded. "Who's the cop?" he asked.

Gretel followed his subtle gesture to the bar. The police officer who'd been at the AMI meeting on Friday was here again. "Officer Stensby," said Gretel. "He's started coming to all kinds of AMI events. My dad loves it; he's always bragging about all the cops and military types who join AMI."

She sipped the champagne, bubbles tickling her lips. Not everyone in America got to feel safer around the police; some people had to worry about the cops even when they were just living their lives and not breaking any laws. Just one more thing she couldn't help but notice these days.

She watched her dad move through the room, shaking hands. When he reached the closest group, she darted forward. "Dad."

Beau blinked in surprise. "Gretel? I wasn't expecting you here." He eyed Alex with a confused stare. "Or to bring a date."

"Alex is a journalism major at Rainier, interning at the *Emerald City Tribune*," Gretel lied easily. Her dad didn't have much respect for bloggers, no matter how successful *Eyes on Empaths* was; he'd be more open if Alex met his standards for *real* reporter. "He's doing a piece on that break-in at Stone Solutions last month."

"That's right, sir," Alex said earnestly, Southern accent in full effect. "How the heck did an empath get in? Stone Solutions must have state-of-the-art security."

"It certainly does," Beau said, chest puffed out.

Alex tilted his head, like he'd heard a sound no one else had. "I heard their only security used to be access cards. But after November's break-in, they must have realized that cards are too easily stolen, right?"

"Absolutely," Beau said. "They've gone to biometric security everywhere. After November, it was top priority to upgrade everything."

Alex nodded slowly, head still tilted like he could hear something more than Beau's voice. "What did they do for Mr. Stone's office? I heard he was hospitalized somewhere secret; did they still get his fingerprints or retina scan?"

Beau cleared his throat. "Of course they did." His gaze went past them, to another knot of people. "AMI has our conference coming up on Monday and I see our marketing head. Excuse me."

"But, Dad—" Gretel started.

"It's okay," Alex said, under his breath. "I got what I needed."

"You sure?" she said, also quiet.

"Definitely." Alex's lips curled in a tiny smile. "Your dad should work on his poker face, though. Those lies were probably obvious to the whole room."

Gretel hadn't picked up on any lies. Alex was so perceptive. "To great stories, in that case," she said, clinking her champagne flute against his soda.

"Hey, aren't you Mr. Macy's daughter? The one who runs *Eyes on Empaths* for him?"

Gretel looked over to see Officer Stensby approaching, holding his whiskey, several inches taller than both her and Alex. "Not *for* him," she said coolly.

"That's Gretel's blog," Alex said, just as coolly.

Stensby looked down his nose at him. "I didn't catch your name."

"I'm Gretel's date," Alex said. "Mr. Date, if you're the formal type," he added, which made Gretel snort behind her champagne. He gestured to an unimpressed Stensby's glass. "Guess you're not on duty tonight."

"It's nonalcoholic," said Stensby, with a note of defensiveness.

Please. Gretel could smell the whiskey from here.

Alex had tilted his head again, in that listening way. "So what are you doing here then?"

"Police business isn't exactly your business, is it?" Stensby said, more sharply.

"If you say so." Alex seemed completely unintimidated by the much bigger Stensby. "We should talk more later tonight."

For some reason, the tone of Alex's voice made Gretel shiver.

It was fully dark when Reece finally made it to the southern end of Seattle and took an exit for Kent.

After Stensby had bailed from the doughnut shop, Reece had taken the rest of his bagel back to the car and checked his phone to discover he'd missed three calls and four texts from Grayson.

Can you talk right now?

A little later:

Call me when you get this.

Later still:

I need you to trust me: go straight to McFeely's as soon as you see this. Once you get there, STAY there. I'm sending you their temporary address. Mr. Lane is expecting you.

And, sugar, if I ever get your auto-response when I'm trying to reach you again, I'm gonna give Eyes on Empaths an exclusive interview and tell everyone you're an unsafe driver.

That was frankly diabolical. But it would be nice to see Dominique "Diesel" Lane, the gentle giant bouncer at McFeely's, and Reece did trust Grayson—maybe *only* Grayson, these days, because as much as he loved Jamey, he didn't trust her to stop him if it became necessary, not the way he trusted Grayson would. And so Reece followed the request and headed to the address Grayson had given him for the temporary location of McFeely's.

He navigated through Kent, past local restaurants and grocery shops to a set of streets that felt more industrial, with parking lots of eighteen-wheelers, a tall contraption that might have been a concrete mixer, and short, wide warehouses with no windows. But as he approached the address Grayson had given him, cars began to line the curb again, and Reece had to park two streets over.

The address turned out to be a warehouse, which looked like every other windowless and unadorned warehouse in the area. But as he approached the door, it was opened before he could knock by a white man with a goatee, almost as tall as Diesel with a thick, strong build, like a teddy bear who could plow through a brick wall. He was wearing black slacks, a black T-shirt, and, inexplicably, a pair of black bunny ears on his bald head. "You Reece?"

Reece nodded warily.

The bouncer held the door open and muffled bass spilled out. "Diesel told me to keep an eye out for you. Come on in."

Reece stepped through the doors into a different world—warm and inviting, with colorful lights set into the ceiling above a carpeted hall and a roped-off line of well-dressed people chattering excitedly with each other. The bass grew louder as Reece followed the bouncer toward the pair of double doors at the far end of the hall.

The doors suddenly swung open, letting the music out into the hall. "Hey, kiddo, you made it."

Reece found himself breaking into a real smile to match Diesel's. He didn't meet many friendly faces these days; it was as welcome as a warm house on a winter day. "Hey yourself," he said to Diesel, raising his voice over the music. "Do you know why Agent Grayson wanted me to come here?"

"Does he ever explain himself to anyone?" Diesel said wryly.

He was also wearing a pair of bunny ears. Reece furrowed his brow, but before he could ask, Diesel was pointing to the crates that had been stacked to form a makeshift bar on the other side of the room. "Ben's on tonight too, if you want to say hi."

Reece carefully threaded his way through the crowd, dodging to avoid any contact with the tipsy people dancing and gesturing. Ben Castillo, the bartender Reece had met in November, was mixing something in shiny cups while a woman with pink hair and tattoos covering her bare shoulders worked the cash register. They were both in gloves—and also bunny ears.

Reece leaned on the bar, which seemed to be made of spare wood, like someone had been about to build a deck and topped off the crates to form a bar instead. "Ben!"

Ben glanced his way and broke into a smile, waving.

And for all that Reece hated this entire business model, this was apparently the one place in Seattle he could go right now and be welcomed so easily and genuinely it made his throat tight. No, the people here weren't empaths in the paranormal way, but you didn't need paranormal abilities to be kind and empathetic, and in that way, people like Ben and Diesel were more exceptional than Reece was. No wonder business was booming.

Ben set the drink on the bar in front of a man in a suit and tie, and then he was making his way to Reece. He put his arms on the bar in a mirror of Reece and then leaned forward, his complicated hair falling over his brown eyes. "Hey, stranger. You want your Shirley Temple?"

Reece really did.

A few minutes later, Ben was putting Reece's drink in front of him. "Is your hot and scary boyfriend here too?"

"My *what*?" Reece said incredulously. "Are you talking about Agent Grayson?"

"How many hot and scary boyfriends do you have?"

Ben had dark circles under his eyes like Grayson, like Reece himself, and there was a tension in his shoulders that hadn't been there the last time they talked. But then, on that terrible night back in November, Ben had been the one to find the body of Stone Solutions' head of IT dead in the McFeely's server room, and Reece knew now it had been an empath behind everything, who'd put this sweet, friendly bartender through something like that.

"What's with the ears?" Reece asked, instead of fighting Ben about Grayson.

Ben touched the headband with bunny ears. "We're all wearing them the first week in the new place, as a tribute. It's heartbreaking, what happened to Bunny; she was a sweetheart and we miss her."

Not a lie. Reece bit his lip. Jamey had told him there'd been more casualties when Cora's thralls attacked the club, but she hadn't given him details about who had died. Bunny must have been one of the employees. She wasn't just a part of the death toll to people who cared about her; Ben's pain was real.

"I'm sorry," Reece said. "That whole night—I'm just really

sorry." He leaned forward on the bar. "Are you okay? You found a body—I can't, I can't even—I'm so sorry."

"It was bad," Ben admitted. "But I'll get through it. Therapy, sleep meds, that kind of thing. That night shook the whole place up, but we're a pretty tight-knit group and we're helping each other."

An empath could have helped too. Could have helped sort through the overwhelming jumble of feelings that accompanied tragedies, or help them through the darkness of grief to find the light, to unbury the good feelings they couldn't find on their own anymore.

Or at least, an empath who wasn't Reece could have helped. Because the last person Reece had touched had almost died and he had no right to get his empathy anywhere near anyone. Possibly ever again.

"Good," Reece said, throat tight again. "I'm glad you have each other."

Ben reached down under the bar and then came back up a moment later. "You want a pair? All the empaths have them—you should too."

He held out a black headband with bunny ears.

And Reece could have protested that everyone in here was faking it for tips. That he was the only actual empath now, in Seattle.

But he hadn't realized just how much he missed Cora, and how very alone he was. How nice it felt to have Ben include him with complete sincerity.

So Reece shut his mouth and took the ears.

"Ben!"

Ben glanced down the bar. "I gotta help Ink," he said ruefully. "But call me sometime, okay? I'm not trying to piss off your boyfriend—we can just be friends."

"Grayson's not my—"

Ben had already disappeared.

Reece sighed and slid the ears onto his head. Imagine Ben actually thinking Grayson was his boyfriend.

He pulled out his phone and turned on the screen, and his new background lit up with Grayson's smoking hot gym selfie.

Wild, the ideas people came up with.

Like many hotels, the Leviathan had restrooms on the first floor, practically hidden from the lobby down a corridor past the elevator. The men's room was empty as Officer Stensby slipped through the door.

He leaned against the sink and pulled out his phone. The screen was blurry; he probably should have stopped a few whiskeys ago. But it didn't matter; if the deposits were in his bank account, then he was done promising Beau Macy he'd be at all the upcoming AMI events; he was withdrawing all of it and buying a one-way ticket to Puerto Vallarta.

The door suddenly opened. He looked up from his phone to see that short guy who'd come to the dinner with Gretel Macy, the one with the annoying Texas drawl—*Alex*, he'd heard Gretel call him.

"Hi, officer," Alex said. "I was hoping I'd catch you alone."

Stensby narrowed his eyes. This kid was bold, shoulders straight and chin up, like he had all the right in the world to follow a cop into the men's room. "What do you want?"

Alex stuck out a foot, hooking the garbage can. "I thought we could chat."

Stensby shoved the phone into his pocket. "Not interested." Wait—was Alex now wedging the garbage can under the handle? So the door couldn't be opened from outside? "What the hell are you doing?"

"I have this thing." Alex kicked the garbage can into place, his gaze never leaving Stensby. "I don't like liars."

Stensby was rapidly going from irritated to pissed, a buzz to his anger that must have come from the whiskey. "I don't know who you think you are or what you think you're doing," he said, starting forward, "but I don't appreciate being cornered."

"Your rage has a hair trigger, what a shock," Alex said dryly.

"To be fair, being around AMI this evening hasn't been great for my temper either, but that just makes it even easier to light you up."

The fuck was this kid talking about? Stensby's anger was rippling over him, clouding his vision alongside the whiskey. "I don't have time for this." A moment later, he had Alex backed against the wall. "You're about to catch a lot more heat than you bargained for."

"I'm afraid you have it backwards, officer." Alex put his hand on Stensby's bare arm.

And the world began to dissolve, leaving only Alex.

"Now, see, Gretel I couldn't thrall," Alex said, as the rage began to shift, replaced by a deep-set ache to serve and please, to devote himself to Alex, that was spreading through Stensby's chest. "I needed her to be able to use her brain. But you seem like the type who traded rational, nuanced thinking for fear and rage long ago, so no need to spare your intelligence, or lack thereof. How about you tell me what you're doing here?"

Stensby was going to tell him *everything*. "I've got this buddy who's been in AMI a long time, and for ages he's been telling me these theories about how dangerous empaths are, like how they can read your mind and shit."

"Always with the mind reading," Alex said, with a shake of his head. "For the record, we can't do that, though we don't need your thoughts when we have your emotions. But go on."

Of course Stensby would go on. He'd go on for hours, if that was what Alex wanted. "I never liked empaths, but I figured if they were *actually* dangerous, the government would do something, right? We sure as hell wouldn't have had that nervous, useless empath consultant right there on the police force. Or so I thought, until the Hathaway murder."

Stensby shook his head. He'd been so naive. "We got called to Stone Solutions. I was one of the first on the scene, and I saw our supposedly harmless empath consultant on his knees next to Cedrick Stone's unconscious body. He didn't look like an annoying, barely functional pacifist on that roof; he looked guilty as fuck. But we were ordered to just…let him go."

Stensby was angry all over again. "They said Cedrick Stone was responsible for that senator's death, but he was covered in blood on that roof, and the papers say he's been in the hospital ever since. Reece is clearly a lot more dangerous than we were told, and they let him work with the *cops*. I said *fuck that* and started going to AMI meetings. I started listening to Keith. But then last week, Keith comes to me and says he heard from someone higher than AMI. And he says they're going to do something about empaths—they just need recruits. And that I could help."

Alex's eyes were fixed on his. "Recruits for what?"

"I don't know and I didn't bother to find out," Stensby said. "Keith put me in touch with someone who offered me a pile of money to get Jamey out of town and I saw my ticket out of all of this empath crap."

"Who's Jamey?"

"Detective St. James," said Stensby. "Reece's sister. She was a detective on the force. And see, I'm not stupid. I know an anonymous benefactor isn't just going to pay me to distract Jamey, they're going to want more, and if I say no, then I'm going to have a little accident somewhere, someday. Dirty money always comes with strings, and that's why I'm going to Mexico tonight, before those strings attach. But I had to do something about Reece before I left, because if half of what Keith says is true, then the whole city is in danger."

Alex tilted his head. "What did you do to this other empath?"

"Car sabotage," Stensby said proudly. "Nothing that could be traced back to me."

"I see." Alex took his hand off of Stensby. "I'm going to need your phone."

"I will give you anything you want," Stensby promised, handing over the phone.

"Yeah," said Alex, narrowing his eyes. "You will."

CHAPTER ELEVEN

From: [REDACTED]
To: [REDACTED]
Subject: Re: McFeely's

Yes, I'm aware of the existence of McFeely's. No, there are no real empaths working there. Yes, impersonating an empath is a crime.

In the past, however, McFeely's has proved useful when it comes to entertaining certain clientele. In the present, at least one of their employees is a person of interest.

The club should be left alone, for the moment.

REECE WAS HALFWAY through his second Shirley Temple and considering a third when Diesel joined him at the bar. He stayed standing, and up close Reece could now see that the smile he was offering was hedged with a tiredness that hadn't been there in November. "How you doing, kiddo?"

"Ben makes the best drinks," Reece said. "What's wrong?"

Diesel startled. "That obvious?"

"Real empath," Reece reminded him, pointing to himself

with one hand as he pulled a maraschino cherry off the ice by the stem with the other. Ben had added several extra cherries, because he was the best bartender in Seattle. "I can listen. I know I talk constantly and I'm super annoying, but I can be a good listener." He bit the cherry off the stem. "I'd love to listen, honestly. It's—been a while since I got to be an empath like that."

"If you like to listen, you really should work here." Diesel clapped him on the back. "And you're not even close to annoying. Trust me."

Not a lie. It was a brief touch through layers of clothes, and months ago Reece wouldn't have picked anything up. Now, though, he caught a flash of something—compassion, maybe, sweet as the cherry in his mouth.

And instead of being able to enjoy it, Reece's stomach soured with guilt. Diesel had no idea an empath had just read his emotions without consent. Just one more reason Reece shouldn't be around normal people, even ones as nice as the staff at McFeely's.

Diesel gestured toward the other side of the warehouse. "I need to keep an eye on the cameras for a bit. Want to join me? It's quieter."

Reece squished his guilt down best he could, picked up his drink, and followed Diesel. More people had joined the dance floor until it took up most of the room, and there wasn't a way through without crossing it. Reece wove his way through the crowd of dancers, gaze darting right and left under flashing lights. The music was good but louder now, especially under the speakers over the dance floor.

Someone bumped into him from behind, and Reece got another distant flash: euphoria over despair, someone dancing, maybe drunk, trying to forget how bad things were. He gritted his teeth and tried to focus. It was pretty easy to keep his eyes on a guy Grayson's height in a pair of bunny ears.

They went through a doorway and into the hall, and then Diesel led the way down the hall. They passed a brightly colored sign that said *Wellness Room—Staff Only Please, Thank You for Understanding!* It was covered in smiley faces and stickers.

Diesel stopped at the next door and opened it, revealing a closet-sized space with three flat-screen TVs. The big bouncer who had let Reece in earlier was lounging in one of the room's two oversized office chairs, watching the screens.

"Thanks, Rocky, I got it," Diesel said.

Rocky flashed them a peace sign and stood, adjusting his bunny ears as he stepped out and closed the door behind him.

"He looks tough," Reece said.

"Tough as nails," Diesel agreed. "He's also got a huge crush on Ben."

That made Reece grin. "So what's eating at you?" he asked, as they sat down.

Diesel watched the TVs for a moment. The closest one showed the street and sidewalk just in front of the warehouse's front door. "Um. Well. My therapist disappeared a couple weeks ago. Actually, you might even know of her, since she's also an empath. Cora Falcon?"

"Oh," Reece said weakly. "Yeah. I know her." Cora had been a veterans' therapist, specializing in PTSD. Diesel was an ex-marine; Reece could guess why he might have been her patient.

"She was amazing," said Diesel. "She was helping me move past—well. The past. But the hospital said she moved. I didn't even get to say goodbye. And now—"

He closed his mouth.

"What?" Reece said.

Diesel sighed. "Just someone from my past, that I knew in the military. He's been hanging around, showing up here a lot. Always hinting that he's got some amazing job and I could too, if I wanted to learn more."

"But you don't want to learn more," Reece guessed. "You're happy here, at McFeely's?"

"People try to be kind here, and there's not enough of that

in the world." Diesel shook his head. "A lot of people would think I'm being stupid, though. Keith—that's the guy's name—he drives a brand-new Hellcat; he clearly is getting paid." He tilted his head, bunny ears and all. "I like my hybrid, though. Or biking, that's even better for the planet."

"You're not being stupid, and that's really hot," Reece admitted. "Can you talk to Evan? I think between the two of us, we could get through to him on carbon emissions. He pretends he's so stubborn but he really does listen."

"Does he?" Was Diesel smothering a smile?

"Yeah, he does," said Reece suspiciously. "Why?"

Diesel shrugged, and oh, he was *definitely* smothering a smile. "It's just sweet: you're this snack-sized perpetual grouch, but Agent Grayson comes up, and all of a sudden, you're lit up like rainbows and kittens. Or you were. You're kind of glaring again now."

Reece narrowed his eyes.

Diesel put his hands up in surrender, though his smile hadn't disappeared. "Anyway, you caught me brooding because Keith reminds me of some shit from the past right when I have to find a new therapist. But I'll be fine; I'm heading to Vancouver for a few days, it'll be a perfect chance to clear my head."

Reece gratefully latched on to the subject change. "What's in Vancouver?"

"International car show," Diesel said. "One of the manufacturers is a new electric car company from Vietnam and I have a guaranteed test drive."

"Are you kidding me?" Reece said. "Oh, I am *jealous*."

"I know, right?" Diesel sounded genuinely excited. "They're going to have models we don't have here in the States yet. I actually won a whole package: VIP pass, hotel—can you believe it? I never win anything."

"Okay, you *have* to talk to Evan," Reece said. "I bet we could get him to a car show—"

There was a knock on the door, and then it swung open to reveal Rocky. "We got a situation trying to form," he said. "Group of dicks talking shit to Ink. Ben's pissed and two seconds from taking them all on by himself."

Reece started to stand. "I can—"

"You can sit back down," Diesel said, getting to his feet. "Rocky's going to send the staff outside for a breather while we take care of this."

"But—"

"Your sister made me guard an office with you in it to keep you away from violence, and I'm pretty sure I will be in for a world of regret if Agent Grayson finds out I let you near a fight," Diesel said. "We'll take care of it, and you can wait here, okay? Unless you're going to break another historical window and rappel to the ground if we leave you to your own devices for a moment?"

Reece flushed. "There aren't any windows in here," he said grumpily.

Diesel gave him a smile that was annoyingly effective at making Reece smile back, and then disappeared through the door with Rocky.

Reece tucked his feet under him to sit cross-legged in the big desk chair. Maybe Grayson had texted again with some kind of goddamn explanation for why he wanted Reece to stay at McFeely's.

But as Reece went to pull out his phone, his gaze was drawn to movement on one of the monitors.

His eyes widened.

At the far end of the screen, the front half of a white Hellcat was pulling into view.

Was this the asshole who'd been harassing Diesel? When Diesel was one of the only people in the city Reece knew genuinely liked empaths? Who, despite knowing Reece only hours, had stood guard at the office door to protect him when violence had broken out at McFeely's in November?

Reece got to his feet. There was a faint ringing in his ears, but he ignored it. Whoever this dick in the Hellcat was, they were going to have a conversation.

He opened the door and hurried into the hall. Even if this was just a temporary club, there would be a door somewhere where the staff could step outside for a smoke break, to make a call, or to get some fresh air. Sure enough, at the far end of the hall was a door with a lit Exit sign that had been propped open a few inches by a large rock.

He slipped out the door and onto a patch of pavement hemmed in by the sides of the warehouse. Someone had dragged a picnic table under a shelter not far from the door, and even though a light but icy rain had started again, at least seven people had crowded around it, squashed tight to each other's sides in the cold. Two women in bunny ears were kissing, someone had a joint, and Ben was passing out steaming paper cups of what might have been coffee, lots of smiles and laughs from around the table.

Reece hunched into his sweatshirt and darted past the group, around the side of the building. As he broke into a jog, heading down the long side of the warehouse toward the part of the street where the Hellcat had been, Grayson's text flashed through his mind.

I need you to trust me: go straight to McFeely's as soon as you see this. Once you get there, STAY there.

Yeah, well, Reece *was* staying here. He was still on the property, wasn't he?

As he rounded the edge of the warehouse, he saw a man in a camouflage jacket and balaclava standing next to the Hellcat, typing into his phone with gloved hands. There was a tense set to his shoulders that was familiar.

Reece skidded to a stop. *"You."*

The man jerked around in surprise.

"You were outside my building." Reece pointed at him. "And now you're *here*? Are you following me?"

"I—"

"You could have just *talked* to me." The man blinked behind the balaclava as Reece stepped closer, gesturing at the warehouse. "Do you know how many people are in that club? How many people might have been freaked out if you came in after me?"

A group of women were walking toward the warehouse doors, and all of them had turned their heads in Reece's direction. The man in camouflage quickly stepped forward, putting a hand in the center of Reece's chest and shoving him back, behind the side of the warehouse and out of sight.

"Keep your fucking voice down," he said, pushing Reece up against the wall with a hand on his neck. "They said you'd come with me without a fight. That you're the one we need. They told me exactly what to do, and unlike their other soldiers, I know how to follow orders, see? That's why they chose me."

He had thick gloves on, a mix of emotions coming through like a staticky radio station—greed, anticipation. Fear.

An ache lanced through Reece's chest. "Hey, you don't have to be scared of me," he said, looking up and past the balaclava into the man's eyes, which were pale in the outdoor lighting and narrowed to angry slits. "I won't hurt you. I just want you to leave Diesel and McFeely's alone."

The man yanked his hand off Reece like he'd been burned. "How are you reading my mind?"

"I'm not," Reece said. "I'm just trying to keep people safe. If you want me to come with you, I will."

"You're supposed to be easy," the man snarled. "Stay out of my *head*."

And then he pulled a gun.

Reece's world shrank, the road and warehouse disappearing as his vision tunneled to only the weapon. Pain erupted in his chest, radiating out like fire from a phantom bullet wound that would tear skin, rend muscle, shatter bone.

This is how Evan would have felt, on that rooftop of Stone Solutions, if the corruption had taken hold and I'd made Cedrick Stone pull that trigger.

This would have been Evan's pain, if I'd made Stone fire that gun on that rooftop.

A man was shouting. In the distance, there were more shouts, more screams, layered over the pounding of feet, growing louder. Reece couldn't understand any of it. Couldn't move, couldn't think, could only stare at the gun.

I almost shot Evan.

Almost murdered him.

The gun abruptly vanished from his line of sight.

Reece sucked in a breath as he heard the gun clatter to the sidewalk, the world rushing back so fast his head spun.

"Don't shoot, don't shoot—"

The words weren't coming from Reece. His gaze zeroed in on the ground. His would-be kidnapper had hit the sidewalk, curled in a ball with his knees to his chest, rocking back and forth as frantic pleas came from his lips.

But there were more people shouting, screaming even, a stampede of sprinting feet. Reece looked up just as the entire group from the picnic table sprinted past, some holding on to each other as they ran. Their faces were locked in expressions of terror; Reece was surrounded by it, tasting it, drowning in it.

He froze. His gaze went back to the man rocking in fear on the ground. He was also terrified.

As terrified as Reece.

Oh no.

He became aware of the buzzing along his skin, his hands vibrating in their gloves, his nerves standing at alert. Aware of a feeling of fear too big to contain, spilling out of him and catching others in its orbit.

Like Cora had been able to project her fury onto three SWAT teams.

And Reece was outside a packed club of innocent people.

He took off at a sprint. He ran to the opposite end of the warehouse, and then down the blocks until he reached his car. He leapt into the driver's seat, slammed the door, and slipped his key into the ignition.

Nothing happened.

He frowned. He bent down over the passenger seat and fumbled to pull up the carpeting from the footwell. A moment later, he had the panel off and was staring into the compartment. Goose bumps prickled on his arms.

Someone had completely disconnected the battery.

Someone didn't want him driving away.

"Too fucking bad," he muttered aloud, as he reached for the wires. A minute later, he had the wires reconnected. He tried the key, and this time the engine sprang to life.

Somewhere behind him, he heard the roar of a supercharged V8. He glanced up at his rearview mirror and saw a white Hellcat swinging around the corner two blocks behind him.

Well, shit. Reece didn't take the time to replace the panel—or even use his turn signal—before pulling away from the curb and speeding off into the night.

Jamey was back in Port Angeles, almost to the hotel to get Liam, when a familiar number flashed on her caller ID.

"The fuck is going on, Stensby?" she said, instead of hello, as she answered.

"This isn't Officer Stensby," said the voice on the other side of the phone. "I'm afraid he's unavailable right now. Is this Detective St. James?"

She paused. That accent was incredibly familiar—a little more subtle, the voice more of a tenor than bass. But familiar. "Grayson?"

"Not Evan, no," said the man. "I understand Officer Stensby

sent you on a wild-goose chase to Port Angeles. Or a wild-empath chase, let's say."

"Who the hell is this?" she snapped. "Why are you calling from Stensby's phone?"

"Officer Stensby has made some unfortunate decisions lately. Including sabotaging your brother's brakes."

Jamey's heart leapt into her throat. "What?"

"Apparently Officer Stensby punctured the brake fluid in Reece's car earlier today. It's likely all drained out by now," said the stranger. "I have a personal interest in Reece's safety, so if you could get in touch with some of the folks back in Seattle and see if anyone can find Reece before his brakes fail, I'd be real appreciative. I imagine you don't want him to die either."

The line went dead.

CHAPTER TWELVE

It's World Traffic Safety Awareness Day! What's that? World Traffic Safety Awareness Day isn't a real holiday? Well, I'm sure we can all agree IT SHOULD BE.

#SafetyFirst #SafeDrivesSaveLives #DriveLikeAnEmpath

—EXCERPT FROM REECE DAVIES' SOCIAL MEDIA

REECE TORE PAST another warehouse and made a sharp right to cut across a parking lot with a concrete mixer and three eighteen-wheelers. A Smart car had about seventy horsepower to a Hellcat's seven hundred; he was never going to win a head-to-head race. His only hope was to lose his pursuer.

His phone was ringing in the center console. He ignored it, his tires squealing as he wove around a sandbag pile and took another corner at a frankly unsafe speed, popping out on a four-lane road lined with strip malls. His stomach swooped as he had to pump the brake pedal twice—which, what the hell, he checked all his fluids and wires weekly at minimum—but then they caught as they were supposed to. Thank God for small mercies; he drove on.

His phone was ringing again. He again ignored it, as up

ahead, the industrial area was giving way to shops and traffic lights. He had to make a choice: suburban streets that would grow more crowded with shops and residents, or the feeder highways that eventually led to I-5. He winced, and then chose the ramp, skidding under an overpass for a sharp left and then up onto the highway.

He cut across the lanes to drift behind an eighteen-wheeler, keeping pace to hide his tiny car in between SUVs in the lanes on either side of him. He glanced in his rearview mirror to see if he could spot the Hellcat's headlights.

Nothing but midrange imports, so far as he could tell.

The ringing of his phone yet *again* was very loud as he let out a small breath. He took the ramp for I-5 north toward downtown; as the interstate spread out, he slowed to match the semi in front of him as they crested a hill.

And that was when his brakes gave out completely.

Reece's eyes went wide.

He jammed his foot down on the brake, which went to the floor without slowing the car in the slightest.

"Shit." He pumped it again, the brake moving uselessly through the air. "Shit, *shit.*"

The road was turning downhill and he was trapped between the SUVs, rolling too fast toward the back of the eighteen-wheeler. Sucking in a breath, he jammed his foot down on the accelerator and jerked his car through the tiny opening in front of the SUV on his left.

The SUV honked but Reece ignored it. At least he was out from behind the semi, but now he was going even faster, cruising downhill at seventy miles per hour with no brakes.

He ran through his options in a panicked list. Nothing but concrete blocks on the left; if he hit them, he risked careening over them and into oncoming traffic and could end up killing someone else in a head-on collision. If he pulled his e-brake, it would slow the car but possibly lock his tires and send him spiraling out of control, again risking a crash and hurting someone else.

There had to be a way off the highway without hitting anyone else.

Red taillights were lighting up around him as cars slowed. More honks split the air as he swerved around a Prius going only sixty in front of him and cut off a BMW in the middle lane. Fuck. The shoulder on his right was also full of concrete blocks—was there a goddamn stretch of I-5 that *wasn't* under construction? He could steer into the concrete and scrape his car along the side, slowing himself with friction, but still too much potential for causing an accident if someone rear-ended him. Maybe he'd get an opening in the blocks and could hit grass, roll his car, no risk to anyone but himself—

There was a new horn, loud and long, and then a souped-up engine opened up somewhere behind him, even louder than the Hellcat had been.

Reece's eyes widened as a black truck flew past on the left and then cut sharply in front of him, filling his vision with the lights and tailgate of an F-150.

His voice came out as a strangled whisper. "Evan?"

Then Reece's phone rang again, and this time, he grabbed it, glanced for a split second at the Caller ID he knew he'd see, and hit speakerphone.

"Evan."

"Don't. Hang. Up." The F-150 stayed directly in front of him, matching his pace and leaning on the horn so that cars moved out of the way. "Status of your brakes?"

"Gone." How the hell did Grayson know that? Where the hell had he come from?

"Stay behind me." Grayson's drawl was as calm and flat as ever, as if they were chatting on Reece's couch, not flying toward downtown Seattle with no way to stop. "When do we get a good exit?"

"No exits," Reece said immediately. Too many curves and stoplights, too many chances to hit other cars, other people. He wracked his memory of airport drop-offs. "We might get a grass shoulder at some point, but no telling for how long before the construction starts up again. And we're heading toward downtown, there'll be even more cars, more construction, and I could hurt someone—"

"You're not going to," Grayson said, steady and still calm. "I know your empathy is sending you into a panic attack at the thought of other people in danger, but you're too good a driver and I'm between you and everyone else. We're gonna get you stopped. It's gonna be okay."

Grayson's voice filling his car was the North Star Reece hadn't realized he needed. His panic was easing enough for him to concentrate on Grayson's words. He was right; if traffic came to a sudden stop, Reece would crash into the bed of the truck, and no, he didn't want to hit Grayson's truck at seventy miles per hour, but there would be a whole bed between them. No one else would get hurt.

They worked a path over to the far-right lane, cars moving out of Grayson's way or the two of them finding pockets to weave around slower cars. Reece's knuckles were probably white in his gloves, his hands fused to the steering wheel.

Finally, the concrete blocks gave way to a guardrail. The hillside was steep on the right; once the guardrail ended, he could get his right-side tires on the grass and the friction would help, as long as he was careful not to go up the hill and flip his car. "Here. We don't have much space."

He put on his turn signal, and Grayson did too, and together they moved into the shoulder. The guardrail ended, and Reece put his right tires into the grass, but the road was sloping downhill and he wasn't slowing. Still too fast for the e-brake; he might lock his tires and completely lose control.

Grayson's voice came over the phone. "Cop up ahead in the shoulder."

"Shit." Reece's stomach plummeted.

"You trust me?"

"Yeah." Not a lie, some distant part of Reece's brain noticed.

"Drive into me."

"What?"

"Carefully, obviously," said Grayson. "I know you got the skills to do it."

Oh, this better work. Reece took a deep breath, then pressed on the gas. His car inched forward, the back of the truck rapidly approaching. His roof wasn't much higher than the top of the tailgate; this was going to wreck the front of his car, but better his headlights than someone else.

The impact rattled Reece in his seat as the front of the Smart car knocked into the F-150's bumper. But Grayson was still moving at almost exactly the same speed he was, and it wasn't hard enough to set off the airbags.

Grayson's drawl came through the phone again. "Ready?"

Reece took a breath as Grayson's brake lights lit up, only a couple feet away, illuminating Reece and the dashboard in red.

"Keep your foot off the gas."

And as Grayson's truck began to slow, Reece's Smart car slowed with him.

"Oh my God," Reece said shakily, watching his speedometer finally sink. "Oh my God, I think I'm in love with your truck."

"We can talk about your kinks later. Gotta brake harder or we're gonna rear-end that cop."

Reece yanked up the e-brake, which screeched as his car coasted over the shoulder and grass, the friction of the dirt dragging on the Smart car's tires as Grayson's truck acted like a giant tugboat slowing a tiny barge. He watched his speedometer fall to twenty, then fifteen, and then finally his car came to a complete stop, half on the grass, the steep hill rising up on his right and cars rushing by on I-5 on the left.

"Evan, Jesus." He slumped in his seat. "I will never complain about your driving again."

Lie. Reece couldn't even groan. He let his head fall forward and land on the steering wheel, taking deep breaths, his heart racing and tears threatening from the flood of adrenaline that had left him shaking.

A moment later, there was a blast of cold air as his driver's door was opened.

"You know which Care Bear you are? Bad Decisions Bear."

Reece broke into a laugh as Grayson's drawl rolled over him, real and unstripped by the phone, unnervingly emotionless, yes, but also familiar, even reassuring. He flopped back in his seat, looking up at the tall, broad silhouette backlit by a streetlamp and the headlights and taillights of I-5.

"That's not a real Care Bear," Reece said, like his heart wasn't still too fast. From adrenaline. Obviously.

"Well, you're not *Good* Decisions Bear." There was just enough light spilling over the grass from the highway that he could see Grayson as he bent forward and held out his hand.

Fuck, he looked perfect.

Reece shook himself. He reached out and took Grayson's hand, closing gloved fingers around his palm as Grayson's hand closed around his. With an easy tug, Grayson helped him out of the car. Momentum carried him forward and he landed close enough Grayson had to gracefully dodge so they didn't touch. But despite Reece's wobbly knees, Grayson's grip on his hand kept him steady.

Reece tilted his head back to look up at Grayson, their hands still joined.

"Hey," said Grayson.

"Hey," Reece echoed, hyper-aware of everything in that moment, the wintery mist cold and damp against his face, the gust of I-5 traffic rushing by, and most of all, aware of Grayson, only a foot away.

He squeezed Grayson's hand. "I want to hug you so much," he said, still breathless.

Grayson raised an eyebrow. "I'd have to carry you off I-5 then."

"Might be worth it." Reece didn't hug him, but he did drop Grayson's hand, and then put both gloved palms on Grayson's biceps. "This is a hug, okay? A big *my hero* hug. I thought you were in Vermont or Maine or somewhere east? How the hell did you find me? How did you know my brakes were out?"

"The tracker that EI wasn't supposed to put on your car, and then a call from your sister, respectively." Grayson's eyes were on his face. "You hurt?"

Reece shook his head. "That was some good driving," he admitted. "Nice moves."

"Nice ears."

Reece's hand flew to his head and found the bunny ears still in place. "They're a *tribute*. To the employee who died at McFeely's."

"If you wore them for a high-speed brakeless thrill ride through Seattle, you don't need to take them off for me."

Reece snorted. He squeezed Grayson's arm and then dropped his hand. Reluctantly, because damn, even an empath in gloves could appreciate those arms. And it was definitely shallow physical arm-appreciation, not touching Grayson generally, that was keeping his racing heart from slowing.

Grayson's gaze followed Reece's hand as it returned to his side, but his face of course revealed none of his thoughts. He pointed at his truck. "Can I give you a ride?"

Reece glanced at his car. Grayson's truck had taken minimal damage, while his poor car was crunched against Grayson's bumper, the headlights smashed, an EI tracker on it, and still no brakes. "Probably a good idea."

He followed behind Grayson up to the truck. Grayson opened

the driver's door, and Reece leaned in to hug the truck's door frame. "You beautiful souped-up angel."

"You know you've got your arms around a truck that only gets sixteen miles to the gallon?"

"Don't listen to Evan," said Reece. "What's a girl like you doing with a guy like him anyway?"

"Planning to steal her away?" Grayson said. *"Again?"*

"I didn't *steal* your truck that night," Reece said indignantly. *Lie.* He winced. "I mean. I gave her back. And look, I'm not even asking for the keys right now. I can admit that I'm shaken enough that you're probably the safer driver. For now. Come tomorrow—"

"Not in your wildest dreams," said Grayson. "Get on in, it's freezing out."

"Freezin'," Reece repeated, as he levered himself up onto the step into the tall truck. He glanced back over his shoulder. Like this, he was a couple inches above Grayson, and it was easy to look into those vault-like hazel eyes. "I could just sit in the driver's seat and not move?" he said sweetly.

"You think I won't move you myself?"

Don't say it, don't say it— "I thought you were saving that kind of thing for our hypothetical hate-sex."

Son of a bitch. Was he ever going to be able to be remotely smooth around Grayson?

But Grayson wasn't mocking the world's most awkward empath. He only casually leaned on the side of the truck, gaze flitting over Reece. "You do realize that every empath on this planet has a million reasons they don't want even hate-sex with the Dead Man?" he said. "No matter how hypothetical?"

"What, because of the empath hunter thing?" Reece scoffed. "That's not a deal-breaker."

"Empath *specialist.* And how is that not a deal-breaker?"

"You could have worse jobs," Reece said. "Like a billionaire hoarding money while other people starve. That's way worse."

"I can't help but notice that once again, you have all the self-preservation of a lemming."

"I can't help but notice that you said *empaths don't want it.* What does the Dead Man want?"

"Are we back to you assuming there could be more to the Dead Man's life than the job?"

They were almost level like this, their mouths nearly aligned and close enough Reece could have leaned forward and kissed him.

And then blacked out and fallen on his face. But still.

"I didn't ask about the Dead Man's job," Reece said. "I asked what you wanted." He hesitated. "Are you able to want things?"

"Wouldn't matter and never will," Grayson said enigmatically. "You getting the rest of the way in? Or am I gonna have to move you after all?"

Reece had more questions, but he let it go for the moment and crawled into the truck, awkwardly maneuvering over the center console until he was in the passenger seat. The hillside was close outside the window as he grabbed his seat belt and buckled it. It was warm in the truck's cab, cozy and familiar, and he shamelessly turned on his seat warmer and cranked it up. "What about my car? It's not going to be towed to Tacoma again, is it?"

"No." Grayson slid into the driver's seat in one graceful movement, pulling the door shut with a thud. "Mr. Lane has a cousin with an auto-repair shop in the Central District."

"He does?"

"Did you think folks call him Diesel for his muscles?" Grayson had his phone in hand. "Your car is going to their shop. I want someone I can trust looking it over."

That was a relief. The overhead light went off, darkening the truck cab so they were lit only by the glow of the dash and control panel. "I don't know what happened. I check everything weekly—"

"Officer Stensby punctured your brake fluid and sabotaged

your brakes." Grayson was still typing in his phone. "And now he seems to have disappeared."

"Oh." Reece wrapped his arms around himself. Up ahead, the police car was still parked on the shoulder, lights whirling under the streetlamp. He hadn't liked Stensby either, but Jesus. At least Reece hadn't tried to kill him. "So was the guy in the Hellcat his friend or something?"

Grayson looked up from his phone and over at Reece. "Hellcat?"

"At McFeely's." Reece gestured up ahead. "Is that cop about to come up here and ask what's going on?"

"No. I took care of that," Grayson said, because of course he had. "What happened to you at McFeely's?"

"I know you said to stay, and I swear I was listening to you, but that guy could have hurt Ben or Diesel or the others, so obviously I had to—"

"Reece." Grayson's voice was still as dead as his nickname, but he'd pitched it quiet enough it wasn't jarring. "Were you in danger?"

Reece hesitated. He looked over at Grayson. "I—"

I was being followed but I can't tell you because I think you only want to protect me because your brother changed you like I changed Jamey and I sent other people into a panic on accident and I definitely can't tell you that either—

"No." *Lie.* Reece forced a smile. "No danger. Ignore me, I'm shaken from losing my brakes."

Grayson's gaze lingered on him for just a second more. Then he reached for his door panel.

All around Reece, there was a chorus of *snicks* as every lock in the truck engaged.

Reece's mouth fell open in outrage. "Did you just *lock me in*?"

"Sure did," said Grayson, in the exact same tone of voice he'd used to ask Reece if he'd been in danger. "Because I'm the Dead Man, and you're an empath lying to me."

"I'm *not*—"

"You just flinched again because you hate the way lies sound," said Grayson, which was gallingly true. "So yeah, you're lying to me, and you're hiding something, and I haven't forgotten you're walking a fine line between pacifist and killer and I'm the last thing between you and the rest of Seattle. And this is reason number million and one that no empath could ever want even *hypothetical* hate-sex with me: I will never be safe for you."

Reece looked away, out the windshield, watching the swirl of the cop car's lights.

"I've got a city to protect, seat-warmers, and no ability to feel impatience," said Grayson. "So the next move is yours, Reece."

Reece blew out a long breath. He should be furious. He should be terrified. But the part of him that had been wound tight since he'd learned about the concept of corruption had loosened, just a little.

He didn't want Grayson to be safe for him. He didn't want Grayson to fall for his lies.

Reece was dangerous; he wanted the Dead Man to be even more dangerous than he was.

"There's been this guy hanging around my building," he said, the truth spilling out of him at barely a whisper, but Grayson would be able to hear it just fine. "He turned up at McFeely's tonight. He wanted me to go with him, and he pulled out a gun, and my memories of what I almost did to you came flooding back."

"What did that do to you?" Grayson said, still quiet and still patient.

Reece swallowed. "I don't know, exactly. But the next thing I knew, he was just as scared as I was, and so were the other people nearby." He let his head fall back against the headrest. "So I ran."

"Why?"

Reece glanced over at Grayson in confusion. "So I wouldn't be influencing them anymore—why else? I had to keep everyone safe from me."

Grayson nodded slowly. "And the Hellcat?"

"Chased me. My battery was disconnected when I got to my car; I think I wasn't supposed to leave. I lost him somewhere back in Kent."

"You lost a Hellcat. In your *Smart car.* Bet this guy is pretty pissed right now." Grayson tilted his head. "How long had he been following you?"

"I don't know," Reece admitted. "I first saw him Friday, then again Saturday night."

"Before Detective St. James left? Your sister went to Port Angeles knowing you were being watched?"

"No." Reece wrapped his arms around himself. "I didn't tell her."

There was a pause. "Did you tell anyone?"

Reece made a face. "No."

There was another, longer moment of quiet. The cop car had cut its lights and was driving up the shoulder, away from them and toward the exit. Grayson glanced out the windshield, then back at Reece. "You up for dinner? Give me a place that's open late and vegan-friendly. I'm buying."

Reece blinked at the subject change. "The Dead Man just caught an empath lying to his face again and now he wants to take said empath out to dinner? How does that not make *you* the Bad Decisions Bear?"

"We're not done with this conversation," Grayson said, which was ominous. He put the truck back in gear. "But I came straight from Burlington and all I've eaten is a pack of mini pretzels."

"So I was right about Vermont," Reece said, as Grayson picked up speed and merged back onto I-5. "And *you* were lying about having endless patience."

"At least I make good decisions."

"Oh please. You just merged without a turn signal—you make *terrible* decisions."

CHAPTER THIRTEEN

CEO Emerson Blackthorne learned long ago that business and feelings can never mix. But when his company becomes the subject of an environmental controversy, there's only one way to save his reputation: a fake engagement to empath Riley Davids, outspoken pacifist and manager of a struggling conservation start-up.

Riley is willing to be a pretend fiancé in exchange for all the trees Emerson has promised to plant to offset his company's carbon footprint. But will all bets be off when this fake engagement sparks real emotions?

—EXCERPT FROM THE BACK COVER OF THE ROMANCE NOVEL *ENGAGED TO THE EMPATH*, CURRENTLY THE SUBJECT OF AN AMI CONTROVERSY

THEY ENDED UP heading to a twenty-four-hour diner that flagged the menu items for all kinds of different diets. Or so Reece promised—Grayson had not been allowed to look at the phone and confirm it for himself while driving.

Reece called Detective St. James on the way. "I'm fine," he said earnestly into the phone, for a third time. "I'm with Agent Grayson and—no, I'm not in handcuffs."

"But I do have them on me," Grayson said, which earned him a withering look. "What? I'm not fool enough to lie to your sister."

Reece rolled his eyes and went back to the phone. "No, I just—yes, okay, the brakes were out, but—yes, but I'm completely safe, so take Liam home and—wait, Jamey, are you *driving*? Briony St. James, we are hanging up right now. Get your eyes back on the road."

Reece ended the call. He hadn't said a word to St. James about the Hellcat or being followed.

Interesting.

St. James' mysterious caller had been interesting too. Grayson had been walking out of the airport when she'd called. She hadn't said much, just that someone had tipped her off about Stensby and the brakes and Grayson needed to make sure Reece was found *right that second.*

He'd taken her at her word and found Reece himself.

He pulled into an empty spot in the parking lot. Reece opened his own door and jumped down before Grayson could get around the truck to open it for him.

"Are you planning to cut this dinner for another felony?" Grayson said as they fell into step together, heading for the diner.

"Only if you ask real nice," Reece said wryly.

He'd left the bunny ears in the truck—a crying shame—and apparently hadn't bothered with a coat or hat that night. He came up to around Grayson's shoulder, so it was easy to see the flecks of frozen rain that caught in his dark brown hair, the real smile that transformed his face when he looked up at Grayson, the wiry build that was the perfect size for Grayson to lift onto any convenient surface or wall and—

He cut the thought right off, but his body remembered too much: the fun two people of different sizes and strengths could have; the way dry wit used to make him laugh; the care that kind people took with your body and heart.

His body remembered the things and people that had made it happy, even if Grayson never felt happiness anymore. And now that they were in person again, his body couldn't stop noticing that Reece seemed to be made entirely of things that had once made him happy.

They reached the entrance, and Grayson got the door for Reece, who looked at him suspiciously. "So where do the manners come from if you don't *feel* like it's the polite thing to do?" he asked, as he walked through the doorway.

A memory started to form: Grayson's dad holding doors for his mom, teaching Grayson and Alex to do the same; the way his mom would tease his dad and smile. He didn't look closer, and it disappeared. "Reflexes are a funny thing."

There were a few other diners scattered about, a couple with matching salads at a table, a group of thirtysomethings eating club sandwiches at the counter. He waited as Reece slid into a booth and then took the other padded bench, his knees grazing the underside of the table as he twisted his legs to avoid any contact with Reece's. He hadn't ever conducted the testing needed to find the limits of his knockout ability. They might have been okay with two layers of denim between them, but they also might have ended up with Reece face down and out cold on top of the condiments.

The menus were laminated plastic, a mix of traditional diner food like corned beef hash and burgers alongside things like tofu scramble and avocado toast. Good, Reece could actually eat. "And you heard me say this is on me?"

Last thing he wanted was Reece to skimp on food because of his budget. He'd never met an empath who became corrupted because they were hangry, but Reece marched to the beat of his own drum. Drove in the lanes of his own highway, maybe. At exactly the speed limit.

A waitress came by with waters, silverware, and a coffee—for Grayson, obviously; the world wasn't ready for a caffeinated Reece. He ordered steak and eggs while Reece asked for a stack of the vegan pancake of the day with extra syrup.

As she left, Grayson leaned forward. "I think we ought to finish our conversation."

Reece winced. "I'm sorry," he said, and it sounded genuine. "I didn't mean to project my fear on all those people, but if I'm not safe—"

"Not that part," Grayson said, which made Reece furrow his brow. "Someone backed you into a corner, pulled a gun on you, and made you relive an empath nightmare. Whatever you did next, I'd never blame you for it."

"Oh." Reece looked a little lost. "Then what do we need to talk about?"

"Why didn't you tell anybody that someone was watching you?"

Reece's eyes widened. "What do you mean?"

He had giant brown eyes, a deeper shade than Grayson's hazel, framed with long black lashes. Very cute. Perfect for wide-eyed innocence, even if it was definitely bullshit.

"You didn't even tell your sister on the phone just now. She's a detective; don't you think she would've wanted to know?" Grayson said, and Reece winced again. "This seems like more than an empath's reluctance to talk to a so-called empath hunter. What's going on?"

Reece looked down into his water like it held some kind of atonement for a guilty conscience. He didn't speak for a minute, and then finally, he said tensely, "It wouldn't have been fair of me to tell Jamey. And it's not fair of me to tell you either."

"Reece, I made you vomit with my voice. I can knock you out with my touch," Grayson said. "What could you possibly tell me that's less fair than that?"

Reece blew out a long breath. "What your brother and I did to you both when we were all kids."

Oh.

"Jamey told me about it. How we manipulated you like Cora did her thralls," said Reece, "so you'd be stronger and faster than humans were ever meant to be. We changed you both, when you were just children, and that is so much more unfair than anything the Dead Man can do."

Grayson considered him. "Did your sister tell you the theory she believes?"

"That baby empaths do it accidentally, out of love?" Reece scoffed. "Yeah. But Cora didn't make thralls until she became corrupted and wanted them to protect her or do her bidding. What better way for the corruption to make sure it's protected when it's young than creating a permanent thrall?"

Grayson raised his eyebrow. "I've watched Detective St. James tell you no without flinching. She's in love with Mr. Lee, moved in with him, might marry him. She has her own mind, and her own feelings, and her own life. She's her own person. She is not your thrall. Not even a little."

Reece bit his lip. "But if some corrupted part of me was trying to turn her into a bodyguard—if that's what your empath brother did to you too—it's fucked up, Evan. It's fucked up what we did to you."

"Do you have a single memory of consciously doing it?"

"Of course not, but that doesn't matter," Reece said impatiently. "We changed your bodies—how do you know we didn't change your minds? Your instincts?" He swallowed. "So I'm not going to ask either of you for protection. Never again."

He looked crushed. And he probably was—there wasn't anyone in the world Reece loved more than his sister, and there probably wasn't anything that could have hurt him more than believing he'd hurt her.

Grayson leaned forward. "My empath brother was three years younger than me. My earliest memory of him is when he was two and crawled into my bed during a storm."

Reece winced again. "Was he using you for protection even then—"

"No," said Grayson. "I was the one who was scared of the thunder. He was trying to make me feel better."

Reece blinked.

"I got a million stories like that, and I bet Detective St. James does too," said Grayson. "So it doesn't matter what you two did to us and it doesn't matter why you did it. Sure, I've got extra strength and speed, and that's my brother's fault, but if you want me to be angry at the toddler who caught pneumonia because he wouldn't stop checking on me when I was sick, it's never gonna happen." He met Reece's eyes. "And I've never been a thrall either."

"But how do you *know*?"

"Because if I were an empath thrall, I wouldn't be able to do my job," said Grayson. "How many times have I had you in handcuffs?"

"How many times have you saved my life?" Reece countered, wrapping his arms around himself. "You came out of nowhere to save an empath tonight. Why else would you have done that if not for your empath brother making you believe you have to? If it wasn't our influence, why would both you and Jamey care so much about protecting people?"

"Why wouldn't we?" Grayson said. "Maybe most of this world acts like other people don't matter. Maybe we got politicians selling human rights to corporations and those billionaires who hoard wealth while children starve. But maybe some of us would rather make the world better instead of worse. Maybe St. James and I see how much stronger and faster we are than everyone else, and it makes us want to be protectors, not bullies."

Reece bit his lip again. "So you think you came tonight of your own free will?"

"I know I did," said Grayson. "I came because it's what I wanted to do."

Reece's gaze darted over his face. Most empaths couldn't stand to look at Grayson at all, his emotionless presence unbearable, and Reece had been the same when they'd first met in November.

Now, though. His gaze didn't linger in one place too long and he didn't look too deep into Grayson's eyes, but he wasn't cringing or looking away. "So you *do* still want things?" Reece finally said. "Even without emotions?"

Grayson's gaze flicked over Reece before he could stop himself. "I told you," he said. "Reflexes are a funny thing. But they're still *my* reflexes, not just the empty motions of some thrall."

Reece picked up his silverware, rolled tight into a napkin. He toyed with it, turning it around in his hand. "You're sure? Like, really really *really* sure?"

Grayson reached out and tapped Reece on the hand. "Yeah, Care Bear. I'm sure."

A ghost of a smile crossed Reece's face.

Grayson lingered for just a second, his fingers against the back of Reece's hand, the glove between them. The only part of Reece he could for sure touch without consequences. His hand was bigger than Reece's, but then, he was bigger than Reece, full stop, which was just one more reason Reece ought to call him when there was trouble.

The waitress was approaching with a tray loaded with plates. Grayson pulled his hand away. "Next time you're in danger, call me, all right?"

Reece snorted. "I told you that *hey, baby, call me if there's danger* line wasn't going to work on me," he said, curling the fingers on the hand Grayson had just touched. "*You're* the danger."

"Oh, I am," Grayson agreed. "But I'm not the only danger out there. I was in Burlington because a killer put gloves on a corpse, so we'd think the victim was an empath."

Reece paled. "I'm so sorry—"

"I know," Grayson said. "But I don't think it's a coincidence that I was supposed to be across the country investigating a decoy empath murder while someone tried to kidnap you at gunpoint. And no disrespect, but you got any idea how easy it is for bad folks to target an empath?"

"What *easy*? Look what happened tonight. I'm dangerous too—"

"If you hadn't lost control of your fear, would you have acted with an ounce of self-preservation and run? Or would you have gone with him without a fight?"

"Don't be ridiculous," Reece said, with a dramatic scoff, but he wasn't quite meeting Grayson's eyes. "Obviously I wouldn't just peacefully go with a kidnapper."

Grayson would've seen that flinch from space. "Reece."

"Well—I mean—maybe it's a little more complicated than a straight no—"

"Mr. Davies."

Reece huffed. "Okay, but what if I resisted or didn't go with him and that guy hurt someone?"

Grayson stared at him until he squirmed. "Call me next time," Grayson said pointedly.

"Yeah, okay, maybe I should," Reece muttered.

The waitress set their food in front of them. By the time she'd turned away, Reece had already upended both of the little silver pitchers of maple syrup over his gingerbread pancakes. "I didn't realize how hungry I was," he said, grabbing his fork.

Grayson picked up his own silverware. "I'm about to say something my manners don't approve of. But how would you feel about a houseguest tonight?"

Reece furrowed his brow. "Who?"

"Me."

Reece's eyebrows flew up.

"I wouldn't normally invite myself over," Grayson said. "But between you getting followed and Officer Stensby sabotaging your brakes, I think everyone from the people of Seattle to the president would want me to keep an eye on you. You shouldn't be alone tonight."

Reece's voice was a little too high as he said, "You know I'm living in Liam's old studio now? His one-room studio?"

"I've slept in my truck plenty of times. I can sleep on the floor."

"Wait." Reece popped a giant forkful of pancake in his mouth. "Why would you sleep in your truck?"

"I'm on the road a lot," Grayson said. "I don't need much sleep. Easier to pull over when I do, catch a couple hours, then keep driving."

"So how often do you go home?"

Grayson took his own bite. "Home where?"

"I don't know," said Reece. "You grew up in Texas, right? Do you still live there?"

Grayson swallowed. "No."

Reece scooped up more syrup-soaked pancake. "So where do you live?"

"When?"

"When you're taking a break from the Dead Man thing."

"The Dead Man doesn't take breaks."

Reece frowned. "But you have a house or apartment somewhere, don't you?"

"I own a house. And I have some acres in the Texas Hill Country."

Reece's eyes narrowed suspiciously. "*A* house, singular. As in, you own one house and only one house."

"Yeah."

"But I know you don't live there," said Reece, "because you bought a house the day we met, and that was a safe house that you bought for *me*. If that's the only house you own, where is *your* home?"

Grayson took another bite. "If I don't take breaks and don't have any sentimental attachments, what makes you think I need a home?"

Reece stared at him. "You live out of your truck?"

"You gotta stop thinking about me like a person," Grayson said. "If your pacifism doesn't like the weapon analogy, think of me like a robot. An automaton. I got reflexes and memories, like I've been programmed. But I'm not a person."

Reece pursed his lips.

"You gotta remember that while I'm here, all right?" said Grayson. "Because otherwise, the only one who risks getting hurt is you."

"I don't *gotta* do a damn thing," Reece said testily. "But of course you can stay with me. You can have the bed; I'll take the couch."

"You keep the bed. I'm gonna spend half the night working anyway."

"Bullshit." Reece pointed at him with his fork. "Between the midnight gym and the flying and the internal clock on East Coast time, I bet you crash the instant you lie down."

"The Dead Man doesn't *crash*."

"I'm sure Evan Grayson does," said Reece. "Just like Evan's the one who has to be a Southern gentleman and give me the bed."

Grayson picked up his coffee. Reece couldn't read him, but he wasn't trying to. All he was doing was making a distracted observation while munching on pancakes that were at least two-thirds syrup. But subconsciously, Reece's empathy was still at work, trying to solve Grayson like a riddle.

Wasn't easy for empaths to manage the aversion to Grayson's presence. Reece, though, seemed to be getting better at it, accustoming himself to Grayson like easing into an icy river one leg at a time because you wanted to swim. Getting to the point his empathy was trying to put together what pieces it had about the Dead Man to form a picture of a person.

The anxiety should have clued Grayson in already, but Reece's empathy was strong. *Real* strong.

Of course, Grayson wasn't a person anymore, not really, and he wasn't someone an empath of any strength could understand. But under no circumstances could they ever find out if Reece could get used to Grayson's touch. If Reece did ever go all the way over to the dark side, Grayson would need every weapon he had to stop him.

Because if Grayson couldn't stop him, Seattle might be fucked.

CHAPTER FOURTEEN

Big Hair, Bigger Feelings: Our Favorite Empaths of the Eighties

—**FEATURED STORY FROM THE DECEMBER ISSUE OF *EMPATHY MONTHLY***

WITH REECE'S CAR out of commission anyway, he directed Grayson to park in his spot in the high-rise's garage. The giant truck was such a tight fit that Reece had to get out before Grayson pulled in, because otherwise he wouldn't have had enough room to open his door.

He stood in an empty parking space, arms folded, as he watched Grayson crack open the driver's door and awkwardly lever his bags out of the truck and onto the concrete.

"Just one more reason I should do all the driving tomorrow," he called, as Grayson had to contort all six feet and five inches of himself sideways to get out of the truck.

"Try all you want, sugar, but I will crawl in through the bed before I give you these keys."

They rode up together in the elevator to the fourth floor, Grayson with a duffel on one shoulder and a messenger bag on the other. "How's the new place?" Grayson asked.

"A lot of people around." A few months ago, Reece would

have loved it; now the pleasure of others nearby was sabotaged by anxiety, because all of them were in danger. From him.

He hesitated, his eyes going to their reflections in the elevator's mirrored wall, to Grayson standing tall next to him, hat in one hand and unsurprisingly fixing his hair with the other.

Except the Dead Man was here. And he'd promised he was even more dangerous than Reece. So maybe tonight, Reece could listen to everyone outside the studio—and even better, someone inside it with him—and not be afraid for them.

The constant knot in his chest loosened, just a little, and he let out a quiet breath.

Grayson met his eyes in the mirror. "What?"

Reece cleared his throat. There would be absolutely no feelings, not in an elevator with a man without them. "Could I touch your hair without passing out? Hypothetically, obviously," he quickly added. "Do you even let other people touch your hair?"

"Some people," Grayson said dryly.

Reece clasped his hands together behind his back, casually and not at all like he was suddenly imagining running fingers through Grayson's hair. "That only answers one of my questions."

"Sure does," Grayson said unapologetically. "Almost like the Dead Man's limit against empathy is one of those national secrets you're not supposed to be guessing."

At the end of the hall, he unlocked the door to the studio, only for Grayson to reach over his head to hold it open for him.

"You know I'm the host," Reece said, as he ducked under Grayson's long arm and into the studio. "Are you ever going to let me act like it—actually, never mind, I already know the answer is no."

"You want to be a host, you can let me borrow your shower."

"Sure." It came out as a high-pitched squeak. Reece quickly cleared his throat. "Sure," he said, forcing a much more normal tone. "And before you make any cracks, yes, I do use it."

"I'm a guest and you're letting me stay in your place. I appreciate you being a sweet Share Bear. I'm not gonna make any cracks about Unwashed Hair Bear."

Reece narrowed his eyes.

"Right back to Glare Bear, huh," Grayson said.

"Take your shower, asshole."

"And now it's Swear Bear."

Grayson set his bags down on the end of the couch. Reece belatedly realized the gift basket was still on the coffee table, now empty except for wrappers. And oh shit, he'd also left out—

"I think I know that hoodie."

"I was leaving it out so I'd remember to return it to you." *Lie.* Well, luckily Grayson was looking at the hoodie, not him. Hopefully he hadn't noticed the flinch.

"Are you wearing it?" Grayson glanced back at him. "I figured you'd burn it to keep the bogeyman away."

Reece shrugged, trying to look nonchalant and not like he wore it every day. "It's a lot nicer than any of mine."

"Then you should keep it."

"What, really?" Reece said, eyes widening. "Is it from your college?"

"Yeah," said Grayson. "But it's not like I'm gonna be sentimental about that."

"Right," Reece said, nonchalant, because he was definitely way too cool and collected to have his own sentiments over getting Grayson's hoodie to keep.

Or any sentiments over having Grayson finally here with him again. There wasn't much space in the studio's living area and they were only about three feet apart, close enough their size difference was even more noticeable than usual, as was the easy strength that practically radiated off Grayson. Reece would have to climb him like a tree to kiss him, but Grayson would probably barely notice his weight. And yeah, it'd be different without the map of emotions to guide his mouth and hands, would be a new challenge to figure out how Grayson liked to be kissed, to get him wrecked and sated.

But damn. They could have a lot of fun.

Reece quickly turned away, walking over to the thermostat. "Towels are in the bathroom. I feel pretty confident in guessing an obscene amount of that duffel is devoted to shampoo and haircare products, but help yourself to anything of mine."

He turned the heat up as Grayson pulled a few things out of his bag and then disappeared into the short hall that led to the studio's minuscule bathroom. A moment later, he heard the shower start. It was nice, knowing he wasn't alone. The studio felt smaller with Grayson in it—in a good way, a cozy way. Maybe he could think about a roommate when the sublease was up. He could put up an ad.

Twenty-six-year-old terminally single empath seeking roommate. No drugs, bad drivers, or movies rated higher than PG. Must be open-minded about bisexuality and sadistic superhuman monsters.

Maybe not.

He walked over to the double bed along the far wall. He didn't have much in the way of blankets or pillows, but Grayson hadn't seemed concerned about his accommodations, had said he often slept in his truck.

Apparently lived out of his truck.

Reece frowned. He didn't know what to do with someone who'd bought a house to keep him safe but didn't have a home for himself.

A few minutes later, Reece had turned the couch into a bed best he could, with his comforter and one extra pillow. He heard the shower turn off and the bathroom door open, and turned before he meant to.

Grayson had poked his head out of the bathroom, a towel draped around his neck, covering his visible shoulder. A mesmerizing flush deepened his shower-warmed skin. "Can you pass me my bag?"

If Grayson had still had emotions, he probably would have felt refreshed and calm, maybe even languid. All that height and breadth would mean endless inches of skin to explore and map, so that Reece could fall into him and lose himself until the world had disappeared.

"Care Bear?"

Reece shook himself. Grayson, of course, didn't have emotions. But his fingers twitched at the sight of wet, bare skin, because he might enjoy touching him anyway.

"Bag. Coming right up." He grabbed Grayson's duffel off the couch and nearly stumbled. "This weighs almost as much as me."

"Then you already know it's not enough for a workout."

"Show-off." Reece held the bag out.

Grayson took it, his hand brushing Reece's glove. "You can take the gloves off if you want. I mean, up to you, but you can't accidentally read me and I'm not the one who'll get knocked out if we get too close."

He disappeared behind the door with the duffel. Having transformed the couch into a bed, Reece shucked his sweatshirt and swapped his jeans for a pair of threadbare flannel pajama pants. He grabbed Grayson's hoodie—his now—and hopped up onto one of the bar stools. He tugged off his gloves and tossed them on the counter, flexing his fingers.

It had been months since he'd read someone. He'd be lying if he pretended he wasn't craving it more desperately every day, to finally get out of his own jumbled-up, spiky feelings and into someone else's.

He glanced at the hall that led to the bathroom.

What had Grayson's emotions been like before he'd lost them? Had he always been stoic and distant? Cold, even? Or was the dry sense of humor the lingering ghost of a man who'd liked to laugh, who'd liked to make others laugh too? Had he always watched sports in silence, or had he been the type to jump to his feet in euphoric cheering when his team scored? Had he always been hard and tough, or had he had soft spots before, let people in close to his heart before it had been taken away?

Was there really nothing left to feel? If Reece could get used to his touch, the way he'd gotten used to Grayson's voice and face—would he be able to find any traces left? Echoes of who he'd been?

Finding out might be worth getting knocked out however many more times.

You do realize every empath on this planet has a million reasons they don't want even hate-sex with the Dead Man? No matter how hypothetical?

Reece shook himself again. Yeah, he'd definitely gone too long without reading someone if he was sitting here bargaining with himself over repeated unconsciousness versus touching Grayson.

Reece pulled on the giant hoodie. The sleeves came down far enough to offer some protection to his hands. Could a hoodie save him from Grayson's Vulcan nerve pinch equivalent? Seemed unlikely, but wearing it gave him an excuse to ask.

A moment later, Grayson emerged from the hall in generic sweats and a plain white T-shirt that he could have bought on the road. His feet were bare, and Reece had a moment of vertigo with the surrealness of it all. "Okay if I get some water?"

"You literally came to my rescue like a guardian angel—well. Guardian enemy, maybe." Reece put his chin on his sleeve-covered hand. "But help yourself without asking, is what I'm saying. I'm a little off my hosting game, finding out the Dead Man is not only real, he also does things like shower and go barefoot."

"Be a peach and ignore it, won't you?" Grayson said. "You're gonna get the idea that I'm human and we already talked about this."

As if Reece would ever be willing to think of him as some kind of robot. Even now, as Grayson passed him on the way into the small kitchen, he could see the shifting of his muscles under the slightly sheer T-shirt. Could smell the faint scent of something so stereotypically masculine he could have walked out of a cologne ad. Could feel a hint of the warmth of his big body as he passed Reece's hand where it rested on the counter.

It didn't matter what he was called or what he said. Grayson wasn't dead.

"I just moved in a couple days ago, so I don't actually remember where I put the cups," Reece admitted. "You might have to dig."

Grayson began opening cabinets, and Reece was going to sit on his stool and pretend he wasn't watching the bizarro sight of the Dead Man rifling through his kitchen.

"Can't help but notice all your top shelves are empty."

Reece rolled his eyes. "Maybe I'm planning to bag someone tall and saving that space for them."

Grayson had his back to Reece, his hair damp and short enough on the back of his head that his neck was bared. A lot of people were sensitive on the back of their neck, or behind their ears, or on their throat. You could skim that skin with kisses and feel the shift of their emotions as excitement grew.

Grayson was pulling a cup off a shelf and turning around. Reece quickly tried to smile like his thoughts were completely innocent. Platonic, even. It wasn't like he was thinking about kissing *Grayson's* neck. He was just—thinking. It could have been about anyone.

Grayson filled the glass under the tap, gaze flicking over Reece. "That definitely fits you better."

Reece held out his arms pointedly, the sleeves flopping all the way forward to hide his hands.

Grayson turned off the tap. "Isn't there a saying? It's not the size that matters, it's how you use it?"

Reece snorted. He folded his arms on the counter, his hands still tucked inside the sleeves. "If it covers my hands, could I use it to protect me from that knockout ability of yours?" he said casually. "How does it work, anyway?"

Grayson raised an eyebrow as he took a sip. "I already told you that you don't get that kind of answer."

"But we're sharing a one-room *studio*. Shouldn't I know the limits?"

"No."

"Come on," said Reece. "Is it just your touch? Or will I pass out if I make contact with any part of your body?"

"Empaths don't get to know the limits of what the Dead Man can do. Especially the ones who keep trying to guess national secrets." Grayson leaned back against the counter behind him. "And you know those big eyes are never gonna work on me."

Reece leaned forward, putting his chin in his hand again. He studied Grayson for a moment, considering. "Oh, of course," he said, in sudden realization. "It's so obvious now that I think about it."

Grayson raised an eyebrow. "You think you figured out when you'd get knocked out?"

"No," said Reece. "It's just obvious that you don't actually know the exact limits of your ability."

Grayson stilled. "How do you figure?"

"Because finding out would have required you to conduct tests on an empath. Knock them out again and again," said Reece. "And you would never agree to put one of us through that."

The kitchen was silent for a moment.

"You are so much more intuitive than anyone gives you credit for," Grayson finally said.

Reece waved it off. "Not at all. I'm not smart like Jamey. She got all the brains in the family. And the looks."

"Nice try, deflecting like that," Grayson said, raising his glass for another sip. "But not only does no one give you credit, you know full well everyone is underestimating you. And you let them."

It was Reece's turn to still. After a moment, he scoffed. "I don't know what you—"

"Drive like an empath?" Grayson said pointedly, meeting Reece's eyes over the glass.

"It doesn't matter how people interpret that," Reece said, dodging his gaze. "All that matters is they drive safer."

"But you know they think it means *drive like a cute little pacifist carefully following all the rules.* Not *drive like a professional joyriding my truck like he stole it—because he did.*"

Reece huffed. "Are you ever going to stop being mad about that?"

"I don't get mad," said Grayson. "I'm just not gonna forget. Just like I'm not gonna forget that the first day we met, you looked me right in the eyes and lied and I fell for it. You think a lot of folks can pull that off?"

Reece tried not to squirm as his conscience prickled. "You know most *folks* think I'm an annoying useless basket case?"

"They couldn't be more wrong," Grayson said. "Empaths might be sweethearts but y'all are also masters of human nature. You're circus ringleaders where the rest of us are monkeys, and you always secretly think you run the show."

"How could I run any shows?" Reece protested. "I'm barely functional. I've never been able to do the things other empaths do, like therapy. I get so anxious and upset people are hurt that I'm useless—"

"No," said Grayson. "You get overwhelmed by your own empathy because it's more powerful than what other empaths are wrangling. Maybe you haven't figured out yet how to fully control it, but that's not because you're weak. It's because you got a Doberman where other empaths have a Chihuahua. And because that empathy's strong, I suspect you already know this about yourself, but you just let people see the anxiety and think what they want."

Reece pursed his lips.

"That's right. I'm onto you now." Grayson set his glass down. "Because I promised you that there's nothing you can do that I can't stop, and I'd be pretty bad at that if I hadn't learned my lesson about underestimating you."

They were quiet again for a moment. "I'm not sure whether I've been complimented or called out," Reece finally said.

Grayson shrugged. "A little of column A, little of column B," he said, which made Reece snort. "Not like you're obligated to correct anyone. If they can't see past their own biases about you, that's on them." Then he added, "And that's not the first time I've heard you call yourself annoying. When are you gonna learn that I don't ever think that about you?"

Reece's lips reluctantly quirked up.

A couple of minutes later, Grayson was stretching out on the couch. Reece made one last effort to get through those manners. "You sure you don't want to switch?" he said, pointing at the bed. "This was Liam's; the mattress is all fancy and squashy. And you can't even lie flat without hitting the arm."

"How can you be so smart and intuitive and yet not realize I need to be the one between you and the door?" Grayson pulled the comforter over him. "Oh, that's right: because when it comes to danger, your common sense pulls a vanishing act."

Reece blinked. "Did you really just call me smart?"

"And once again, when I'm talking about your safety, I might as well be talking to a rock."

"You did call me smart." Reece paused for a moment, still standing, lingering by the end of the couch. Screw it; they were friends—frenemies—complicated—but the point was this was all platonic and he could tease Grayson. *Platonically.* "And somewhere back around your circus analogy, I think you said I was cute."

Grayson seemed to hesitate. He looked up at Reece, his head on the pillow, damp hair a deeper brown against his forehead. He looked younger than usual, his real age, same as Reece's. And for just that moment, Reece thought maybe he wasn't seeing only the emotionless void but Grayson's real eyes, the red threaded around hazel, the bags underneath. Not a scary urban legend; just a tired man with too much weight on his shoulders.

"Maybe I did," Grayson finally said. "Maybe you deserve to

hear that your sister's not the only one in your family who got brains *and* looks."

Reece let out a surprised laugh. That was not the response he'd expected.

And *that* was a compliment.

He climbed into the bed and flipped off the last light. He didn't have a lot of blankets, but he had the soft sweatshirt, and had turned the heat up enough for Grayson to be comfortable, which had made the studio cozy and warm. The city lights were sparkling through the big windows, those pinpoints of red, yellow, orange, and blue. "I bet you say that to all the empaths."

"All the ones who have my number."

Son of a bitch. Reece fought off the pleasant shiver that had just danced over him, light as a caress. Grayson's voice was softer and quieter, the lack of emotions camouflaged, and in the dark the deep drawl seemed so intimate it had left goose bumps on Reece's skin. "How many is that?"

There was a beat.

"One."

One.

"I'm the Dead Man," Grayson said. "Empaths don't *want* my number. Most empaths, at any rate. The ones with sense."

Reece bit his lip before he could smile.

Having Grayson only feet away made him feel better all the way to his bones. Grayson wouldn't let him hurt anyone. Grayson would keep everyone safe. For the first time since March, Reece felt like he could actually sleep.

He cleared his throat. "So then I'm also the only empath with your number *and* your hoodie? Does that mean we're going steady? Because if we're going steady, you should let me drive your truck tomorrow."

"Good night, Reece," Grayson said pointedly.

Reece let out a soft breath and closed his eyes. "Thanks, Evan," he whispered, knowing Grayson would hear it and understand.

CHAPTER FIFTEEN

It will never matter that the empaths, in their original state, abhor violence; all of them have the potential to evolve into killers. The fact of the matter is, we can wait like scared rabbits for the pacifists to turn on us, or we can prepare to fight back.

We must be ready to defend ourselves: there's no cost too high to pay.

—PARTIALLY BURNED NOTE FOUND IN THE ASHES OF A LABORATORY

THE QUIET RING woke Jamey instantly, years of sleeping lightly and responding to emergency calls jolting her awake. She grabbed her phone and silenced it before it woke Liam, who was sprawled on his back next to her, fast asleep since they'd gotten back from Port Angeles only a few hours ago.

Holding the phone to the side so the screen light wouldn't be in his face, she glanced at the caller ID. Lieutenant Parson?

It wasn't even six a.m. Whatever Parson was calling about, it wasn't good news. She quickly got to her feet, slipping out of the bedroom and into the hall before answering.

"Lieutenant," she said, keeping her voice down. "What's going on?"

"Jamey, it's Stensby." Parson's voice was muffled, like he was calling from a car, and he sounded shaken. "They just found his cruiser crumpled and smashed out by Lake Sammamish."

Jamey's breath left her in a rush. A complicated flood of emotions tore through her: years of working closely together intertwined with the betrayal of learning he'd lied to her and tried to hurt her brother.

She stepped into the kitchen and leaned back against the counter. "Was he in it?"

"No." Parson was a little hoarse. "No one has seen Stensby since an AMI dinner yesterday evening."

Jesus. Was Jamey's mystery caller involved? Responsible? "I don't understand," she said. "I'm not on the force anymore. Why are you calling me?"

"I don't know what kind of friends you've made since you left," Parson said tightly. "But Stensby's disappearance has been flagged for forces higher than the SPD. And I'm supposed to give you whatever help you want."

That was definitely Grayson's team at work. And maybe Jamey should stop pretending she wasn't itching to work with them, Grayson and all.

She watched the clock on the microwave flip from 5:43 to 5:44. "Send me what you've got," she said.

The vibration of his wristwatch woke Grayson. He cracked his eyes and glanced at the screen to see *Detective St. James* on the caller ID.

He reached down to the floor next to Reece's couch and grabbed his phone.

"Grayson." He kept his voice the barest whisper. She'd hear it.

"They found Stensby's cruiser abandoned out by Lake Sammamish."

Grayson raised an eyebrow.

The studio was quiet at that hour, only a few cars outside,

the hum of the refrigerator, Reece's soft breaths. Grayson sat partway up, enough to see Reece sprawled on the studio's double bed. Still fast asleep—peacefully asleep, even.

Grayson lay back down. "Got any details?" he said, keeping up the whisper.

"It's smashed up like it went a few rounds with a junkyard car crusher, apparently," she said. "And no one has seen Stensby since the AMI dinner last night."

Interesting. "Any leads on your caller?"

"Because he's likely somehow involved?" she said. "No." She paused, then said, "He had an accent just like yours."

She hadn't mentioned that the night before, but then, their conversation had been short by necessity. "A lot of people do."

"Not around here," she said. "He had your accent and he said he had *personal interest in Reece's safety*. Does that describe anyone you know?"

"No," Grayson said honestly. "I've met a lot of people interested in empaths, but I don't know any other Texans who'd be personally interested in your brother."

"I'll send you Stensby's number, but whoever was on his phone last night, they're not answering. Calls are going straight to voicemail now; they probably chucked Stensby's phone in the ocean." She sighed. "So you're back in Seattle, then? Reece said he was with you last night; I trust you checked his apartment to make sure Stensby didn't sabotage that too?"

Grayson glanced over at Reece again, gaze lingering. "Definitely saw the apartment, yeah."

"That wasn't what I asked." Her voice had taken on a note of suspicion. "Where's Reece?"

He ran a hand over his face. She wasn't gonna like this. "About five feet away from me."

There was a pause. "Five feet."

Grayson cleared his throat. "Yes, ma'am."

"Where."

"His new apartment."

"You're in his apartment." No, she didn't like this at all. "Your next sentence better promise me he's handcuff-free."

"He is." Grayson propped himself up on his elbow. "I slept on his couch. Thought he ought to have someone with him."

"Because of Stensby?"

"Because of him and whoever's been following Reece."

"Following Reece?" St. James sounded shocked. "He didn't tell me that part."

"No, he—"

"And *you* didn't tell me that part either," she said, more darkly. "Instead of calling for my help, you decided Agent Empath Hunter ought to sleep over at my empath brother's house. For *safety*," she added, with a depth of sarcasm that could only have come from Reece's sister.

Oh. He could have called her instead of inviting himself over. She'd been on her way back from Port Angeles; he could have taken Reece to her house and waited for her, then gone to a hotel or caught a few hours of sleep in his truck.

His gaze darted to Reece again. He'd slept in Grayson's too-big hoodie all night. The hood was bunched at the back of his head on the pillow, and his face was the most peaceful he'd ever seen it.

No, Grayson definitely needed to be the one who stayed over. To protect Reece—which was of course to protect the city *from* Reece. Obviously.

"Who was following him?" St. James said.

"Don't know yet," Grayson admitted. He gave her all the details Reece had given him, from the chase to the emails to the man outside the building.

"Shit," she muttered, when he finished. "Aisha told me the body in Vermont wasn't really an empath. Someone wanted you in Burlington. Or didn't want you here. Can't imagine why anyone wouldn't want you around when you're so good at sharing vital information about their brother's stalkers."

Maybe Reece had learned his sarcasm from his big sister, not the other way around. "The real Marie Pelletier is still missing from Montreal."

"I know," St. James said grimly. "Aisha said she's going to visit her roommate and get more details. Meanwhile Reece gets his car sabotaged and almost gets himself empath-napped. I still don't understand why he didn't tell me any of this."

"Got himself twisted up thinking he thralled you as a baby," Grayson said, which made St. James groan. "Think I straightened him out on the whole empaths and their siblings, though."

"Maybe he'll listen to you where he didn't listen to me," she said grudgingly. "Obviously you know what you're talking about."

Memories started to rise: a ranch set on acres of rolling, tree-covered hills; the smell of horses; tumbling out of a barn hayloft and already so different from other kids that he only skinned his knee when he should have broken his leg. His tiny brother, putting too many Band-Aids on the cut, lisping through his missing front teeth, *Gonna take all your pain away so you don't hurt anymore.*

A different part of Texas, flat and endless; his brother, bigger now, but still so much smaller than he was; the scorching heat of flames underground, and the sound of gunfire.

Nothing hurting anymore.

"For the record, I didn't tell Reece the parasite theory," St. James said. "I still think it's fucked up."

Grayson blinked, and the memories were gone. "Lot of fucked-up empath theories out there."

He hesitated. He barely knew St. James, when it came right down to things, but he trusted her and had done from the moment she'd pulled a gun on him to protect her empath brother.

"Brand-new one catching fire, according to the EI director," he admitted. "Predator theory."

"Are you fucking kidding me?" She sounded aghast. "Please tell me that's not what it sounds like."

"You know it is."

"Have the people who come up with this shit ever met an empath?" She muttered a curse. "Let me talk to Reece."

He glanced back at the bed, at Reece sprawled peacefully in the hoodie. "He's sleeping like a baby right now. How often do you think that happens?"

"Are you *bragging* that you made him feel safe enough to sleep?"

"No." Was he? "'Course not," Grayson said, and he was definitely talking to St. James and not himself. "I'm just saying we oughta let him sleep a little longer."

"Right," she said, drawing the word out skeptically. "I got coordinates from Lieutenant Parson; I'm going to join him at Stensby's car, see what I can learn. Don't bring Reece there."

Obviously Grayson wasn't bringing Reece to the scene of any kind of violence, but she was probably still mad at him so he let it go. "If you're taking care of that, I'll find whoever's been tailing Reece."

"Start with the coffee shop across the street," said Jamey.

"Pretty sure a man in camouflage and a balaclava wasn't sipping gingerbread lattes or peppermint mochas on spy duty," Grayson pointed out.

"No, but the coffee shop has been running a holiday promotion this week—tag them on social media and get a free cookie. Check their accounts at the times Reece saw him; bet you'll find at least one photo of beaming tourists with Balaclava Camo Man in the background."

Oh. "That's a good idea," Grayson admitted.

"Almost like I was a detective," Jamey said dryly. "And what do we do with Reece?"

"I was gonna bring him with me," Grayson said.

"With you. And you think my empath brother should spend the day with an empath hunter because *why*, exactly?"

Grayson's gaze darted back to Reece, the slow rise and fall of his chest, the sleep flush across his cheeks. "Because protecting your brother is how I protect Seattle."

"Mmm," St. James said, disbelief clear in the sound. "Fine. But Agent Grayson?"

"Yeah?"

"You're from Texas, aren't you? Don't you tell a story down south, of dads on their front porches with shotguns, protecting their innocent daughters from the unfeeling assholes who'd break their hearts just to get laid?"

Grayson hesitated. "We might?"

"Just remember: I'm a hell of a lot scarier than that."

She hung up on him.

He lay back against the pillow. That could have gone worse. Maybe.

He pulled up the coffee shop's social media account on his phone and scrolled back to see the pictures and tags from Friday afternoon, when Reece had been moving in. Outside the studio's big windows, the morning was dawning in a palette of silvers and whites: steel-colored sky and mercury rain, milky clouds and pale flecks of sleet.

His dreams had none of the depth or dimension of a Seattle winter morning. He only ever dreamed of a flat, unchanging gray. The doctors theorized it was the same sort of thing as the phantom sensations sometimes experienced by people who lost limbs. Grayson's emotions were gone, and his mind had conjured a phantom gray to fill the empty space where his dreams used to be.

Over his scrolling, a new text message alert appeared at the top of the phone screen.

Director Traynor: Didn't get your update yesterday. What's the latest in Burlington?

The Empath Initiative and Stone Solutions would expect to be told that the murdered woman in Vermont wasn't an empath. They'd expect to be told that the Dead Man had left.

Grayson raised his eyes from his phone to Reece, still peacefully sleeping on a bed that was very much in Washington, not Vermont.

The next thing I knew, he was just as scared as I was. So I ran.

The Empath Initiative and Stone Solutions also would have expected the Dead Man to do something about an empath who'd projected his emotions onto others—they'd expect the Dead Man to bring the empath up to the Polaris empath prison, to make sure innocent people weren't at risk. Even if the empath was still a pacifist and had been in the most danger of all.

Grayson's gaze lingered on Reece.

The Empath Initiative and Stone Solutions might've expected Grayson to hand Reece over to be locked up, but how was that the right thing to do? When Reece had only lost control because he'd been held at gunpoint, and had still run away on his own to protect everyone else? When Reece had been put in this dangerous, complicated liminal state by the Stone Solutions CEO in the first place?

Was Grayson really supposed to trust any of them with Reece right now?

He sent a response to Traynor.

Grayson: Burlington's cold.

Grayson: Nothing else to report.

He went back to the coffee shop's social media account, and then paused. There was a picture of three people, holding up their Christmas-themed coffee cups, and behind them a figure in camouflage was lounging against the wall of the building.

Grayson zoomed in on the background. This had to be the man. His face was hidden by the balaclava and he was holding a phone to his ear with a thick glove, the kind with hard knuckle reinforcement.

He took a screenshot and then got up and dressed, and was moving silently through the kitchen when Reece stirred. Grayson tipped some kind of crunchy frosted cereal into a bowl as he watched those big brown eyes flutter open.

"Morning," he said, to orient Reece and remind him he was here. Reece had been pretty deeply asleep, and it wouldn't be very nice for an empath to be surprised by the Dead Man in their kitchen.

Reece, though, didn't startle. He just turned his face in Grayson's direction. "Hey."

Grayson grabbed the cashew milk. "Took you up on that offer. I'm helping myself to everything I want in this apartment."

If Grayson had been like everyone else, Reece would've heard that lie. There was something in the apartment Grayson wanted a lot more than Reece's vegan sugar-bombs. Didn't help that Reece was stretched out on the bed with messy hair and soft eyes, bundled in that too-big hoodie that fit him better. No gloves between them. Reece had touch-starved himself into misery out of worry for others, and Grayson's body would have happily volunteered for all of the touch Reece could need or want.

But it obviously wasn't an option, for those million and one reasons that formed the gulf between the Dead Man and an empath, especially an empath flirting with corruption. His touch was dead enough to knock Reece out, and even if it was possible to get past that, possible for Reece to get used to his touch the way he'd gotten used to his voice, they couldn't find out, because the Dead Man had a responsibility to keep the world safe and keep all his weapons against a potentially corrupted empath.

The two of them couldn't touch.

And they *shouldn't* touch.

Grayson's mind knew this.

His body, however, didn't much care about those *couldn'ts* and *shouldn'ts*.

His body wanted to break the damn bed.

"I got some investigating to do this morning," Grayson said, veering the subject far away from those thoughts. He'd tell Reece about Stensby a little later; at least let him wake up before having to stomach that.

"Oh yeah?" Reece rolled onto his stomach, wrapping his arms under his pillow, his expression too innocent. "Somewhere we need to drive to?"

"Somewhere *I* might need to drive to, maybe," Grayson said dryly.

"Oh, come on," said Reece. "What's a boy have to do to get your truck keys?"

Grayson took a bite. "Steal them."

Reece sighed dramatically and rested his chin on the pillow, gaze on Grayson. "So what's the news you're not telling me?"

Grayson's eyebrows went up. "What makes you think I'm not telling you something?"

"Because you're standing exactly like Jamey does when she's stalling on sharing something I won't want to hear," said Reece. "You two are so much alike."

Grayson leaned back against the counter with his bowl. Another thing to keep in mind: St. James gave Reece a window into Grayson that most empaths didn't have. Another reason the Dead Man couldn't afford to lose any more of his defenses when Reece was concerned.

"Just spit it out," Reece said. "Waiting makes the anxiety worse."

"If you say so," Grayson muttered. More clearly, he said, "Officer Stensby's car turned up smashed to pieces last night. Stensby himself is missing."

Reece went very pale. "Is it—does it have anything to do with—"

"What he did to *your* car?"

Reece swallowed and nodded.

"Don't know," Grayson said honestly. "Your sister tasked me with stopping you from turning up on the scene like you have a bad habit of doing."

Reece frowned. "I have Stensby's number," he said, reaching for his phone. "I can call—"

"Someone else has his phone," Grayson reminded him. "Whoever called your sister to tell her that Stensby had sabotaged your brakes."

"Then I'll call whoever that person is," Reece said. "Maybe they're still with Stensby, or maybe they know what happened—"

"Or maybe the pacifist empath *doesn't* call the number of a man who tried to kill him," Grayson said bluntly, "and he lets his detective sister with her superhuman strength handle it."

Reece huffed.

"Detective St. James tried calling and got voicemail; she thinks the phone's probably been ditched in the ocean somewhere," Grayson said. "I got another job anyway, which is figuring out who was behind the wheel of that Hellcat."

"So what's *my* job?" Reece said.

"Looking cute in that hoodie. And you're already real good at it."

Oh, Grayson should not be saying that kind of thing; it was just adding fuel to the fire that wasn't supposed to be burning for Reece in the first place. But a smile curled on Reece's lips, easing some of the distress from the news about Stensby.

Then his smile faded. "I talked to Stensby yesterday, at that bakery in Everett. Looked right into his eyes. And the guy in the balaclava; I looked right into his eyes too."

Grayson stilled. In other circumstances, this conversation might be about to go south real fast. But Reece's voice had gotten smaller, and he'd hunched into the hoodie.

"So, um." Reece bit his lip. "That means I might be able to use that insight ability, right? Like I did in November, to figure out what was going on with Senator Hathaway's PA, and to figure out what was going on at McFeely's? The ability you said helps empaths connect the dots about people in ways no one should be able to?"

Grayson shrugged, watching him. "It helps a certain kind of empath connect the dots, usually."

Reece buried his face against the pillow. "I don't want you and Jamey to have to do all this work because of me," he said, somewhat muffled. "I don't want to put either of you through this. And I could make it so much easier on you both, but I don't want to use insight either—it's too much, too violating, I don't ever want to use it on purpose—"

"Good," Grayson said, which made Reece still. "That's a *good* thing. I told you, back on the Hathaway investigation, that I wasn't willing to throw empaths on the altar. I'm not willing to use empaths in ways that could hurt them or corrupt them. I meant it then, and I mean it now."

Reece lifted his head, just enough Grayson could see his eyes. "Even if it could solve the case?"

"There are no circumstances worth the consequences," Grayson said. "Insight isn't an option and never will be, because using it on purpose is a one-way street. You ever cross that line, you're not coming back, Reece. And then the Dead Man will have to step in."

Reece swallowed. "Okay," he said, blowing out a breath. "But you have to let me help you and Jamey somehow."

Reece shouldn't be put through more stress, but there was a plea in his voice, and he'd already seen the guy in camouflage. Maybe he'd see something in the picture Grayson hadn't.

Grayson set the bowl on the counter and picked up his phone, unlocking it and walking over to hand it to Reece. "Tell me what you make of this. And take the phone *carefully.*"

"I *know.*"

Reece stretched out his arm, still lying on the bed on his stomach as he gingerly took the phone. Their fingers came within two inches of each other, and Grayson should have just texted him the link because this was torturing his body with what it could never have.

He stepped back—not as far as he ought to have—as Reece considered the picture. "His gloves are weird."

"Tactical hard knuckle gloves," Grayson said. "Could be military."

"Not the knuckles," said Reece. "Last night, when he had his hand on me—"

"He laid hands on you?"

Reece glanced up. "Yeah," he said. "He was *scared* of me." He winced. "I mean, even before I projected and made him afraid."

Someone had been who-knew-how rough with Reece and the empath was more upset that the man had been scared. Grayson bit back several choice words about that and instead said, "You felt his fear?"

"Through the glove," Reece said. "But it was—patchy, if that makes sense? Like a radio signal that's not coming all the way through? He seemed really surprised I felt anything at all."

Interesting. Grayson dropped onto the couch, reaching into his bag and pulling out his laptop.

Reece tilted his head. "Does that mean something to you?"

"Man in military gear, afraid of empaths, thought he could touch you without you feeling his fear." Grayson popped some words into the search engine, and then turned the laptop around to show Reece. "And look at this: we got a brand of tactical gear that claims their gloves can even block empathy."

Reece raised his eyebrows. "I thought the materials in empath gloves were highly classified."

"They are. And Stone Solutions guards that secret like dragons guard gold." Grayson turned the laptop back to himself and added some more search terms. "But there's a market for fakes for folks who want to buy offensive protection. Your stalker must have believed the gloves would work against your empathy and been real surprised to find out they didn't."

"Bet he's an AMI member," Reece said bitterly. "Xenophobes are the easiest prey. They're so afraid of others they'll pay for everything from guns to AMI dues."

"Or fake empath gloves, apparently." Grayson pulled up a website. "There's an airsoft course to the south that sells this brand in their shop."

Reece swallowed. "Some of the SPD officers are airsoft fans. Like…well."

"Stensby?"

Reece nodded. "But last night—airsoft guns aren't supposed to hurt anyone, but that's not what the guy had, his gun didn't have the orange tip—" He was breathing faster.

"Hey." Grayson closed the laptop. "You don't have to do this."

Reece furrowed his brow.

"You don't have to help with any of this. You don't have to even think about it," Grayson said. "Putting an empath through stress or violence is never my first choice. I've got that safe house. You can go there anytime you want."

Reece chewed on his lip. And then he shook his head. "I think everyone is safer if I'm with you."

"You're not," Grayson pointed out.

"I'm counting on that. I don't want to be safe; I want other people to be safe *from* me," Reece said, without flinching. "I don't want to be alone with my head. I want to come with you today, wherever you go."

"Even if I'm going to an airsoft course?"

Reece nodded. "I'd rather be with you."

He hadn't flinched when he said that either. Grayson's words slipped out before he could stop them. "Pretty sure there are other things we could get up to with a day together."

There was a moment of silence.

"Hypothetically," they said, as one.

Gretel had not made good drinking decisions at the Leviathan. Even after a dose of painkillers and two cups of coffee, she was still in bed, scrunched low on the pillow with glasses in place as she read through headlines on her laptop.

SPD Patrol Car Found Wrecked by Lake Sammamish

The line that had her stuck was buried in the next-to-last paragraph. *The SPD has not made the officer's name public, but sources tell us the patrol car was assigned to Officer Jared Stensby, who could not be reached for comment.*

Why couldn't he be reached? She'd seen him just last night, at dinner at the Leviathan Hotel.

She reached for her phone, scrolling through texts from the night before.

> Alex: Sorry I have to cut and run, something came up. Make your dad pay for a car home if that champagne hasn't worn off, okay?

She snorted. If she hadn't known it was Alex, she'd have thought that text came from Reece Davies; the empath went off about that kind of thing like it was a reflex.

She sent him the link to the news article, with a note.

Gretel: Weird coincidence, right?
Did you see Officer Stensby
when you left last night?

She switched back to the laptop and over to her *Eyes on Empaths* inbox. Three different readers had sent notes about the empath club, McFeely's—apparently there had been a panic outside the club involving several of the employees.

Proof of empath mind control?? one of the notes was titled.

Mmm, probably not. Gretel had a tag on her blog devoted to McFeely's—not least because a reader sent in countless pictures of the wildly hot bouncer—but she wasn't sure she believed the companions at McFeely's were real empaths. Still though, the reviews said the staff were good listeners, and the club's whole schtick was being a *judgment-free zone of acceptance.* Frankly that sounded like a damn good time; maybe one day she'd stop by and hope she wasn't recognized.

She tabbed to her dad's email and scanned through, pausing on one.

The member lists are appreciated, and congratulations to AMI for its growth. Keep us posted; we're always interested in hearing about your recruits.

It was from a generic email address. Gretel sighed, loud and frustrated. Beau didn't even care about his members' privacy enough to protect them from randos asking for member lists. This was probably some shady marketer and now every AMI member would be put on targeted spam lists.

She shook her head and kept reading.

The body lying dead in a Burlington park wasn't an empath, which meant it wasn't Marie Pelletier. Except the real Marie

Pelletier might not have died in Burlington, but she still hadn't been seen in days.

Aisha made her way to Marie Pelletier's home in Montreal's Rosemont–La Petite-Patrie borough. Her roommate, Chantelle, was also a librarian, and let Aisha come into their small two-bedroom flat.

"This is not like Marie at all." Chantelle had a soft Quebecois accent, and Aisha could hear the genuine distress in her voice. "Why wouldn't she call? She doesn't make people worry, you know?"

"I know," Aisha promised. Empaths preferred to worry about others.

A cute tabby cat, maybe the one from Marie's pictures, appeared from behind the couch. Chantelle bent and scooped the cat up. "And then we get calls asking why she was in Burlington. Burlington! Why would she lie to us?"

Aisha tilted her head. "What do you mean?"

"She was going to BC," Chantelle said. "She had a job interview at the museum, curating historical records."

Aisha frowned. "Isn't that far for a job interview?"

"Marie's sister lives on Vancouver Island. She would move to the moon to be closer to Simone," Chantelle added, which made Aisha smile. "Prince Rupert is a smaller city, but Marie could take the ferry from there to Port Hardy, and it was a big opportunity for an empath. Marie was excited." She frowned. "Why would she have gone to Burlington instead?"

Aisha's heart was beating a little bit faster. "So you think she went to Prince Rupert?"

"I thought so," Chantelle said. "She texted to say she'd made it to her hotel." She awkwardly balanced the cat in a squishy hug as she grabbed her phone off the coffee table. "Look, see?"

She held up the phone, a text chain on-screen in a mix of English and French.

At the Alder. Time change, ugh. Trying to sleep for the interview tomorrow, wish me luck!

Aisha spoke some French and Arabic, thanks to her mom, but an American dad and lifetime in Seattle had left her rusty in both. "Sorry, my French is pretty basic. What does she mean by *Alder*?"

Chantelle shook her head. "It's the hotel name, Alder Inn. Small and local—she liked to support that kind of business."

Aisha nodded slowly.

"You are with the American empath agency, yes?" Chantelle shifted the cat, who was sniffing her chin. "You are looking for her? You will check Prince Rupert?"

"Yes," Aisha said firmly. "We're not letting this go."

As she stepped out of the stairwell and into the lobby of their building, she called Jamey.

"Hey." Jamey's voice had an echo, like she was on speakerphone in a car. "I'm getting close to Lake Sammamish, where they found Stensby's cruiser. How's it going in Montreal?"

Aisha frowned. "Marie Pelletier's roommate said she went to Prince Rupert, not Burlington. Job interview, apparently."

"In BC?" Jamey sounded as surprised as Aisha had felt. "And no one mentioned this to us?"

"Seems like whoever talked to Marie's roommate assumed she'd lied to cover up a trip to Vermont," said Aisha. "Which sounds like a ridiculous assumption to me, more so than ever now that we know it wasn't her in Vermont."

"But someone wanted us to think the body was hers," Jamey said. "Or at least, they wanted Grayson out of Seattle at exactly the same moment that Stensby lured me out of town and a different asshole went after Reece. I don't think I believe Stensby could pull all of that off alone."

The lobby held the mailboxes and had a small seating area by the window, a striped couch that looked vintage and a couple of armchairs where patches of velvet had been rubbed away over time. Aisha sat down, eyes on the window. "You think Marie and Stensby and the guy after Reece could be connected?"

"Maybe," said Jamey. "Although I don't know what to make of the anonymous call from a mysterious Texan—a second mysterious Texan, like Grayson wasn't enough."

Aisha was a doctor, a medical examiner these days, and could tell you when a death looked suspicious. But Jamey was a detective, had the kind of mind that could take *suspicious* and unravel its mysteries. Aisha watched the snow fall for a moment, then said, "There's another twist that you don't know yet. I'm not supposed to tell you, but fuck it—I don't like the coincidence."

"What coincidence?"

Aisha dropped her voice to less than a whisper. "The facility we talked about last night, in BC, where Cora Falcon is being held with the other corrupted empaths. It's on an island that's a hundred, maybe a hundred and fifty miles away from Prince Rupert."

"Don't people *live* there?" Jamey said, in shock. "Tons of the North Coast is First Nations land, or protected wildlife refuge."

"This island is uninhabited," Aisha said. "Nothing on it but a ghost town from the Gold Rush days. And then they built Polaris underground, in an old mine. It's not a fail-safe, but it helps dampen the empathy."

"Same as the heavy metal threads in the empath gloves." Jamey let out a long sigh. "And Marie just happened to have a dream job offer in Prince Rupert, the biggest and most accessible mainland city in that area? How could that be a coincidence?"

"It can't," said Aisha, and then added, "and you can't ever tell Reece where Polaris is."

Jamey went quiet.

"If you want to see it yourself at some point, for whatever reason, Grayson can probably make that happen," Aisha said. "But no empaths can know where the corrupted empaths are being kept."

"...okay," Jamey finally said. "You're right, there's a million reasons you don't ever want the pacifist empaths showing up at a facility for corrupted empaths. So are you heading to Prince Rupert tonight?"

"We'll see how close I can get. Airports I'm looking at are pretty small, and it's snowing here and probably at plenty of connections across Canada right now."

"Send me your itinerary," said Jamey. "I'll see what I can learn from Stensby's car. There's also that creep who went after Reece, but Grayson's claiming he'll deal with it while we're handling this."

"God help the creep, then," Aisha muttered.

Jamey snorted. "Grayson will have to be careful about being nonviolent; he's got Reece with him. And I don't like that at all, but part of me apparently still trusts Grayson to handle it." She sighed. "Probably because Grayson went straight from the airport to find Reece on the highway—managed to *save* Reece from failing brakes. And I talked to Reece last night, and he actually seemed happy, like it had cheered him up to be reunited with Grayson again. So... I don't know."

"Does *I don't know* mean it's still not a *yes* to being an official part of the team...but it's not a *hell no*?"

"Maybe," Jamey said wryly. "Montreal has amazing Lebanese food, right? Send me a picture and make me jealous. And call me again later."

CHAPTER SIXTEEN

"...and Duncan has the puck, lines up the shot—Henderson out of nowhere, smashing him from behind!

Oh, Duncan didn't like that, he's taking a swing—he's got Henderson's helmet off, you can see the red on the ice, and now West is getting involved with Grande, this is looking like a big one, folks—

Hang on, we're getting word that a fan has just collapsed, possibly fainted. Paramedics are rushing into the stands and—

Are you kidding me? Who brought an empath to the game?"

—TRANSCRIPT EXCERPT,
***HOCKEY NIGHT IN CANADA* BROADCAST**

"WHAT THE HELL was that?"

"What was what?"

Reece gestured behind them. "You just flew over that bridge without slowing at all. Don't you know an overpass can ice in inclement weather?"

"This is Seattle. All of your weather is inclement."

"It is *not*."

"I got here last night and it has yet to stop raining."

"Then you should know the rain could have frozen on the overpass and you need to exercise a little caution and stop driving like you're on some sunny country back road—although I hope you also know your current speed isn't legal on any road in Texas either."

"Maybe you're trying to backseat drive your way behind my steering wheel," Grayson said, "but, sugar, you can keep right on trying 'cause it's not gonna happen. I'll just add *unrepentant backseat driver* to your EI file and keep the keys."

Obviously Reece wasn't trying to annoy Grayson into handing over the truck keys. Obviously he was way too mature for something like that.

He sat back against the seat with a huff, then huffed again. He'd swapped the giant Texas hoodie for a warmer fleece, and folding his arms was now annoyingly less satisfying without the dramatic flare of too-long sleeves. "But you're not even driving her in the right terrain mode. It's like you don't even care about traction control or throttle response or public safety."

There was a moment of silence, then Grayson fiddled with the buttons. "There. Weather mode. Better?"

Grayson wasn't sharing emotions, but that hadn't felt passive-aggressive. It felt like Grayson had actually listened to his empath bitching and taken him seriously. "Maybe a little," Reece grudgingly admitted. "EI already knows I'm a backseat driver anyway, don't they? Everything I've done from birth to today is in some EI file."

"It's supposed to be." Grayson had kept his eyes fixedly forward as he said that.

"That's not exactly the same thing as saying *yes*," Reece pointed out. "Is there something you know *isn't* in my file?"

"Why would there be?"

"Don't dodge the question," Reece said. "I don't care if you're the Dead Man—that won't work on an empath. What's missing from my file?"

Grayson didn't answer for a moment, like he was choosing his words, because it didn't seem to matter that Reece couldn't hear the difference; Grayson tended to evade or misdirect instead of outright lie. An echo of who he'd been, perhaps? Maybe he'd been an honest person before he'd become the government's tool?

"You already know I've never met another empath like you," Grayson finally said. "One who's got some of the enhanced abilities but kept the pacifism. It wasn't supposed to be possible."

"Okay," Reece said slowly. "So what are you saying? You haven't told EI yet that I accidentally projected emotions last night? Or you haven't added *any* of my new weirdness to my EI file?"

Grayson cleared his throat. "That would be the second one."

Reece stared at him. "EI doesn't know any of it? You're keeping government secrets from me—and secrets about me from the government?"

Grayson shrugged, like that wasn't a huge fucking deal that probably broke who knew how many laws and put Grayson squarely against EI. "You're not supposed to be possible, and a lot of people would treat you like a science experiment if they knew. But you're not anyone's lab rat. Look, I'm gonna slow down on this bridge, just for you," he added, like he hadn't left Reece reeling.

They left I-5 a bit before Tacoma and drove through neighborhoods and retail strips until the city thinned out. Grayson finally turned into a gravel parking lot full of Jeeps and more pickup trucks and pulled his own truck into an empty patch of wet grass.

"No Challenger," Reece observed.

"Can't imagine he'd drive a Hellcat into this mud." Grayson put the truck in Park. "If you're coming in with me, I'm gonna need a favor."

"Sure," Reece said easily.

Grayson cut the engine and turned to face him. "Look me in the eyes and say, *Evan, I'm not gonna wander off.*"

Reece opened his mouth, then closed it.

"You want me to phrase it another way?" Grayson said. "How about *I could be in danger, Agent Grayson, so I promise I'll stay with you.* I'd even take *I know you're trying to keep me safe, Mr. Dead Man, so today I'm gonna make good decisions for a change.*"

Reece folded his arms. "Why do you want me to say those things?"

"You know why."

"Because you think they're going to be *lies*?"

"Are they?"

"No." *Lie.* Reece winced.

"That's what I thought." Grayson leaned toward him. "You gonna make me remind you that you got *stalked* and *chased* last night by someone who might be somewhere around here? That you need to let me deal with him?"

"What do you mean, *deal with him*?"

"Don't you worry about that," Grayson said. "Reece, I gotta do my job. I'm trying to make sure you stay an angel, but I don't know what that man wanted with you and you know I can't let Seattle end up with another serial killer. You would have let your kidnapper right into your home, so tell me something that's gonna convince me I don't need to literally handcuff you to me today."

"I told you already, I *want* to be with you," Reece said heatedly. "I don't trust anyone but you right now. Do you need to hear that this means I don't want to *wander off* anywhere you're not? That I plan to glue myself to your side? That if touching was an option I'd happily get so close I'd be inside you—" He stuttered, his face going red. "Um. I mean. Metaphorically only, obviously."

Lie.

Oh, come *on.*

There was a moment of silence, then Grayson cleared his throat. "Well, I'm convinced," he said, a little more gruffly than normal, as he opened his door.

There was a small building at the end of the parking lot that looked to be both the airsoft course check-in and a store that sold gear. Past the building, the course itself was fenced off with chain-link, with shipping crates and hollowed outbuildings disappearing off into the tall trees. Beyond the fence came a chorus of excited shouts and the sound of air guns popping, over and over again, meant to sound like real gunfire. Getting closer. Getting louder.

Reece's feet didn't seem to want to move. *Not real*, he frantically told his blood pressure, which was rising so fast he could feel it. *Air guns. Not real guns. Not real, not real—*

A hand suddenly grabbed his, fingers intertwining with Reece's gloved ones.

He looked up in surprise.

"You didn't hear me calling your name," Grayson said, squeezing Reece's hand.

"Oh," Reece said weakly, and wow, hey, the air gun fire was ever-so-slightly lost to the new rhythm of his heart beating in his ears.

"I got something that might help." Grayson dropped his hand, then pulled something out of his pocket. "If you don't have a playlist, you can listen to one of mine."

He handed Reece a small white box. "You *saint*," Reece said, scrambling to get the earbuds out. "Put on whatever you got; anything is better than gunfire."

Reece popped the earbuds in and the world was instantly, blessedly muffled. He exhaled in a rush. "How can I say thank you?" he said, tilting his head back to look into Grayson's face.

"Stay put for once," Grayson said wryly.

Reece huffed but couldn't help smiling up at him.

"The *fuck*," a man's voice said, from their left. "Take that fucking gay shit back to Seattle."

Reece turned, pulling out an earbud and opening his mouth, but Grayson was faster, straightening to his full six feet and five inches. "Come say that to my face," he called back, voice particularly flat and gravelly.

The man's mouth worked uselessly for a moment, then he ducked into his SUV.

"The speed limit in a Washington parking lot is fifteen miles per hour!" Reece yelled after him, as the man's taillights disappeared too quickly. He looked back at Grayson. "It's like I walk around with a big sign that says *Awkward Annoying Bisexual*," Reece said, scuffing at the gravel with his tennis shoe. "I can't, um. Can't believe he actually thought *you* were my boyfriend, though."

"I know," said Grayson. "Hell of a compliment, that he thought I could bag a guy like you."

That startled Reece into a laugh.

"Come on," said Grayson. "Earbuds in, music up, and let's see what we can learn."

Reece followed close behind Grayson into the building, steady beats in his ears. Most of the space seemed to be used for the store, with racks of camouflage coats interspersed with other clothes and tactical gear—balaclavas, goggles, knee pads. On the far left was a wooden counter, a brown-haired woman behind it.

Grayson went over to her. Reece averted his eyes from the archway that led into the next room with its big *Guns for Sale* sign, and quickly walked over to the display of tactical gloves instead. He found the brand, reading the feature list on the tag: *hard shell protection, textured for grip, touch-screen technology, top rated for anti-empathy defense—effective as what the empaths themselves wear!*

Reece swallowed hard. He didn't want to make anyone afraid

at all, let alone so afraid they'd pay this price to con men to defend themselves against empaths they'd probably never meet.

They should be afraid of you, a little voice in his head said. *Not just afraid. Terrified.*

Reece's fingers tightened on the glove, his teeth clenching.

"Hey."

Grayson's voice was barely audible over the music, but it drove away the awful thoughts. Reece turned to find Grayson only about a foot away. He pulled one of the earbuds out, just a little.

"Apparently the manager didn't show up today." Grayson pointed to the wall.

Reece followed his hand, eyes landing on a framed portrait above a small plaque reading *Keith Waller, Manager.* He stared at the man in the picture: close-cropped blond hair, a lighter shade than Grayson's honey-brown; broad shoulders with a familiar tense set; pale eyes that were narrowed at the corners.

Reece had seen those eyes, boring into him above a balaclava.

He quickly pulled his gaze back to Grayson. "I think that's him," he said quietly.

Grayson straightened up, looking out the shop windows and into the airsoft course. Reece followed his gaze and groaned out loud.

A small stand-alone structure, like a garden shed, sat a little ways into the course and off the edge, with a big sign reading *Manager's Office.* No way to reach it without crossing some of the ground currently full of shouting and air gun–armed airsoft enthusiasts.

Reece wrapped his arms around himself. "We have to search that, don't we?"

"I'll think of something," Grayson said, which was not at all the *no* Reece had wanted to hear.

Jamey parked Liam's car close to the coordinates Parson had given her, seeing yellow tape and a crowd of uniforms up ahead.

The air was wet and cold as she approached, coat zipped shut and a warm winter headband over her ears, her curls pulled into a messy bun.

Parson was waiting for her at the edge of the yellow police tape.

"Has anyone talked to Stensby yet?" she asked.

Parson shook his head. "Still no contact since last night's AMI dinner. I'm told he hasn't appeared at the station and he's not answering his phone."

Someone had called her last night from Stensby's number, someone who'd known he'd sabotaged Reece's car. Could Jamey's caller have been with Stensby at the Leviathan? Could they still have the phone? Jamey had tried calling back several times the night before, and again that morning, but no one had answered, not Stensby, not the man with the Texas accent like Grayson's. Apparently all her mysterious caller had felt like communicating was the one cryptic request to save Reece.

Parson handed her a pair of latex gloves and took her past the yellow tape. She recognized several of the officers on scene, their confused gazes following her as she walked with Parson.

As she approached the car, her eyebrows went up. From Parson's description and the pictures, she'd assumed the cruiser had been in an accident, maybe hit a tree. But up close, there seemed to be no single point of impact—in fact, there were too many to count. Every window was broken, every door smashed, the hood dented and crunched in multiple places.

Jamey tilted her head. "How did this happen?"

"To be honest, we're not sure yet," Parson said. "Damage is spread over the vehicle like it was done systematically, but at this level..."

He trailed off, but Jamey understood. The force had seen its share of cars smashed by the baseball bat or golf club of a drug dealer's goons or an angry ex, but Jamey didn't know many people strong enough to total a car to this extent. She could do it, and Grayson could. Diesel, the McFeely's bouncer, possibly.

Stensby himself? Maybe. He was taller than she was, close to Grayson's height, and in good shape. But this amount of damage had an unhinged edge to it that left her uneasy.

She opened the driver's door with glove-covered hands before she crouched and put her head inside. She closed her eyes and breathed in through her nose.

Whiskey. Not strong, but definitely present in the cloth seat, like traces of a spill. Had Stensby gone on a drunken rampage, destroyed his car, and was now somewhere sleeping it off?

She scanned the cabin. There were crumbs on the floor by the pedals, and a few crumpled napkins on the floor in front of the passenger seat. She gingerly cracked open the top of the center console with gloved fingers and found a pack of gum and a couple of folded bills. She snapped several pictures with her phone, then straightened up and shut the car door.

"Stensby's laptop was still on his desk at the department," said Parson. "The Empath Initiative has it now. He's going to be pissed as hell if he comes back to find EI in his business. I'm not happy about it either."

Parson gestured to the back of the cruiser. "There's a suitcase in the trunk."

The trunk no longer closed, the latch busted like the rest of the vehicle. Jamey found the suitcase, a carry-on that was already unzipped by whoever had searched before her. She lifted the top and delicately ruffled through the contents: tank tops and T-shirts, shorts and flip-flops.

"He's packed for somewhere a lot warmer than here," Jamey observed, uncovering what looked like a bathing suit. "Was he planning a trip?"

"Not one the force was aware of," Parson said flatly. "He didn't have any time off scheduled."

Whatever Stensby had been packing for, he hadn't included so much as a sweater. He'd clearly been planning to cut town for somewhere warmer. He wouldn't have driven his police cruiser out of Seattle—maybe a flight, then?

Out of the corner of her eye, she caught an outline of something deeper in the trunk, something small and dark and hard to see in the pale gray of a winter morning. She lowered the top of the suitcase and reached over it, hand closing around a small cylinder wedged into the crack where the carpeting met the side of the car.

She withdrew the item: a black metal pen, with a firearm logo and the phrase *got your six*.

The logo matched the one Grayson had sent her that morning—the airsoft course that sold the so-called anti-empathy gloves, where he and Reece were headed.

She snapped a picture of the pen. "What the fuck is going on, Stensby?" she muttered under her breath.

Once upon a time, Grayson had enjoyed an occasional game of airsoft. Obviously not with his empath brother, but he'd gone a few times with friends in college. On a course like that, he could let go more than usual, not hide his own differences quite so deep.

That had been in the Before Days. Now he didn't enjoy anything, and he was a lot more familiar with actual guns than air guns. But he remembered the rules, and he could aim an air gun as well as any other weapon.

"Come on," he said, after he'd paid for gear for both himself and Reece. He kept Reece's air gun for himself—Reece wasn't gonna touch even a replica firearm without possibly puking right on the spot—and led the way out to the edge of the course.

Reece had gone very pale as they crouched behind a crate. "I don't know about this, Evan," he said, and it was possible he was gonna vomit even without touching the replicated gun.

Grayson quickly scanned the field. Eight players dashing around the course, with more possible in the buildings or woods. The trees helped make decent coverage to the manager's office, but he'd need to clear the path—preferably without Reece seeing any of it. They weren't sneaking in anywhere if Reece was having a nervous breakdown in the middle of the course.

He crouched again. "It's gonna be okay," he promised Reece. He handed over his phone. "Keep those earbuds in and crank the music up until you can't hear anything else. Just trust me."

Reece furrowed his brow, but he took the phone, gloved fingers brushing Grayson's. He fiddled with the phone for a moment, then flashed Grayson a shaky thumbs-up.

Grayson straightened just enough to see over the crate, his gun in his right and Reece's gun in his left. Respawn point was in the opposite direction of the manager's office and he could send all eight players there at once.

He glanced down at Reece, who had closed his eyes and was lightly bobbing his head along to the music. Probably the best chance he was gonna get. He cocked both their guns and stepped out from behind the crate.

Three minutes later, he was diving back behind their hideout. He grabbed Reece by the hand again, and Reece's eyes flew open.

Come on, Grayson mouthed at him, tugging.

Reece reached for his earbud with his free hand. "I hear shouting. Did you piss someone off—"

"Keep that in," Grayson ordered, and pulled him to his feet.

They darted across the course, Grayson stopping just once to push Reece behind a plywood structure while he fired at a group of three who'd just emerged from the woods. Then they were running up behind the manager's shack on the edge of the course.

Reece pulled out the earbuds. "How are we getting in?" he asked, as Grayson examined the dead bolt. He was still slightly too pale but looked a lot steadier on his feet now that the air gun fire had stopped. "We don't have long before everyone's back, right?"

"I might be able to kick this down," Grayson said, as he accepted the phone and earbuds back. "Wouldn't be subtle, though."

"And I bet we can get in without any destruction of property." Reece pointed up to one of the high windows. "Is that unlocked? I could climb in through there, if I had a boost."

Grayson eyed the window. "You sure? It looks a tight fit to me."

Reece cleared his throat.

Grayson gave him a flat look. "That's a serious question that's pertinent to your safety, not just a sex joke."

"I promise I take you talking about tight fits *very* seriously," Reece said. "Come on. You keep bragging about all that enhanced strength; can you lift me up?"

Grayson stood on his toes and tried the window, which slid to the side to make a narrow opening. He looked back at Reece consideringly. "Lifting you is never gonna be a problem. Lifting you without touching you might be."

"But shoes should be safe, right?" said Reece. "And let's be real—if it goes awry, you can still kick down the door, with the bonus that your day will probably actually be *easier* if I'm unconscious."

Grayson couldn't really argue with that. He stepped closer to the shack, crouching down so Reece could get his foot up into his hands. They weren't touching, not really—just three points of contact: Reece's shoe resting in his cupped palms, one of Reece's gloved hands on each of his shoulders. No skin-to-skin contact, just light, soft pressure on Grayson's hands and shoulders.

And Grayson was as aware of every inch of Reece as if they'd been naked in a bed. He didn't do much touching these days beyond fights, and gloves or not, he hadn't had someone's hands this gentle on him in a long time.

"You've, um. You've got really nice shoulders." Reece's fingers curled into him, each one lighting a spark under his skin. "I mean. Just saying. They're a good, um. Handhold."

Oh, great. Now he was thinking of a dozen other positions they could get into where Reece would be gripping his shoulders tight.

Reece cleared his throat. "Maybe you better lift me up."

"I think I better." Grayson lifted, and confirming how damn easy it was to manhandle him was not helping *anything.*

Reece twisted, putting his hands on the ledge and poking his head through the window. "There's a desk just below I can land on. I'm going in."

"Sure, sure," Grayson muttered under his breath, as Reece ducked under the frame and levered himself through the narrow opening. "And I'll just stand here. Watch you squirm in through that window on your stomach. Notice how flexible you are. Think about *tight fits.* This is fine, this isn't gonna haunt me."

A minute later, Reece was unlocking the dead bolt. Grayson stepped inside to join him.

"Waller's got AMI propaganda—who could have seen that coming?" Reece said, bitter and sarcastic, pointing to a bulletin board with tacked-up flyers.

"I'm not sure AMI is the one who put him up to coming after you." Grayson crouched, looking under the metal desk for anything taped underneath.

Nothing he could see, but there was an unopened package on the floor, maybe the size of a shoebox. Reece hovered at his side as Grayson picked it up and set it on the desk. It was addressed to Keith Waller with the airsoft course's address and postmarked two weeks earlier from Vancouver, British Columbia. No return address. Grayson broke the tape and lifted the cardboard flaps to uncover—

Empath gloves.

"These look real," Reece said, as Grayson picked them up. "Big, though—those would fit *you*."

He was right, and he was right that the gloves were the real deal. Grayson could smell the coppery metallic scent, feel the stiffness under his fingers.

"I've never met an empath who'd need that size gloves," Reece went on. "What are they for?"

"Don't worry about it."

"Why?" Reece said suspiciously. "You think it's something I won't like—oh." His voice had tightened. "Of course. They're not for empaths; I bet Stone Solutions makes these for people who have to handle empaths. Mr. Airsoft Manager was probably supposed to be wearing these when he dealt with me."

Grayson stilled. "How—"

"That wasn't insight."

Reece hadn't flinched as he said it. But still. "You came to that conclusion real quick," Grayson pointed out.

"Well, yeah," Reece said, like it was obvious. "I was manhandled onto a roof last month by non-empaths wearing empath gloves. It left an impression." He looked up at Grayson with big, earnest eyes. "I'm not using insight," he said again. "But I'm glad you're checking." More quietly, he added, "I keep telling you I want you to watch me, Evan. I know I'm dangerous and I don't want to hurt anyone."

Reece had successfully lied to Grayson before, but Grayson hadn't known his tells then. Now he still hadn't flinched, and his queasiness on the airsoft course had been real, Grayson was certain of it.

"You're right," Grayson admitted. "Stone Solutions has a line of gloves intended for folks who handle corrupted empaths and they come in larger sizes. But you can't order any kind of real empath gloves online, and those are all made right here in Seattle. These were shipped from BC."

"For all the good it did them," Reece said bitterly. "This guy still trusted his own brand more than the scientists. A mistake."

He turned away, toward a filing cabinet. "Want to bet Mr. Paranoid Airsoft Manager doesn't trust the internet and keeps everything on paper?" Grayson heard a drawer open behind him. "Bingo, he has a file on me. Ugh, with *pictures*—can I burn this?"

"Let me take a look through it and then I'll buy you the matches myself." Grayson set the gloves to the side, going through the rest of the contents of the box. No note, packing slip, or explanation. They were packed in tissue paper that could have come from anywhere. But this had been shipped from Vancouver, meaning the most likely place it could've come from was Stone Solutions Canada.

He straightened up. "What do you think about—"

He paused.

Reece had vanished.

CHAPTER SEVENTEEN

Cute but Concerning: An examination of the legal potentialities of the common law doctrine of attractive nuisance as the substantive basis of tort liability in matters of empathy.

—RAINIER UNIVERSITY LAW REVIEW,
VOLUME 24, ISSUE 2

DIESEL FROWNED AS he replayed the previous night's security footage for a third time. Reece had burst out of the building and gone straight up to the guy leaning on the Hellcat. The man wore a balaclava, but from his height and breadth, it could have been Keith, showing up for—what, exactly?

The camera didn't have sound, but Reece was clearly pissed. Not afraid, though, even when the man—twice Reece's size—shoved him back around the side of the warehouse.

Diesel switched cameras, frown deepening as he again watched the asshole in the balaclava pull a gun on Reece. *Then* the fear on Reece's face was clear, but it was the man in the balaclava who hit the ground a moment later, trembling. At that same time, all of the staff outside had broken into screams too and gone sprinting off into the freezing night. They'd come back maybe twenty minutes later, confused at their own terror and paranoia, no ideas beyond *maybe it was the weed.*

Diesel wasn't so sure. He paused the video on Reece, who was staring down at the man in shock. "What happened to you last night, kiddo?" he muttered out loud.

There was a knock on the open door. Diesel turned to see Ben, balancing a box half his size. "You're supposed to be on your way to Vancouver and that cool car show," he chided, as he wedged his foot on the door frame and got his knee up under the box to support its weight.

"I'm still going." Diesel closed the video and stood. "Show doesn't start until tomorrow—I'll leave early in the morning."

"Your hotel package starts tonight—"

"But it'll keep. And give me that." Diesel reached out for the box swamping Ben.

"You deserve a break more than anyone I know," Ben protested, letting him take it out of his hands. "There's at least a dozen of us here right now to get this place ready for tonight. Frodo is scrubbing down the bar himself. We were all so excited that you won this trip—why aren't you taking it?"

"I will," Diesel promised again. "But just wanted to check on this place or I'd be all distracted up there anyway. We still don't know what spooked you last night." And someone had held Reece at gunpoint. Diesel wanted to show that to Frodo, the owner of McFeely's, before they told the staff, who'd probably be equal parts freaked and furious. Ben especially; he was sweet but also loyal, and he didn't tolerate people messing with his friends. Something clinked in the box as Diesel hefted it up. "What's in here?"

"Bottles for recycling." Ben rolled his shoulders, head tilted back to look up at Diesel. "I'm cleaning up the bar."

"Go get Rocky," Diesel said. "He's going to be so mad if he finds out your tiny ass moved a bunch of heavy stuff and he didn't get to help."

Ben snorted, but he had started to smile. "Where is he?"

"Cleaning out the Wellness Room." Those two had been eyeing each other since Rocky had started at McFeely's three weeks ago. Diesel would be staying out of the Wellness Room for at least another hour.

Ben disappeared into the Wellness Room and Diesel went the opposite way, down the hall and out the side door, the same one he'd watched Reece storm out of on the security footage. He carried the box past the picnic table, light droplets falling on his hair and sweatshirt as he headed for the back of the warehouse, to their staff parking area and the dumpsters.

As he lifted the lid of one of the recycling bins and tossed the box of bottles in, somewhere behind him, a car door opened. He glanced over his shoulder to see four men approaching, an average-sized man in front in a long dark coat and three larger men in puffy camouflage coats that didn't quite conceal the outline of their firearms.

Shit. Diesel let the lid fall as he straightened. "Can I help you?" he said, as the men approached.

"Mr. Lane," said the man in front. He didn't have a hat, his brown hair in disarray and his glasses sliding down his nose. His eyes were pale blue and narrowed. "You were supposed to be on your way to Vancouver by now."

Diesel's gaze darted over the group. He'd seen his share of rough folks over the years. People with bad intentions, people itching for a fight. But this man and his group made Diesel's stomach twist in a new way.

Keith had mentioned powerful contacts—the kind who paid well enough that he'd bought the Hellcat. Diesel's good fortune at winning a trip out of the blue suddenly seemed like a lot less of a lucky shot.

"Plans change," Diesel finally said.

"Indeed they do. Sometimes people shirk their duties and vanish into the night, and other people don't take their scheduled trips, and you're forced to make moves sooner than expected." The man looked over to the warehouse. "We've learned a lot about you, Mr. Lane. You like empaths—not just the pretend ones you work with, but the real ones. You like their compassion and their pacifism, and they like you right back. Your empath therapist at the veterans' hospital wrote glowingly about you in her notes, and I'm sure Reece Davies would love to count you as a friend."

The recycling bins were at his back, but broken bottles wouldn't do Diesel much good against guns. "What is this about?"

"Your warm relationships with real empaths. It's a hard quality to find in an ex-marine, you know." The man nodded toward the warehouse. "Lots of people inside right now, aren't there?" he said, too lightly.

Diesel took a breath through his nose. That hadn't been subtle.

"Why don't we go for a drive together?" said the man. "Unless you'd rather introduce us to your friends?"

Most people didn't find their way to a place like McFeely's unless life had given them a reason to crave kindness. Everyone inside had a past of their own that could be dug back up and used against them.

Diesel let out his breath. "Let's go, then," he said tightly.

The man with the pale eyes smiled. "I knew you were the right recruit for the job."

Reece didn't look back as he sprinted into the airsoft gear shop and then across the parking lot. He had found Waller's file on him in that cabinet, and it was one thing if some wannabe kidnapper was watching Reece.

But that creep had taken pictures of *Jamey and Liam*.

Fury threatened to choke him; Reece shoved it down. Last night, he'd been so scared that he'd projected his emotions onto others. Fear had been bad enough, but he could not risk projecting anger, not with all these people around, not with air guns and maybe real weapons nearby.

He crossed the gravel lot, an uncomfortable combination of hot from exertion and cold from the icy wind hitting his sweaty skin. But Grayson's truck was right in front of him and it looked like a fortress. Reece practically ran the last few steps to the truck, using the dented bumper to climb over the tailgate and into the bed. He sat on the ridged floor, bringing his knees to his chest in a tight ball, his back against the wheel well.

He breathed the cold, wet December air and willed it to cool his temper before he lit up the entire airsoft course with rage. What was he doing, pretending he could be out among normal people? Acting like a sheep when he was turning into a wolf?

He stuck his hands out in front of him, staring unseeing at the black gloves.

Waller thought he was some kind of badass. He had no idea how dangerous Jamey was—and even less idea how dangerous Reece really was. No idea the risks he was taking by messing with Reece's family.

He reached for his right glove and tugged it off. The air was icy against his fingers, but it felt good.

Waller had thought his airsoft gloves could protect him against Reece. What a fucking idiot. The only protection anyone in Seattle had against Reece was his own willingness to stifle his abilities with the empath gloves.

What would happen to creeps like Waller if Reece decided he was done wearing them?

His phone was ringing in his pocket. Reece shook his head, thoughts slipping away. By the time he'd dug it out of his jeans pocket, it had stopped ringing. *Missed call Evan Grayson* it said on-screen.

A text came in.

Grayson: You better feel guilty enough about taking off that you're gonna tell me exactly where you are.

Reece winced.

Reece: Truck.

His gaze lingered on his phone, his new background with the hot gym picture Grayson had sent from Vermont; the flush to Grayson's skin, the sweat-dampened hair, the warm hazel shade of his eyes.

Footsteps were already approaching, big feet moving rapidly. And here he was, making giant metaphorical heart-eyes over Grayson's selfie.

Reece quickly stuck his phone in his hoodie pocket just as Grayson appeared on the other side of the tailgate. "What is it with you and running off behind my back?" He folded his arms on the top of the tailgate. "You couldn't wait thirty seconds to tell me you're going?"

Grayson's eyes were so much harder to look at in person, with their missing emotions, but Reece could meet them for longer now, could take in the shades of gold and warm brown against the winter day's endless steel.

"I'm sorry," he said, and meant. "I opened that drawer, and Waller had pictures of me, but not just me—Jamey and Liam too."

"Oh." Grayson leaned forward on his folded arms on the top of the tailgate. "That pissed you off."

It wasn't really a question, more of an understanding. Reece nodded anyway. "I was—*really* mad," he admitted. And after last night, I just—rage and weapons didn't seem like a great combination, and I thought I better get some distance from other people. Fast."

"So you came here?"

"Yeah." Reece hunched his shoulders. "I wasn't really wandering off. I was just coming to wait for you."

Grayson nodded slowly. "You still feeling on edge?"

Reece took a slow breath, in and out, trying to parse out his feelings. Grayson's arrival had helped him calm down, but anger was still simmering, ready to rise up. "Probably safest if I'm not around anyone else for a while," he finally admitted. "Except you, obviously. I still want to be around you, you're the only one that makes me feel—the only one I want to—maybe it can be just the two of us for a bit?"

He winced. "Wow. I can't believe I topped your terrible pickup line, but *hey, baby, call me if there's danger* isn't half as bad as *hey, baby, let's be alone so I don't accidentally send strangers into fits of rage.*"

"Hey now," said Grayson. "You don't know what kind of lines work on me. Maybe I'm into it."

Reece huffed a surprised laugh that eased the anger even more, a small smile on his lips as he looked up at Grayson.

Grayson stepped back, and then the tailgate was coming down. "Come on." He extended a hand. "We can bicker over who has worse lines in the truck. It's freezing out."

Reece started to move his hand, then felt something cold in his pocket—*felt* the cold, because that was the edge of his phone against his bare skin.

Shit. "Are we going somewhere?" Reece said, stalling as his mind raced. Why had he taken off his *glove*?

"Those gloves we found gave me an idea," Grayson said. "Not sure what you're gonna think, though."

There was a chime. Grayson dropped his hand, turning slightly to the side as he checked his watch. Reece took advantage of the moment and hurriedly slid down the bed until he was perched on the edge of the open tailgate, his legs hanging off the end, tucking his hands out of sight under his thighs just as Grayson turned back to him.

"What idea?" Reece said, in the most normal tone he could manage.

"I happen to know that the president of Stone Solutions Canada, Vivian Marist, is here in Seattle at least through tomorrow, giving a keynote speech at an AMI conference in place of Cedrick Stone," Grayson said. "That box in Mr. Waller's office held real empath gloves and they were shipped from BC. I think I need to do some undercover searching at Stone Solutions Canada. You want to come to Vancouver?"

Reece blinked.

"Drive's only a few hours," Grayson said. "We can stop by your place, grab my stuff and anything you need."

"You want to run away to Canada with me?" Reece's heart didn't skip a beat. Definitely no beat-skipping, heart-fluttering here.

"It's a lot closer than Texas," Grayson said. "And the safe house is in BC. If we need to get you there, it'll be closer still."

Reece was panicking outside clubs and losing his temper in airsoft courses. Had to worry he might accidentally project those emotions onto other people. Had taken off his glove. In *public*.

It would be better for everyone if he went somewhere that kept other people safe.

He took another breath through his nose, then blew it out. "When this is done," he said quietly, "I'll go to the safe house."

If you come with me, he wanted to say.

But he didn't. Grayson was the Dead Man. He had responsibilities to the entire country, not just to a single empath. By rights Grayson should just send Reece up wherever the Stone Solutions facility was in Canada and leave him there, and every minute he hadn't was a minute Reece didn't deserve.

But it wasn't fair. It wasn't fair that Grayson had to be so alone, that he wasn't supposed to share pictures of himself, that he didn't have a home. He'd given up his entire life, given up his *heart*, so that he could do the dirty work that governments and corporations couldn't be trusted to do.

Come with me.

Let's really run away.

Maybe your emotions aren't completely gone.

Maybe I can find out.

Reece bit it all back. "Vancouver first, though. I'll go undercover into Stone Solutions with you—"

"Reece." Grayson put his hands on the tailgate, on either side of Reece. And Reece's breath caught in his throat as he was suddenly boxed in between Grayson's arms, their faces level with only inches between them.

They weren't touching. But they were so close, close enough he could feel Grayson's warmth, smell that faint cologne, hear his breathing.

"You paying attention to me?" Grayson said.

Reece swallowed thickly. "Undivided," he promised, his voice too high.

"If you think you're coming with me anywhere but the hotel, you're gonna have to convince me I can trust you," Grayson said, and he was *so damn close*. "You understand? We came here to investigate someone who literally tried to empath-nap you last night and we still don't know why. I can name a lot of moments you should've stayed put, but today had a big neon sign saying *sit your lemming ass down and talk to Evan*."

Grayson's arms were almost touching his on either side. Reece could have easily closed the inches between them and kissed him.

"I am trying to keep you out of trouble, but you are making sure I got my work cut out for me," Grayson said. "So tell me you're gonna at least *try* to make a good decision now and then, okay, Care Bear?"

"Okay," Reece agreed dazedly.

"Good."

Grayson suddenly seemed to realize how close he'd come. He stilled, and with so little space between them, Reece could sense the way his arms and shoulders had tensed and flexed.

Reece ran his tongue over his dry lips, and Grayson's gaze darted straight to them.

Want to make a bad decision with me?

Reece didn't say it. Instead, he cleared his throat. "Should we start our great Canadian adventure?"

Reece watched Grayson's chest rise and fall, his breath a vibration between them. "Yeah." Grayson straightened up. "Come on."

The picture of perfect manners as always, he held out his hand to help Reece down from the tailgate.

And Reece took it.

Their fingers interlaced as their palms pressed together. Grayson's hand was big and warm, calloused at the bases of his fingers, and at the touch of bare skin every part of Reece, from his suddenly alight nerves to his empathy, was automatically reaching, searching, desperately wanting—

Oh shit, he remembered, just as Grayson said, "Where's your glove—"

And then everything was black.

CHAPTER EIGHTEEN

...and then the Dead Man bent over Reece the empath, pinning him tighter to the hood of the Smart car. "I have to protect Seattle from dangerous empaths like you," he said, in his deep, broody, and accented voice. "But I never thought defending the world from empaths would mean getting this close to one."

Reece squirmed on the car hood, but the empath was never going to escape the Dead Man's hold: the bigger man was just too strong. And that shouldn't have been so sexy, but it was, because Reece wasn't going to escape his feelings either.

(continued in the next comment)

—EXCERPT FROM *HUNTING FOR LOVE*, AN EMPATH/EMPATH HUNTER FANFICTION

ONE MOMENT, Grayson was offering Reece a hand down from the truck.

The next, he was scrambling to catch him before he tumbled off the tailgate.

He got an arm around him just as Reece listed into him,

boneless and unmoving as a rag doll. Grayson tilted him enough to glimpse his face, already knowing what he'd see.

Closed eyes. Slack expression. Because Grayson's arms were suddenly full of unconscious empath.

He shifted Reece back to center, the full weight of his head resting against Grayson's chest.

"Bad Decisions Bear," he muttered.

He held Reece up for a moment, weighing his options. Reece himself didn't weigh much, light and easy in his arms, soft in the hoodie and warm with that empath extra body heat. He was right up under Grayson's sensitive nose, but for all of Grayson's ribbing about his unwashed hair, he smelled good.

But Grayson would ignore all of that. Reece was unconscious; Grayson would behave with impeccable professionalism and keep the touching to an absolute minimum.

Starting with dropping the hand he hadn't realized was still loosely intertwined in his own.

Grayson immediately let go, slipping his arms under Reece's to steady him as he considered their options.

Reece had been game for driving up to Vancouver. But they'd also been planning to stop by Reece's place first and that probably wasn't an option anymore; Grayson wasn't going to leave him alone and passed out in the truck, not when Waller knew where Reece lived, but folks would notice if Grayson carried Reece up and down from the studio with bags for two, and it'd be better if they didn't leave a trail.

But waiting wasn't ideal either, not when they only had a limited amount of time to search at Stone Solutions Canada before Vivian Marist returned to Vancouver. Reece would probably be unconscious still for some hours. Grayson couldn't even be sure how many hours; he'd never knocked the same empath out twice before.

He could find somewhere safe for Reece to stay and leave him behind; maybe take him back to Detective St. James' house.

But Reece was dangerous in ways no empath ever had been before. And he knew it and wanted to stay with Grayson, even when it meant a trip to an airsoft course or Vancouver. Because he trusted Grayson to keep everyone safe, even when he didn't trust himself.

Grayson bent forward, enough to get his left shoulder aligned with Reece's stomach and lever him up and over as he straightened. Looked like they were heading to Canada, and it was Reece's own fault that he couldn't ask for the truck keys or complain about Grayson's driving.

He worked his right hand into his pocket to pull out his phone. Pictures of the Dead Man were classified. They weren't supposed to exist. But Reece had pulled this stunt and ought to see for himself where it got him.

He held the phone up and out to the side to get the back of the truck and both of their faces in frame, so there was no question who it was tipped over Grayson's shoulder.

"Guess who gets to wake up to this in their texts?" he said, as he snapped a picture.

The missing glove was in the truck bed, lying innocently where Reece had been sitting. Why it wasn't on Reece's *hand* was a good question, but Grayson wasn't gonna find out until Reece was conscious again.

Balancing Reece on his shoulder, Grayson grabbed the glove and stuck it in his pocket before closing up the tailgate. He carried Reece over to the passenger door and got it open.

He leaned forward again, awkwardly hunching and twisting to keep Reece's head from bonking the door frame, then set the still out-cold Reece on the passenger seat.

"Very Bad Decisions Bear," he told him, as he reclined the seat enough that Reece wouldn't fall forward or slump off, then buckled him in—there'd be weeks of lectures if he forgot that part.

He straightened up and considered Reece, the lopsided look

of one glove. After a moment, he reached for Reece's left hand and pulled that glove off too. He stuck them both in the glove box, then slipped his coat off and put it over Reece. With Reece now secured and supine, Grayson shut the passenger door and went around to the driver's side.

It was a short trip onto I-5, but even at midafternoon, the rush hour traffic was already starting. Without Reece's chatter to fill the truck, Grayson put on music as he inched north, but even that wasn't enough to tune out his thoughts.

Reece had taken off a glove in public. EI and Stone Solutions both would have some pretty big opinions about that.

They'd have even bigger opinions about Grayson taking an empath up to Stone Solutions Canada behind their backs.

But someone had sent Keith Waller those real empath gloves, manufactured by Stone Solutions and mailed from Vancouver. Considering what had happened in November, and what had been done to Reece in March, Grayson wouldn't've trusted Vivian Marist and Stone Solutions with anything right then.

But maybe he ought to tell Director Traynor at the Empath Initiative.

Traffic moved forward just a little, and Grayson moved with it.

What was EI gonna do differently, though? If Traynor knew what was going on, he'd send the agency's biggest weapon—and that was the Dead Man. Nothing would change.

Except Traynor would want to hand Reece over to Polaris. Reece might have Polaris in his future, if the corruption ever set in all the way, but he didn't belong there now. Not when he was still the sweet pacifist who'd nearly been kidnapped last night, yet ran and hid in Grayson's truck just now so he wouldn't risk anyone else getting hurt. Who'd said *maybe it can be just the two of us* to the Dead Man.

So no. Grayson couldn't tell Traynor either.

He eyed the traffic. He could hit the shoulder and pass everyone, but there wasn't gonna be anything they could do tonight, and Reece needed time to wake up anyway. They'd get in to Vancouver when they got in, find somewhere to get a toothbrush and a change of clothes.

Find a hotel room for the two of them to share, sleeping only feet apart as they had last night. That would be fine. Wasn't like Grayson had spent the night hyperaware of Reece in that too-big Texas hoodie, soft and trusting and almost close enough to touch.

Grayson forced his fingers to loosen on the steering wheel.

It'd be just fine.

From Lake Sammamish, Jamey pulled into a rest stop to think, sitting in Liam's car and taking in the snow-dusted evergreens. She'd sent Grayson and Aisha both the pictures of Stensby's car, including the suitcase and the pen from the airsoft course. No one had heard from Stensby all day and all leads seemed to stop at the smashed cruiser.

Her phone beeped with a new text from Grayson.

Seems like the airsoft manager might have been the one chasing Reece in the Hellcat last night. We're following a lead to Vancouver.

We. Jamey raised her eyebrows.

Jamey: Reece is going with you to BC? Where the Mysterious Facility for Corrupted Empaths is located?

Grayson: Yes. But I'm not taking your brother there.

A straight answer. Interesting.

A cardinal was hopping through the branches, bright red against the white snow. He chirped, and his mate chirped back.

Another text came in from Grayson.

He's not my prisoner. He's free to go anytime. He said he wanted to come with me today.

And now Grayson was *explaining* himself to her, like he wasn't the Dead Man with an empath, but a good Southern boy promising to have his date back by curfew.

Also interesting.

But Grayson could go from gentleman to ruthless killer in a heartbeat. If he thought Reece was a threat, Grayson wouldn't hesitate to lock him up with the other corrupted empaths where he couldn't hurt anyone.

Which was, of course, exactly why Reece trusted him and wanted to be with Grayson.

She watched the birds hop from branch to branch. If she was being fair, she probably ought to acknowledge that whatever complicated person he was now, Grayson could have easily already taken Reece up to the BC facility, left him there, and never looked back. And he hadn't done it.

What he had done was taken a bullet for Reece.

She looked back at her phone.

Jamey: Take care of him.

Grayson was following the trail from the airsoft course, and it seemed like Stensby's path was twisted into that trail. It couldn't be coincidence that the airsoft manager had gone after Reece the same night Stensby had lured Jamey out of town and Grayson was supposed to be across the country investigating the murder of Marie Pelletier—who hadn't gone to Burlington at all, but was supposed to be in Prince Rupert, where Aisha was now headed.

Jamey ran a quick flight search from Seattle to Prince Rupert, scanning through the list with a frown. She should have realized her options would be slim; past Vancouver, the rugged network of mountainous islands that made up the British Columbia and southeast Alaskan coasts were vaster and wilder than most people realized, the towns smaller and more remote. Prince Rupert was a decent hub for the area, and you were still lucky to get one direct flight a day out of Vancouver.

After a moment, she texted Liam.

Jamey: If I told you we could charge everything to Grayson, can you figure out how to get me to Prince Rupert by morning?

Then she called up Aisha.

"Hey, you," the other woman answered, and Jamey could hear voices in the background. "How are—"

"I'm in," Jamey said. "Count me as part of your Vanguards."

"Yes," Aisha said, and Jamey could almost hear the fist pump. "We are officially the most badass super-secret spy team in the Pacific Northwest."

"How much competition could we possibly have?" Jamey frowned. "How would we even know if we had competition if we're all secret—you know what, never mind. Are you on your way to Prince Rupert?"

"On a layover in Toronto right now," Aisha said.

Jamey's phone beeped. She glanced at the text from Liam.

Consider it done.

She grinned. "Then I'll meet you there tomorrow," she said to Aisha, which earned another *yes.* "Flights are limited so it could be late afternoon, but Liam might be able to wrangle something earlier with his charter connections. Learn anything new?"

"Simone Pelletier, Marie's sister on Vancouver Island, is a paramedic, and she volunteers with Search and Rescue."

"Go Simone," Jamey muttered, then paused. "Wait."

"I had the same thought," Aisha said. "It's an interesting career for an empath's sibling."

"You think the sister could be like me? Like Grayson? Maybe we can get in touch with her and meet her—"

"I tried," Aisha said, more quietly. "I got Simone's number from Marie's roommate. Simone isn't answering calls or texts, not from me, not from Chantelle either. Maybe she's on her way to meet Marie in Prince Rupert, or maybe she's off the grid on a rescue."

"And maybe we might believe that," Jamey said, "if there weren't a million other coincidences piling up. Did you already tell Grayson that the missing empath has a sibling who could be like us?"

"I'm calling him after you," Aisha said. "I got a text that he and your brother are following a lead from the airsoft course."

"According to Grayson, the manager of the airsoft course was probably the one chasing Reece in a Hellcat last night," Jamey said. "And Stensby had a pen in his cruiser from the same airsoft course."

"Did they know each other?" Aisha mused out loud. "Could the airsoft manager have been the one who called you from Stensby's phone?"

"He would've had to call at the same time he was literally trying to kidnap Reece, and Reece didn't mention any Texas accent," Jamey said. "I think the caller was someone else. But who? And how did he know what Stensby had done to Reece's brake fluid? Stensby knows damn well he could be on the hook for attempted murder here. He's not a fool; he's not going to be out there telling people he sabotaged Reece's brakes."

"Your brother could have been hurt or worse, and we never would have known who was behind it," Aisha agreed. "So who was your caller, and how did they get that confession out of a cop like Stensby?"

Jamey snorted. "I don't suppose there's a corrupted empath around that sounds just like Grayson."

The line went very quiet.

"Not anymore," Aisha finally said. "But obviously Grayson's brother would have fit that bill, once upon a time."

Jamey sat back against the car seat. "Grayson only mentioned him to me once. Said his brother was dead but never said how."

"He's never told me either," Aisha said. "I know the Grayson brothers were prisoners somewhere out in Middle-of-Nowhere, West Texas. I know some twisted and unethical scientists were involved. And I know the whole facility was annihilated, and Evan was the only one who made it out of that West Texas bunker alive."

Jamey swallowed.

"I'm pretty sure Cedrick Stone knew most of the story," Aisha said, "and maybe there are others at Stone Solutions or the Empath Initiative who know more than me too. But I'm not sure there's anyone alive who actually knows exactly how Alex Grayson turned Evan into the Dead Man. Evan says it's better people don't know it's even possible."

"He's probably right," Jamey admitted. "Imagine what people like Stone would do if they knew how to make more Dead Men."

"Build an army to fight the empaths," Aisha muttered. "And all of us would lose."

Wasn't *that* the truth.

Stensby was in the backseat of the white Challenger Hellcat, eyes closed contentedly. It'd felt so good to smash his cruiser up for Alex. Lake Sammamish had been his idea, to distract everyone. Then Stensby had called Keith, who was in a rage from losing Reece. It'd been easy to lure Keith to some sketchy strip mall in Kent so he could meet Alex, and now all three of them were a *team*.

They were idling outside an older gas station in Bellevue with Alex behind the Hellcat's wheel. He'd given Keith instructions and the other man had gone inside. Stensby was happy to wait in the backseat. He was happy to do anything, as long as it was what Alex wanted. Keith understood and felt the same way now.

"Gretel sent a text. Says her dad keeps giving AMI membership lists to anyone who asks." Alex was lazily scrolling through his phone. "For someone who keeps yelling about privacy, Beau Macy sure doesn't seem to care about anyone else's."

How had Stensby ever disliked Alex's accent? He loved his voice. Maybe Alex would keep talking forever. "I'm probably on that list."

Alex glanced up, meeting Stensby's eyes in the rearview mirror. "I'm sure you are. Keith too. Makes you wonder what they're using these lists for, doesn't it?"

"You should ask for them," Stensby said dreamily. "You should introduce yourself to all of AMI."

"You've had worse ideas." Alex glanced at the gas station's doors. "Here we go."

An alarm split the air. The doors burst open and Keith came running out, thick wads of green bills in his hands. Behind the gas station's glass windows, Stensby could see a lot of red.

"You're a terrible kidnapper but luckily an excellent robber," Alex said, over Stensby's cheering, already throwing the Hellcat into Reverse as Keith leapt into the passenger seat and slammed the Hellcat door. "And I hope you're both ready for our next stop."

CHAPTER NINETEEN

Name: Vivian Marist (filed on behalf of)

Title: President

Location: Vancouver

Description: Business dinner

Other attendees: Holt Traynor (Empath Initiative); Victor Nichols (Polaris Empathic Research Facility)

—**STONE SOLUTIONS CANADA EXPENSE REPORT**

REECE BECAME AWARE he was in a moving vehicle before he even opened his eyes. "Where are we?"

Grayson's voice reached his ears. "Almost to the border."

Reece opened his eyes. He was in the passenger seat of Grayson's truck—seat belt fastened, thank goodness, it wouldn't do to risk him flying around the truck and distracting Grayson from the road—reclined and covered with Grayson's big coat. "Did you say *border*?"

"We decided we were running away to Canada. Or maybe

you don't remember that part, because thirty seconds later you'd knocked yourself out colder than this weather."

Reece winced as events came rushing back to him. "Oops?"

"*Oops*, he says." Grayson gestured to the glove box. "Your gloves are in there. You don't have to wear them around me, but you do need to remember you took them off before you go touching me."

Why had he taken them off in the truck bed? Reece reached for the memory, but it slipped away.

The memory of Grayson's skin, though. That was seared into his brain. "You have really nice hands. Like, they're all big, and warm," Reece said, and then his brain caught up with his mouth. He cringed. "Jesus, sorry, my brain's still fuzzy, ignore me slobbering over your hands. *Please.*"

Grayson's eyes darted to him, then back to the road. "I didn't hear any slobbering. I heard you trying to flatter me into forgetting you're not supposed to take your gloves off in public. And I didn't forget, but you were also supposed to stay put, so I guess I'm just gonna add more lines to that long list of things you're already in trouble for."

Reece's shoulders relaxed. Grayson wasn't going to make fun of him for being so desperately untouched. "So what's an empath got to do to get out of trouble?" He made a face. "That sounds like the start of a bad porn."

"Or a real good one," Grayson muttered.

Reece snorted. "Don't tell me you've got a thing for bad empaths. That would make your job very difficult, wouldn't it?"

"Sure would," Grayson said, eyes fixed forward.

Reece sat up, bringing the seat upright with him as he held the cozy coat blanket in place. Night had fallen while he'd been unconscious, the highway a dark sea with red taillights. At some point the rain had become big fluffy white flakes of snow that caught in the truck's headlights and landed on the windshield. The seat warmer was on and Grayson had cranked the heat up, making the truck cab feel like a glimpse of summer in the heart of winter. Reece could almost imagine driving through a warm night in Texas, windows down and sunroof open. Parking somewhere they could lie in the bed and stargaze together.

He shook his head quickly, to clear it of those kinds of thoughts. Lusting after Grayson he might be able to deal with; feelings were absolutely off-limits. "Any chance you've got something to drink stashed around here?"

Grayson gestured at the cup holders, where a pair of paper cups with lids and straws were sitting. "I hit up a drive-through in Bellingham. Told the cashier you were a deep sleeper."

"Now that's a bald-faced lie." Reece picked up the cup and took a sip. Vanilla cream soda. He smiled around the straw.

Grayson twisted, one hand on the steering wheel and eyes on the road while he started to reach into the backseat. "Got you some kind of veggie—"

"Hands on the steering wheel," Reece snapped. "I'll get it."

"Sugar, you can't reach the backseat. Not without unbuckling your seat belt, and I know you're not gonna do that."

"Excuse you, *honey*," said Reece, and he'd been aiming for sarcasm to match Grayson's patronizing, but damn. That had rolled off the tongue a little too easy. "I can too reach." *Lie.* He pinched his lips together, ignoring the rumbling in his stomach. "I'll just wait until the border."

"Empaths." Grayson put on his blinker.

"What are you doing?"

"Feeding you." He pulled onto the shoulder and popped on his hazard lights. He stretched one long arm into the seat behind Reece and came back with a paper bag in hand. "Here. And take it *carefully*, unless you want to spend a few more hours unconscious."

Reece chanced a glance at him. In the dark of the truck's cab, he couldn't see the missing emotions. Just his partially lit face, the high cheekbones, the line of his jaw. The lips Reece could lose himself in until nothing existed but Grayson.

"Thanks," he muttered, painstakingly avoiding Grayson's hand as he took the bag. He dug in and found a veggie burger, Tater Tots, and three fruit-filled pastries. Reece might have been the endlessly awkward mayor of Weirdo Town, but Grayson understood him, neuroses, quirks, and all.

He popped four Tater Tots in his mouth as he pulled out his phone. "Did you already tell Jamey—aw, fuck." His cheeks flushed. "You took a *picture*?"

"Thought you'd want to see it."

"I thought pictures of you were classified!"

"They are."

Reece narrowed his eyes. "So now there's a top secret picture of me ass-up over your shoulder?"

"There sure is," Grayson said. "You would've been face down on the pavement if I hadn't caught you. And remember you only got yourself in that position because you went and knocked yourself out."

Ugh, that was an annoyingly fair point. "And you needed to carry me like this *why*?"

"So my hands were free to open the truck," Grayson said, like that had been a stupid question with an obvious answer, which in fairness it probably was.

Reece's gaze stayed on the picture, how unbothered Grayson looked by his weight, the way his arm wrapped around his thighs to hold him in place.

It was infuriatingly *hot*. Reece could extrapolate a whole damn night from this one image, bickering but laughing as Grayson carried him across the studio to toss him down on the bed, Reece's mouth on his until they were both kiss-drunk, his hands on Grayson until he'd mapped every inch. They could have so much fun together.

If they weren't who they were.

Reece took a breath through his nose. "Tell me you let Jamey know where we are but without the picture."

"Being the Dead Man doesn't mean I have a death wish," said Grayson. "I know better than to send your sister photographic proof of me manhandling you."

How about you come over here and manhandle me some more— Reece shook his head to try and clear away that wildly unhelpful thought. "What's our plan for the border?" he asked, like a subject change could somehow make him stop wanting Grayson. "I don't have a passport."

Grayson cleared his throat. "You don't actually have anything but your phone, your wallet, and the clothes you got on."

Reece groaned. "I didn't even think of that. What was your big plan there?"

"We're going to Canada, not the moon. Last I checked, they have stores." Grayson gestured at the glove box. "And the border plan is in the first aid kit."

Reece furrowed his brow but got the kit out of the glove box from under his gloves. Opening the hinge lid revealed a shallow tray of supplies, and under the tray was—

"How many passports do you have?"

"Enough to do my job." The road was more brightly lit now, a line of cars up ahead waiting at the single open booth at the border. "I change the truck license plates every few months. It'll come back as a rental if they run them."

Reece picked up the top passport, the darkest green in the dim light with *México Pasaporte* on the front. "Won't these all have your picture? Not only can I not remotely pass for you, don't you think the border agent is going to notice if the pictures match?"

"The pictures aren't identical, but if they do notice, then I have actual government credentials I can pull out. But I want to keep us under the radar, and EI doesn't know about these identities."

Keep *us* under the radar. Meaning EI still didn't know the two of them had run off to Canada. Reece side-eyed Grayson. "Does EI have any idea you keep all these secrets from them?"

"Wouldn't be secrets if they knew."

"But you're *the Dead Man*. Aren't you, like, an EI agent, in a way? Doesn't Stone Solutions have you on their payroll?" Reece gestured at the border. "You can't tell me any of them would be happy with you, if they knew about this."

"I'm not exactly in the business of making folks happy."

"But what is EI going to do when it learns you're cutting them out of the loop?" Reece pressed. "What is *Stone Solutions* going to do if they find out? Are you going to get in trouble?"

"You know I can look out for myself." And before Reece could argue, Grayson nodded at the stack. "We're almost at the border. Give me the US one for León Collins—I have a beard in that picture. You take the Canadian one."

Reece pulled out the blue passports from the stack and opened one up to find a version of Grayson with dark brown hair and glasses. "Thirty-one-year-old Teodoro James, born in Victoria," he said, reading from the page. "Nice disguise, but I will never pass for half this hot and you know it."

"I don't know anything of the sort." And before Reece could process that compliment, Grayson was adding, "Pull the coat to your chin and face the window. Pretend to be asleep."

Reece groaned, but it wasn't like he had a better option. "If we're going to be around another person, let me put my gloves back on—"

"You can't," Grayson said.

"But I have to—"

"We're here because you almost got empath-napped," Grayson said, cutting him off. "And there is a Canadian empath out there who's still missing. So far the only thing we've learned that you and Ms. Pelletier from Montreal have in common, besides being empaths, is that y'all both have sisters who picked careers saving people. That's not much to go on, and until we know what's going on, we can't risk anyone learning you're an empath. All right?"

Reece sighed, but nodded. He passed the two passports over, then stuck the others back in the glove box. He reclined the seat a bit, pulled the coat up high, and rolled on his side, just as Grayson pulled past the Peace Arch and into the line.

This late on a freezing Monday night, the border line was short, and before too long, Reece could sense the light on the outside of his eyelids. He peeked through his lashes over the dashboard. They were next in line, and he could just make out the border agent in the booth, the lines in her forehead, the tenseness in her shoulders. In a near-silent whisper that only Jamey or Grayson would still be able to hear, he said, "Can you ham up the Southern thing? Lay it on really, really thick?"

"Maybe. Why?"

"The border agent looks like an introvert who's had a long day and is very tired of people," Reece said, in the same whisper. "Last thing she's going to want to deal with in her line is a chatty Southerner who won't shut up. Annoy her enough and she might be itching to push us through and be rid of you."

The car in front pulled away, and Reece closed his eyes fully. He felt the truck move forward, then heard the window lower.

The woman's voice came. "Passports?"

"Yes, ma'am, here you go." Grayson's voice had suddenly become less deep and a lot more friendly than Reece had ever heard it. "How's your night going? They got heat in that little booth there to keep y'all warm in all this snow? We don't get much snow in Texas, but we do get ice storms, and then we don't have the salt or plows ready to go like y'all do, though I reckon one of those storms would shut things down even up here. Hail too, and graupel—bet y'all haven't even heard of that."

The agent grunted, and Reece could almost taste her grumpiness. "Business travel or personal?"

"Personal as it gets. The long-distance thing gets real old, real fast." Grayson had dialed the accent up to thick as molasses. "My boyfriend—that's Theo there, asleep in the seat, you've got his passport—he came down to see me, like a—we call them Winter Texans, but do y'all call them snowbirds here, like Yankees do, or maybe y'all call them snow geese in Canada, because of the Canadian geese?—anyway, we met online and then Theo came to Austin for American Thanksgiving—you can see I used to have a beard in the picture, had to shave it for the relatives, I'm thinking of growing it back but that's a whole other conversation—and now it's my turn to visit Vancouver Island; I didn't even know there were islands in Canada before I met him. Do I need to wake him? Baby, we're at the border. Can you tell the agent why you were down in Texas with me and how we're going to your place in Oak Bay? Oh, and tell her that whole long story about how I didn't know you could drive cars onto the ferry 'cause I thought you rode dog sleds in Canada."

"It's fine, I can see him," the agent said hastily. "Welcome to Canada."

Reece bit his lip hard, trying not to smile and ruin Grayson's unexpectedly good performance.

A few minutes later, the truck was moving again. Reece opened his eyes. "You took my advice," he said happily, as he brought the seat back up.

"When it comes to people, I put my money on the empath's opinion every time." Grayson's voice had dropped back into its usual gravelly register, and his accent seemed downright subtle now, in comparison.

Reece settled into the seat as they drove down the dark highway, the more sparsely populated marshy area just before the explosion of Vancouver. "The boyfriend thing was an inspired touch."

That sounded casual, didn't it? And not like he was still a bit giddy over it?

"To be honest, I wasn't sure I was gonna pull it off," Grayson said. "Been a while since I've been anyone's boyfriend."

You looking to be one again, by any chance? Ready for someone to take you off the market? Reece cleared his throat. "I thought you were really convincing," he said. "I mean, you're calling Theo baby, waking him up all sweet—I bet León's got him smitten."

"I bet León wouldn't know Celsius from centimeters, but he drove all the way up here from Texas in December," Grayson said. "Theo's definitely his baby."

"See?" Reece said. "Very convincing boyfriend. Bad driving boyfriend, on both sides of the border, but convincing."

Grayson glanced at him. "What *bad driving*?"

"That speed limit sign you just blew past was for eighty *kilometers* an hour. Not miles."

There was a pause.

"We're in Canada for five whole minutes and you already forgot which part of your speedometer to watch?" Reece said. "Or does Evan not know Celsius from centimeters either?"

"Hush," Grayson muttered, as the truck slowed.

CHAPTER TWENTY

Introducing a streaming service that's pacifist-approved! We've got you covered for peaceful playlists with Paciflix, the first streaming service to offer tailored recommendations for adults, kids, AND empaths. Movie nights are for everyone now!

—ONLINE ADVERTISEMENT

THE DARK HIGHWAY soon turned to city outskirts, and then the busy traffic and streets of the southern suburbs. Grayson found his way to a store that sold outdoorsy clothes and gear, a brand he'd seen other empaths wear, and pulled into the parking lot. "We've got eighteen minutes until they close."

Reece hesitated. "I should put on my—"

"Undercover," Grayson reminded him. "There are not enough empaths in this area for you to go running around broadcasting it to the world."

"But—"

"We're down to seventeen minutes and we both gotta grab what we need. Come on."

Reece frowned. "But I know this store. This is really quality stuff. As in, too nice for my budget."

"This store offsets its carbon footprint, only sells fair trade products, and I'm gonna expense it all to Stone Solutions. Either you pick out clothes or I will, and if it's me, everything is gonna have bears on it."

"Well played," Reece muttered, opening the truck door.

Inside, Reece immediately disappeared into the hoodie racks. Grayson browsed the camping gear, picking up a pair of travel grooming kits—whether Reece would ever use the comb or brush remained to be seen—as well as a pair of backpacks. They had an expansive selection of winter hats, and he got a new one for himself that would actually fit his head, along with a scarf and a hat for Reece that he hid at the bottom of the stack and hopefully wouldn't get noticed until it was too late and had already been bought.

Fourteen minutes later they met in the middle of the store. Reece's face was barely visible behind his stack of fleece and flannel, his cheeks more flushed than usual and his hair sticking up, like he'd tried on something with a hood. He was smiling almost shyly. "The fabrics in here feel really nice."

Because he always wore his gloves, so he never got to touch things.

Just like he never got to touch people.

Grayson stood still for a moment, gaze on that shy smile, the messy hair. Then he blinked. "You get everything you need?"

Reece nodded, then jerked his head toward the register. "Come on. That cashier has probably been on her feet for eight hours and is desperately hoping we're going to check out in the next two minutes so she can close up on time."

The cashier was probably around thirty, a short woman with a soft, curvy build and glasses. She didn't look annoyed with them, though; in fact, she was smiling as Reece put his stuff on her register counter. "We're getting out of your hair, I promise," he said to her.

"You're fine," she said, still smiling as she began to ring

clothes up. Her gaze kept going to Reece, like a magnet. "How is your night going?"

Reece began chatting with her. Grayson pulled the backpacks over, ostensibly packing their new stuff but subtly watching the two of them.

Reece's shoulders were relaxed, his smile bright, gesturing unselfconsciously as he talked. He looked happy.

And so did the cashier, as she went on enthusiastically about the fabrics in one of the hoodies, how it was made with 100 percent recycled materials, her motions animated and her eyes still going to Reece as much as possible.

Could Reece be projecting again? It obviously wouldn't have any effect whatsoever on Grayson and he wasn't able to tell. Before Reece, Grayson's experience with empath projection was with corrupted empaths purposefully influencing others with things like rage or fear.

He hadn't extrapolated the possibilities of an uncorrupted empath accidentally projecting an emotion like contentment or happiness.

Before he could decide what, if anything, he should do, Reece had turned to him, holding up a tightly packed, oval-shaped bag, hunter green with a drawstring. "This is for you."

Grayson blinked. "Is that a…sleeping bag?"

"An extra-long, Big and Tall sleeping bag." Reece pointed at him. "I didn't see so much as a blanket in your truck. I bet you've spent a lot of cold nights alone on the side of the road, and maybe I can't get you a house but I can get you this. So no arguing."

"Sir, yes, sir," Grayson muttered, but he didn't argue.

The cashier took Grayson's credit card as he took both backpacks, and a couple minutes later, they were back at the truck. Grayson got the passenger door first, so Reece could climb in, then moved to open the back door and set the sleeping bag and both of their new bags on the backseat.

His gaze lingered on their bags together. A memory rose up: an older truck, loading it up with a tent and gear, the man in the University of Texas T-shirt tossing in a travel hammock.

"They had *kayaks* in there." In the passenger seat, Reece still sounded enthusiastic, his normal Grumpy Bear attitude gone for the moment. "Have you ever gone? Jamey and I go sometimes in the summer; my arms are pretty useless, but it's so great to get out on the water."

Grayson blinked and the memory vanished.

But Reece was still there, looking over his shoulder at Grayson and smiling brightly. "With the right straps and the tailgate down, you might be able to fit a kayak in the bed of this truck, if you were camping."

"I used to love camping."

The sentence slipped out. Grayson blinked at himself. His body apparently continued not to need his brain's permission to notice that Reece reminded him of so many things he'd once liked.

"Oh yeah?" Reece tilted his head. "Did you used to go with, like, a girlfriend or something?" His eyes were lit only by the truck's interior glow, not quite enough for Grayson to make out whatever he might be thinking or feeling.

"Just friend-friends, in college," Grayson said. "I did have a crush for a time on one of them, but I was pretty sure he was straight, and I would never have crossed that line."

"You seem to have a lot of lines you don't let yourself cross," Reece said.

Grayson shut the backseat door instead of answering.

Not long later, they were pulling into the parking lot of a small hotel, the kind that had advertised to business travelers and extended stays. Grayson had booked it from the road while Reece had been solidly unconscious, and he never needed to know it had happened behind the wheel.

Reece glanced at it. "You didn't pick some downtown luxury place?"

"One, I told you we're undercover. Two, when I'm undercover, no one valets my truck. Three, we're *undercover*, and I know I already said that but seems like you're missing the point—"

"All right, all right." Reece opened the glove box and pulled out his gloves. "I learned my lesson about leaving these in a glove box, though. I'm bringing them in."

He unbuckled his seat belt, twisting halfway in the passenger seat to reach into the backseat. "Just sticking them in—oh, you've got to be kidding. How'd you sneak this past me?"

"Did you find your hat?"

"This has *bear ears*."

"Practically had your name on it. And now you'll be all set for your next felony and won't have to steal mine."

Reece twisted back around, turning the hat over in his hands, a surprisingly big smile on his face. "You think you're so funny, but you know what?" he said, as he leaned over, closer to Grayson. "I'm into it. I'm going to wear the shit out of this hat."

Grayson side-eyed him. "You didn't flinch."

"Because I wasn't lying." Reece pulled the hat on. "You like it?"

Well, damn. It somehow suited Reece, managing to be charming instead of ridiculous, and Grayson really hadn't needed more reasons to be slapped in the face with how cute Reece was right before they shared a hotel room.

Grayson could hear the unhappy crying of an overtired toddler from the parking lot. And sure enough, as the front doors slid open, there was a young man in the lobby, a fussy toddler in pajamas in his arms as he walked back and forth in front of the decorative gas fireplace.

As Reece walked in, the toddler abruptly stopped crying. She turned toward Reece with big eyes.

"Aww, it's a baby!" Reece waved at her. "Hi, sweetie!"

The toddler blinked and then broke into a smile. She rested her head on her dad's shoulder and waved back at Reece.

The young dad mouthed *thank you* at Grayson. He was also smiling, his tired strain from moments before vanished.

Oh, Reece was definitely projecting.

Grayson had no protocol for this. Did he need to interfere? Get Reece away from other people immediately?

But projection wasn't anything like thralling. The effect was transient, and maybe projecting rage or fear was dangerous, especially in a corrupted empath's hands, but Reece wasn't trying to manipulate anyone. Projecting a good feeling wouldn't be any more harmful than playing a song someone really liked and momentarily cheering them up.

And if Reece knew he was projecting, he'd be crushed. All his happiness would be gone. Maybe he'd stop projecting, or maybe he'd start projecting sadness instead, but none of it was worth stealing away his happiness. Reece wasn't hurting anyone; Grayson would leave it alone.

Funny, though. Of all the situations that could make an empath happy enough to influence other people, Grayson would never, ever have thought *running away undercover to Canada with the Dead Man* could make that list.

They checked in at the front desk under León Collins' credentials. Like the cashier at the store, the front desk clerk also seemed bright and cheerful, as if having Reece in the lobby was the best thing that could have happened to his night.

"Third floor or higher, please," Grayson requested.

"And a king bed," Reece added.

Grayson side-eyed him. "I got us two doubles."

Reece waved it off. "You won't fit on a double. Your long legs will hang off. I'll sleep on the sofa bed."

Grayson was being bossed around by an empath half his size wearing a backpack and a bear hat. "I know you like your bad decisions—"

"You're the one trying to make a bad decision," Reece said, and he didn't flinch, so he honestly believed that outrageous sentence. "You just flew in from East Coast time and then drove for hours. You got bad sleep on my couch last night, you've been sleeping badly for who knows how long, sometimes in your *truck*. Tonight you're sleeping on a decent bed that fits your ridiculously huge body."

"I don't think you're going to win this argument, Mr. Collins," the front desk clerk said, as he slid the keys across the counter. He added, to Reece, "I like your hat."

"He likes my hat," Reece said to Grayson.

Lord help him. Grayson *was* making bad decisions.

Their studio room on the third floor looked like countless others Grayson had slept in, with a kitchenette, a small living area, and a king bed just past the couch. Though the empath in bear ears curiously examining the instant apple cider packets by the coffee maker was, admittedly, new.

"We're up high so no one can come in the window, and now I need to be between you and the door," Grayson said, as he locked the door behind him.

"You're literally engaging all the locks right now and we can put a chair under the handle. Stop trying to find excuses and accept you have to be comfortable tonight." Reece had already set his backpack on the couch and was heading for the thermostat. "Let me warm it up in here."

Defeated by bear ears, Grayson crossed the room and set his own backpack on the bed. "I know you're doing that for me."

"Obviously," Reece said. "I run hot as a furnace."

Grayson knew that already. Having Reece in your bed was probably as cozy as having a heated blanket. A *cuddly* heated blanket that would be wrapped around you all night, seeking out all the touch he could get.

Except, of course, for the part where he'd pass out again the instant he touched Grayson. There would never be a warm and cuddly empath in Grayson's bed, and he needed to remember that.

Grayson unzipped his backpack as Reece wandered into the bathroom. "Looks like all the soaps and shampoos are citrus-scented. Will that bother you? Jamey's usually okay with that, but I don't know about your nose."

"These ones are fine." Grayson had stayed at most hotel chains enough times to know which brands and scents of toiletries they carried. But this part was again different, having someone around so familiar with Grayson's enhanced senses that they'd ask if he was okay with scents. "Are you actually going to take a shower? Do we need to put this on the news? *Eyes on Empaths*, maybe?"

Reece met his eyes in the bathroom mirror and flipped him off.

As the shower ran, Grayson changed into sweats and stripped down to his T-shirt. There was a for-purchase basket of overpriced snacks and sodas on the kitchen counter and he took all of it back to the king bed. He set the basket in the middle of the comforter, then sat on the side of the bed farthest from the couch and picked up the remote.

What am I doing? some part of his brain asked, as he flipped through channels. *Am I expecting Reece is going to—what, exactly? Eat hotel snacks and watch television? On this bed? With me?*

One of the stations was running a special from Canada's best-known empath stand-up comic, and at least some of the snacks were vegan. And the bed was a king, wide as the truck cab, plenty of space for them to sit side by side without touching.

None of that is going to happen, the voice in his head said. *You're drawing from memory, that's all it is, because Reece reminds you of things you liked in days long gone. But you don't watch television. You're not hungry. And most of all, you feel nothing. Put the food on the coffee table for Reece and go to sleep.*

The bathroom door opened. "Hey, Evan?"

Grayson glanced over.

Oh. Shit.

Reece had one of the white hotel towels wrapped around his waist and not a stitch of other clothing on. His arms and chest were covered in beads of water and his damp hair was the darkest of browns, almost black. He seemed distracted by his thoughts, not even looking at Grayson, just chewing on his lip. "I'm not doing anything weird right now, am I?"

Empaths. So caught up in feelings they went oblivious to anything else.

"*Weird* can mean a lot of things, sugar," Grayson said, and admittedly it might have come out a little bit tense, because maybe Reece hadn't clocked that he was almost naked in a bedroom, but every muscle in Grayson's body sure had.

Reece huffed. "I mean, I'm not like, projecting again or anything, am I? I feel a little buzzy, but I've been such a mess for months that maybe I just forgot what good feels like."

It wasn't fair, that Reece had been put into this state where he couldn't remember when he'd last felt good. It also didn't seem fair that Reece couldn't remember he had no *clothes* on when they had this giant bed right here, but Grayson would just keep on noticing for both of them, apparently.

"At some point, we probably ought to have another conversation about your lack of survival instinct, if you're feeling good around the Dead Man," said Grayson, trying to sound very casual and not at all like his body was clamoring to sweep Reece up into his arms and toss him down on the bed. "But even if you were projecting, it couldn't affect me, so what would it matter?"

"Your consent and boundaries matter too—"

"Reece," Grayson interrupted. "You can relax. Don't worry about it. It's just us."

"I guess it is." Reece's same small, almost shy smile from the store was back, like he had any right to be even cuter. Then he suddenly frowned. "You okay?"

Oh, great. Grayson cleared his throat. "Obviously."

"You seem tense," Reece said. "It's hard to tell because usually people's emotions will show what their body is going through loud and clear, and I can pick those up in a million different ways. But with you I can't just fall back on habit, I have to pay close attention to all the physical signs. And I think your shoulders look tighter, and your voice is a little higher, and you might have this little tick in your jaw—"

"Look, I found candy," Grayson said, holding up the snack basket.

Reece lit up. "Be right there."

He disappeared back into the bathroom, then emerged again a minute later, mercifully dressed this time in some of the new clothes they'd bought, flannel pants and a T-shirt.

His gaze went to the television, where the show with the empath comic was returning from a commercial break. "Oh, I love her." He was already scrambling across the room. "I can't believe you found her special. Is that licorice?"

They settled on the bed together, Grayson on one side under the covers, Reece lounging on top of the comforter on the other side. The snacks were in the two feet of no-man's-land between them.

Reece was grinning at the comic as he worked his way through the candy. "I saw her live when she came to Seattle. A few other empaths came into town for it; we went to her show and then we had an epic game night. Such a great time."

Because when empaths were left alone, they just lived their lives like anyone else. It was only when people like Cedrick Stone started fucking around that Grayson had to step in and stop sadistic killers.

Buzzy, Reece had said. So was he still projecting? Well, Grayson had meant what he said about it being a nonissue at the moment. Obviously Grayson wasn't going to feel it, no matter how much happy contentment might be pouring off of Reece like the vibrations of a purring cat.

Grayson slipped another inch down under the covers, resting his head on the pillows. Reece was a little in front of him, legs up on the bed, leaning back on his arms. He turned to look back over his shoulder, his smile like sunshine. "You would not believe how long it's been since I've just relaxed and watched television. Thanks for finding something I can handle."

He turned back to the show. Grayson slid down farther, until he was horizontal and the covers were up to his shoulders. It was a decent mattress, a soft pillow top and big enough only his toes were off the end. A lot of scents, but good ones, clean sheets and citrusy shampoo and candy, and Reece had a soft, bright laugh to go with the scents. For once, Grayson was around an empath who was content and happy, and even if Grayson couldn't feel any of it—not Reece's projections, nothing of his own—his body could still sense things like safety and peace.

He let himself close his eyes.

Stensby leaned forward as Alex drove the Hellcat past the front doors of Stone Solutions and pulled into the closest parking spot, one with a big sign that read *Reserved.*

"Keith and I were here a couple days ago," Stensby said, as Alex cut the engine. "There's a decent amount of security at night: cameras, patrolling guards, that kind of thing."

"We can take care of that," Alex said, looking over his shoulder at Stensby. "And thanks to our friend Mr. Macy, I know the security around Mr. Stone's office hasn't had the grand finish they've promised the public. Keeping a CEO in a secret hospital is all well and good until you need his fingerprints and retina scan to finish your security upgrade."

He looked back to Keith. "If you two could go in and handle the cameras first, I'd be mighty appreciative. Let Officer Stensby take the lead; in that police uniform, he's as good as a Trojan horse. Night shift security will let him right in."

Stensby led the way to the building. He'd read a detailed report on Reece Davies' arrest at Stone Solutions the night he'd broken in. According to the report, Stone Solutions' security control room was on the first floor, full of monitors and all the hardware that ran the system. He'd noticed the room for himself just the other night at the AMI meeting.

They only had to wait at the main sliding glass doors for about three minutes before a security guard came hurrying over. A moment later, the doors were sliding open for them.

"Hello, officer," the security guard started. "Can I help—"

Stensby headbutted him full in the face.

The man staggered backward. He stumbled into the lobby and crashed into one of the chairs, falling to the ground in a heap. Keith was on him as he fell, grabbing the nightstick from his belt.

"What—" the guard started, garbled through his mouthful of blood.

Stensby grabbed his own nightstick, heavy and deadly. This would handle both the guard and the security equipment nicely.

A few minutes later, Stensby returned to the car. Alex was leaning against it, phone in hand. "Welcome back," he said, pocketing the phone as Stensby hurried toward him. "Are we cleared for entry?"

"Yes, sir." Stensby held up a security card. "We took care of the first guard and I lifted this. Keith's gone hunting for the others."

"Excellent," Alex said, taking the card and pocketing it.

Stensby would do anything for him.

They crossed through the lobby, Alex calmly stepping over the crumpled body of the guard on the way to the elevators.

They rode up to twenty-two. Stensby had only been on the first floor until now, and his eyes widened as the elevator door opened into a suite that took up the entire level. The front area was set up for entertaining, with a living room set, a fully stocked bar, and an endless view of Bellevue city lights. There were doors around the walls that might have led to a private office and bathroom, maybe private elevator to the roof's helipad, and even a panic room, if Stensby had to guess.

Alex tried one of the doors. "Locked."

How *dare* a locked door get in Alex's way. "I got it." Stensby drew back his foot in sudden rage and kicked the door. It flew open so hard it bounced off the wall, hanging precariously on its hinges.

"Appreciated, I'm sure," Alex said.

Stensby followed Alex into the office and waited as he surveyed the giant desk, the endless bookshelves, the art on the walls.

Alex tilted his head, staring at the giant flatscreen that took up a sizable chunk of the right wall. It displayed a map of North America, with blue circles dotted all over the United States.

"And what do we have here?" Alex muttered, stepping forward. "Oh, isn't this quaint. They track the empaths."

Stensby stared at the map. Some of the dots on the map were moving very slowly, like a flight map on an airplane. Alex stepped forward, reaching out so his finger hovered over the Seattle area.

"Just one of us in Seattle now, although somehow I very much doubt that Reece Davies is actually chilling in the shoulder of I-5."

"We used to have a second empath," Stensby said. "Cora Falcon was her name. She was a therapist at the veterans' hospital, but she disappeared the same night Senator Hathaway was killed."

Alex's gaze flicked up, from Seattle to Alaska and then back down as he traced a finger up along the British Columbia coastline, where there were four red dots. "And what do we have here?"

He made a flicking motion, spreading his fingers, and the touch screen zoomed in on a green space quite far north of Vancouver. "What are four empaths doing on an island off the North Coast?"

"I know that island, I've gone fishing up there," Stensby said. "Used to be a Gold Rush hub, but now there's nothing there, just a ghost town and some empty mines. I can't think of a reason empaths would be there."

Alex zoomed in even closer and then touched one of the circles. A profile popped up: a pretty woman of maybe thirty, dressed in pink scrubs, with long brown hair and big brown eyes. *Cora Falcon*, the tag read.

"Well, that's a weird coincidence," said Stensby.

Alex was looking at Cora's image. Was it Stensby's imagination, or did he feel prickles of anger against his skin? "Go get Keith."

"Of course," Stensby said excitedly. There was nothing he wanted more than to do things for Alex.

Alex glanced over his shoulder. "And then we're going to need a ride."

CHAPTER TWENTY-ONE

Looking for a multiplayer experience for your gaming system—but want something combat-free? Look no further than our newest release, Cooperation Co-op, *created in partnership with the makers of* Dragons Without Dungeons! *Explore our open world and help villagers solve conflicts via peaceful methods like using your words.*

—ONLINE ADVERTISEMENT

THE GRAY IS endless as always, flat and unchanging in every direction. Too thick to walk through, too wide to walk around, too high to climb—

Too high to climb?

Grayson's eyes opened. He took stock of his surroundings: hotel room; king bed; candy wrappers in the trash; soda cans separated for recycling.

Reece fast asleep on the couch, breaths soft and peaceful.

Grayson silently got out of bed without so much as looking at the clock, going straight to the shower. He got it running extra hot and stood in the spray, staring at the white shower curtain, the white tile, the white porcelain bathtub.

He'd dreamed of gray. He always dreamed of gray; he was never going to dream of anything else again.

But for the first time, there had been something different in the dream. Instead of the color alone, it had been as if he'd stepped backward, gotten a little distance, and seen that the gray in front of his face had the form of an endless wall.

Had the gray always been a wall, and he'd just been too close to realize what he was dreaming of?

He washed his hair with the citrusy shampoo, letting his thoughts organize themselves like books on a shelf.

Maybe it *was* a wall. Maybe the scientists were right, and it was like when a limb was removed and the wound was cauterized. The emotional part of Grayson had been destroyed, irreparably severed, and so maybe his brain was visualizing a wall to stem the bleeding and cope with the loss.

It didn't actually matter if he was dreaming of incorporeal gray or a gray wall. At the end of the day, it meant the same thing: Evan Grayson was gone.

And that was a good thing. The world couldn't afford to lose the Dead Man. No one needed Evan Grayson and no one wanted him back.

He stepped out from the steamy bathroom with a towel around his waist and crossed over to his backpack for clothes. As he dug in the bag, his gaze stole to the couch. Reece must have switched over from the king bed at some point, but Grayson didn't remember it happening, and it'd been a long time since he'd slept that deep. Reece hadn't bothered to open up the sofa bed; presumably he'd put the sheet over the cushions, but now it was crunched up at his feet and his comforter kicked to the floor, since he'd probably been roasting in the room he'd set to a Southerner-friendly temperature. His phone was discarded on the coffee table next to him, the message light blinking.

Reece himself was stretched out on his stomach with one arm hanging off the couch. Grayson was used to seeing him in oversized hoodies, but now the T-shirt had ridden up enough to show a sliver of the skin of his side and lower back, and the flannel pajama pants seemed molded to the contours of his legs and ass.

Grayson forced his gaze back to his own backpack. He might be making the occasional bad decision when it came to Reece, but he drew a line at eye-fucking him while he slept, no matter how good the view.

He got dressed and opened the curtain enough to let some of the gray early morning light in. He made a cup of coffee in the machine on the counter and added all the creamers, then sat on one of the bar stools, toes touching the floor as he unlocked his phone.

Reece had texted him a picture: a selfie with the bear hat back on his head and flashing a peace sign at the camera, which was carefully tilted to include Grayson very obviously fast asleep behind him. There was a message with it:

> Jamey wanted proof that I was safe, so for the record, I DID send this one to her. She said to tell you she's sending it to someone named Aisha.

No one was supposed to have pictures of Grayson, and now in the space of a couple days, Reece had three. Grayson should delete this one, and the one of the two of them at the truck, and the gym photo he'd sent from Vermont because Reece had been upset.

He raised his gaze from the phone and eyed the empath on the couch. Reece was still trustingly asleep, his slow and peaceful breathing filling the room.

He looked back at the picture, at the two of them only about a foot apart on the bed. At Reece in pajamas and the bear hat, the rare smile on his face, the camera capturing an evening when he'd been content and happy enough to project those feelings onto a store clerk, a front desk receptionist, and a toddler and her dad.

Grayson's thumb hovered over the delete icon.

Then again, it wasn't like Grayson ever shared his phone with anyone, and was there really a point in deleting pictures when other people had them too?

He moved his finger and hit Back instead.

Dr. Easterby had sent her itinerary to Prince Rupert, along with an unexpected text.

There's going to be a big bill
for charter flights, but it's worth it:
Jamey's officially part of the team.

Grayson hadn't thought St. James would ever forgive him for arresting Reece—twice—and he wouldn't have expected her to. It was good, though; Dr. Easterby deserved to work with someone like St. James, who had the extra strength and speed but still had her heart.

Grayson: Call me in if you need me.

He had several emails from Stone Solutions and the Empath Initiative that gave him pause. There had been a break-in at the Bellevue campus of Stone Solutions the night before.

The police suspect arson, Vivian Marist had written. Perhaps the Dead Man's attention is still on ensuring Vermont's empaths don't see so much as a photo of the Burlington murder, but if our foremost anti-empathy weapon could concern himself with a trifling thing like arson at the nation's biggest empathy defense facility, I can have the jet sent for you.

Grayson considered her message. Arson and a break-in at Stone Solutions was a problem. But Reece was also still a problem, in a dangerous liminal state no empath had ever managed before, accidentally projecting emotions without even realizing it.

With a snap of her fingers, Marist could have the police, ten SWAT teams, the FBI—anyone she liked—coming to their aid.

Reece didn't have anyone but Grayson right now.

He heard the rustling of a sheet as Reece shifted. Grayson glanced at the couch and found Reece's eyes partially open, watching him.

Grayson closed Marist's email without answering. He owed Reece some choice words about the picture, but what he said was, "Hey, Care Bear."

Reece's lips curved up. "Hey."

Seemed like his sweet side came out in the mornings. Maybe Reece was always slow to rise. Maybe he was the kind of person who liked having someone in their bed, lazy wakeups that led to kisses that led to both of them getting up late.

Or maybe Grayson's mind just insisted on spiraling straight into the gutter around Reece.

But it'd be so easy for Grayson to cross the room and get down on his knees next to the couch. Bury his fingers in that thick dark hair and steal a sleepy morning kiss. Run hands over Reece, to that bare lower back, up under his shirt, across skin that would be soft and fever-hot from that higher empath body temperature. Grayson could follow the path his hands had traced with his mouth, his fingers slipping under the waistband of those pajama pants, which would probably slide down easy—

Real easy, yeah. Because Reece would have been knocked *unconscious* back at that first kiss. Grayson needed to cool his thoughts, because none of that was ever happening. Reece was off-limits in every possible sense.

Reece stretched lazily. "Did you know you're too big for that stool?"

Grayson really needed to stop watching the way Reece's

movements pulled his clothes even tighter to his body. "I'm too big for everything."

Reece snorted.

Grayson gave him a flat look. "That wasn't a sex joke."

"If you say so."

"I wasn't talking about my dick."

"Maybe we should make room for him in the conversation." Reece rested his chin on his arm, eyes wide and innocent. "A lot of room, apparently."

"What we're *doing*," Grayson said, "is getting your empath ass up so you can eat something way too sweet for breakfast, and then we can get going. And you've got messages on your phone."

"You can check them if you want," Reece said, yawning.

"I don't know your passcode."

"I don't have one."

"You don't—*why* don't you have one?"

"They're annoying. Besides, who'd want to look at my stuff?"

At some point, Grayson was gonna need to have a conversation with Reece about basic safety. A second conversation. A tenth conversation, or whatever they were up to now. "Read your messages, then put a lock on your phone."

Reece rolled his eyes. "Fine," he said, swiping his phone off the table. "They're pointless, though. Too easy to guess."

"No, they're not," Grayson said.

Reece lifted his gaze, then went back to his phone. "You use your brother's birthday."

Grayson stilled. "How did you—"

"Because you told me back in November that he passed away," Reece said, more quietly, as he keyed in whatever new passcode he was adding. "And that the Dead Man is vengeance. It's not hard to figure out."

Grayson blinked.

"You keep thinking you're so unknowable," Reece went on. "But that's not true. Maybe I can't read you like most people, where it's as obvious as the colors of a rainbow, but your memories keep you from a flat dead gray. You're quicksilver, and I'm starting to see every glint and shimmer."

Grayson sat still for a moment, then picked up his phone.

"You're changing your code now, aren't you," Reece said, eyes on his own phone and typing with his thumbs.

"Shut up."

"I knew it."

"You'll never guess this one."

"Whatever you need to tell yourself, *sugar.*" Reece held his phone out to Grayson. He was frowning. "The text was from Ben. Look at this."

Grayson took the phone to read Reece's message chain with the McFeely's bartender Ben Castillo.

Ben: Any chance you've heard from Diesel?

Reece: No, why? I thought he was supposed to be at that car show.

Ben: He is but he disappeared yesterday without saying goodbye and hasn't answered any texts. It's just not like him.

Ben: Will you check with your boyfriend too?

"Diesel had won a whole package to a car show here in Vancouver." Reece's frown had deepened. "But that airsoft manager, Keith Waller, was hassling Diesel too. We should check the show and see if we can find Diesel."

"Agreed." Grayson was still looking at their message chain. "You have a boyfriend?"

The question had tumbled out of his mouth before he'd known he was going to ask it.

"What? Oh." A hint of color appeared on Reece's cheeks. "No, no, I—I mean, it's actually—um. Ben thinks—well." He rubbed the back of his neck. "You."

"Me what?"

"Ben thinks it's you. That you're my hot, scary boyfriend," Reece said awkwardly. "It's my fault; he said something at McFeely's and I didn't correct him."

"Oh." Why had Grayson even asked that question? Why had the thought occurred to him? Maybe they'd run away to Canada together, but that was part of the job. Didn't make Reece's relationships any of Grayson's business.

He considered the phone and text chain for a moment.

He must've asked because he'd been surprised. After all, it sure would've been surprising if he'd missed that Reece had a partner when they'd practically been breathing the same air for thirty-six hours.

He held the phone back out to Reece, whose face was still lightly flushed.

"I should set Ben straight about the boyfriend thing," Reece said, taking the phone. "I'll do it now."

He was still sprawled out in pajamas, looking soft and warm, like he should've been waking up in someone's arms, not alone on a couch on a would-be kidnapper's trail.

"Why?" Grayson heard himself say. "You could just tell Mr. Castillo that I haven't seen Mr. Lane either but that we'll check the show. We can tell him the rest some other time."

"You think so?" Reece seemed to brighten. "Yeah, I mean, there are a lot more important things than correcting everyone who thinks we're boyfriends, right? Who even knows where they get such a wild idea?"

"Who knows," Grayson said, gaze lingering on Reece.

★ ★ ★

It had snowed in Vancouver the evening before, delaying flights, and Aisha had opted to head from Toronto to Calgary instead, and then up to Terrace for the night.

She'd caught a few hours' sleep at a cheap motel, then taken the earliest bus from Terrace to Prince Rupert, head propped against the window as she drank rapidly cooling bus station coffee, watching the darkness rush by until the late winter sun finally rose, lighting the forested mountain landscape in gray.

From the bus station, she'd taken a taxi to the address Jamey had sent. She and Liam had caught the last commercial flight from Seattle to Ketchikan the night before, and Liam had wrangled schedules and favors with his family's charter until he had one of the floatplanes for that morning.

Now, Aisha was walking across the parking lot of the two-story building that held the offices of a local roofing company and the Prince Rupert hub of Archipelago Air. At the edge of a parking lot was a wooden ramp down to a small dock on the gray waters of the inlet. Two people in rain gear were already down on the dock, smoking in front of a small metal shelter on floats.

Jamey's last text had been fifty minutes ago, saying the sun was theoretically up even if the rain hadn't stopped and they were taking off. Aisha stood at the top of the ramp and wrapped her arms around herself, watching the sky. The clouds were low, hiding the tops of the evergreen-covered mountains around her, and even though it wasn't raining at that moment, the air was wet and cold.

She heard the plane before she saw it, the thrum of the motor that seemed to echo around the landscape. A moment later, the small plane, red and white, appeared, flying just beneath the gray cloud line. She waved up at it and made her way down the dock.

Ten minutes later, the plane was touching down out in the strait, water spraying up around the floats. She waved again, just able to make out someone waving back at her from behind the propeller and windshield as the plane taxied to the dock.

The people in rain gear stepped forward as the plane pulled up to the dock, and a couple minutes later the plane was secured and Liam and Jamey were climbing out.

"I take it back." Jamey had a flushed, happy grin as she stepped onto the wooden planks, and her eyes were bright. "I'm not joining the Vanguards; I'm quitting everything to move to Alaska, get my pilot's license, and work for the Lees."

Liam grinned. He'd switched the long, camel-colored wool coat Aisha had previously seen him in for a puffy parka and winter hat, his look definitely less *public relations* and more *Alaskan bush pilot*. "Nothing like flying."

"You are joking, though, right?" Aisha said, reaching out.

"Mostly," Jamey said, as they hugged hello.

Liam opted to stay behind at the office to handle some paperwork. Jamey and Aisha got another taxi back into town and to the museum, where they were shown around by a friendly woman with a gray bun and giant glasses.

"Ah yes, spawning," Aisha said, trying to sound knowledgeable as they paused by a display of the life cycle of salmon. "You know, one of our friends just interviewed to work here."

The woman blinked. "She did?"

"Just a couple days ago." Jamey's eyes were on the woman's face. "Her name is Marie. Curls like me, glasses—sound familiar at all?"

The woman gave them a sweet, confused smile. "Are you sure you have the right museum? We haven't had an opening in nearly a year. We certainly haven't done interviews recently."

Of course they hadn't. "Well, shoot," Aisha said lightly, exchanging a look with Jamey. "We must have the wrong place then."

From the museum, they tried the Alder Inn, where Marie had supposedly stayed. But when Jamey had asked about her friend Marie from Montreal, the front desk man had seemed sincere when he said he hadn't seen her.

"Are you two staying long?" he'd added, glancing between them. "I'm off work soon and could help you look around. Or we could get drinks instead. I'm sure your friend will eventually turn up; you said she's pretty too, right?"

Jamey had given him a flat look and they'd left. Thirty minutes later, they were inside the warmth of a local coffeehouse, which overlooked the busy harbor. In these small Pacific Northwest towns, the water sometimes seemed like an extension of the town, its own kind of Main Street. Aisha watched a floatplane take off, parting the tops of the waves under its pontoons until it lifted and took off into the sky.

"Was Marie Pelletier ever here at all?" Jamey sipped her triple shot latte. "Or did someone send that text about the inn from her phone, pretending to be her?"

Aisha shrugged helplessly. She raised her gaze to the forested mountains on the other side of the harbor, like she could see past them and over to Haida Gwaii. "We need to talk about the other possibility."

Jamey followed her gaze. "We admittedly don't know much," she said, "but nothing we've heard sounds remotely like this was a corrupted empath."

"Agreed," said Aisha. "Marie shouldn't be in Polaris. But what a fucking hell of a coincidence."

Jamey's lips tightened. "You've been to this Polaris facility before?"

Aisha nodded. "I try to go a couple times a year to check on the empaths."

"Even though they're all corrupted?"

Aisha ran a hand over the scar on her neck. "Yeah." She cleared her throat. "I haven't been up since Cora Falcon was admitted. I can call for a company ride over without anyone blinking; there's a satellite office here with a helicopter on call."

She made a face. "Getting you in might be a little trickier. Security is—well. What you'd expect from a prison for sadistic superhuman killers. I can't just add you to the guest list, and breaking in would take planning, or an army."

Jamey frowned. "In theory this should be nothing but a quick visit for you, everything in order, right?" she said. "Except we're missing an empath who's supposedly lying dead in Burlington, Vermont. And I don't really want to let you go alone."

Aisha bumped her with her shoulder. "Look at you. You're like the extra badass version of the friend who makes you text that you got home safe."

"Shut up," Jamey said good-naturedly. She took another sip of her coffee, gaze still on the mountains. "Can you show me on a map where the facility is? And where we could, in theory, land a floatplane without being seen?"

Aisha nodded.

"Then Liam and I can be our own ride," Jamey said. "And if it turns out you do need me, I can also be the army."

CHAPTER TWENTY-TWO

...as the debates around the Empath Initiative heat up in Washington, many have opinions about the purpose and future of the nascent agency.

"It's simply good policy to be sure that our empath policies will first and foremost protect those of us without empathy," said defense contractor Charles Stone. "After all, the best defense is a good offense."

Mr. Stone's son, Cedrick, recently received a large government grant for empathy-related research and development.

—EXCERPT FROM A TWENTY-FIVE-YEAR-OLD ISSUE OF *THE EMERALD CITY TRIBUNE*,
"No end to debates surrounding empath agency"

GRETEL PULLED HER BMW into the Stone Solutions parking lot, a good distance from the edge of the police tape marking off the front doors. There were cruisers everywhere, along with a fire truck, an ambulance, and a black armored car that might have been a SWAT team.

No news crews. Obviously they'd be trying to keep this quiet—on the heels of an empath breaking in and the questionable involvement of Cedrick Stone in a senator's death, it didn't bode well for public opinion if Stone Solutions couldn't keep out an arsonist.

She stared at the building up ahead. From what she could see, the fires seemed to have been put out, but how much research had been lost? Product destroyed?

She scanned the area beyond the yellow tape. The SPD public relations front man, Liam Lee, her go-to source for information, was usually on-site and easy to spot in the sea of navy and black in his preferred camel coat. Today, though, he didn't seem to be here. At least she had his number; maybe he'd have a statement for her.

He was also dating Reece Davies' sister, Briony St. James, formerly a detective with the SPD. Gretel had initially started following Detective St. James' career thanks to her dad's ranting about the SPD having an empath's sibling on the force, but you couldn't read about all the amazing, almost superhuman things St. James had done and not wind up her fangirl.

Maybe Liam would also loop in Detective St. James to figure out what the hell was going on.

She eyed the SWAT team's armored car for a long moment and then picked up her phone and looked at her messages again, at the text from Alex: a picture of Officer Stensby and a big blond man in a camouflage coat, the one she'd seen Stensby with at AMI meetings. The two men were standing next to the door of an office with a giant plaque that read *Cedrick Stone, CEO.*

Alex: I did promise you a story.

The car show had been easy to find online, and was taking place at the convention center. Reece and Grayson navigated downtown from their hotel, the buildings getting taller and the traffic bumper-to-bumper with morning commuters.

"Stone Solutions Canada's offices are around here too," Reece pointed out, as Grayson took them down a narrow street between towering glass high-rises. "I suppose they don't put their *Protecting American Minds* motto on their Canadian offices."

"They don't," said Grayson, as they idled at a red light. "But be glad we're checking on Mr. Lane first, because you're still gonna find Stone Solutions Canada plenty annoying."

"Of course the empath hunter already knows that."

"Empath *specialist*," said Grayson. "But I'm warning you because I do need you to remember what being undercover in Canada means."

Reece furrowed his brow. People were rushing by on the crosswalks, bundled in coats, their gazes on their phones. "You don't want anyone to know you're the Dead Man?"

"That's part of it," said Grayson. "But more importantly, even if people did know who I was, I don't have the operational exemptions here that I have in America. The Empath Initiative has no reach here and I don't have the right to preempt any Canadian jurisdictions."

"So?"

"So," Grayson said, "our plan after the car show is to walk into an empath defense office. *Undercover.* That means no gloves, and it's still illegal in Canada."

Reece frowned. "So you could get in trouble if they find out you brought me in with you?"

"I already told you I can take care of myself. I need the empath to stop worrying about others and think about himself for a moment." Grayson looked over at Reece. "It's not a stretch to think we might run into something that will piss you off. But if you get in trouble, like you have a bad habit of doing, they're not gonna be keen to let me pull you out of it."

"Oh." Reece squirmed. "Am I too much of a liability to bring? Is it better if I'm not there?" He sighed unhappily. "Wouldn't be the first time or place that would be true."

But Grayson shook his head. "Just warning my resident pacifist that I could end up with an argument on my hands. I still think you're safer with me and it'd be my choice to stay together, because I'm pretty good at winning fights. But if you want to wait in the truck, you can, and my only request would be that you lock the doors."

Up ahead, the light turned green. "My feelings haven't changed. I'd still rather be with you," Reece said quietly, as Grayson drove on. "I'll just watch my mouth today."

Lie.

"I saw that flinch," said Grayson, as he pulled into a public parking garage with an outrageous per-hour price. "And you try to say you're not Bad Decisions Bear."

Reece huffed. "How many years ago did you come up with that, anyway?" he said, instead of acknowledging Grayson might have had a point.

"What do you mean?"

"You know," said Reece. "How long have you been calling empaths *Care Bear*?"

Grayson's gaze darted to him, then went right back to the ramps leading them down into the underground garage as he shrugged vaguely.

"You just missed an open spot," said Reece. "And what the fuck was that?"

"The spot was too tight. And what was what?"

"Are you kidding me?" Reece gestured at him "You hesitated. It was noticeable enough to see from space."

"I doubt that." Grayson turned the corner, then cleared his throat. "And it's just you."

"It's just me what?"

"The *Care Bear* thing. It's—I didn't plan it or anything and—well. It's just you."

Reece blinked. And then he felt himself starting to smile.

"You're about to be insufferable, aren't you?" Grayson muttered, heading down yet another car-lined ramp.

"Well, *yeah*," said Reece. "The Dead Man gave me a *nickname*."

"It just happens," Grayson protested. "One side of my family's Latino and I grew up in Texas. I either know you by your formal name or you've got a nickname, there's no middle ground."

"What do I get to call you?"

"Agent Grayson."

"Aw, baby, you don't mean that."

"You want to go back to being Mr. Davies?" Grayson said, as he finally pulled into an open spot on the fourth level.

"What I want is to drive," said Reece. "I could have fit us into that open spot on the second floor."

"I thought you were finally gonna watch your mouth."

"I thought *you* were finally going to accept which one of us is the better driver. Guess we both set ourselves up for disappointment."

Grayson shifted into Park. "You know, most folks would say the last person an empath ought to sass is an empath hunter."

"Probably," Reece agreed. "So it's a good thing you're just a specialist."

Grayson cut the engine. "You're making me consider a career change, sugar."

Aisha had left Jamey and Liam in Prince Rupert, and now rain lashed the Stone Solutions helicopter as they flew below the cloud line, over the patchwork of islands like scattered puzzle pieces along the BC coast. Evergreen-covered mountains sprouted up straight from the sea, shorter than the Rockies Aisha had left behind but tall enough that snow dusted their tops. Around the islands, the ocean was slate gray, the sky above them hidden by the thick layer of paler gray clouds.

The Polaris Empathic Research Facility—a nice name for the corrupted empath prison—had been built into an abandoned iron-and-copper mine, dozens of miles from the boat routes that traversed the Inside Passage and invisible from air or sea. From land, if you knew where to look, you could find the new camouflaged windows and skylights that marked the empaths' quarters, that ensured they had light, and views, and fresh air. It had been expensive to create glass that was reinforced with empathy-dampening tech, but Grayson had been clear with the Empath Initiative's Director Traynor: all empaths had to be treated well, even the corrupted ones, or there would be no Dead Man.

The new requirements hadn't made Grayson any friends at the agencies, particularly not with Dr. Nichols, who'd run Polaris since its creation two decades earlier. But then, Grayson would tell you himself that he didn't have any feelings about that.

Aisha breathed through her nose, trying to settle her stomach as the helicopter flew over a rocky beach, inward toward the island's core, and started its descent. The tops of trees came closer and closer through the raindrop-streaked windows, and she caught a flash of black moving within the green—one of the island's many bears, perhaps.

"At least the weather's not bad," Tasha, the pilot, said.

Aisha turned and stared at her.

Tasha shrugged. "Rain's not sideways," she said. "Happens often enough in fall and winter."

There was a small helipad created on a crumbling concrete foundation that had once upon a time been a lodging house for miners. Today, greenery twisted along the remains of the walls, and two people in slickers and tall galoshes were waiting for their landing. A third person stood apart, a white man with brown hair and glasses, dressed in a long raincoat somewhere between khaki and green and holding a large umbrella open over his head.

Dr. Victor Nichols, who ran the facility. He'd come personally. Interesting.

One of the men in galoshes opened the helicopter's passenger door. Nichols stepped forward and offered his hand. "Dr. Easterby. This is a surprise."

Aisha took his hand and let him help her down from the helicopter, not trusting her unsteady stomach or legs. His hand was cold, as were the pale eyes studying her. "My apologies for the short notice, Dr. Nichols," she said, affecting a courteous tone she absolutely didn't feel. He didn't like her much; the feeling was mutual. "Agent Grayson felt the visit couldn't wait."

She'd never actually come without Grayson before. There was no cell service, just the company satellites, and for safety's sake it always seemed better to come with company. But if Marie Pelletier had somehow become corrupted and been brought here, they needed to know. And Aisha wasn't alone; she had Jamey on her way.

Still, dropping Grayson's name had the desired effect of making Nichols straighten.

"Of course," he said, more deferentially. "We're at his disposal."

"Great," she said, smiling blandly. "Lead the way."

An umbrella was produced for her, and she followed Nichols across the helipad and onto the dirt.

"How long are you staying?" Nichols asked, as they passed the rusted walls and crumbling bricks that used to be a storage facility for equipment.

"I was only planning on the day," she said. "Agent Grayson is expecting a report tonight."

In other words, *everything better fucking be in order with the empaths, asshole.*

Beyond the remains of a handful of buildings was the mouth of the mine—not much taller than Grayson, looking for all the world like a cave or break in the rocks. No hint to all of the surveillance right there at the opening, from drones to infrared technology scanning for body heat, or to the state-of-the-art facility hiding just within.

Aisha's stomach still hadn't settled, but the bumpy helicopter ride was most likely to blame. She took another breath and followed Nichols into the mine.

Just beyond the mouth, there was a solid iron door with a touch pad next to the handle. Nichols scanned his thumb, then hefted open the door so they could step into the lobby. There was of course no receptionist, but there was a check-in desk at one end of the lobby, and a white man in a lab coat was behind it, working at a computer.

Nichols looked down at her without smiling. "Did you have a specific request while here?"

"I'd like to visit with the new residents."

"We've only added one empath since your last visit, and that's Cora Falcon." Nichols' mouth had pinched. "Were you expecting someone else to be here?"

Was she? Marie Pelletier had been in Prince Rupert and now she was missing. It was a hell of a coincidence, but surely Polaris wasn't kidnapping empaths off the street without involving Stone Solutions and the Dead Man?

"No one else," Aisha finally said. "But I'd like to see Ms. Falcon straightaway."

Nichols stepped across the lobby to the desk. "We're visiting our newest guest," he said to the man in the lab coat, whose eyebrows went up. "Will you page down and let security know?"

Page *down*? "I'd rather you didn't," Aisha said. "And I'll conduct the visit on my own, thank you."

Nichols took a breath through his nose. "Very well," he said. "I think you shouldn't have come today. But it's your funeral, as the saying goes."

He didn't waste another moment with her, turning and striding away so abruptly that Aisha felt the raindrops that flew off his coat.

The man on the other side of the desk slid a visitor key card over to her. Aisha could see the badge that hung around his neck now: *J. Higgins*. "You do know Ms. Falcon is fully corrupted? That she's extremely powerful and dangerous?"

"I know everything I need to know." Aisha took the card. "Can I see the roster of empath residents?" Maybe Marie wasn't going to be on it, but she needed to be sure.

"I'll pull together an inmate list," Higgins said, although he hadn't looked Aisha in the eyes as he said it, and she hadn't missed his switch from *residents* to *inmates*. "Cora Falcon is in medical, sublevel two, end of the hall."

"Medical?" Aisha said in surprise. "Is she hurt?"

"*She's* fine," Higgins said testily. "Her victims? Not so much."

But what the hell is she doing in medical? In the basement? Why didn't Nichols say anything about this, just now?

Aisha didn't say it, instead gesturing above their heads. "The empaths are supposed to live on the top level."

"Where they have the windows and pretty views while the rest of us work in a literal mine?" Higgins scoffed. "There have been a few changes around here the last few weeks. We're not putting mass murderers in resort rooms anymore."

Cora is only a mass murderer because Cedrick Stone and his buddies made her one for profit. Aisha bit her tongue. Grayson was going to be very interested to hear about all of this, once she had a cell signal.

She turned her back on Higgins, heading for the elevator in the corner.

Taking Reece to a car show was apparently like taking a kid to a candy store. Or, well, taking an empath to a candy store. A Canadian candy store powered by electric vehicles.

Whatever the country or metaphor, Reece had lit up like the Fourth of July. The show was a big one, with nearly two dozen manufacturers represented, and Grayson found himself being tugged by the sleeve from one end to the other.

"Evan, come look at the hybrids—"

"Evan, we don't have this tech yet in the States—"

"Evan, they're doing test drives—"

At one point, Reece dragged him over to a cluster of American brands. As Reece crawled inside a tiny hatchback, Grayson found himself eyeing an F-150 Lightning.

But the Dead Man didn't get excited about horsepower, or torque, or towing capacity, or the number of electric and hybrid trucks at a show. They were here with a purpose and on a mission.

He stepped forward, to the hatchback, and ducked awkwardly to fit his head in the passenger window. Reece was sitting in the driver's seat, examining the center console.

"Are we ever gonna look for Mr. Lane or are you fixing to play all day?"

"I've *been* looking," Reece protested. "I haven't seen that Vietnamese company yet."

Come to think of it, neither had Grayson. He straightened up, scanning the room again.

Reece pointed. "There's an attendant there. I'm going to ask."

He climbed out from the car. Grayson took a step after him, and then on his wrist, his watch buzzed with an incoming call from Detective St. James.

He kept one eye on Reece and the attendant as he answered the phone. "Grayson?"

"Where the hell are you?" St. James said, her voice layered over a loud motor. "It sounds like a circus in the background."

"Car show, which your brother is treating like the circus," Grayson said. "Mr. Lane apparently cut town without saying goodbye and now he's not answering his messages; it's making his friends nervous. He's supposed to be at this show and we're looking for him. Where are *you*? It sounds louder than a car."

A few feet away, Reece was gesturing to the attendant.

"We're in the air again," St. James said. "Keep me posted about Diesel. He tried to keep an eye on Reece when Cora's thralls were tearing up the club; I like him and I owe him. But I'm about to lose my signal, so listen—Gretel Macy, the *Eyes on Empaths* blogger, called Liam. She asked him for a statement on why Officer Stensby was at Stone Solutions last night."

Grayson blinked. "First I'm hearing of that."

"She says she has photographic evidence, but she won't tell us how she got it." St. James hesitated. "You remember that someone with your same Texas accent called me from Stensby's phone, right? Someone who had gotten Stensby to confess what he'd done to Reece's car—"

Her words were garbled for a moment, then she came back online. "—and now Stensby turns up at Stone Solutions last night. That's a lot of empath connections. Could a corrupted empath be involved?"

"One who just happens to sound like me?" Grayson said flatly.

"Well—"

"I know where you're trying to lead this conversation, detective," Grayson said. "Except there's no chance. He's dead."

"But are you absolutely sure? There's no way your brother could—"

"I'm completely sure," Grayson said, more quietly. "And I can *be* completely sure because I was there. If you take my meaning."

St. James went eerily silent. "Are you implying—"

The line went dead.

Grayson waited a moment, gaze on his phone, but she didn't call back. If she was flying up on the North Coast, she wasn't likely to get a signal again for a while.

"You were where?"

He glanced up. Reece was standing less than a yard away, arms folded.

"Texas," Grayson said, fingers tightening ever so slightly on the phone. "You learn anything?"

"There aren't any Vietnamese manufacturers here," Reece said. "There were transportation issues due to the weather and the company that was coming had to cancel like a month ago."

Grayson raised his eyebrow. "So someone promised Mr. Lane a test drive of a vehicle that wasn't going to be here?"

"Seems like it." Reece frowned. "But why? Why would anyone lie to Diesel? And where did he go, if not here?" He nodded at the phone still in Grayson's hand. "What did Jamey think?"

Grayson blinked. "How did you know who that was?"

"Your body language is more relaxed when you talk to Jamey than when you take other calls," Reece said. "She's probably the closest thing you get to a peer, isn't she?"

Grayson blinked again.

"I think if Jamey were here, she'd be thinking that we can't find Diesel, but we know someone shipped big empath gloves from Vancouver to that airsoft manager, the same guy who was bugging Diesel," Reece said. "And she'd still want to search Stone Solutions Canada. I think we should go there next."

He was looking up at Grayson from under the bear hat, eyes big and earnest, apparently unaware of how easily he understood people, even for an empath, or how damn dangerous he could potentially be, even as a pacifist.

But the Dead Man could not—and would not—forget.

CHAPTER TWENTY-THREE

...of course the Empath Initiative has jurisdiction over the empaths, but the FBI needs to stay in the loop. If for any reason they need more manpower, we can back them up.

And since Stone Solutions is so deeply intertwined with EI, I just think it just makes sense for ~~me~~ us to stay close with Stone Solutions too...

—EXCERPT FROM INTERNAL FBI MEMORANDUM, SIGNED BY ASSISTANT DIRECTOR JACOBS

BEFORE HEADING INTO Stone Solutions Canada's high-rise, Grayson made them stop at a coffee shop across the street, where he ordered nine drinks, a baker's dozen of pastries, and eight sandwiches.

"How hungry *are* you?" Reece asked, as they stood to one side and waited for Grayson's order.

"It's not for me," Grayson said. "We gotta walk into a high-rise like we belong there. Guards are less likely to think we're suspicious if we look like the office interns who got sent on a coffee run."

"Right, right," Reece said skeptically. "Because you look so much like an office intern, standing six foot five with endless shoulders."

"I'll hunch," Grayson said.

"Doesn't fix your gorgeous face and perfect hair. Have you considered that going undercover might mean you need to be a little less hot?"

In the end, they got their bags of food and their drinks slotted into cardboard trays, and with Grayson hunched over, his hat pulled to his eyebrows and the drinks in front of his face, Reece could grudgingly concede people might not pay him too much attention.

He, on the other hand, felt wildly conspicuous as he stepped through the automatic doors into the ground floor of the high-rise. He clutched the bags of food tightly in his bare hands and followed Grayson a little more closely than he probably should have, considering that if Grayson stopped suddenly, there was a chance Reece would bump into him, and their clothes might not be enough to keep him from passing out.

The lobby was generically fancy, with clusters of modern furniture set along the two-story glass windows that framed the thick traffic along the street. A large sign on the wall by the elevator bank read *All visitors must check in with security.*

Reece glanced out of the corner of his eye at the end of the lobby, where there was a security desk with a trio of guards behind it.

Just walk on in like you belong here. Why his thoughts had to take on a Southern accent when he was taking Grayson's advice, Reece was sure he didn't know, but he kept his eyes on Grayson's back and followed him to the bank of elevators to wait with a cluster of people in business casual attire, most of them carrying winter coats.

They stepped into the elevator, and Reece watched Grayson's eyes go to a woman in a cardigan, who'd just pressed the button for the twenty-fourth floor. When the elevator stopped at twenty-four, Grayson cleared his throat.

"I'm sorry, ma'am, but could you get the door for us?" Grayson said, as they followed Cardigan out of the elevator and into a small waiting area. This definitely wasn't the main floor of Stone Solutions, because the door had only a small sign and a card scanner. "We got a delivery from a happy client."

She glanced at Grayson. And then her gaze lingered, because Reece was right—he could try and hunch all he wanted, but he was still stupidly attractive. It worked in their favor this time, though, because Cardigan smiled and said, "Sure!"

A moment later, she'd scanned her card. Despite his full hands, Grayson somehow managed to gracefully twist in to hold the door for her with his shoulder. "Appreciate it," he said to her.

"Anytime," she said, with a little too much sincerity. "Do you work here? I don't think I've seen you around."

Because I would have fucking noticed someone as hot as you, Reece could practically hear her finish.

"Does running errands all day count as working here?" Grayson said, dodging the question as gracefully as he'd gotten the door. "You should come by the staff kitchen in a few minutes; one of these might have your name on it."

"Yeah, cool," she said, her gaze still on him, and boy, it was a good thing an empath like Reece was way too emotionally evolved for a caveman feeling like possessiveness over someone who wasn't even his boyfriend and he couldn't even touch.

Way too emotionally evolved.

Yes he was.

Cardigan turned down a hall, and Reece followed Grayson as they continued straight. "You know where you're going?" Reece said quietly.

Grayson nodded. "I've been here before. Anyone asks, we're office services."

"If your office serves up catwalks, sure," Reece muttered.

As they moved down the hall, they picked up a line of workers that followed them into the kitchen like they were white-collar Pied Pipers. "From a happy client," Grayson lied again, as they set their stash on a round Formica table, and no one asked further questions as they descended to claim free food.

Reece carefully twisted around the crowd so he wouldn't make contact with anyone as he and Grayson slipped out of the staff kitchen.

"Marist has an office on the twenty-sixth floor," Grayson said quietly, as they stood against the wall.

"And how do we get up to her office?"

Grayson held up a key card.

"Wait," Reece said. "Did you steal that?"

Grayson jerked a hand toward the office kitchen. "No one was looking past the lattes in there."

Reece frowned.

Grayson gestured with the card. "Don't act like you've never swiped one of these yourself."

Reece sighed and followed Grayson down the hall.

From the Polaris lobby, Aisha rode down to the second level beneath the ground, nearly the mine's lowest save for sublevel three, which was only for storage and the morgue. She stepped out into the hall, immediately chilled. The air was colder down here, and there was nothing but artificial light, the kind that made time meaningless. It wasn't a long hall, and Aisha could see a security guard at the far end. He straightened up as he saw her.

"Dr. Easterby, with the Stone Solutions Seattle office," she said, as he stood. "I'm here on behalf of Agent Grayson."

The man flinched. "Understood, doctor. If I could just…"

Aisha didn't hear him. Her gaze had gone past him, to the room he was guarding. The room held a single bed, which held

Cora. She looked exactly like her pictures, pretty enough to make people look twice, except now her big brown eyes were closed, long brown hair spread out on the pillowcase around her. An IV on a stand was connected to her wrist while a monitor beeped softly.

Aisha knew, logically, that Cora had been behind more than a dozen deaths in Seattle in November. But looking at her, all she could feel was sympathy for the sunshiny therapist who'd been kidnapped and lost the love of her life in the most horrific and traumatizing way.

"Is she being *sedated*?" Aisha demanded.

"She's a mass murderer with emotion-control powers," the guard said back sharply.

"That's literally the entire reason this place was built in an old mine full of empathy-dampening metal residue," Aisha said, even sharper. "I'm going in."

"Doctor—"

"It wasn't a *request*," Aisha said.

"If you're opening that door, I have to lock down the whole floor."

"Then lock it down," Aisha said. "Go get a coffee or something and leave me and her alone."

The guard threw up his hands, muttering something Aisha ignored as he finally turned, heading away down the hall toward the elevator.

Aisha swiped the access card Higgins had passed her, and a moment later, the door was sliding open, letting her in and then closing behind her.

Cora didn't react. Her chest rose and fell with slow breaths as the heart monitor beeped at a concerningly sluggish speed. Aisha distractedly registered the whir of the blood pressure cuff tightening, then relaxing as she stepped to Cora's bedside and picked up her chart.

Her mouth tightened. Sedating a corrupted empath did take

a large dose and was tricky to maintain; their jacked-up corrupted empathy would burn through invasive medication like a wildfire. But there weren't any studies about the long-term effects of sedation on empaths, and Cora was being pumped full of sedatives at a dosage better suited to a horse.

Aisha glanced back at Cora. She wasn't just sedated; she was cuffed to the rails of the bed with padded medical cuffs. This deep in the mine, there were metals in the very walls. It wouldn't block Cora's strongest powers, like hearing lies, and Aisha's safety wasn't guaranteed, but the room itself was almost like an empath glove, and Cora would be groggy and disoriented and unable to touch her.

Aisha stepped close and carefully worked the IV out of Cora's wrist. Then she stepped back and waited.

It didn't take long for Cora's eyelashes to start fluttering. Aisha cleared her throat. "My name is John Doe. I'm a middle-aged white man from Chicago."

Cora slowly turned her head toward Aisha, blinking.

"You could hear that lie, right?" Aisha said. "Despite the location and the drugs? Sorry, I know this is a surprise and you don't know me, but I don't know how long we have and I just want to be sure you know I'm being completely honest with you."

She stepped closer. "My actual name is Aisha Easterby. I'm a doctor, I live in Seattle, and I work with the Dead Man. I understand if that puts you off, but again, I want to be honest."

Cora studied her for a moment, through half-open eyes. When she spoke, it came out as a hoarse whisper. "What do you want?"

"To check on you," Aisha said.

Cora managed to look skeptical even through the drug haze. "Thirteen dead. From *me*. Check on them."

"Oh, I know you were behind all those deaths, and I'm sorry for many of them," Aisha said. "But some of them deserved what they got for what they did to you."

Cora stared at her for a long moment. "Dr. Harleen Quinzel and the Joker," she finally muttered.

Aisha's lips twitched slightly at the reference. Cora had been a therapist and psychologist; of course she was familiar with that particular origin story. "That depends on whether you like pigtails," Aisha said, before she meant to.

That drew a soft huff from Cora, like that had surprised her. "You don't belong in this place, Harley Quinn." She was beginning to sound more alert, likely the corrupted empathy working quickly to rid the sedative from her system.

Aisha gestured around them. "You don't belong in *this* place. You're not supposed to be in medical unless you need the care, and you're sure as fuck not supposed to be cuffed to a bed and sedated."

"Think worse shit is happening here," Cora murmured, arching her neck a bit as she looked up at the ceiling.

Aisha frowned. "What do you mean, *worse shit*?"

"Just a feeling." Cora made a small gesture toward herself with the fingers of her cuffed hand. "Empath intuition. Whatever."

"Not whatever," said Aisha. "What do you think is happening here?"

"Why would you care?" Cora muttered.

Aisha frowned. "You think I don't care what's happening to the empaths here?" She began unwinding the scarf from her neck. "Obviously you can see this scar. It's not my only one, and I bet an empath like you is already starting to guess how I got them."

Cora turned her head back in Aisha's direction, her gaze flicking over her with something like new recognition.

Aisha took a breath through her nose, keeping her voice steady. "Once upon a time, some very bad scientists thought it would be an interesting experiment to find out what my pain would do to my empath boyfriend."

Cora seemed to still.

"Peter didn't take it well. At all," Aisha went on, hoarse herself now. "And he didn't survive the transformation. So when I say that I know you're a victim too, that what was done to you was more monstrous than anything you did, and that I care whether or not you're okay, you can hear that I believe it's the truth."

Cora's gaze was now on Aisha's face. Finally, she said, "I've felt people, in my sleep, their emotions so strong they burn through this place. Some are new. Some are gone." She tilted her head. "And the freak who runs this place is a sadist." She met Aisha's eyes. "I would know."

Shit. "Okay," Aisha said, as she rewound her scarf around her neck. "I'm going to look. And I'm going to get you out of this fucking basement," she promised. "I'll be back."

She could feel Cora watching her as she left.

Reece followed Grayson down a couple halls until they found the office supply room, where they grabbed a couple empty laptop bags and loaded them with miscellaneous cords. There was a set of fire stairs nearby, and they took those up two flights and then used the key card to unlock the door at the twenty-sixth floor.

They poked their heads out, looking up and down a door-lined hall. At the far end was a door with large interior windows on either side. It looked like the office behind them took up the entire side of the building. Through the glass, Reece could see a desk with what looked like Marist's personal receptionist behind it.

"So are we still office services?" Reece whispered.

"No," said Grayson. "Now we're from the Help Desk."

Reece gave him a searching look. "We're IT support?"

"That's right."

"Evan," Reece said patiently. "I can pass for an intern on a coffee run or office services picking up the mail. I cannot pass for IT. I can barely work my phone. I am the reason help desks are necessary."

"You got a better excuse for us to go poking around Ms. Marist's office?"

Reece sighed.

He once again let Grayson lead the way as he knocked courteously on Marist's door and then inched it open. "Excuse me, ma'am?" he said to the secretary. "IT got a call to service Ms. Marist's printer while she's in Seattle?"

The secretary had a harried look on her face as she glanced their way, confused. "You did?"

"We sure did." Reece met her eyes, hoping his own looked innocent and sympathetic. "You must be so busy trying to deal with everything while she's gone. We'll try to be quiet and stay out of your way."

The secretary's face smoothed out. "Thanks, I am busy," she agreed. "Do whatever you need to."

Reece followed Grayson through the wooden door to the secretary's right and into an office that was decorated almost aggressively professionally. Diplomas hung on the walls, along with tastefully bland art and a handful of framed photos. One wall was taken up by an enormous screen, which was currently dark.

"I don't think I'd have pegged the president of Stone Solutions Canada to need a giant television in her office," Reece said, keeping his voice barely a whisper as he and Grayson crouched down by the printer. "Doesn't really fit with the rest of the decor."

"It's not a television, it's the empath map," said Grayson. "Mr. Stone had them installed in every office."

"Empath…map?"

"It shows where all the empath trackers currently are."

Reece narrowed his eyes. "Oh, it's *Stalker TV*, how cute," he said bitingly. He turned his gaze to the framed photos. "And are these the stalkers?" He straightened and stepped closer to the photos. "I recognize Cedrick Stone."

Grayson joined him at the wall. "If by *stalkers* you mean all the directors of the various empath organizations, then yeah." Grayson pointed to the center photo, of a pretty, polished blonde woman with a perfect smile standing on a dizzyingly high suspension bridge next to a handsome Black man. "That's Vivian Marist herself, with Assistant Director Jacobs. He's the Empath Initiative's liaison with the FBI."

"And they're fucking," said Reece.

Grayson blinked. "What?"

"Those two." Reece tapped the picture of Marist and Jacobs. "Secret relationship that they're hiding from their work colleagues. You can't tell? It's written all over them, even in a still picture, how they're leaning into each other like they can't help themselves. Not to mention it's Marist's only casual picture and she's put it in the nicest frame, right at what's probably her eye level. I bet she's in love."

"I did not know any of this," Grayson muttered to himself.

"What about this one?" Reece gestured at a different photo, the largest one on the wall. It was a professional, posed shot, with the Seattle skyline behind them. A caption at the bottom read *Dedicated to Keeping You Safe*. "Who are these two assholes with Marist and Cedrick Stone?"

"The big man next to Cedrick Stone is Director Traynor."

Reece raised an eyebrow. "Why is the director of an empath organization built like you?"

"Ex-military," Grayson said. "Used to be a general. If I work for anyone, it's him; the role of the Dead Man was his idea."

"Was it." Reece sized up Traynor in the picture. Unlike the poised, corporate smiles of Stone and Marist, Traynor's face was carefully blank. "Who's the guy next to Marist and what does he run?"

"Director Nichols," said Grayson. "He runs a—research facility."

"I see." Reece narrowed his eyes at the man in the picture, who had brown hair and pale eyes. Something about his expression gave Reece the creeps. "And what kind of *research facility* is *dedicated to making people safe* but also makes the Dead Man stumble over telling an empath about it?"

"It's—I mean—"

"Back on the rooftop of the Seattle Stone Solutions, Cedrick Stone mentioned they were going to send Cora to a place where they did research." Reece's eyes narrowed further. "He said it was here, in BC. Does this creep run that place?"

"Reece, stop," Grayson said, more quietly. "Your empathy is trying to discover secrets the people of Seattle and Vancouver can't afford for you to know. There might be a day when it's not safe for them that you know. Understand?"

Reece took a breath, trying to calm his blood pressure. "Was your brother sent to that place too?"

He hadn't realized he was going to ask that question until it had already spilled from his lips.

For a moment, the only sound was the hum of the fluorescent lights above and the clicking of computer keys as Marist's secretary typed in the next room.

"No," Grayson finally said. "Everything that happened with Alex happened in Texas."

I know where you're trying to lead this conversation, detective, Grayson had said on the phone at the car show, to Jamey. *Except there's no chance. He's dead.*

Grayson had paused to listen, then added, *I'm completely sure. And I can* be *completely sure because I was there. If you take my meaning.*

You were where? Reece had asked.

Texas.

"Your brother died in Texas." Reece jerked his head to look

over his shoulder, back at Grayson. "Is that what you were talking about earlier, with Jamey?"

"Reece—"

"You're certain your brother is dead because you were *there*?"

Grayson didn't answer for a moment, standing in the middle of the office, framed by the window's gray skies and mountain landscape. "Alex was the most dangerous corrupted empath I've ever met," he finally said. "And the Dead Man always does what he has to do to save people. I wasn't safe for my brother and I'll never be safe for any empath, including you. You gotta remember that. Always."

Reece stared at him.

He could read between those lines just fine, read the neon sign Grayson was unsubtly flashing for both him and Jamey.

He expected them to take his words to mean that Evan Grayson had caused Alex Grayson's death.

And someone else, even Jamey, might actually believe it.

But Grayson might as well expect Reece to add one plus one and get three.

"Evan," Reece said again, his voice a little lower. "What happened to you and your brother?"

Grayson's gaze flicked over his face, like he was trying to confirm if Reece had swallowed the lie he'd just tried to tell.

"I'm not gonna give an empath details they shouldn't be hearing, you know that," he said. "I don't have feelings about what happened, so it's not worth dragging into the light. You want to help, keep an eye on the secretary so I can dig in Ms. Marist's files and see if they've started making and mailing out extra-large empath gloves here, like the ones that turned up at the airsoft course. Then I might need to get back to Seattle and go looking for Officer Stensby—wherever the Dead Man is needed."

Reece watched him walk over to the desk, bending his tall frame to open a drawer. His gaze went to the picture on the wall, of Stone and Marist, of Traynor and Nichols. These were the leaders in empathy defense. People who claimed to be protecting innocents from empaths, but when they had learned of the horror that happened to the Grayson brothers, they'd taken advantage, descended on Evan like vultures, treating him like he wasn't a person anymore, just a weapon, until even Grayson believed it.

Reece slipped a hand into his jeans pocket and pulled out his phone. Keeping an eye on Grayson, he opened his messages—but not his texts with Jamey.

Instead, he opened the last message he'd gotten from Stensby, about a bakery in Everett, and sent a new text.

I'm not sure who has this phone now.

But I think I want to talk to you.

CHAPTER TWENTY-FOUR

We can bandy around words like "singular" and "unique" but it will never make them true. Replication is key to any study: if it can be done, it can be duplicated.

Nothing—and no one—is an exception.

—COMMENT BY [REDACTED] ON [REDACTED] MANUAL

THE FREAK WHO *runs this place is a sadist. I would know.*

Cora's words replayed in Aisha's head as she stepped out of the fire stairs into Polaris's top level, where the empath quarters were supposed to be. She'd been up to this level before, to check on the three other empaths who lived here. They knew her too, would call her name when she entered, because their empathy always picked it up when someone approached.

Today, however, all she heard was silence.

Her footsteps seemed unbearably loud as she walked down the hall. The heat had been turned off on this level, and her breath was a visible puff in front of her as she swiped her key card and stepped into the residential area. She approached the closest room, the walls made of glass like the medical rooms.

Her spine stiffened, her stomach plummeting.

It was empty of the furniture it was supposed to have. Instead, there were two steel tables under the skylight in the middle of the room, covered with sheets, the outline of a petite body under the first, a second, taller body under the other.

"No, no no *no*," she whispered, hurrying forward. She hadn't heard about any recent empath deaths. There shouldn't be *any* bodies here.

Her hand was shaking as she unlocked the door and stumbled across the room. She reached the table and yanked the sheet back.

Marie Pelletier, unquestionably dead, her corpse at least a day old.

"Marie." Aisha could feel the ache welling her throat, her chest. She grabbed the other sheet and pulled it back, already knowing what she'd see: another woman, younger than Marie but with the same curls and delicate features. They were unmistakably sisters, Marie and Simone Pelletier.

"Oh no," Aisha whispered. "No, I'm so sorry, so sorry."

She glanced up, seeing the telltale red dot of a security camera in the corner. She had minutes, maybe seconds now. She sprinted to the corner of the room, with its window, beneath its high skylight, and pulled the two-way radio Liam had given her out of her coat.

She'd be fired for this—probably arrested too—but something in this mine was rotten to its depths, and it wasn't the corrupted empaths.

"Code red," she said into the radio, desperately hoping Liam was right and he'd pick her up. "Code *red*."

"Enjoying your discoveries?"

Aisha whirled around to see Victor Nichols had appeared in the doorway. "Victor," she said, breathing too hard. "What have you done?"

"What have *you* done?" he countered, gesturing at the radio in her hand. He seemed more curious than concerned, watching her with his pale eyes behind his glasses.

Aisha ignored the question. "Where are all the other empaths? André, Faith, Timothy—where are they?"

"I'm afraid they and their partners didn't make it, same as the Pelletier sisters," Nichols said easily. "Trial and error; you're a scientist, you should appreciate that."

"Trial and error for *what*?" Aisha snapped.

"To protect ourselves." Nichols spread his hands. "Here, on this island, we're like the ancient humans with the saber-toothed tigers. Only we've evolved beyond spears—we're depending on our minds to create weapons against the empaths."

"Oh my God. Are you behind the predator theory that's spreading?" Aisha's gaze went to Marie, the sweet librarian who'd loved her cat and was now lying dead in Polaris. "Empaths are *pacifists*."

"Until they're evolved," said Nichols. "And then they become perfect predators, able to hide among us, to *control* us. This is a war, Dr. Easterby, and the empaths are going to win if we don't find a way to stop them."

Two more people appeared in the doorway behind him: Higgins from earlier and one of the men from the helipad.

"But that brings us back to our original question," Nichols said. "Who were you trying to contact on that radio?"

"The Dead Man, obviously," Aisha lied. Maybe Nichols could still be scared into sense.

But Nichols lit up. "Oh, good," he said. "That's perfect, actually. A little ahead of schedule, but we can be ready for him."

"What?" Aisha said helplessly.

Nichols didn't answer, instead motioned to Higgins, who stepped forward. He had a syringe in hand, and given the sedatives Cora had been on, Aisha could guess where this was going.

There was a tiny chime, and Nichols suddenly looked at his watch. His lips tightened. "Deal with her," he said crisply to

Higgins, as he spun around and headed for the door, movements quick and tight.

Aisha tried to squash the tiny ray of hope. Even Jamey wasn't that fast. She couldn't be, could she?

"Put her with the other one," Nichols said, as he disappeared through the morgue door.

Other one?

Aisha looked from the syringe to Higgins, who had the gall to smile at her. "He did say you shouldn't have come today, Dr. Easterby."

Nothing had turned up in Marist's office linking a pair of gloves from Vancouver, British Columbia, with a Washington airsoft course, and the secretary was starting to give Reece and Grayson impatient looks. Whoever had Stensby's phone hadn't texted back yet.

They were facing more dead ends, and Reece was getting very tired of those. A Canadian empath was missing, and someone had wanted Reece to go missing too.

They needed answers.

Grayson stepped close to him, close enough Reece's skin broke out in prickles of want. "I want to search a few more places, but it's gonna be more obvious," he said, in a whisper. "Think you could distract the secretary for a few minutes?"

"Sure, sure," Reece said quickly, like he wasn't thinking how nice it'd be to reach out and slide his arm around Grayson, fainting be damned.

He stepped out of Marist's office and into the reception area, where the secretary was texting on the phone. As subtly as he could, he pulled the office door mostly shut behind him, enough to hide Grayson. "We're wrapping up," he lied, as he leaned over a reception chair and pretended to go through one of the messenger bags.

She glanced up, meeting his eyes and giving him a smile and a thumbs-up before going back to her phone.

She probably made Marist's appointments, sent emails on her behalf. Probably knew a lot more than anyone ever gave her credit for. Maybe Marist had asked her secretary to run errands for her—errands like mailing a package to an airsoft course outside of Seattle.

Marist seemed to have taken her computer down to the AMI conference in Seattle, but they could probably get a good amount of information from her secretary's computer.

Reece hesitated.

What would it take to get the secretary to leave?

There was, of course, a way Reece could find out.

He bit his lip. No. No, he couldn't think about using insight on purpose. He shouldn't think about it. It was a hard line; Grayson had said so.

You're in Stone Solutions. The company that might have hired someone to kidnap you. That was going to hurt Jamey. That kidnapped Cora and purposefully corrupted her. They hurt your fellow empaths.

And Cedrick Stone would have hurt Evan.

Reece cut his eyes to the partially open office door that hid Grayson. The last couple times Reece had used insight, he'd puked all over himself. Grayson would notice that, and maybe they were sort of flirting and sharing a truck and a hotel room, but Grayson had made it clear that the Dead Man's amnesty wasn't going to extend to Reece using insight on purpose.

But then, the last couple times, using insight had been an accident, brought on by stress. If he did it on purpose, could he stay more in control? So that Grayson wouldn't even know?

He looked back at the secretary, and before he could think on it further, his gaze went unfocused, absorbing details about her.

High heels, skirt and tights, all crisp and neat, dressed up despite the winter weather and business casual attire of the rest of the office, her posture tense as she perches on the edge of her chair—

Hair in a smooth updo and heavy eye makeup, but faded lipstick on chewed-on lips—

Pretty nails as she's glued to her phone, her face set in anticipation every time her fingers stop moving, the occasional small and furtive smile stealing through—

She has an office crush.

Reece's stomach swooped. He clenched his teeth hard as he took a stabilizing breath through his nose. *No puking*, he ordered himself, as he forced the nausea down.

He pushed himself up from the chair. "Some interns brought coffee and stuff," he said, trying for a friendly tone. "Did you get any?"

"Hmm?" she said distractedly, not looking up from her phone. "Oh, no, I'm not hungry."

"You must be the only one, then," Reece said casually. "I think the whole office turned up in the break room."

She paused, looking up at him. "Really?"

"Yeah," said Reece. "They were all still hanging out when I walked past, making happy hour plans and stuff. Must have been, like, everybody who works here."

"Oh." She put her phone in her purse, then stood. "Coffees too, you said?"

A minute later, Reece was alone in the front room—and she hadn't locked her computer when she left. He kept an eye out on the hall as he bent over the desk.

What would Jamey start with, if she was standing here? The answer came as easily as the secretary's office crush: expense reports and time sheets, looking for a record of a trip to the post office.

He began opening programs until he found one with saved receipts. The box the gloves had been mailed in had been postmarked two weeks earlier. He scrolled backward until he could scan the entries in the system for that date.

Nothing from the post office. But there was a receipt from a

Vancouver restaurant, for—Jesus, Marist had spent *how much* on dinner? Reece read over the entry, gaze lingering on the description.

Business dinner.
Other attendees: Holt Traynor (Empath Initiative); Victor Nichols (Polaris Empathic Research Facility)

All three of them had been in Vancouver the day the gloves had been mailed to the airsoft course. Reece leaned closer.

"Mr. Davies."

Reece froze. He glanced up, trying—and almost certainly failing—to keep an innocent expression. "Evan. Hey. Find anything else?"

"I think we got a bigger question right now." Grayson was leaning on the bookcase, his arms folded. He was watching Reece with a completely inscrutable expression. "Like whether this is the part where I ask if you're being a bad empath?"

"Depends," Reece said lightly. "Are we making that porno after all?"

Grayson's gaze flicked over him, almost like an automatic motion, like he couldn't help himself.

"Because I could be really bad for you," Reece said, just as light. "If that's what you're into."

"You're not going to get me to take that bait." Grayson's tone was as unreadable as his expression. "What are you doing?"

Reece had to stick to the absolute truth. The way Grayson was watching him, he'd see any tiny flinch. "I thought our secretary friend might have some useful information on Marist on this computer," Reece said carefully. "No one thinks about the people further down the chain and the piles of dirt they have on their bosses."

"That's fair." Grayson was still considering him. "How'd you get her to leave?"

"Told her about the drinks in the break room."

"Oh yeah? And how'd you know that would make her leave?"

Reece swallowed. "Who doesn't like coffee?"

The air between them was charged, almost tangible. *This is what you want,* Reece reminded himself. *You want Grayson to be suspicious. You want him to know when you're lying. You want him to catch you—to* stop *you.*

Didn't he?

Grayson moved closer, up to the other side of the desk. He put his hands on the surface, leaning in to mirror Reece. "Sugar," he said patiently, without the slightest inflection or change in his tone, and somehow it sent warning bells off in Reece's brain all the same. "You haven't forgotten who or what I am, have you?"

"No, *sir,* Agent Dead Man," Reece said, with all the sass he could muster.

"Then I suggest you come clean," Grayson said. "Because you might be adorable in a bear hat, but I told you, I'm not gonna underestimate you anymore. And I'm not gonna fall for your lies again."

There was a moment of silence between them. Reece realized his fingers had balled into fists.

All flight, no fight.

He knew that was bullshit now.

Grayson's blank hazel eyes were staring him down. It wouldn't matter to him that they'd driven up to Canada together, bought clothes together, shared a hotel room and watched television together. That Grayson understood him better than anyone ever had, in all of Reece's life. None of that mattered to Grayson at all.

But it mattered to Reece.

He closed his eyes. "I used insight to figure it out."

Grayson somehow went even more silent. After a moment, Reece cracked open his eyes to find Grayson's unreadable gaze on him.

"On purpose?" Grayson asked.

"I don't know," Reece said honestly. "I know I hate this company. Cedrick Stone was going to do terrible things to Jamey, and I watched him aim a gun at you. And I was thinking about that, and the next thing I knew, I was using insight to figure out how to get the secretary to leave so we could look at her computer."

He hesitated, then said, "I don't want you to underestimate me or fall for any lies. I don't want to do this shit. I want you to stop me when you have to."

"I know." Grayson leaned forward, and they were just that little bit closer. "And I know you got the corruption pulling on you on one side, but you got me on the other. And as long as I'm here, I'm never gonna let you leave Care-A-Lot without a fight."

Reece swallowed. "And you're real good at winning fights," he said, echoing Grayson from the morning, the words sticking just a little in his throat.

"I try." Grayson held up a small, black rectangle. "And to your earlier question: I found this behind Marist's group photo."

"Flash drive?" Reece said, eyes widening.

Grayson nodded. "How about we take a look?"

Gretel sat in her car, her dad's voice coming through the Bluetooth speakers.

"I know it's frustrating when your FOIA requests don't get anywhere," Beau said. "But maybe there isn't a story here."

Gretel ground her teeth. "There *is*," she said. "I've dug plenty up in the public records already. Have you ever looked at how much funding EI gets from the military? It's weird. Suspicious."

"Why would it be?" Beau said. "Empaths are dangerous."

"They're pacifists," Gretel said. "So what is EI doing with piles of military money? That they pass on to Stone Solutions?"

"Stone Solutions makes the gloves—"

"More money than that. There has to be more they're doing."

Gretel glanced at her phone, at the inexplicable picture Alex had sent, of Officer Stensby and the big blond man in camouflage outside Cedrick Stone's office at Stone Solutions. She hadn't heard from Alex since.

"Come on, Dad," she tried again. "Don't you wonder why someone always seems to be calling and asking for your AMI member lists? Asking about how many cops and soldiers AMI's got?"

Beau sighed. "I don't have time to talk you out of a new obsession every week. Every time we talk, it's some new story—"

"And you make me send them all to AMI," Gretel said, teeth clenched. "You trust my work. And I'm telling you, something is going on with the empaths. Something someone is not telling us. Something big."

Beau was quiet for a moment. "Okay, honey," he finally said. "I'm listening."

CHAPTER TWENTY-FIVE

Polaris has always been more essential to the population's safety than anyone has wanted to admit. Cedrick Stone can emblazon anything he likes with Stone Solutions' "Defending American Minds" motto, but the true defense against empathy has always been here, on my island in Canada. We are the ones who contain the danger, and we are the ones who will figure out how to defeat it.

—EXCERPT FROM VICTOR NICHOLS' JOURNAL

"CODE RED. Code *red*."

Jamey had given Aisha's directions to Liam, and they'd flown over the Inside Passage ferry route before crossing an island to land on a lake maybe half a mile away from the mine that held Polaris.

They'd just touched down when Aisha's voice came crackling out of the plane's radio.

"I have to get to her." Jamey was already reaching for the .44 Magnum Grayson had given her back in November, leaning forward in her seat so she could wrap the holster around her waist.

Liam was bringing the plane across the lake's surface. There was no dock for them to taxi to; she'd have to be ready to leap. "I wish I could come," he said.

"Are you kidding? You're *vital,*" Jamey said. "We only have a shot here because you're our escape route. I've busted a lot of crooks and trust me: a crime is only as good as your getaway driver. Flyer."

"Why is it so hot when you talk like that?" Liam had the plane nearly up to the shore. "You got the flares? Send one up like a bat signal as soon as you need me; I'm not going to take my eyes off the sky."

Jamey kissed his cheek. When Liam had the plane close enough to the lake's edge, she opened the passenger door and braced herself. "Wish me luck."

"I'm going to tell you to be careful and come back safe with Aisha, that's what I'm going to do." Liam leaned over and kissed her, on the lips this time. "Give 'em hell, baby."

She smiled and then leapt for the shore. The mud was slippery, but she'd been ready for that and kept her feet, darting off into the tree line. She worked her way through the forest until she heard noises up ahead: a helicopter taking off; rotted wood and metal collapsing, voices.

But not just any voices. Screaming.

She slowed her steps, making them silent as she slipped through the trees. But with a plummeting stomach, Jamey thought she might know what she was hearing. Moments later, she could see them: at least ten people, some of them tearing at each other in a rage, way too much red on their faces.

Empath thralls.

But *here*?

Her eyes widened as they landed on familiar red hair. Shit, that was *Stensby* there in the group, yelling at the others. What the fuck was Stensby doing here?

She whirled around, putting her back to the tree and taking a silent breath. Okay. She was breaking into a top-secret empath prison to rescue her friend and doing it through a raging crowd of murderous empath thralls. All in a day's work. Apparently.

She patted her pocket, confirming she had the flare, and then pulled the Magnum out of its holster.

"Stay safe, Aisha," she whispered. "I'm coming."

Reece offered to watch for the secretary's return—probably still feeling guilty about accidentally using insight, which yeah, he ought to've felt guilty for approximately forever, so Grayson let him stand guard. As Reece watched the hall and elevators at the far end through the glass, Grayson popped the flash drive he'd found into the secretary's laptop. With any luck Marist had some kind of record of the oversized empath gloves that had gone to Keith Waller at the Seattle airsoft course.

But as Grayson scrolled through files, he didn't see anything that looked like production orders.

He did, however, see something that had no business being on anyone's flash drive, anywhere in the world.

"Evan?"

Grayson heard Reece as if from a distance as he opened the file.

"You went all quiet. Did you find something?" Reece had come up next to him. He blinked at the screen. "What's that?"

Memories began to rise. Grayson ignored them, flipping through pages in the document like he was reading a dictionary.

Reece was frowning. "I see some pictures, some words that don't make sense. Is that in code?"

"Abbreviations. Might as well be code if you don't know them." In his shoes right now, someone with emotions might have been screaming, Grayson distantly realized, as he calmly clicked through page after page, flicking away the memories before they formed like flies on a hot summer day. No one would need emotions to not be interested in reliving these particular moments.

"There are comments in some of the margins." Reece leaned in and read one out loud. *"'Now a perfectly engineered weapon for these predators.'"* His gaze turned flinty. "Someone with the initials *VN* wrote this. *N* for *Nichols*, as in the guy on Marist's wall? The one you don't want me asking questions about his research facility?"

He didn't wait for Grayson's answer, pointing to the reply to Nichols' comment. "*'The irony.'* That's from *HT*, who's that?"

"Holt Traynor, the Empath Initiative director." Grayson quickly clicked forward, before Reece could ask who *predators* referred to.

The next section of the file was older pictures, the West Texas landscape, a bunker underground, a room that had since been burned to ash.

"Is that a—dentist's office?" Reece's frown had deepened. "That's a weird chair. What's it for?"

Grayson immediately hit Back, away from the room, returning to the landscape. "Don't worry about it."

"Why would I worry about a chair?" Reece's gaze had gone to Grayson. "What am I really looking at?"

Grayson cleared his throat. "Aren't you supposed to be keeping watch?"

"What are you trying to distract me from now?" Reece said suspiciously. "What is this document?"

"Something I would never explain to an empath," Grayson said. "Which is why you're going back to your watch."

But Reece wasn't moving. "Evan, I am getting bad vibes from this," he said, pointing to the screen, and there was a new tightness to his voice. "And you're acting like you know what all this is, and I don't like that. I *really* don't like that."

He'd gone very tense, and Grayson could practically see his blood pressure ticking up. "I do know what this is," he admitted, trying for part of the truth that would calm Reece down.

"But it's fine. It's not like I have any feelings about those memories."

"Oh, I see," Reece said, and he sounded *more* upset, not less. "So this is bringing you the kind of memories other people would have feelings about? Should I guess what kind of feelings people normally have seeing creepy documents found on hidden flash drives in corrupt corporations?"

Well, shit. "Reece—"

Reece tapped the screen. "What is this? And what does it have to do with you?"

His eyes were on Grayson's face, and he wasn't flinching away from the lack of emotions. On the contrary, he'd gotten close enough that Grayson could feel the heat pouring off him.

Grayson shouldn't confide in an empath. But standing here, in Stone Solutions, reading a file annotated by the directors of the Empath Initiative and Polaris, the person Grayson trusted most was the partially corrupted empath who wanted to stay by his side.

"It's a broken instruction manual, more or less," Grayson confessed. "How to make a Dead Man."

Reece's eyes widened. "It's about *you*?"

Grayson glanced back at the screen, still showing the photo of the hidden entrance to a bunker in fuck-knew-where West Texas, where the sky went on for a million miles over red rocks and jackrabbits.

"You told me once that your brother was the one who made you the Dead Man," Reece said, not much more than a whisper. "You said he became corrupted. That you tried to get him help, but you asked the wrong people."

Grayson's gaze stayed on the photo. "There was a time when my empath brother was the sweetest, sunniest person I'd ever met," he heard himself say. "And then, one night when Alex was home from college, someone broke into our ranch and murdered our parents in front of him."

Reece didn't speak, just waited, big eyes on Grayson. Still not flinching.

"I was away, in Austin, and I'm pretty sure now the killer planned the strike for when I was gone, because they were trying for corruption on purpose," said Grayson. "But even still, I don't think they were prepared for what they unleashed. Alex was turned, exactly like Ms. Falcon, and a lot more people died before I could find him. And while I was looking, I talked to a pair of scientists who told me if I brought them my brother, they could use me to bring Alex back."

In the picture, the mountains on the horizon were rocky and red, a world away from the mist-draped green mountains outside Marist's skyscraper window. "A lie, it turned out. I just didn't know it then. Corruption is permanent, and all they wanted was to see if they could use me to make Alex even more powerful."

The sun was bright in the picture. There'd been no windows in the bunker, no way to see the outside world. "But those scientists weren't prepared for Alex either. I walked in there thinking I was going to save my brother and walked out unable to care that I hadn't."

"You're glossing over a whole lot there, Evan." Reece's voice had gone hoarse.

"You don't need the gory details. And you won't find them in this useless manual, because no one knows how Alex managed to destroy my emotions," Grayson said. "And no one ever will, because he's gone now."

The memories were threatening like a tidal wave now—the fire, Alex, the sound of the Magnum.

Grayson place his finger on the screen, over one of Nichols' annotations.

Completely emotionless.

Can do whatever needs to be done.

"Stone Solutions, the Empath Initiative, others—they came

looking for us. But they were too late. And when they found out what had happened, they created the Dead Man, because they all know the truth." Grayson looked at Reece. "That I'm capable of anything to defend people from corrupted empaths—that I made sure Alex was gone."

He expected Reece to flinch away from him. Expected to hear him make a sound of horror.

He wasn't expecting Reece to look him dead in the eyes and say, "Liar."

Grayson drew back. "What?"

"You're lying," Reece said. "I can't hear it, but I know it."

"But—"

"You want everyone to think you killed your brother, even me," Reece said. "I don't know what really happened in that bunker, or why you're lying, but save your breath; I know you better than that. You didn't do it."

Grayson stared at him.

Reece reached for the flash drive. "These fuckers can't be trusted with this. We're taking it with us."

"We?" Grayson put his hand on the desk, in between Reece and the flash drive, and Reece was forced to stop before they made contact.

"Move your hand, I'm taking that drive," Reece said.

"Did you just miss the part where I told you what was done to my brother?" Grayson said. "You think I'd let you set foot anywhere near the Dead Man's past?"

Reece's mouth pinched.

"In fact," said Grayson, "where you're standing right now is too damn close. Seattle is too damn close. You got a place in the south that you've always wanted to see? SoCal? Mexico?"

"Evan," Reece said warningly.

"I got a couple folks I trust," said Grayson. "We get you set up somewhere else—anywhere else—and then I'll take care of this."

"I'm not going down south." Reece stepped closer. "I'm not going anywhere."

Grayson had to tilt his head down so their eyes stayed aligned. "You said you'd go to a safe house. I'm just asking you to go a little early—and a lot farther away."

"And I'm telling you *no*," Reece shot back. "You said I wasn't your prisoner."

"You're not," said Grayson. "But that doesn't mean you're gonna come to all the awful places the Dead Man has to go."

Reece moved right into Grayson's personal space, close enough to raise a concern about accidentally making contact. His cheeks were flushed and his shoulders tense. "Try and stop me."

"Reece—"

"I will steal your truck again before I leave you to face whatever's going on here alone," Reece said tightly, and he didn't flinch, so he wasn't lying. He tilted his head back, looking up at Grayson. "Cedrick Stone was going to use Jamey to corrupt me all the way. He was going to do that by tor—by tor—" He broke the word off with an angry sound. "By hurting her in every terrible way he could think of. Is that what happened to you and your brother? Did they try to use *your* pain to make your brother more powerful?"

There was a muffled crash down the hall, like someone in another office had just thrown something against the wall.

Grayson took a breath. "Reece—"

"And these creeps put details in a fucking document, like you're some kind of lab experiment?" Reece demanded, pointing at the laptop, his bare hand coming dangerously close to brushing Grayson's arm.

Another crash, then another.

"I think you might need to take a couple deep breaths," Grayson said.

"Stop trying to distract me," Reece snapped. "What happened to you?"

In the hall, someone threw open their office door so hard it swung one hundred and eighty degrees to smash into the wall. With a shout, a petite redhead in sensible shoes and dress pants threw herself out of the office and at the door across the hall. A moment later, a man's yell split the floor.

Grayson's gaze flicked back to Reece. His dark brown eyes were glittery bright as he glared up at Grayson, his chin high and movements jerky. "It doesn't matter what happened," Grayson said. "I keep telling you, it's not worth getting angry over something done to a man without feelings."

"And I'm not listening." Reece's voice was darker, more gravelly than normal. "Because you're worth everything."

More yells were coming from down the hall. At the far end, the elevator doors were opening. "Reece," Grayson said, trying to keep his voice soft, "I think you're projecting your anger and setting off the floor."

Reece didn't seem to hear him. "The more you refuse to answer, the more I know I'm right," he said, too loud, as the four people who tumbled out of the elevator were already swinging at each other.

"Care Bear," Grayson said, and Reece finally blinked, finally looked at him and seemed to hear him. Grayson leaned down, holding his gaze. "You're starting a white-collar brawl."

"What?" Reece glanced out the windows and froze. "Oh shit." His face went from red to white and then back to red. "And I'm still pissed. I know you were hurt and I can't stop being furious."

Grayson grabbed his shirtsleeve. "Come on." He tugged Reece into moving. "Get behind me."

They stepped into the hall, and Grayson had to immediately dodge the coffee mug that came sailing his way.

"Shit," Reece swore again. His skin was mottled and sweaty. "I have to get under control. Oh, watch out!"

The petite redhead in the pantsuit was coming at Grayson, swinging a small purse that could probably barely bruise.

Meanwhile, three men from the elevator were heading straight for Reece, who wasn't moving and hadn't even seemed to notice them. Just a wide-eyed little lemming, completely oblivious to any danger to himself, breathing too hard and looking around in a panic.

Grayson dodged the woman's purse and stepped in front of Reece in one motion, throwing up a hand to block a punch from one of the men. Another man had grabbed a large potted plant off a marble-topped table and was bringing it around like an Olympic discus.

"Fire door," Grayson said, twisting to get his elbow in between the plant and Reece's head, so that the pot shattered against the edge of the table instead.

"Evan, your arm!" Reece said, without even looking at the ceramic pot that had barely missed his temple. "And this guy—sir, I am very angry right now, but if you hit me you might hurt yourself—"

"Reece, would you *stay put* for once, don't step any closer to him—"

The man swung the broken ceramic pot at another man at the same time someone else was swinging at the woman, and if Reece had to watch this much longer, he'd start hyperventilating.

Reece wouldn't be able to see pain on Grayson's face, though. He pivoted, putting himself between the men and taking the blow himself. Pain erupted across his right shoulder blade as the broken ceramic pot tore through his sweater, but he ignored it.

"Reece," he said loudly, "open that fire door and get your ass moving. We're getting you out of the building."

Reece swore but cooperated. As soon as he was through the door frame, Grayson stopped pulling punches. Two minutes later, the hall was littered with unconscious bodies and he was taking the steps down to catch up.

"So many stairs," Reece groaned, as they scrambled down twenty-odd flights.

"Be glad it's down, not up."

They finally hit the ground floor. Reece shouldered open the door and they stepped right into a packed lobby.

Every head turned in Reece's direction.

Chaos erupted.

"You're *still mad*?" Grayson said, as several people in various states of business casual began swinging at each other.

Reece winced. "I don't like exercise and it was a lot of stairs!"

Five office workers with coffee cups and bagels were approaching Reece and Grayson, fury in their eyes. Grayson reached into his jeans pocket. "Here."

Reece's eyes went wide as he caught what Grayson had just thrown at him. "These are your truck keys!"

"I'll handle the lobby." Grayson stepped in front of Reece, eyeing the oncoming horde. "Get the truck. *Be careful.*"

Reece was, mercifully, already running toward the front doors. Grayson pushed up his sleeves and dove into the fight.

CHAPTER TWENTY-SIX

...and now the whole team is asking for a giant grant for their proposed research on empath sexuality, which apparently will be titled "Empaths: The Modern-Day Incubus."

EI is NOT funding this.

—INTERNAL MEMORANDUM AT THE EMPATH INITIATIVE

"PSST. HEY. Pretty brainy tough chick. Can you open your eyes? I think I know you."

Aisha thought she knew that voice too. Her eyelids felt like lead, but she forced them to crack open.

She was on her side, maybe on a bed. Her glasses were digging into her face. Across from her was a big man, and she did know him. He bounced at McFeely's, and she'd met him a few weeks back on that wild November night, after Agent Nolan had discovered empaths could be corrupted and Grayson had needed a place to stash the agent until they figured out what to do with him.

"Diesel?" she said in confusion.

"I never got your name." Diesel's voice was thick, like he was fighting the same drugs she was. "But you don't forget a girl who brings you a bound and gagged FBI agent the first time you meet."

She huffed what might have been a laugh in less dire circumstances. "Aisha." She could see their surroundings now—looked like they were locked in one of the medical cells, like the one Cora had been in. "How are you here?"

"Group of men showed up at the club, didn't give me a choice," he said. "That was yesterday—or was it? They keep upping my sedatives, I've been out of it since we left Seattle."

"Shit." Aisha tried to move her head, but consciousness didn't want to come easy. "They grabbed you. Why?"

"Because I like empaths. That's what they said." Diesel sounded so lost and confused. "That guy with the glasses, Nichols—he said it's a hard quality to find in a marine." His arms flexed. "I've tried to get up," he said. "But even with the sedative, they've got me zip-tied to the bed."

"It's okay." Aisha had to hold on to hope that Jamey was coming. Jamey would never leave them here. "It's going to be okay; we'll make it out—"

An alarm split the laboratory, so loud Aisha flinched.

"Emergency," said the same flat feminine voice that was used through all of Stone Solutions' systems. *"There has been a security breach. Initiating lockdown mode."*

"Oh shit." Aisha tried to sit up, then flopped back down to the pillow. "Jamey."

"Jamey?" Diesel blinked. "As in Detective St. James? She's here?"

"She wanted to back me up." Aisha gritted her teeth. "God, I hope she's okay—"

Her words became a choked gasp of horror as Higgins suddenly appeared, stumbling into the glass wall like a bird smashing a windshield. He was covered in blood, his lab coat torn and stained.

Jamey hadn't done that.

"Higgins?" Aisha said hoarsely. "What the fuck?"

Higgins drew his head back. And then he smashed it into the glass, headbutting it so hard cracks splintered out across the cell.

"Jesus Christ," Diesel whispered.

Aisha swallowed. Some of the blood dripping off Higgins was his own, cuts visible on his neck and face. He drew his head back again, aiming for the glass, and she cringed, screwing her eyes shut. There was only one thing she could think of that would make a person attack themselves like that—

"Dr. Higgins," a new voice said, a tenor that was accented in a Texas drawl like Grayson's. "You're killing yourself too fast."

Aisha's eyes popped open.

A young man was leaning against the glass wall, and he didn't just sound like Grayson, he looked just like a shorter version of him, the same blond-brown hair and defined jawline. Aisha had seen a picture of him, long ago.

She felt the color drain out of her face. It couldn't be. But there was no mistaking Alex Grayson for anyone else.

"This facility has killed a lot of empaths and you've been an eager participant," Alex said to Higgins. "So I'm going to need you to draw your death out. Get creative with how you make yourself suffer."

"Yes, sir," Higgins said, and his tone was *eager.*

He scrambled off down the hall, out of their sight. On the bed across from her, Diesel was watching, expression like he was caught in a fever nightmare. Aisha took deep breaths through her nose as Alex approached the glass.

"You're not empaths," he said, in that Texas drawl, casual as if they were meeting at a party somewhere. "Who are you?"

"I'm a bouncer," said Diesel. "At an empath-themed club."

"Not the answer I was expecting," Alex said, eyebrows up. "But truthful. Interesting."

"Get the sense I shouldn't lie to you," Diesel said. "You give me that feeling, you know? Like when you see a scorpion or a black widow, the feeling that says *size is irrelevant, do not fuck with this thing.*"

"Smart," Alex said. "You're also trying to distract me and draw my attention so maybe I won't hurt anyone else. It won't work, but it's brave and chivalrous of you to try."

Aisha tried to swallow again around her dry throat. "He also used to be a marine," she said, nodding at Diesel. "I'm a doctor. But I do work for Stone Solutions."

"Also truthful," Alex said, nodding. "Two truth-tellers in here, I appreciate that."

"I'm not stupid enough to lie to a corrupted empath." She couldn't seem to stop the trembling in her voice, but then, he'd already be well aware of her fear. "I know who you are. You're Alex Grayson. And you're supposed to be dead."

His gaze swept over her, his eyes the same hazel as Grayson's behind the glasses. "The only way you'd know who I am is if you're involved in some morally questionable shit through Stone Solutions. But that's fine," he said calmly. "A lot of people like you are dying today. What's one more—"

"Not them," another voice cut in.

Aisha's gaze went to the end of the glass cell. Cora was standing there, dressed in a blue Polaris jumpsuit, her eyes on Alex.

Diesel was staring at Cora in bewilderment. "Cora?" he said, in full recognition, sounding shocked through the sedative. "The hospital said you'd left. Are you okay?"

The veterans' hospital, Aisha realized. Had Diesel been Cora's therapy patient, once upon a time?

Alex tilted his head at Cora. "The doctor works for Stone Solutions."

Cora looked at Diesel, then Aisha. Their eyes met for a split second, then Cora was looking back at Alex. "They both go free."

Alex looked at Aisha, and it was like being sized up by a tiger deciding whether to eat you. But then he stepped back, away from the glass. "Yes, ma'am."

"Cora," Aisha said.

"Detective St. James is here and she's almost reached this room," Cora said to Alex, not looking at Aisha. "My last fight with her didn't go well anyway; let her have these two."

Aisha tried to sit up. *"Cora!"*

But Cora and Alex had disappeared.

The tires screeched as Reece pulled the truck up in front of the high-rise, drawing looks from Vancouver pedestrians just as Grayson came sprinting out the high-rise's front doors. He jumped into the passenger seat and slammed the door so hard the truck rattled. "*Drive*, Reece."

Reece was already pulling away from the curb and back into the thick throng of downtown traffic.

Grayson shifted in the seat. "Did you just forget to use your turn signal?"

"I didn't *forget*." Honks erupted as Reece cut across three lanes to take the first turn. "I have other priorities."

Grayson's eyebrows went up. "It's the law in Canada too."

"You came barreling out of that building running from two dozen pissed-off office lackeys caught in my anger projection! Getting you away from all of them is my only concern right now."

Reece jammed his foot on the gas and darted through an opening in the traffic, missing a Skyline by inches as he whipped the truck into an alley. A minute later, they popped out onto the next street.

"Oh." Grayson didn't seem to know what to do with that. He sat back in the passenger seat, then immediately sat forward again. "Go straight at this light."

"I know where I'm going," said Reece. "Don't backseat drive."

"*How* do you know where you're going?"

"I looked at the city maps last night while you were sleeping."

Grayson turned to stare at him.

"It helps to be familiar with the roads when navigating a city." Reece barreled through a red light, ignoring the fresh honks as he ran the tires up onto the sidewalk to cut around a line of cars waiting to valet at a hotel. "You can pay more attention to traffic."

He took the next left, then reached down to the door. A moment later, there was a small chime.

"What did you just do to my truck?" Grayson said.

"Saved my seat position to your memory seats." Reece glanced over to find Grayson still staring him down. "Don't give me that look. I saved it to spot two."

"Oh, spot *two*, how considerate."

"Hey now," said Reece. "I think we can both agree that in this partnership, I own the sarcasm."

"Yeah? I own the *truck*."

"Just think of how much easier this will be for all the times that I'll be driving," Reece said breezily, ignoring that. "But make sure you put it back in position one next time you drive, because I think you're too tall to even get in the truck where I have it right now."

Grayson sat back, then immediately sat forward again, shifting to put more weight on his left shoulder. "Are you still angry?"

"No." Reece gave him a tentative smile. "I know the MPGs are bad, but damn, your truck is fun."

"All right," Grayson said, a little grudging. "Enjoy yourself."

Reece took them out of town and onto the highway. They drove in silence for some time, Grayson on his phone, flipping through screens, texting who knew what to who knew who as the city flew by. Eventually, high-rises gave way to smaller buildings and ungodly expensive houses. On their left, the bay was a choppy dark gray under pale gray clouds, the mountains rising out of the ocean into snowcapped peaks.

They passed a sign for a hiking trail, and Grayson suddenly seemed to realize they'd left downtown well behind. "Where exactly are you going?"

"North," Reece said. "There's a ferry terminal—I figured that was a good place to be while we plan our next step in the investigation."

"The investigation I said you weren't coming on," Grayson said.

"But then you handed me the truck keys," Reece said. "So I'm calling the shots now. I'm taking us to the ferry and I'm afraid you're just going to have to sit there and look pretty."

Grayson might not have feelings, but he sure could communicate the flattest looks Reece had ever seen.

"You're really good at looking pretty," Reece said sweetly.

Grayson sat back in his seat with some force. Then he immediately sat up again, and Reece thought he heard the smallest hiss of breath.

"Wait—are you hurt?"

Grayson shifted. "Define *hurt*."

"Jesus Christ, Evan." Reece put his turn signal on to move into the far-right lane.

"What're you doing?"

"What do you think I'm *doin'*? I'm looking for a place to pull over so I can see how badly you're injured."

Grayson huffed. "I'm sure it's fine—"

"No." Reece cut him off, holding up a warning finger. "Don't even think about trying that macho bullshit with me."

"But it's not worth you getting upset—"

"Stop telling me what you are and aren't worth," Reece snapped. "And I am an empath in a truck with a hurt person. I haven't *begun* to get upset."

"But, Reece—"

"Would you stop *arguing*? Just sit back, shut up, and let the empath show you some goddamn fucking empathy."

Grayson opened his mouth.

"Try me," Reece said warningly.

Grayson shut his mouth.

The road was curving, and Reece could see a small turnoff onto the forested mountainside. Under a Do Not Enter symbol, a sign read *Emergency Vehicles Only.* Reece took it without hesitation.

Grayson glanced around them. "We're not allowed on this road."

"You think I care about driving laws when you're hurt?"

"Empaths," Grayson muttered.

The service road backtracked south from the highway, through thick trees up the side of the mountain. There was a spur off the road, not quite a real shoulder but wide enough for a vehicle. Reece pulled into it and looked around, but there were no other cars to be seen. He put the truck in Park but left it running and the heat on as he turned to face Grayson. "Where are you hurt?"

"My back," Grayson grudgingly admitted.

Reece frowned. "Can you recline your seat a little? And twist?" He got up on his knees on the driver's seat as Grayson started moving, and then Reece caught sight of his shoulder. "Fuck."

"What?"

There were spots of dull red on the back of Grayson's sweater, soaked through the fabric.

Reece took a breath through his nose, his heart rate speeding up. "Blood." It came out too high, too tight, and he was lightheaded now. He winced. *"Fuck,"* he said again, clenching his jaw. "What kind of empath am I? I hate this about myself, I *hate* it. You're hurt, and you need help, and all I can do is panic about how much pain you're in when I need to do something about it—"

"Hey." Grayson flipped back around to face him, probably not-accidentally hiding the bloodstains again. "You're a good empath, that's the kind of empath you are."

"But other empaths can help with pain, can be therapists, can work in the ER—"

"Empaths are allowed to be different from each other, just like everyone else. They can have different ways of showing their—" Grayson cleared his throat "—goddamn fucking empathy."

Reece groaned, covering his face and finding his skin clammy with sweat under his bare hand.

"Care Bear, it's fine."

"It *isn't*," Reece said into his hand.

"I told you, your empathy is overwhelmingly strong," Grayson said. "It makes the anxiety worse. It's not your fault."

"And now you're injured but having to comfort *me*."

"I'm just gonna hop in the backseat for a moment." He could hear Grayson opening the glove box. "I got the first aid kit; I can take care of this cut and change my shirt so you don't have to see the blood. It'll take five minutes, tops."

Reece sat on his knees, miserably chewing on the tip of his thumb as he watched Grayson climb out of the passenger door and get in the truck's backseat, crawling across the long bench and into the more spacious area behind Reece's seat, which was admittedly much farther forward than the passenger seat Grayson had been sitting in.

He was definitely moving gingerly. How deep was he cut? He wasn't going to be able to adequately clean and bandage a wound on his back. It could get infected and Grayson would be in even more pain and it would be all Reece's fault for not having the goddam fucking empathy to be there the way Grayson needed him.

He pulled his thumb away from his teeth.

No. No, fuck that.

"Where're you going?" he heard Grayson ask, as Reece left the engine running for heat, and opened his door and jumped down from the driver's side.

Reece slammed the driver's door and walked around to the passenger side, then opened the backseat door. "I'm coming to help you."

Grayson had already stripped off his sweater and the T-shirt he'd had underneath. He still had them in hand, holding them against his left shoulder and that side of his bare chest in an awkward way.

Reece made a spinning motion with his hand. "Turn around."

"Reece—"

"Not even you can properly bandage up your own back," Reece said stubbornly. He took a breath. "I can do this."

He paused.

Grayson eyed him. "No flinch?"

"No lie." Reece's own chest immediately felt lighter. "I can do this, I really believe I can do this, I can help you," he said, relief flooding him. "Turn around."

Grayson's gaze lingered for a moment. Then he did turn around.

The late afternoon light through the truck's many windows was soft against Grayson's skin, lighting the jagged, bloody line that crossed his right shoulder blade. It was a mix of brown where the blood had dried and bright red where it still seeped from a wound. Reece took a breath, held it, and then blew it out. His blood pressure was high, but his stomach wasn't roiling and his head felt normal. He wasn't going to throw up or pass out.

"Is it bad?" Grayson asked.

"It's not *good*," said Reece. "But maybe if we bandage it up, you won't need stitches or anything." He reached out automatically, then paused at the sight of his own bare fingers. "I wish I could touch you," he said quietly. "I wish I could take your pain away."

Grayson glanced over his shoulder. "You're gonna handle this with a first aid kit instead of empathy. That's still gonna help."

"I hope so." Reece got the kit out of the bag, grabbing disinfecting wipes, antiseptic, and the biggest bandages. Then he pulled his gloves out of his own new backpack, because he wasn't going to be able to help Grayson if he couldn't touch him. "Relax your shoulders if you can."

Grayson finally lowered his hands to his lap, still holding his sweater.

Reece slipped his gloves on. His hands were unsteady as he tore open the packet for a wipe. "I know we have to do this part, but it's going to hurt you more."

"You already know I can't feel any fear about that," Grayson said. "And I'm not gonna flinch. Pretend you're cleaning a statue or something."

"A *statue*." Reece scoffed. "I'll admit you're sculpted like something out of ancient Rome, but I can feel your warmth from here. Hell, I can smell you."

Grayson glanced over his shoulder. "I didn't get that sweaty."

"Oh my God, you're so vain," said Reece. "You smell *good*. Really, *really* good. I just want to keep breathing you in," and okay, whoops, he probably shouldn't have let that last part slip out. "I'm just saying: stop trying to pretend you're anything but living. No statue smells like the hot guy in a cologne ad."

He shifted closer on the bench seat, until they were only maybe a foot apart. With Grayson turned sidewise on the seat so Reece could get to his back, his broad shoulders filled the small space. There was more blood seeping from the cut now, without the shirts to absorb it. Redder, and too vivid against the gray light.

Reece bit his lip. He needed to clean it, but his hands were still shaky and the alcohol in the disinfecting wipe was going to be painful. "Can I…" He hesitated.

"What do you need?"

Somewhere along the line, the emotionless drawl had definitely shifted from unsettling to reassuring. Reece swallowed hard. "This is going to sting. Can I just touch you, like normal touch you, for a moment? Before I have to hurt you?"

His voice was unsteady too, and maybe it was a weird request, but Grayson must have understood because he nodded. "Sure. If you got those gloves on, you can touch me however you want."

"Give a boy ideas, why don't you," Reece muttered under his breath. Grayson shifted slightly, and Reece *really* needed to remember that super-hearing.

He reached out and carefully ran his fingers over Grayson's shoulder blade, just above the gash. He traced up and across Grayson's shoulders, avoiding the cut as he watched the play of muscles beneath his hand.

No, he wasn't made of stone at all. Jesus, what Reece wouldn't do to feel the warm, soft skin under his bare fingers. There would be no emotions to feel, but he'd still be touching Grayson.

"Damn, Evan," he said, trying to keep his tone teasing. "You really aren't kidding about regularly lifting things that weigh a lot more than me, are you?"

"Nope."

Was it Reece's imagination, or had Grayson's voice changed? Tightened, just a little? Maybe Grayson couldn't feel the emotion of fear, but his body could still feel the physical sensation of pain, and Reece needed to get it together and take care of that cut.

He reached out, gently as he could, to clean the cut with the disinfecting wipe, his own shoulders so tense they hurt. It had to sting, but true to his word, Grayson didn't flinch. His steadiness helped Reece's blood pressure, his breathing slowing and evening out as he wiped away blood.

"It's not as bad as it looked," he said with relief. "At least, in my empath opinion, which is decidedly not a medical opinion. But the bleeding seems to be slowing." He spread antibiotic ointment on the gauze, then carefully put it over the cut, using the gentlest of pressure as he taped the gauze in place.

He leaned in close, running his fingers along the edges of the tape to make sure they were flat. "How's that feeling?"

"Fine."

Oh, Grayson's voice had definitely gone tighter.

Reece glanced up. Grayson's shoulders were tensed in a way they hadn't been before he'd treated the cut. "Did I do something wrong?"

"No."

That was clipped and strained even for Grayson. "Did I make it worse?" Reece said worriedly, running his fingers carefully over the area around the cut.

"No," said Grayson. "Cut's better. Good job."

"What *good job*? It's not a good job if you're still hurt!"

"I'm fine."

"You're *not*."

"I *am*. No reason to fret."

"Of course I'm *frettin'*," Reece said, hearing his own voice gone higher and more strained. "I've never seen you like this. Your voice is all stressed and you're completely tense—"

"Yes, sugar," Grayson said, slow and patronizing and still tense. "Because a real cute guy has his mouth right by my neck and his hands all over me. It's pretty much the opposite of hurt."

Oh, Reece's mouth formed. And then the corner of his lips turned up. "So the cut is okay? It's the—" he cleared his throat "—*real cute guy* who's the problem?"

"He's been a problem since we met," Grayson muttered.

"Mmm, sounds like he's a real dick," Reece said innocently.

"You talking about dicks isn't gonna help anything."

Reece's smile grew. He wasn't hurting Grayson, he was making him feel good, and that had heat blooming under his collar, spreading through him. Grayson's body was still taut, but now that Reece knew the cause, he could see what was really happening: muscles tensed not with pain but with anticipation; tiny shifts not away from his hands but toward them; skin not blanched but flushed.

That buzz of *want*, his permanent companion around Grayson, was growing, layered in his ears over the truck's engine.

Before he meant to, Reece skimmed his hand up to Grayson's shoulder, drawing a quiet but audible inhale. "I might be your problem but you're mine," he said softly, knowing the words would ghost over the back of Grayson's neck. "I can't get through a thought these days without you finding your way into it."

Grayson's head tilted almost imperceptibly, like he was welcoming Reece's breath across his skin.

"And you leaning into my touch isn't helping me pull my hands away," Reece said, his voice a little rougher, as he skated his fingers down Grayson's bicep. "It just makes me wish I could give you everything your body wants."

He got to see a small shiver run over Grayson. "Dangerous thing to say around an empath hunter, isn't it?"

"Is that what you are?" Reece said, with mock surprise, as he trailed his fingers back up Grayson's arm, nice and slow, muscle ridged under his gloves. "Funny how you can conveniently switch between specialist and hunter now."

"Funny how your lips keep getting closer to my ear."

Reece smiled again, this time sly. "Do they?" he said, light but pointed. "Or is it that *you* keep getting closer to my lips?"

He honestly wasn't sure who was moving closer to whom, or maybe they were being drawn together like magnets, or gravity.

"Does it matter?" Grayson said, barely a whisper. "We're gonna get the same result if we touch: you out cold, and me reminded why I need that weapon against you."

The truck was quiet except for the mingled sound of their breaths, and Reece became aware of the tic in his own jaw, the strain of keeping the scant remaining inches intact between his lips and Grayson's skin.

Inches that had to stay, because there were a million reasons they couldn't be crossed.

Reece swallowed and forced himself to take his hands off Grayson and pull back. "I'm going to let you turn around."

Grayson took another audible breath and then nodded.

Reece made enough room for him to move, sitting on his heels as Grayson turned. Grayson rested against the door, facing Reece and backlit by the fogged window. There was a pink flush to his cheeks, hazel eyes bright and focused on Reece. The sweater seemed forgotten in Grayson's hand and his chest was bare, flushed like his face, and before Reece could stop them, his eyes had followed the planes of his chest down the line of his abs to his jeans, where Reece could see exactly the impact his words and touch had had on Grayson.

"Oh no," Reece said weakly. "This is worse."

Grayson opened his mouth.

"Don't talk," Reece ordered, forcing his gaze back up to golden hazel eyes. "If you open your mouth and you sound half as wrecked as I feel, I will lose it."

"I gotta talk," Grayson said, and *fuck*, he did sound wrecked. "I gotta talk some sense into you. The title of Reece's Worst Decision has got some stiff competition, but pretty sure this moment right here would win."

Reece tried to shake off the shivers Grayson's deep voice had left on his skin. "You're not a bad decision," he said, his own voice deeper too. "And I'm not flinching when I say that, because I'm *not* lying."

"You believing it doesn't make it true. Doesn't make me good for you." Grayson sounded unsteady. His breaths seemed to be coming faster than normal. "I'm way too dangerous, Reece."

"But I'm dangerous too." Reece barely recognized the sound of his own voice. "Could get more dangerous at any moment. At least you look like what you are. People think empaths are sheep, but you know you and I are both wolves."

As he spoke, Reece's gaze again swept over the addictive view of Grayson spread out and shirtless. Grayson's hand twitched, the one holding the sweater, a tiny movement but like he'd suddenly remembered something. Reece's gaze darted in the direction the movement would have gone—and he abruptly realized why Grayson had originally had his sweater pressed against his left shoulder, what he'd been hiding before.

"Oh my God."

Reece was reaching out before he could stop himself. Grayson quickly and gracefully shifted, stretching one long leg out along the floor and the other against the backrest so Reece fit on the narrow bit of seat between them, safely boxed into the space made by Grayson's legs as he leaned forward.

"This is from the bullet, isn't it? The one you took for me, at the Seattle marina, to stop me from seeing the death when the snipers killed FBI Agent Nolan." Reece touched the round scar with gloved fingers, light as he could. "Why the hell were you hiding this?"

"Reece," Grayson said thickly, "I know your empath feelings are getting riled—"

"You're damn right my feelings are *gettin' riled*."

"—but I don't think you understand just how hard having your hands on me makes it to keep *my* hands to myself—"

"Don't change the subject."

"Who's *changing the subject*? You're between my legs, leaning over my dick, and trust me, I don't need emotions for any of the things you're making me want—"

"You're trying to distract me, and A for effort, but I need an answer." Reece looked up, meeting his eyes. "Why were you hiding this scar from me?"

After a moment, Grayson was the one to look away. "That night was rough for you. A lot of violence and bad discoveries. I didn't want to make you remember it."

"Evan." Reece's fingers were unsteady where they rested against the scar. "You think I could ever forget what you did?"

"Considering it was minutes after I had cuffs on you—"

"Don't try to shrug this off like it's no big deal when it's the biggest deal," Reece said heatedly. "You got this scar protecting me from corruption. You *took a bullet for me.*"

"You believed saving my life was worth more than your freedom." Grayson's soft, deep drawl carried through the truck. "A bullet was more than worth a chance to save your heart."

Reece's hand was trembling now. "And you say I make bad decisions," he said hoarsely.

Grayson met his eyes again, and for a split second Reece could almost imagine he'd seen a flash of courage and steel, a glimpse of the man Grayson had once been. "That wasn't a bad decision."

"Neither is this." Reece put both his hands on Grayson's chest. "Neither are *you.*"

Grayson's arms twitched, like he'd had to stop himself from putting them around Reece. He could feel Grayson's heartbeat, strong beneath his hand. His own body was burning hotter and higher, heat rolling out from Reece's core through his limbs. His empathy was waking up too, the temptation of another person's pleasure too much to resist.

Reece shifted, just that little bit closer. "Did you notice we're fogging the windows?"

"*You're* fogging the windows," Grayson said. "You got any idea what it's like to have all your empath body heat this close?"

"Why don't you tell me?" Reece leaned in to brace himself on Grayson's chest with light pressure. "In fact, why don't you tell me again how hard I'm making it to keep your hands to yourself?"

Grayson swallowed something that might have been a groan. "I already told you my dick doesn't need emotions to want you," he said, low and gravelly. "But try to remember that only one of us is gonna get knocked out if we touch each other."

"True." Reece leaned forward an inch. "But try to remember that only one of us is wearing gloves that let him touch the other."

Grayson's mouth snapped shut.

"That's right, *sugar.*" Reece held up one hand. "You can't touch. But I can."

Grayson was staring at his hand. "But you're gloved. What would an empath get out of that?"

"Don't tell me you already forgot." Reece put his hand back on Grayson's chest, anticipation already threading through him, his own jeans uncomfortably tight. "I get to make you feel good. It's only literally what my empath fantasies are made of."

Grayson seemed to be recalculating everything he'd ever known about empaths. He arched, a small movement, but then, he didn't exactly have much room to move with Reece between his legs. "And I'm supposed to—what, exactly?" He looked up. "Just lie here and let you drive?"

Reece leaned in, bringing their faces closer, still braced against Grayson. "I'm a really good driver," he said, dropping his hand three suggestive inches lower, onto his stomach and closer to the hard outline filling his jeans.

Grayson's Adam's apple bobbed as he swallowed, his gaze flicking over Reece's face. "Care Bear, your eyes."

Reece could guess his pupils were huge, over-dilated, as if they could take in every bit of Grayson like light. "Haven't you seen plenty of empath eyes when the empathy kicks in?"

"Yeah," Grayson whispered. "But never like this."

"Like what?" Reece let his hand drop one more inch. "Like one of us is losing his mind thinking of all the ways he's going to take you apart?"

Grayson's eyes had gone softer, his gaze on Reece through blond lashes, and the flush on his face had deepened. His chest rose and fell under Reece's hand with every breath. "Your eyes are pretty," he said, like a whispered confession. "But tell your empathy it's wasted on me. There's nothing to feel."

Reece leaned in even more, bringing their lips so close together he could imagine the taste of Grayson's mouth. "How about you let the empath worry about the feelings?"

He felt the ripple in the air as Grayson shivered, and a fresh bolt of desire wove through Reece. He skated his hand down Grayson's stomach, coming to rest on the waistband of his jeans, and felt Grayson shift again beneath him.

"How about you just focus on letting me make you *feel* good?" he whispered. "Better yet, let me make you feel the best you've ever felt in your damn life. Let me burn this truck up finding every little touch that makes your body pant and sweat."

"I wish I could kiss you."

Grayson's breathy words danced over Reece's lips as Grayson drew back an inch, like he had surprised himself by saying that.

Reece shifted so his mouth was close to Grayson's ear instead. "I bet your kiss is addictive," he whispered, moving his hands to the button on Grayson's jeans. "Bet you're unbelievable in bed. Bet you show off your strength, give people the night of their lives."

He popped open the button and Grayson arched, small and constrained so their bodies didn't touch beyond Reece's hand. "Bet you know how to use this," Reece said into his ear, as he inched the zipper down. Grayson grunted in the back of his throat as Reece's gloved hand dragged over his hard cock on top of the fabric. "And I was right; it's *big*."

"I'm *six-five*." Grayson's voice was unsteady. "And remember who's not six-five in this truck."

"Stop threatening me with good times." Reece slipped his hand into the open zipper, wrapping gloved fingers around

Grayson over whatever briefs or boxers he had on, and the choked-off moan that filled the truck went straight into his bloodstream. "Jesus, the way you'd look with me on your dick. It'd be so fucking tight; I'd make you feel so fucking good you couldn't talk."

Grayson's head fell back against the fogged truck window. "Is this empath dirty talk?"

Reece's lips curved up. "Damn right it is."

He lifted his hand just long enough to shove it back down under the elastic band, closing fingers around Grayson's hard cock. Grayson made the most amazing noise, relief and pleasure and want all wrapped into one.

"This is not a sanctioned use of empath gloves," Grayson said, his voice cracking.

"I knew something was missing from the owner's manual."

Reece ran his fist loosely along his shaft. Grayson made that noise again, and Reece wanted more, more noises, more shivers, more pleasure.

He shifted back on his heels enough that he could watch Grayson's face, and began to stroke—tighter, slower, tailoring every motion to the symphony of Grayson's reactions. He didn't need emotions; he could follow the map in the sounds from Grayson's mouth, the flush on his cheeks and the fluttering of his lashes, the parting of his lips and the panting of his breath.

He would have given anything to touch him skin-to-skin, to crawl inside him and drink him in. But he wouldn't have given this up for the world.

Outside the truck, a blue-gray twilight was falling, the impressions of white snow and evergreens beyond the fogged windows fading into the evening. There was the hum of other cars zipping along the highway beyond the trees and the truck's engine was rumbling still, deep vibrations through the cozy cab, this space they'd carved out for the two of them.

Grayson arched, just an inch, and Reece moved with him,

speeding up and watching his eyes squeeze shut, his muscles flex with pleasure.

"You're close, aren't you?" Reece whispered, and Grayson groaned. "Fuck, I could come just from watching and listening to you."

Grayson tilted his head, eyes still tightly closed. "More empath dirty talk."

"Yeah, but it wasn't a lie."

"Maybe not." Grayson opened his eyes. "But I got another idea."

And Reece's world was suddenly spinning as Grayson grabbed him by gloved wrists and tumbled him over. Reece's back hit the bench seat, hands pinned above his head, and then Grayson was balanced over him, big and warm and close.

"Wha—" Reece started helplessly, his brain still buzzing from the manhandling and the closeness.

Grayson let his hands go, and then a moment later, something stroked firmly over his dick.

Reece sucked in a breath as pleasure ricocheted through him and he arched up automatically into the touch. "Holy shit," he panted, looking down his body. "How—"

"Your empath gloves are made with heavy metals. And here we got a metal zipper." Grayson ran his thumb up Reece's hard length again, tracing the zipper, and Reece groaned. His hands scrabbled uselessly against the backseat as Grayson did it again, and again.

Then Grayson was undoing Reece's jeans with surgical precision, inching the zipper down without ever touching his skin. "Give me your hand."

"Why—"

Grayson reached for Reece's gloved hand, covering it with his own bigger one, and lifted their hands together. "'Cause I'm driving now."

And then he was wrapping Reece's hand, still enclosed in Grayson's, around his own dick.

"Fuck." Reece's curse rattled off the truck's windows. "Are you jerking me off with *my own hand*?"

"Mine is never gonna fit in your gloves. Consider this stealing your keys. So to speak."

Grayson used his grip on Reece's hand to move them both, stroking over Reece's cock, and Reece's eyes rolled back. "Holy shit," he said, panting. "You didn't have to—I really would've—"

"I know," said Grayson. "Empaths are such givers. And I bet plenty of folks are happy to just take, but you deserve someone who gives right back to you."

That hit Reece right in the chest. "But—"

"And this is plenty self-serving." Grayson kept up the pace, controlling Reece's gloved hand, and fuck, it was *good*. "You think I'm not aching for you too? Does that empath brain need to hear that touching you makes my dick harder?"

Reece groaned, because maybe he had needed to hear it, and all of it together, from Grayson, made his blood feel like fire.

He fumbled with his free hand until he found Grayson's dick again. "Fuck," Grayson breathed, his hand stuttering where it was wrapped around Reece's, because Reece was completely undoing him and that thought launched Reece precariously close to the edge.

"Swearing?" Reece said, breathing hard as they found a rhythm together. "Where'd your Southern manners go?"

"Hell if I know." Grayson's hand sped up, and Reece helplessly arched so far off the bench seat that Grayson had to shift so they didn't make contact.

"Oh my God, how are we not going to touch?" Reece said, his voice raw. "I want to kiss you stupid, I want to ride your dick, like fuck, you have no idea how bad I want you."

"I promise I've got some idea."

Grayson looked more wrecked than Reece had ever seen

him, adjusting his knee between Reece's legs on the seat so not even their jeans brushed. He leaned down, filling every inch of Reece's vision with that broad chest and shoulders, with his flushed face, damp hair sticking to his forehead, hazel eyes gone deep and shiny.

"I can't believe I ever thought it was hard to look at you," Reece said, and he might have been babbling. "I can't get enough now, can't stop looking."

Grayson's face was right by his, their lips an inch apart, breathing each other's air even while they couldn't touch. "I can practically taste that empathy, the way it's pouring off you."

It was; Reece could feel it escaping him, stronger than it had ever been before, and he couldn't have reined it in for anything. "I can't stop it—"

"You don't have to. You can let it go, with me," Grayson said, and as that spiraled Reece's emotions higher, inseparable from the pleasure in his body, he added, "Better hope no one else walks by, though. We ever do this in a city, you're gonna cause a population boom all by yourself."

Reece did laugh this time, and how could this person with no emotions make him this happy, make him feel this damn good?

"If we could touch, I'd fucking climb into you, lose my goddamn self, it'd be heaven." Reece's mouth was just spilling at this point, too overwhelmed by the closeness and the fire building in his stomach to hold anything back. "I want you so damn much. I'd let you call me Care Bear forever."

Grayson made some kind of sound, not an emotion, but something with an edge Reece hadn't heard before. "Reece—"

"Let me make you come," Reece begged. "Let me watch while you're touching me, please—Evan, please—"

Grayson twitched, and their lips came so close to brushing that Reece might have actually gotten lightheaded. And then Grayson was coming, body stiffening, and maybe it wasn't an emotion but that was *bliss* on his face, Reece could fucking *see* it—

It was too much. Reece tipped over the edge too, swept up into the undertow of the best orgasm of his life. The truck's cab blurred then disappeared, and for a moment, he was lost to the flood of pleasure that took over.

He came back to himself to find Grayson still hovering over him, barely inches between them, flushed and sweaty and stunning. And when he spoke, his drawl was the softest rumble, a caress of its own.

"You staying with me, Care Bear?"

And Reece was living moments in duplicate, the words the same ones Grayson had once said to anchor him after a panic attack, now an even sweeter anchor, and Grayson didn't have emotions but he somehow still had compassion, and it made him the most beautiful thing Reece had ever seen.

"Fuck it," Reece said out loud, and kissed him.

Time stopped. Grayson's lips were soft, and so warm, sweet like lip balm with a faint hint of salt from sweat, and he was *kissing Reece back.*

And Reece's empathy completely leapt from any semblance of control, lunging for Grayson like Reece could somehow read him with his lips, like it was ready to smash through any wall in its path to get to Grayson's heart—

And then everything was black.

CHAPTER TWENTY-SEVEN

...for the first time in history, there will be a shield against these creatures who wield emotions like weapons. The Dead Man is, as his moniker implies, dead inside, and the change appears to be as permanent as corruption itself.

—NOTE FOUND AT [REDACTED], TEXAS

GRAYSON'S BRAIN CAME scrambling back online too late, catching up with his lips just as he felt Reece's mouth go slack and slip away.

He stared down at Reece, whose eyes were now closed, his head lolled against the backseat of the truck cab.

"Did you just—" Grayson cut himself off. Reece couldn't hear him and it was a stupid question in the first place, because obviously he *had* just knocked himself out by kissing Grayson.

Oh, but they'd just done plenty more than kiss. Done enough that Grayson's head was still fuzzy and spinning. It *was* his head, wasn't it? Or was it his heart, beating too fast? Adrenaline or the afterglow, maybe, still thrumming through him.

Reece's face was relaxed, unusually vulnerable, his grumpy outer shell gone so that he looked every inch the gentle empath he was inside. His lips seemed extra soft without their perpetual frown. Grayson licked his own lips without meaning to, unexpectedly sweet, because of course Reece tasted like the sugar he loved.

"Care Bear—" He cut himself off again, half because talking to an unconscious Reece was pointless, half because he'd been distracted by Reece's hair where it was damp against his forehead. Grayson had made him sweat. The thought sent a ripple of want over him, a spark compared to the fire that'd been burning moments ago, but with the potential to become a conflagration all over again.

He shook his head to clear the thought, trying to focus. Why was he dizzy still? There was no time for that. He needed to clean up, needed to figure out next steps. He wasn't going to think about how easy it would be to dip his head and brush his lips over Reece's cheek or temple, where his skin would be warm and silky. Definitely wasn't going to let himself get anywhere near Reece's lips again.

This wasn't a fairy tale—or if it was, Grayson wasn't the prince who'd wake up Sleeping Beauty; he was the poison apple who'd cast the spell.

"I *am* gonna call you Care Bear forever," Grayson informed him, Reece's words caught in his memories like a photograph. "You're gonna be Bad Decisions Bear for life."

But Grayson had made the same bad decisions, hadn't he? Let his body take over, found a way to touch Reece, had kissed him back. Still wanted to kiss him, even now. Wanted to stretch out on the backseat and pull Reece all the way on top of him, wrap arms around him and let himself doze off.

Maybe if Grayson held him long enough, Reece would get used to the touch and he'd wake back up, and they could run away together to the safe house on Salt Spring Island, just the two of them, and forget the rest of the world.

He blinked.

What memory had caused *that* thought? Grayson had slept with plenty of people, but it had always been casual. A lot of people wanted his size and strength in bed, but even before he'd been the Dead Man, he'd been too different from anyone else to ever find someone who'd want him long-term. There'd never been anyone serious, someone he could run away with.

How had his mind come up with a memory able to influence him into a thought like that?

He shook his head again. No point in even answering that question because it was out of the question. Being able to knock an empath out with his touch was one of the Dead Man's weapons. Grayson could not risk losing it when it came to Reece.

And right now, he needed to handle this situation. Get them back on the road. Pull on a shirt without bloodstains.

Find a towel.

And probably burn Reece's gloves.

A few minutes later, the backseat held no signs of their moments together, and Grayson had the passenger door open. He leaned through the door frame, awkwardly reaching in to get his arms under Reece's knees and upper back. He lifted him off the seat, bridal style this time, and pulled him out of the truck's backseat.

Snow had started to fall again, tiny spots of cold on the back of Grayson's neck, the big, soft flakes catching in Reece's dark hair. An occasional car could be heard on the highway, but the forest's edge was quiet, and everything was cold and wet, but Reece was warm and the air was clean and bright, the scents of ocean and snow mixing with cedar and pine.

He set Reece carefully on the passenger seat, just as he had the day before. As he bent over to buckle him in, his gaze stole to Reece's face again.

Maybe in another universe, Grayson wasn't the Dead Man, and people left empaths the hell alone. Maybe in that universe, he'd be capable of being what someone like Reece deserved, and their moment in the truck would become more than a memory that occasionally surfaced—it would be the start of something amazing. Maybe in another universe, Grayson was still capable of happiness.

Because none of that was true in this one.

He straightened up and shut the passenger door. But as he climbed into the driver's seat, his phone began to ring. He closed his own door and picked it up from the console to see *Holt Traynor* on the caller ID.

Grayson palmed the phone for a moment, then answered. "Grayson."

"Why didn't you tell anyone you were going to Vancouver?"

So EI had figured out where he was. Stone Solutions probably knew by now too. He cleared his throat. "Director—"

"Someone took a picture of you at the auto show and posted it publicly on *Eyes on Empaths*. Apparently you have *fans*," Traynor said, with an edge. "Unacceptably careless, Evan. You're a classified weapon; you know full well there should be no pictures of you."

The snowflakes were landing on the windshield and hood, melting away into water.

"I don't know if you were involved in the fight that broke out in the Stone Solutions Canada building today and got everyone sent home," Traynor went on, "but those questions are going to have to wait. We have a situation."

"What kind of situation?"

"The kind where we need Agent Grayson to be the goddamn Dead Man."

Grayson sat back against the driver's seat. "What are you—"

"Your brother is alive."

Grayson blinked.

"Your brother, Alex Grayson, one of the deadliest corrupted empaths we have on record, is alive," Traynor repeated. "You said you pulled the trigger. You assured us he was dead."

Grayson watched the snow fall for a long moment. "I guess I was mistaken," he finally said.

"I guess you were," Traynor said tightly. "Alex Grayson has thralled a police officer and an ex–army major. He set a fire at Stone Solutions. He's responsible for multiple murders in Seattle, and if reports are to be believed, he's just getting started. The entire city is in danger, so I repeat: Are you ready to be the Dead Man?"

Grayson's gaze darted to Reece, then back to the windshield. "Yes, sir. Tell me what I need to know."

Jamey hadn't counted on breaking into Polaris at the same time the place was crawling with empath thralls, but at least she didn't have to worry about stealth.

The empath thralls out front had been raging at each other, letting her sneak past to the mine's entrance. The front door must normally be formidable, but it had been wide-open, the thralled scientists apparently rolling out the welcome mat before turning the forest into a cage match.

Had Cora escaped and done all of this? One of the other empaths, perhaps?

Back in Prince Rupert, Aisha had drawn a rough map of Polaris from memory and given it to Jamey. She followed it now, making her way across what looked like a lobby of sorts. It was empty, but bloody footprints tracked across the carpets in several directions.

There was a door at the back, and this one was closed. Blood was smeared on the handle. Jamey held the Magnum at the ready, then smashed the door with her booted foot, hard enough that it flew off its hinges.

The small room behind the door was also empty, save for a desk at the far end, where the corpse of a woman in a bloody lab coat was sprawled unmoving, her eyes staring blankly at nothing. A pink lanyard was draped around her neck with a card on it like a pendant.

Jamey winced, but she couldn't afford to be squeamish. She stepped forward, and gingerly pulled the swipe card off the woman's body.

Jamey.

Jamey straightened. That wasn't an empath thrall screeching with lethal levels of rage. She strained her ears, trying to pick out the words.

Jamey, are you here—Jamey—

It was coming from beneath her feet. Jamey darted out of the room and found stairs tucked back in a short hall off the lobby. She shouldered the door open, sprinting down to the next sublevel and kicking open that door too, gun at the ready.

"Jamey!"

"We're down here!"

Aisha and—was that *Diesel*? The McFeely's bouncer?

"I'm coming!" she called back. She sprinted forward and nearly slipped when her boot skidded in liquid. Oh, she wasn't going to look at the floor, no sir, didn't need to see what she'd just slipped in, she could guess just fine.

At the far end of the hall was a cell with glass walls. The glass had splintered like a windshield struck with a giant rock, except there was red threaded through the cracks and Jesus, whatever empath was behind this house of horrors was not fucking around.

But behind the glass were two beds, and Jamey's breath left her in a rush of bone-deep thankfulness to see Aisha, alive, and Diesel in the other bed.

"Jamey." Aisha looked like she might cry from relief. Her ponytail was a mess where it was wedged against the pillow, her eyes glazed behind crooked glasses. She looked secured to the bed by zip ties, an IV in her arm.

"St. James, thank God." Diesel also looked drugged to the gills, skin glistening with sweat, similarly restrained and hooked up to an IV. "Can you get me loose? I can help you."

"I don't think either of you is going to be in shape to do much of anything but stumble around," Jamey said grimly, "but we'll work with it."

A scanner stood just off to the side, and Jamey tried the swipe card. A moment later, the door beeped and sluggishly slid open.

"Jamey," Aisha said again.

"Hey, doctor," Jamey said, pushing Aisha's glasses into place as she leaned over the bed to get her loose. "You know what they gave you in these IVs?"

"Expensive shit," Aisha said, sounding hazy. "Gonna take a while to burn off. But, Jamey, the empaths who lived here. They're gone."

Jamey cursed as she snapped the tie on Aisha's closest wrist. "Escaped?"

"Dead." Aisha shook her head despairingly. "Even Marie and her sister."

"But this place is crawling with empath thralls." Jamey yanked the tie off Aisha's other wrist. "Who made them?"

"Cora," Aisha said. "And Alex."

"*Alex?* As in Alex *Grayson*?" Jamey raised her eyes heavenward. "Evan told me he was dead. Hell of a mistake to make."

"Alex must have come to find the empaths but only Cora was left." Aisha met her eyes. "They were here. Alex and Cora. They spared us."

They'd what? Jamey had questions, but they'd have to wait; Aisha sounded like she was still half-under. Aisha was already reaching for her own IV to pull it out, and Jamey quickly stepped over to Diesel's bed and his bound ankle.

"Did you just—rip that zip tie off? With your bare hands?" Diesel said, his voice thick but shocked. "Goddamn, St. James," he added, with admiration. "What do you do on arm day?"

Jamey snorted. "I'll tell you, assuming we get out of here. Let's find a place I can set off my bat signal and just pray the empaths leave us alone."

CHAPTER TWENTY-EIGHT

Sugar and spice and everything vice: we keep telling you it's what empaths are made of.

Maybe it's time for more folks to learn it for themselves.

—A.G., UNTITLED BLOG

THE SNOW WAS falling in bigger flakes that melted as soon as they hit the asphalt. At a small gas station off the highway, Grayson sat in the driver's seat, waiting for the truck to fill at one of the two pumps. Vivian Marist had been the one to send him a video clip from the Leviathan Hotel. He'd watched it three times, but there was no mistaking it.

It was Alex, with his arm around Gretel Macy, winking at the camera.

This was probably another moment where someone with emotions might be having a lot of them.

Grayson went back to his messages, to the confirmation that a boat would be waiting for him about twenty minutes north. Still no response from Detective St. James or Dr. Easterby about meeting Reece at the safe house, but he'd give them a few more minutes.

It was for the best. Director Traynor and Vivian Marist might not have figured out yet what Alex had wanted with Officer Stensby or where he'd gone from Stone Solutions, but if Grayson's theory about corrupted empaths seeking each other out was right, then Grayson knew what Alex had wanted and where he'd gone.

Polaris.

Grayson would need to head straight there, and Reece absolutely could not come.

He'd just driven out of the gas station, heading for the highway, when there was a soft rustle from the passenger seat. Reece was stirring.

Grayson looked at the truck's clock, which confirmed what he'd already suspected. He set the phone in the console. "Look who's waking up."

Reece made a grunt, then opened his eyes. He turned in Grayson's direction, a small smile just visible in the streetlights. "Hey, sugar."

"Being cute isn't gonna get you out of trouble. You know what you did."

"Oh, come on, it's kind of funny," said Reece. "You're like a reverse Prince Charming—your kiss puts the princess to sleep."

"*My* kiss? You remember who kissed who, don't you? You used my lips to knock yourself out and I should've left you unbuckled in the back."

"Way harsh, Evan." Reece's tone was warm, and his eyes were still softer than usual. "So we're not going to make it awkward?"

"That would require me to be capable of feeling awkward. So no. Doesn't mean I'm not gonna chew you out for pulling yet another stunt like this."

Reece only smiled softly. "Worth it."

"Empaths," Grayson muttered.

"I'm not fucking kidding. Hours of unconsciousness is a tiny price to pay for a kiss." Reece glanced at the truck clock and blinked.

Grayson looked back out the front windshield. He didn't need to spell it out. Reece was coming to the same realization.

"Except I wasn't unconscious for hours," Reece said slowly, sitting up and bringing the seat with him. "It hasn't been much more than an hour, has it? Just like the time I was out yesterday afternoon was shorter than that first night."

Grayson nodded once, and turned the wipers on to brush the snow away.

"Your touch isn't knocking me out for as long," Reece said. "I'm getting used to it, like I got used to your voice."

"You were right, back in Seattle." *You're right so much more than you give yourself credit for,* Grayson didn't add. "I refused to put an empath through the testing. I didn't know if it was possible for me to ever touch an empath without knocking them out."

"But it seems like it might be."

Grayson glanced at him, then back at the windshield. "Seems like it."

The truck was silent for a moment, a silence that turned weighty and sad.

"Well, fuck," Reece finally said, his voice thick. "I'm too close to corruption and it's not fair to millions of people if I take away one of your weapons against me. I can't ever touch you again."

Grayson turned on his wipers to flick away the snowflakes as they landed. He would've liked to haul Reece right into his lap, or take him away somewhere where they could lock themselves in until they could touch. But it was never going to be an option for them.

Reece rubbed a hand over his face. "You already figured this out, didn't you?"

"Yeah." Grayson shifted, feeling the pressure of the seat against the cut on his shoulder blade that Reece had so carefully treated. "But for what it's worth, you sure can kiss."

A bittersweet smile played on Reece's lips. "Back at you."

They were quiet for another long moment, in the dark cab

of the truck as the snowflakes still fell all around them. Even the road they were on seemed empty, only the occasional engine of another car braving the weather.

Reece finally let out a long sigh. "Where are we?"

"A little bit north of the Horseshoe Bay ferry." Grayson picked up his phone. "Also, I got some other news. Alex is alive."

Reece stared at him.

Grayson probably could have broken that more gently.

"Your brother is alive?"

Grayson handed him the phone. Reece watched the clip in silence, his eyes huge. "That's your brother. That is definitely your brother, he looks just like you. He's alive. Jesus. Are you okay?"

"Obviously," Grayson said. "I'm not gonna have feelings about it. I'm not gonna have feelings about anything, Reece. Don't look for them."

Reece jerked his head up. "Maybe not," he said, more tightly. "But I was right. You didn't kill him. You lied to everyone when you told them you did."

Outside the truck, the night sky was black-and-white. Grayson's memories were blue, like the West Texas sky, red like sunlit peaks on stone mountains. Red like fire.

"You were right. I didn't kill Alex," he said, and it sounded like a confession.

"What really happened?" Reece asked quietly.

Grayson watched the road pass under his headlights, more of the same thousands upon thousands of solitary miles he'd driven since that day he'd been changed into the Dead Man. "Alex and I were taken to a bunker somewhere out in West Texas. To this day I don't know exactly where it was. The people who took us said my pain was going to bring my real brother back, but Alex said they were lying, that they only wanted to use me to see how powerful they could make him, and then they'd kill us both."

"Evan." Reece's voice was so gentle—not a hint of Grumpy

Bear right then, just Tenderheart Bear through and through. "I'm so sorry."

"Don't waste your sympathy on me," Grayson said. "I don't feel sorrow. I don't feel regret. I don't feel anything." He moved into the left lane, passed a car. "Alex said he thought he could make me even stronger, strong enough to break us out, but it'd mean trading my emotions away. And I said yes."

"You let him make you the Dead Man?" Reece whispered.

"*He* wasn't lying," Grayson said. "And it was my fault we were in that bunker. The change worked, and I got us free, but I hadn't counted on Alex turning around and lighting the whole place up, thralling every last person in that bunker. In hindsight I should've—corrupted empaths don't really turn the other cheek."

The sound of the truck's engine was deep and the night was cold, but Grayson's memories still held the bunker's high-pitched screams and fire's heat. "Outside the bunker, Alex could feel it when the Empath Initiative and Stone Solutions showed up to rescue us, and he was laughing, because it meant dozens of new people for him to thrall. I knew Alex was still dangerous, still corrupted, and I needed to stop him before he hurt them. I had him in that room, at gunpoint. And then..."

Grayson trailed off. Reece waited, and the truck was quiet, just the windshield wipers layered over the engine.

"It happened very fast," Grayson finally said. "I didn't have feelings stopping me from using that gun, but I—I still had my memories. And my finger wouldn't pull the trigger. I wasn't ready for that and he escaped."

"You let him go."

"No," Grayson said quickly. "There was nowhere for him *to* go in that bunker, and there was fire everywhere. He was as good as dead."

"Then why lie about it?" Reece said. "Unless, of course,

you lied and told everyone you'd killed your brother because it would keep them from looking for him."

"That's not what it was," Grayson said again. "Maybe your empathy is looking for answers based in feelings but you're not gonna find them with me."

Reece looked like he wanted to say a lot more to that, but he bit his lip. "What does your brother want with Gretel Macy?"

"He apparently let her go unhurt, for whatever reason. But now he's got Officer Stensby and the airsoft manager, Keith Waller, under his thrall, and no one's seen them since they broke into Stone Solutions, left the night shift security dead, and set another fire in their wake."

Reece winced.

"Yeah, Alex is my brother, but I gotta stop him," Grayson said, more quietly. "This is why the world needs the Dead Man."

Reece held up the phone. "The president of Stone Solutions Canada sent you this. The same one who's got that broken Dead Man blueprint on a hidden flash drive." There were too many emotions in his voice for Grayson to pick them all out. "Is this the message from all the empath agencies? Did they tell you that you have to come be the Dead Man—against your own *brother*?"

"Yeah, they did, because yeah, I do," Grayson said. "What happened with Alex taught me that corruption is permanent. I might've hesitated that first night in that bunker, Reece, but I learned my lesson and I'll never flinch like that again. If I have to take my brother down, I will. If I have to take you down, I'll do it too."

"But isn't it just so convenient for Stone Solutions and the Empath Initiative that it's always you?" Reece's eyes had narrowed at the corners. "How nice for a bunch of cowards who want someone to hide behind and don't care what happens to you in the process."

"This is what the Dead Man does. I'm just a weapon—"

"No," Reece said sharply. "I don't care what all those assholes keep telling you. I know it was written all over that manual on that flash drive, calling you *a perfectly engineered weapon for these predators*, but you're more than a weapon, they've just always been afraid of us."

"Don't take that comment for more than it's worth," Grayson said. "Traynor told me about that new theory and it's obviously wrong—"

"What do you mean, *new* theory? It's not *new*, it was right there in that manual," Reece said, over Grayson's protest. "And you're *not* a weapon. Weapons don't have compassion and kindness, but you still do. I know you do, because it's keeping me off that ledge of corruption. *You* are keeping me off that ledge. Understand? So you have to be careful, because if anything happened to you, I don't know what I'd do."

Grayson didn't know what to say to that. Reece was so intuitive, even about Grayson; unusual for him to be wrong like this. Maybe he just couldn't bear the thought of a human weapon, even if that's all Grayson was now. "I do try to be careful," he finally said. "But it's not always gonna be an option. Sometimes I'll have to do things, or go places, where there's danger."

"Ugh, is this about to be your big *and I can't take you with me because I can't put you in danger too* speech?" Reece sounded extremely disgruntled. "I'm surprised it took this long. You know you could have just found a hotel room in Horseshoe Bay while I was knocked out and left me there when you had the chance."

"Unconscious and alone? When you're more on edge than ever, and got a bad habit of running straight into danger?" Grayson shook his head. "You're too close to becoming fully corrupted, and if you turn, it's gonna put countless others in danger. I wasn't gonna leave you all by yourself when I want you to be—"

The streetlight rippled through the truck, lighting Reece in the shotgun seat, because after thousands of miles of the same Dead Man roads alone, something had changed.

"When you want me to be what?" Reece prompted.

When I want you to be safe.

"I—" Grayson's tongue tripped again. "When I, uh. When I want you to be at the safe house."

He looked back at the road. That was what he'd been going to say all along. Of course it was. He had a temporary passenger; nothing had actually changed.

Reece folded his arms.

"It's a better spot for you to be than a hotel," Grayson said. "It's fully stocked with food, clothes, everything you'd need to lay low for a bit. Even vegan candy."

"I'm not that easy," Reece said.

"I had some clothes in my size delivered too," Grayson said. "You can swipe another one of my hoodies."

"Hmph."

Grayson had one more card to play, but he'd wait until they made it to the pier.

They drove in silence for a few minutes, the dark forest rushing past on the right, the black ocean on the left.

"Are you *sure* you're okay?" Reece finally said. "I know you're the Dead Man, but you just found out your brother is alive—"

"I told you, Reece," Grayson said. "Don't make the mistake of thinking I can have feelings. I'll tell you again: Alex was the most dangerous corrupted empath I've ever met. I'm gonna stop him, and if it comes to it, I will stop you too. Nothing will ever change that."

Reece huffed.

"You gotta be careful around me," Grayson said. "Do you know what the word *careful* means or do I need to define it for Bad Decisions Bear over here?"

"Oh, please," said Reece. "How can you tell me I need to listen to you and be careful when in the same breath you're telling me you're the biggest danger around?"

"Because what did you just do in the back of a pickup truck with the *biggest danger around*?"

There was a moment of silence.

"Well, shit," Reece muttered.

Victor Nichols typed frantically into the phone as the pilot, Tasha, took their helicopter south, toward Vancouver.

"Sir," Tasha started tentatively. "Are you sure we shouldn't go back to Polaris?"

"Quite sure," he said curtly.

"But I heard the alarm—and the others have no way off the island—"

"Just fly the fucking helicopter where I tell you to," he snapped, and she fell silent.

Nichols finished his message and sent it out.

Polaris was compromised by Alex Grayson.

He's alive.

I told you the Dead Man would betray us.

He's a failed experiment, as dangerous as the empaths themselves.

No more stalling; we take him out now.

Five minutes later, a single-word response came in.

Agreed.

CHAPTER TWENTY-NINE

From: Victor Nichols <vnichols@polarisempathicresearch.com>
To: [REDACTED]
Subject: Re: Progress

Your support for my projects is, of course, appreciated; Polaris could have never accomplished all that it has without you. This research has been but the tip of the iceberg; there's so much more to come.

REECE CHEWED ON the tip of his thumb as he watched Grayson take an exit and follow dark roads down the mountainside toward the water. His thoughts were in turmoil, as if his intuition knew something his mind hadn't grasped.

Evan lied to everyone about Alex.

Just like he lied to all of them about me.

People in power don't like being lied to.

They don't like what they can't control.

Keeping one eye on Grayson, he carefully pulled his phone out of his pocket. He tilted the screen away from Grayson and checked to see if anything had come in while he'd been unconscious.

His eyebrows flew up. His message to Stensby's phone had gotten a response.

Pleased to meet you, Mr. Davies. I apologize for the delay; I've been a bit tied up today.

Grayson was navigating a tight turn with the big truck. Reece quickly typed a response.

This is Alex Grayson, isn't it?

The phone lit back up a moment later.

Yes, sir. Cora says to tell you hi, by the way, and that we didn't hurt your bouncer friend from the club.

Cora? Bouncer friend from the club—was that *Diesel*? Alex and Cora were together and they'd been with Diesel? Grayson hadn't mentioned any of that.

Jesus, his fingers were itching to text Alex back.

Reece forced himself to turn the phone face down on his lap as Grayson turned in past a chain-link fence and into a tiny parking lot. At the far end was a small wooden dock with a very nice boat. Grayson drove toward the water, stopping a few feet back from the dock, and nodded toward the boat. "That's my ride."

"Don't make me jealous." Reece wasn't going to put a name to the bone-deep sense of protectiveness and affection that now ran through him in Grayson's presence, but he would admit to himself that he'd left any semblance of *platonic* back in Seattle.

And something in him was shouting that he needed to think, needed to understand, or Evan was the one who would pay the price.

He cleared his throat. "So you're taking that boat? *Alone?*"

"I'm pretty sure I can guess where Alex is going," said Grayson, "and I'm gonna want my own ride there. I have to go, Reece. And it has to be alone."

Reece shook his head. "After everything that's happened, after everything I said, how can you think I'll let you go by yourself—"

"Because if I bring you to the rendezvous with Stone Solutions or the Empath Initiative, they're gonna want to take you to the same place," Grayson said, more quietly, "and then they're never gonna let you leave."

Reece's fingers tightened on his phone. "You're talking about the prison for corrupted empaths, aren't you?"

"You know I'm not going to answer that."

Reece didn't need him to; it was obvious. Cora was supposed to be at that prison; if she was with Alex, was he already there? But why in the hell would *Diesel* be at an empath prison? There was so much Grayson hadn't told him.

"What do you mean, rendezvous with Stone Solutions *or* the Empath Initiative?" Reece said, asking a question Grayson might actually answer.

"Because I gotta pick one," Grayson said. "I got one location from Director Traynor of the Empath Initiative, and a different location from Vivian Marist of Stone Solutions Canada."

"They sent you different locations?" Reece frowned. "That's weird, isn't it?"

"They're usually a lot more in sync, yeah," Grayson said. "But then, they're usually not dealing with my corrupted empath brother coming back from the dead."

Reece's frown deepened. "I guess," he said reluctantly.

"I can get to both rendezvous points by land or sea," Grayson said. "You got an opinion which place I should go?"

Yes, you do, something in Reece's mind said. *You have to figure out what it is.* He screwed his eyes shut, trying to think.

Grayson cut the engine. "I know you're fighting me on the safe house because when it comes to danger, you're only ever thinking of others. But if you'll go to the safe house, I'll make you a deal."

There was a jingling sound. Reece opened his eyes to find Grayson holding up the truck keys.

And then he held them out to Reece.

Reece's eyes widened. "No fucking way."

"Drive back to the ferry terminal and catch the next ride over to Nanaimo," Grayson said. "I'll text you where you're going from there."

"You're loaning me your *truck*?" Reece said. "This isn't a hoodie, which means you'll definitely have to come get it back, right?"

"Yeah, I am, and yeah, I will," Grayson said. "Deal?"

Reece stared at the keys.

He's sparing me.

Like he spared Alex.

He's never been an empath hunter.

He's been protecting us since the beginning.

Reece quickly reached for the keys before Grayson could change his mind, carefully taking them without making contact with Grayson's hand. "Do me a favor?"

"Sure," Grayson said easily.

"Look me in the eyes and say *Reece, I promise I'll come back to you.*"

Grayson hesitated.

"You want me to phrase it a different way?" Reece said lightly, echoing Grayson's words from the airsoft course. How had that been only yesterday? "How about, *Care Bear, I know I could be in danger, so I promise I'll only make good decisions for a change.*"

"What are you talking about?" Grayson said. "I always make good decisions."

"You literally just handed me your truck keys."

"Didn't you tell me you're a real good driver?" Grayson said lightly, as his gaze flicked down to Reece's lips, the motion likely too subtle for most people to notice in a darkened truck cab but a giant billboard for an infatuated empath.

Reece couldn't stop himself from leaning closer. The feeling of being caught in Grayson's gravity, like the moon and tide, had only become stronger. "I need to know that you're going to be safe. Promise me, Evan."

Grayson exhaled, and Reece felt his breath ghost against his cheek. "I'll try," he said, soft and low. "Gonna check the boat. Wait in the truck where it's warm; I'll be right back."

Reece sat in the passenger seat as he watched Grayson walk down the dock, lit by the truck's headlights. In Reece's hand, the metal of the truck keys was cool against his skin because he wasn't wearing his gloves.

They hadn't found the record of gloves they'd been looking for in Stone Solutions Canada.

But they'd found an attempt at a *How to Make a Dead Man* manual.

Reece frowned, watching Grayson in the boat as he poked around, lifting the seats and checking beneath them—body turned at a funny angle, meaning he was probably making sure whatever weapons he'd asked for were there, but not wanting Reece to see them.

Stone Solutions, the Empath Initiative—they all thought Grayson was the weapon.

And now Evan is in danger.

Reece ground his teeth. Why? Why did he keep thinking

that? The answers were there, he could almost taste them, like he could see the shadows on the ground but not what cast them.

Stone Solutions had used Cora's fiancé to corrupt her, and she'd come into her stronger empathy powers too late to save him. Same for Alex and his parents. But Reece had already been twisted by scientists, and his empathy could find out what he wanted to know.

If he was willing to use insight.

His fingers tightened on the keys.

Insight isn't an option and never will be, Grayson had said, *because using it on purpose is a one-way street. You ever cross that line, you're not coming back, Reece. And then the Dead Man will have to step in.*

There are no circumstances worth the consequences.

"Bullshit there aren't," Reece said under his breath.

Grayson had been willing to take a bullet to protect Reece from corruption and still had the scar. He'd throw himself between Reece and corruption like a shield and pay the price before he let Reece use insight to protect him.

And maybe he was right, that using insight was a one-way street.

But so was losing Evan.

Reece took a bracing breath. "The Dead Man can take me down if I turn," he whispered into the truck cab. "If corruption gets ahold of me and I can't come back from this, the Dead Man can stop me."

Not a lie. Reece believed that.

He closed his eyes and deliberately reached for the power crackling at the back of his skull.

Why do I think Evan is in danger?

His eyes popped back open wide, the dark truck cab suddenly brighter as Reece's pupils dilated.

Alex and Cora didn't hurt Diesel, but why would a bouncer and ex-marine be in an empath prison—

Not just a prison. A research facility. Run by a man who left com-

ments on a broken Dead Man blueprint, who could have sent Keith Waller the empath gloves from Vancouver—

Waller is ex-army and had been trying to recruit Diesel too, and has not just fear but also greed in his eyes as he says that Reece is who he needs, that unlike others, Waller knows how to follow orders—

Waller was going to kidnap Reece, just after an empath from Montreal also went missing. And the one thing Reece and Marie have in common is a sibling, just like Alex, who made the Dead Man—

Stensby thinks Reece should have been locked up for his crimes and wants to know why the Dead Man protected Reece from consequences, hints that someone told him Agent Grayson can't be relied on because his priority is protecting empaths—

Someone doesn't trust Evan.

Someone's been trying to figure out how to make more Dead Men to replace him.

Someone would have learned today that Evan lied about his brother and they'll want to replace him—

Now.

"Reece?"

The truck door had opened, cold air swirling in. Reece took a deep breath through his nose, dots connecting themselves in his mind to create the terrible picture. And through it all, fury was building, a rage so hot he could taste it.

You can't tell Evan, his mind ordered. *He will know you used insight. It won't matter that he protects empaths and it won't matter what you shared. If he knows you crossed this line on purpose, he will do his job, arrest you, and take you in to Stone Solutions.*

He won't listen to you when you tell him where to go.

And he's the one who'll get hurt.

"Care Bear?"

For the next two minutes, you have to be more dangerous than he is. It's the only way you'll save him.

Lie to Evan. Lie so he doesn't suspect. You won't flinch this time; you'll love the way these lies sound because they're going to keep Evan safe.

"Sorry," Reece said, and his voice didn't quite sound like himself. A little deeper, a little more gravelly. "I just—today has been a lot. Tense and anxious, like usual, that's all."

Lie. Reece held Grayson's gaze, his expression and body steady.

"Oh." Grayson's gaze flicked over him. "Understandable."

Reece pointed out toward the dock. "I hope you can drive a boat more safely than a car."

"Are you actually giving me a hard time about my driving when I'm loaning you my truck?" Grayson said, automatically glancing where Reece was pointing.

"You wouldn't know what to do with me if I stopped," Reece said, as he swiped his hand across the center console. "Don't forget your phone. But don't text from behind the wheel of a boat either."

"Unbelievable." Grayson took the phone Reece was offering him. "What would you do if you didn't have me to sass?"

"Don't know," Reece said lightly. "I guess I'll just have to make sure you're always here."

They climbed out of the truck, coming around to the front, lit in the headlights.

"Go to the location Vivian Marist sent you," Reece said, and his voice had gone gravellier still.

"Marist?" Grayson blinked. "Surprised to hear you pick Stone Solutions over the Empath Initiative. I was thinking if I had to pick, I'd meet Director Traynor."

"No," Reece said firmly. "Go to Marist."

His anger was like a living thing—not at Evan but at everyone who had used him, who would use up anyone they could get their hands on to fight their battles for them.

But Grayson did need to be far away from Reece as soon as possible, for his own safety.

Grayson's gaze was on him again. "You promise you're going to go to the safe house?"

Reece held his gaze again. "I promise." *Lie.* He stayed steady. "Be safe, okay?"

Grayson nodded. Reece stepped back, leaning against the front of the truck as he watched Grayson climb into the boat. When Grayson looked back one last time, he waved, then watched as the boat pulled away from the dock and headed out into the strait.

Reece hauled himself back up into the truck's driver's seat. The rage was vibrating just under his skin. He could feel power spreading through him, black lightning crackling from the base of his skull.

He couldn't have stopped it any more than he could have stopped a tidal wave.

And he didn't want to.

Grayson's enemies weren't going to give up just because he didn't show tonight. They'd be going after Grayson, and he'd be in terrible danger—unless Reece took care of it.

Well. Not *just* Reece.

"So the Empath Initiative sent Evan a second location," he said out loud, as he pulled the phone out of his pocket. "I don't think this meeting is going to go quite like they planned."

Aisha had managed to give Liam coordinates to Grayson's safe house on Salt Spring Island, and then she and Diesel had fallen almost instantly asleep on the tiny backseat of the floatplane.

Outside the plane was the blackness of night, only the occasional light on the islands or water below. Jamey looked over her shoulder, where Aisha had listed heavily into Diesel while he slept against the window. "They're out."

"We'll get them to the safe house," Liam promised. "They can sleep it off. Diesel is probably going to have a lot of questions."

"I have a lot of questions for Evan," Jamey said, but she wasn't angry. Grayson was an enigma who couldn't be trusted, but he hadn't killed his brother. And yeah, they were in a terrible mess now, but her last doubts about what kind of man Grayson was had disappeared.

And speaking of, she needed to call the instant the plane's antenna picked up Wi-Fi again. She held her phone, watching the signal. They were heading south, toward Vancouver and the city sprawl; she'd be able to call soon.

Despite the snow, the wind wasn't high, and the water wasn't nearly as choppy as it could have been. Grayson set a speed of thirty knots and started heading south, toward Vancouver and the location Vivian Marist had sent him.

He pulled out his phone.

Except—

Except it was a little too light in his hand. Slightly too small against his palm. He lit up the phone and found himself looking at a lock screen. The numbers one through nine stared mockingly up at him, because he'd made Reece set a passcode but hadn't asked what it was.

Don't forget your phone, Reece had said in the truck.

He'd given Grayson the wrong phone. On purpose? *Why?* Grayson patted himself down but it just confirmed what he'd already guessed: that he had Reece's phone and Reece, presumably, had his.

And now Grayson couldn't unlock it.

He sat down in the seat behind the wheel, a little harder than necessary.

"Reece," he said into the wind. "What's going on?"

CHAPTER THIRTY

I've thought about your proposal. I have some conditions but yes, I accept. I can't let what happened to Alex happen to other empaths.

Call me the Dead Man if you want. Obviously I don't have feelings about it either way.

—NOTE FROM EVAN GRAYSON TO HOLT TRAYNOR

THE EMPATH INITIATIVE had sent Grayson the address of a warehouse on the water, just north of Horseshoe Bay. Reece took his time getting there. After all, he wanted everyone else to have plenty of time to arrive.

He brought the truck down the hill and into the parking lot, then drove to the middle of the lot and cut the engine.

He rested his fingers on the steering wheel and closed his eyes.

If Cora had done it, maybe he could too.

Sure enough, a moment later, he was picking them up: emotions around him. Fear, anger—oh, that was excitement and anticipation, and in more than one person. There were a few twisted fucks in this crowd who enjoyed the thought of throwing down with an enhanced superhuman like Grayson. They would have been briefed on Grayson and be ready to fight him.

Unfortunately for them, tonight that was going to be like bringing the proverbial knives to a gunfight.

The driver's door was yanked open.

"Don't move, Agent Gray—Reece Davies?"

Reece opened his eyes. He looked over to his left, and stared straight into the eyes of Holt Traynor, the ex–army general turned Empath Initiative director.

"The thing even an empath specialist forgets about empaths," Reece said, holding up Grayson's phone, "is that when I need to crack a password that I'll—" he cleared his throat "—*never guess*, I don't actually have to guess that impossible password. I just have to figure out what password *Evan* thinks I would never be able to guess." He shrugged. "And *that's* easy: 2273-2327." He stage-whispered, "It spells *C-A-R-E-B-E-A-R*."

Traynor's lips tightened into a flat line. "Where's Agent Grayson?"

"Far away," Reece said, keeping his eyes on Traynor's. "Where you can't hurt him."

Traynor's nostrils flared. "What are you—"

"Was it your idea to send Keith Waller those gloves from Vancouver?" Reece said dangerously, feeling the rage bubble up again. "So that if Evan ever found out, he'd think the trail led to Stone Solutions? He was already suspicious of them, after all; he'd be quicker to believe they were the ones trying to recruit big, ex-military test subjects."

Traynor's fingers tightened on the door frame.

"How much of it was your idea, and how much do you just sign off on?" Reece said. "Maybe you don't want to know the gory details, but you approve everything that's done to us? You think any experiment is worth finding out how to stop us, because we're predators?"

"I don't know what you're talking about." *Lie.* Traynor

averted his gaze, but it was too late. Reece's empathy was finally running free, connecting puzzle pieces until he could see the entire picture clearly.

"I'm still trying to figure out why you lied to Evan about that predator theory. I mean, why tell him it was new?" Reece shrugged lightly. "The only theory I've come up with is pretty sick. Want to hear it?"

Traynor's eyes narrowed.

"I was thinking that maybe you didn't want Evan to realize you'd bought into this *empaths are predators* theory years ago," said Reece, "because then maybe Evan might start to wonder if you'd ever been motivated to try to create an anti-empathy weapon. Whether, to that end, you might have sanctioned certain experiments to find out what corrupted empaths could do to their siblings."

"Mr. Davies," Traynor said warningly.

"Most of you are pretty scared of Evan, after all," Reece said. "You wouldn't want Evan wondering if you'd been responsible for what happened to Alex Grayson. You would have hidden how ecstatic you must have been when the Grayson brothers exceeded your wildest hopes."

He tilted his head. "But it didn't turn out how you wanted, did it? Evan was supposed to be your Frankenstein's monster, your perfect weapon, but he's got a mind of his own. You should have known nothing you tried would work. You can never take our siblings from us."

"Parasites," Traynor spat at him. "Changing, entrapping your own siblings—"

"Maybe," Reece said. "Maybe we've molded them into our perfect bodyguards since childhood. Or maybe it's the love: you could take away Evan's emotions but not the years of kindness and compassion from his little brother, an adoration so strong it changed Evan. Either way—you can't have him."

"Evan is a failed experiment who betrayed us," Traynor

snapped. "We learn from the results and dispose of failure. Happens all the time. What was your big plan here, Davies?" He gestured around them, weapons cocking in the night. "I didn't come alone: I have an army with me, all their guns pointed at you. They'll kill you before you can make a move against any of us. And you don't have the Dead Man here, protecting his precious empaths. You can't hide behind Evan now."

"Oh, I know," Reece agreed.

"So you just decided to hand yourself over?" Traynor said. "Give us the chance to run some experiments on you?"

"No," Reece said, drawing it out. "I've been stalling. My friends needed time to arrive."

Somewhere at the back of the parking lot, there was a scream.

"You should have left the Dead Man alone, you know." Reece smiled at Traynor. "Yes, Evan has been protecting us from you. Because it was the only way to protect you. From *us*."

Grayson had brought the boat back to the dock, but Reece and the truck were gone. He'd walked up to the road, but no Reece, and with the phone still locked he couldn't call him, or St. James, or Stone Solutions, or even for a damn ride.

Finally, with no other ideas, he'd gotten back in the boat, gone back out to the strait and started heading south, toward Vancouver and the location Marist had given him. He'd been on the water long enough that he'd come up on the edge of downtown, and the dock Marist had picked for their rendezvous was in front of him when Reece's phone started ringing.

He snatched it up, seeing Jamey on the caller ID with a picture of Detective St. James. Luckily, even locked he was still able to answer.

"Grayson."

"You've got *Reece's* phone?" St. James groaned. It was very loud in her background, the whine of a motor. "What the fuck happened?"

"I'm not sure I know," Grayson admitted. "I got a boat. My brother is—"

"Alive, yes, trust me, we know."

Grayson blinked. Up ahead, he could make out vehicles in the parking lot, and two tiny figures on the end of the dock, waiting for him. Vivian Marist, bright blond hair and white puffy coat. FBI Assistant Director Jacobs next to her in a long black wool coat.

"Oh," Grayson said. "Well, I figured if Alex broke into Stone Solutions, he was probably looking for—"

"The location of Polaris, yes, and guess what, he found it, and he's already been there, wrecked that."

Grayson took a moment to process that. He watched Marist and Jacobs on the dock, and yeah, they were standing pretty close together for work colleagues. Reece might've been right about them.

"Okay," he finally said into the phone. "Guess maybe I don't need to head up there right this second anymore. But I gave Reece the truck. I thought he was going to the safe house—"

"My brother is with your brother and Cora Falcon." St. James's voice had gone very tight. "Have you seen the news?"

"No," Grayson said slowly. "Reece switched our phones. I haven't been able to unlock his."

"There was a series of murders at a warehouse by Horseshoe Bay maybe thirty minutes ago." St. James sounded like she was fighting back an overwhelming emotion. "Director Traynor of the Empath Initiative was at the scene but now he's missing. I haven't heard from Reece, but according to the news, there's mayhem happening in downtown Vancouver. A high-rise is on fire, on the same street as Stone Solutions Canada."

Grayson stilled. He looked at Marist and Jacobs, who were waving at him, a frantic edge to their movements.

He grabbed the steering wheel and turned the boat around. "I guess I know where I'm going, then."

He heard shouts behind him; he ignored them, taking the boat away from the dock and out into the strait, pointed at the lights of downtown Vancouver.

"Evan," St. James said warningly. "Liam's flying over the Georgia Strait; he's going to drop me off downtown and then take Aisha and Diesel to the safe house."

"Aisha and Diesel?"

"I'll explain everything," said St. James. "But *wait for me*."

Reece had become corrupted, just like Cora Falcon, just like Alex. And now the director of the Empath Initiative was missing.

Up ahead, the city lights twinkled. He'd be there in minutes. "Sorry, Jamey," he said quietly. "But I have a job to do. And this time, I have to finish it."

"Evan—"

Grayson hung up, and pushed the boat to full speed.

CHAPTER THIRTY-ONE

He keeps his friends close—and his enemy even closer.

—**TAGLINE FOR THE 2001 TELEVISION DRAMA** ***THE EMPATH ADVERSARY***

AFTER THE CONFRONTATION with Director Traynor, Reece had driven south, back to Vancouver. Alex and Cora had grabbed their own rides, big black government SUVs that could each fit several of Traynor's now-thralled soldiers.

The three of them had parked along the curb at the edge of downtown, close to the convention center where Reece had been with Evan only half a day ago, and then Alex and Cora had turned their thralls loose.

Traynor apparently had a specific taste in his backup: big, armed men who liked violence. Reece watched, lips curled in a new kind of smile as ten of those men disappeared with a roar into the streets of Vancouver.

"We'll keep everyone busy," Cora promised, as the three empaths stood at the edge of a small green space. At night, the water beyond the city's edge was black, glittery lights reflected in its surface. She tilted her head, and for a moment, she could have been a therapist again, not an empath prison escapee with blood speckling her jumpsuit. "How are you feeling, Reece?"

Reece's entire body sparked and buzzed, like he'd drunk electricity. The night was cold, but it didn't bother him; he'd always run hotter than non-empaths, and now he felt the burn like he was made of fire. The phrase *bloodlust* came to mind, like he finally understood what other humans must have been feeling when they seemed to crave violence and mayhem.

For the life of him, he couldn't imagine why he'd fought corruption off so long.

"I feel ready to raise a little hell," he said.

Somewhere down the block, someone screamed.

"I didn't say *thank you* yet," Reece said. "For showing up when I needed you."

"I owe you the thanks right back. The score with Traynor is mine to settle." Alex was running a hand over the side of the F-150. "I haven't seen this thing in two years. I can't believe Evan kept it."

Cora looked back at Alex's SUV, where Traynor was still unconscious in the back. "What should we do with Traynor?"

"I'm still deciding. Just like we're still deciding what we should do with our Polaris escapee Victor Nichols, when we find him." Alex looked at Reece. "Nichols has been sending you ominous emails, you know. *Stress-testing*, he called it in his notes. Who knows the extent of what he's been willing to do to empaths—or their siblings. And speaking of my brother."

He looked back at Reece and Cora. "We may run into him at some point, but I think we'd all rather it wasn't today."

"This will be fast," Reece promised. "I just want Vivian Marist's flash drive with everything they've tried to figure out about how Evan became the Dead Man."

"I can't wait to read about myself," Alex said wryly.

"I hope there are more files on there," Reece said. "Maybe they've got the names and locations of more empaths."

Three more screams rent the air, echoing off the high-rises.

"They sent a bunch of people from Stone Solutions Canada home today after the fight," Reece said. "The flash drive might still be in Marist's office."

Cora cracked her knuckles. "We'll buy you time to look."

Grayson parked at a pier not far from the convention center, certainly stealing someone else's slip, then took the gun from the under-seat storage before he left the boat behind and sprinted up the street lined with hotels and high-rises. Even if he hadn't known where Stone Solutions Canada was, he could have followed the screams.

He turned a corner downtown, running at top speed past the parking garage he'd parked in with Reece that morning, bickering over who got to be behind the truck wheel. Now, several of the cars along the curb were on fire, and people were screaming and tearing down the sidewalk.

He didn't see Alex or Cora Falcon, but coming out the front doors of the Stone Solutions high-rise was a familiar silhouette.

"Reece."

Grayson's voice cracked, but then, the street was full of smoke from the cars.

Reece whirled around. For a moment, the shock was evident on his face; unlike everyone else on the planet, with their emotions picked up by Reece's corrupted empathy like ships on a radar, he wouldn't have been able to feel Grayson approaching.

Grayson gestured around them. "What are you doing?"

Reece looked from the cars on fire to the broken glass on the street to a pair of thralls locked in a fistfight farther down the sidewalk. Then he smiled in a way Grayson didn't recognize at all.

"Oops," he said dryly, without an ounce of regret.

That was it then. Another pacifist empath was gone.

Reece was lost.

"You're fully corrupted," Grayson said, stating the obvious.

"Oh, come on, it was inevitable." Reece spread his hands. "To be honest, I don't know why I fought this side of me so long. Give me power over anxiety any day."

Out of the corners of his eyes, Grayson could see at least half a dozen other people on the street, all of them big men in camouflage, turning slowly in his direction with malice in their eyes.

"How?" Grayson said, before he could stop himself.

"You know what's funny?" Reece said, which wasn't an answer. "Before I turned, I said to myself, *the Dead Man can stop me if I become corrupted*. And it wasn't a lie: I believed it, I believed you'd come, and you wouldn't let me hurt people, and so I could pay the price for corruption and no one would lose but me."

He waved at the chaos around him. "Now, though, I can see that I underestimated myself, just like you kept telling me. My empathy is strong. And my empathy got used to *you*."

Around the street, the thralls were moving in. Grayson counted seven of them, all close to his own size, and all of them would have strength and speed jacked up from the corrupted empathy in their systems.

"I'm not like other empaths with the Dead Man now," Reece said. "Your voice doesn't bother me. The sight of you doesn't bother me. I don't want you to stop me—and I don't think you can."

Grayson took a step forward. "Come here and touch me then."

Reece scrambled backward, up onto the curb behind him. The thralls moved closer, a living wall between them. At least one of them had blood already welling in his eyes.

"Don't worry," Reece said, anger flashing in his eyes, "I'll figure out a way around that too."

"Wouldn't count on it, if I were you." Grayson put a hand on his waistband, on the top of the gun. "I can guess why you came back here, to Stone Solutions Canada. Do you have Vivian Marist's flash drive in your pocket?"

"No." Reece didn't flinch. Instead, he smiled again, the one that wasn't his, and pulled something small and black from his jeans, holding it up. "You know, I kind of like the way lies sound now."

Grayson wrapped his fingers around the gun's grip. "Give me the drive."

Reece took a deliberate step backward. "I don't even get a *please*?"

"Hand it over. Now," Grayson said, voice unwavering. "You know I don't have feelings about you. I will do what I have to do to take that drive back."

"Sorry, sugar." Reece took another step back. "Finders keepers."

"You could say the same about corruption." Grayson kept his gaze on Reece as the thralls got closer. "Corruption found you and it's gonna keep you. It's permanent. There's no saving you now; my only option is to stop you."

Reece tossed the drive up in the air, then caught it. He looked straight at Grayson, eyes narrowed. "You can try."

Grayson raised the gun and sighted down the barrel, so all he could see was Reece.

Reece froze.

Memories started to rise: *Reece in the Smart car, Reece in the studio, Reece in the hotel—*

Reece under him in the backseat of the truck, his lips against Grayson's.

Grayson shoved every last memory down. He had a job to do, innocents to protect; there would be no memories stopping him this time.

He cocked the gun, index finger curled on the trigger, gaze locked on Reece's face, the rumpled dark hair, those big brown eyes, his soft lips.

"Last chance, Reece," he said, without a hint of emotion.

Not a single memory rose.

But something in Grayson's chest twisted—and the gun faltered.

The seven thralls were on Grayson in the next breath. He was forced to fight, ducking and dodging and throwing punches of his own as sneakers echoed on pavement—Reece sprinting away down the street, ducking into an alley and disappearing from view.

CHAPTER THIRTY-TWO

For years, readers have come to Eyes on Empaths *to get the TRUTH. But today we're coming to you to say that we think that we might not be getting ALL of the truth.*

Why are so many of our tax dollars going into anti-empathy defense? Who decided the organizations that monitor pacifists should be connected to the military? When were these decisions made?

And most importantly: What's really going on with the empaths?

Eyes on Empaths *promises to find out.*

—GRETEL MACY, BLOGGING FOR *EYES ON EMPATHS*

AN HOUR LATER, Grayson was sitting on a bench in a park along the dark water's edge, watching the lights of the boats bobbing out in the black. It was cold and wet, the dampness seeping into him, but he hadn't moved.

Finally, he heard the approaching footsteps. He stayed in place. He'd wanted her to find him.

"I am furious with you," St. James said tightly, from behind him. "Just so you know."

Grayson grunted in acknowledgment.

She sat next to him on his bench. There had been a thickness to her voice that wasn't usually there, and her eyes were puffy and bloodshot. She'd lost her brother to corruption. He hadn't just failed Reece; he'd failed her too.

They were silent together for a moment, then St. James said, "You came here after the empaths. To do your job."

"I did," he admitted.

"But you let Reece go."

"I let him go."

She wrapped her arms around herself. "Why?"

A small skiff was just visible in the edge of the city lights, chugging along, never minding that it wasn't as big or fancy as the other boats. "It's—complicated." Grayson watched the little boat for a moment. "He and I are—we're—well. I've made some complicated memories, when it comes to him."

"Mm," she said. "You know what else is complicated, though, right?"

"What?"

"Feelings," she said, her voice still tight, still too thick.

When he closed his eyes, he could still see Reece on the other side of the gun barrel. He didn't remember having any memories, but he must've. What else could have stopped him from pulling that trigger?

"I can't have feelings," Grayson said. "They're gone. Alex destroyed them."

"Alex was also supposed to be dead," she said. "How'd that work out for Vancouver?"

They went quiet again, except that Grayson could hear her quiet swallows, a sniff she'd probably blame on the cold.

"I don't know how Reece became corrupted," Grayson confessed. He owed St. James the truth. "He told me to join Vivian Marist, not Director Traynor, and then switched our phones and went after Traynor himself. I still don't know why. I don't know if my word is worth anything to you, but I swear, if I could have stopped it—"

"You never would have let him fall, even if it meant putting yourself in a bullet's path again. I know. I believe you." St. James blew out a very long breath. "And maybe that's part of the answer."

Grayson looked at the phone in his hand again, like the dark screen held any answers.

St. James stuck out her hand. "Give me Reece's phone."

Grayson tilted his head but held it out. She took it, typed something in, then handed it back. "Here. Nice selfie; watch me not ask why my brother has it."

The screen was lit up and unlocked. The wallpaper was set to the picture Grayson had sent Reece from the gym back in Vermont. "How'd you unlock this?"

"Reece hates passcodes. When he has to set one, under duress, he only ever uses the exact same thing."

"Which is?"

"It's 123456."

"I really ought've been able to guess that," Grayson muttered. His thumb went, unbidden, to the text message icon, opening up their text chain. He looked at the last message between him and Reece: the selfie Reece had taken of himself at the hotel, in the bear hat and pajamas, Grayson fast asleep in the background. Reece had been happy enough that night to project it onto others; if you looked for it in the photo, you could see the true happiness in his smile, the way it extended all the way to his bright eyes.

Grayson turned off the screen and set the phone on his lap. "I gotta be honest. I don't know what to do next."

"Yeah, well, lucky for you, you've got me on your team," said St. James, and Grayson turned to look at her. "Because I know what we're doing now. We're going to find them."

"Corruption is permanent," Grayson said. "Irreversible."

"So was your brother's supposed death, but he's still here," she said. "So was becoming the Dead Man, but you just let Reece go. Maybe I'm choosing to believe none of it is as permanent or irreversible as you've always believed."

Grayson lit the phone screen again, illuminating the picture. His gaze lingered on Reece's smile, and when he licked his dry lips, he could almost imagine he still tasted Reece's kiss.

"Empaths made us who we are," she said. "I say we use all our empath-given skills to find them. My brother. Your brother. The world's scariest therapist."

There weren't supposed to be pictures of the Dead Man out in the world. Grayson touched the picture, so it filled the screen. His thumb hovered over the delete button.

"We're not gonna be the only ones looking for the empaths," he pointed out. "They targeted the Empath Initiative. They set fire to Stone Solutions. They're gonna have the world after them."

"So we get there first. We find them, we save them, and we bring them home. Pinky-swear on it." She held out her hand again, this time with her little finger extended. "I mean, come on," she added, raising her chin, her eyes defiant and daring. "You're supposed to be an empath hunter. Cowboy the fuck up and hunt some empaths."

Grayson wasn't like St. James. He didn't feel hope that they could save Cora, or Alex, or Reece, because Grayson didn't feel anything. He couldn't.

He touched his chest, over his heart, where he'd felt a twinge the moment the gun had faltered. And then, instead of hitting Delete, he replaced the wallpaper of himself with the picture of Reece, where he'd see that smile every time he opened the phone.

"We bring them home," he vowed, and linked his pinky with hers.

***

Reece sat in the driver's seat of Grayson's F-150, phone in hand, Alex in his ear.

"Cora and I found a yacht," said Alex, which was probably a nice way to say they'd thralled the owner and were now having a luxury ride back to the States with Director Traynor and their ten thralled Canadian foot soldiers. "You're sure you'd rather drive?"

"Yeah," Reece said. "We'll want the truck in Seattle."

"And you're sure it's not just that you need time to clear your head after running into Evan?" Alex said shrewdly.

Reece cleared his throat. "I handled Evan. He won't be a problem for me."

Lie.

Reece froze.

"Good," Alex said, sounding pleased. "We've got big plans, Reece. We can't let him get in the way. See you in Seattle."

"See you." Reece hung up. He palmed the phone for a moment, then looked up at his own eyes in the truck's rearview mirror.

More slowly, he repeated, "Evan isn't going to be a problem for me."

Lie.

"I'm not attached to what happens to him."

Lie.

"There is no part of me that still wants him."

Lie.

Reece took a breath through his nose. There was no part of him that was still a pacifist. Corruption was complete. Irreversible. He had evolved.

If you're so certain, say it out loud, said a little voice in his head.

Reece tightened his jaw. But before he could say it, Evan's phone—Reece's now—went off. He glanced down to see a text from his own name on-screen. Evan must have finally figured out how to unlock the phone.

Reece opened the message up.

You know I'm not gonna let you go that easy.

Reece considered the words, gaze lingering. Then he sent two texts back and put the truck in gear, tires pealing as he left downtown Vancouver behind.

Come and get me then.

And hope I don't get you first.

★ ★ ★ ★ ★

AUTHOR NOTE

The Sugar & Vice series' alternate universe takes inspiration from the real Seattle and Pacific Northwest, but apart from the setting, all people, corporations, organizations, and abilities described herein are intended as entirely fictional.

ACKNOWLEDGMENTS

So much gratitude for so many wonderful people who help me in so many ways:

To C—I am forever blessed that we found each other;

To my family and friends—I am so grateful for your love;

To Arianna—friend, cheerleader, and fully amazing, with extra thanks for inspiring the setting of Chapter 13;

To my Canadian author crew, especially Vanora, for their kindness, commiseration, and the willingness to dive deep into fictional French Canadian empath agencies, and to Rachel & Jenn, for sharing their hockey knowledge (and friendship too!);

To my readers—thank you for taking a chance on me (and Reece & Grayson!), and for bringing your brightness and enthusiasm to these books;

To Mackenzie Walton, whose edits always shine a light on the right path forward;

To my agent, Laura Zats, and to Stephanie Doig and the art, marketing, and production teams at Harlequin;

And to T, who brings boundless joy and sunshine to my world.